CLANDESTINE

CLANDESTINE

A St-Cyr and Kohler Mystery

J. ROBERT JANES

MYSTERIOUSPRESS.COM

INTEGRATED MEDIA

NEW YORK

Cover design by Neil Alexander Heacox

978-1-5040-0934-8

Published in 2015 by MysteriousPress.com/Open Road Integrated Media, Inc.
345 Hudson Street
New York, NY 10014
www.mysteriouspress.com
www.openroadmedia.com

This is for Mike Bursaw,
of Mystery Mike's in Carmel, Indiana,
and for Steele Curry in Calgary, Alberta.
Over the years, each in his own way
has been immensely kind and supportive.

Acknowledgments

All of the novels in the St-Cyr & Kohler series incorporate a few words and brief passages of French and German. Jim Reynolds, of Niagara-on-the-Lake, very kindly assisted with both; the artist Pierrette Laroche, on occasion with the French. Should there be any errors, however, they are my own and for these I apologize.

Author's Note

Clandestine is a work of fiction in which actual places and times are used but altered as appropriate. As with the other St-Cyr & Kohler novels, the names of real persons appear for historical authenticity, though all are deceased and the story makes of them what it demands. I do not condone what happened during these times, I abhor it. But during the German Occupation of France in World War II, the everyday common crimes of murder, arson and the like continued to be committed, and I merely ask by whom and how were they solved.

CLANDESTINE

*To the old French saying, 'Opportunity makes the thief,'
must be added, 'Murder has its reasons, death its answers.'*

1

L'Abbaye de Vauclair, thought St-Cyr, and here he was facing it again but in an entirely different way.

Down through the encroaching forest, up against the ruins of the monastery and definitely not where it should be, an armoured Renault van with open doors awaited. Even from a distance and through a heavy downpour they could read the necessary: BANQUE NATIONALE DE CRÉDIT ET COMMERCIAL, SIÈGE SOCIAL, 43 BOULEVARD DES CAPUCINES, PARIS.

A difficult address, given the implications such could have these days, but an even more formidable crime if given the needs of the Résistance, considering that only two days ago Dr. Julius Ritter, Gauleiter Fritz Sauckel's forced-labour man in France, had been shot dead as he stood on the corner of the rue des Réservoirs in Paris's 16th arrondissement, home and/or office space to so many of the Occupier.

'Oberg's going to scream his head off, Louis. Boemelburg will be in a rage, Berlin on the line again and blaming them both for not having kept "order",' said Kohler.

Lately Hermann's bosses had caused him to worry more than usual and with good reason. Karl Oberg was the Höherer SS und Polizeiführer of France, Walter Boemelburg being its Gestapo chief. It was a Friday. Sometimes those could be good days, if a Saturday half-day and Sunday break could be allowed, though now, it being 1 October 1943, that was highly unlikely. But since the bodies were not with the van and there was no immediate rush, they could take their time and he could fill Hermann in on the ruins and everything else.

'Why us, Louis? Why when we damn well know the end is in sight and that idiot of a carpet-biter is still bent on destroying everything?'

Hermann never missed an opportunity to nail the Führer with the latest descriptive. Like a lot of other things from home, he had ways of finding such and conjuring them when needed, but 'spring' really was coming, an Allied invasion all but certain since the war in Russia was going very badly for the Wehrmacht, and Berlin and lots of other cities in the Reich were persistently being bombed by the RAF at night and the USAAF during the day. It would be wise to take his mind off things and focus it on what was needed. '*Ah bon, mon vieux*, Rocheleau, the local *garde champêtre*, awaits. Somehow he has managed a small fire and will be warming us a welcoming cup of *le thé de France.*'

Lemon balm! No sugar, of course, but no saccharine, either. Just the herb water and a few bits of leaves. The rural policeman.

'Hermann, the nervousness you continue to exhibit requires the calming that tea will bring. Be your generous self. We may not just need what he will begrudgingly tell us, but everything else he will attempt to hold back.'

After an initial gust of flame to start the fire, that thin pillar of smoke had continued to rise well beyond the van and was now all but lost among the ruins. 'He's in what remains of the refectory,' said St-Cyr. 'That's appropriate, where the monks used to take their meals. Corbeny, his village, is but five or so kilometres to the east. Rocheleau will know the ruins well.'

Longing for a cigarette if one had it to light and could do so in such a deluge, Kohler held this partner of his back a moment. 'Now be so good as to tell me how you even knew it would be lemon balm?'

It was a logical enough question, given the state some of the Occupier had got themselves into, though Hermann wasn't really one of those, not with the past three years of their having worked together day after day solving common crime and doing so honestly in an age of rampant dishonesty. 'Ah, because the monks left a herb garden that has not only maintained itself over the forgotten years, but peacefully conquered the adjacent land.'

'Peacefully? *Bitte, mein Lieber,* don't rub it in. You've been here before.'

'First in September 1914, but that was a little before your side decided that the only way to hold Falkenhayn's line after the First Battle of Ypres was to invent the abominable trench warfare that would tragically dominate the next four miserable years of that other war you people caused us to declare.'

Credit given where credit was due, eh? 'The Great War, was it, and not the Franco-Prussian?'

'Both, but the later one, of course. Now take a few drags of this reserve I've kept hidden. Let me cup my hands over the match you will have to light.'

'I've run out. We'll need his fire. And that second visit?'

They were both edgy, and with good reason, for the SS of the avenue Foch and Gestapo of the rue des Saussaies could be far from calm and the partnership would be blamed no matter what. 'April 1917 when, in five days, 29,000 of our boys were killed, myself having been spared due to the sniper's bullet that nearly took off my left shoulder. Nivelle had ordered Mangin "the ferocious" to attack that ridge behind me. Nivelle's plan was simple. After all, he was a general. In the first three hours we were to take the entire 3,000 metres of the steep and heavily wooded limestone scarp that forms the other side of that ridge, and never mind the natural caves, the ancient and more recent quarries, and even the German trenches, entanglements of barbed wire and machine guns we had to face. In the second two hours we were to cover this side—it's easier going downhill, isn't it?— therefore an additional 2,000 metres of the flat valley floor in which these ruins lie were called for. Though the official casualties were 130,000, and of yourselves some 163,000, the French figures should, I think, rightfully be 187,000 with 40,000 dead before that "engagement" was broken off. Nivelle went out in disgrace, Pétain came in, and now we're still stuck with that pitiful octogenarian.'

Who had all but elected himself prime minister of France in June 1940 and had settled the government in that playground of the Empress Eugénie, the spa town of Vichy which the partnership knew only too well, having been there early last February.

'*Travail, Famille et Patrie*, Hermann.'

Work, Family and Country, not *Liberté, Égalité* and *Fraternité*.

'*Traison*, Louis. *Famine et Prison,* that's what the graffiti artists recently slapped on the boarding that surrounds the Palais du Luxembourg to keep away the grenades someone might throw at the headquarters of the Luftwaffe here in the West.'

In June 1940 Reichsmarschall Göring had taken it over and had had that fence put up when so few would even have thought to throw such, but now . . . ?

'That ridge is the Chemin des Dames, Louis, with the "walk" your Louis XV made atop it for his daughters when they went to visit the duchess of Narbonne at her Château de la Bove. There are strategic viewpoints along its thirty-five or so kilometres and it separates the valleys of the river Ailette, here to the north, from that of the Aisne to the south. We're probably a little less than 150 kilometres to the northeast of Paris, maybe 35 north from Reims and 15 south from Laon.'

Good for Hermann. He was now prepared to focus on the job at hand. 'Just don't "Chief" me in front of Rocheleau. I prevented him from throwing his weapon away and running but foolishly failed to report him to his superior officer.'

'Must you continue to attract old enemies I then have to put up with?'

'Detectives always do, Hermann. It's part of the job. We're just not paid for it.'

Founded in 1134 at the request of the Benedictine bishop, Barthélémy du Jur, l'Abbaye de Vauclair had been extremely successful for over 600 years only to then be auctioned off for next to nothing after the Revolution. Turned into a farm, its substantial church had become a barn, the whole of its buildings being used and decaying to then be put up for sale a last time in 1911, only to be reduced to the present rubble during the offensive of April 1917 and subsequent battles, for the oft-stagnant front had run right through here.

'Come on, Hermann. It's time these two old soldiers, one from each side of this present conflict and the last one, met our *garde champêtre.*'

'I'll let you ask the questions. That'll put him on edge.'

Hermann generally needed to have the last word but this wasn't one of those times. 'Then I'll start by asking him why Joliot, the coroner from Laon, is not present.'

Rocheleau, felt Kohler, was a little man with damned big glasses whose black Bakelite rims made him look like an owl that had just been surprised while tearing apart a chicken it should never have touched.

'Rocheleau . . .' began Louis.

'Sergeant St-Cyr! Ah, the years they have taken their toll, but the mind will be as nimble as ever. I knew when I heard the car that you would have seen the smoke and found me. A deluge like this brings back memories of the battle, *n'est-ce pas*? I've placed stones here near the fire for yourself and Herr Kohler. A little warmth for the soul. *Le thé de France* and the ersatz ham in welcome.'

Like the rifle with its pig sticker's lance that was leaning against the ruins, the tin mugs were antiques, felt Kohler: dented, banged back into shape and still imprinted with their French Army logos. The bugger even had a *poilu*'s rucksack and wore boots of the same, since the French never seemed to throw out anything. No medals, of course. Just the dark blue of a somewhat untidy cop's uniform and a bicycle, the rain gear having been hung aside and the arch of stone above looking solid enough.

'*Ah bon*, Inspectors,' went on Rocheleau, 'the steaks will soon be ready. One for each of us to bring a little warmth of their own.'

Thumb-thick slices of rutabaga, felt Kohler, were being fried in lard when, having come from a farming community, Rocheleau should at least have had potatoes with a few eggs and rashers of bacon. Reaching for some sprigs he must have gathered, the cook tore off bits to sprinkle over the repast.

'A little thyme and oregano, to better the flavour, eh, Herr Detective Inspector Kohler? Don't burn the fingers. *Bon appétit.*'

And why was he serving up even such?

The answer came quickly enough. 'Food is the great leveller, Hermann. It lubricates even those matters that are less than obvious. Rocheleau, our sincere thanks for such a consideration but please be so good as to tell us when you arrived, what you found and why Coroner Joliot, an old and much valued colleague, is still not present?'

There must be no hesitation, not with this former comrade in arms. 'At 0900 today I received instructions by motorcycle courier from Laon to come here, touch nothing and keep everyone else away but yourselves. I was even brought the rifle with its bayonet and six cartridges.'

While Boemelburg must have sent word that they would be in charge, that motorcycle alone would have meant the Wehrmacht whose local Kommandant would have been duly notified by the Préfet of Laon or vice versa, the former being the only one who could have sanctioned the rifle. But Hermann would already be thinking the investigation was only going deeper and deeper. 'And did anyone else attempt to intrude?'

With St-Cyr it would have to be said. 'Father Adrien, our village priest, insisted on blessing them before consigning their souls to heaven.'

'And was curious, Hermann. Our priests always consider it a duty to find out as much as possible about what has happened in their parishes and what might still be happening. He touched the victims, did he, Corporal?'

Ah merde. 'Only with his cross and maybe sprinklings of holy water from his little bottle.'

'In a deluge like this?'

'Should that matter?'

'Of course not. Now be so good as to tell us that you covered the bodies with the tarpaulins that courier had instructed you to bring along from Corbeny.'

Bon! St-Cyr hadn't asked about Father Adrien's other bottles. 'I did, yes.'

'And while you were busy, did the father duck his head into that van or did he step right into it to have a better look?'

Sacré nom de nom! 'Me, I was not nearby but he wouldn't have touched anything. When I returned, he said that God would find it hard to forgive the killers. Then he rode off on his bicycle.'

'Killers?' asked that Sûreté.

'*Oui.* Since the bodies were not lying together or even beside the van, Father Adrien concluded rightly, as I also did, that the shots must have come from two assailants.'

'And where, precisely, did he find the bodies?'

And never mind who had first been busy hauling that canvas, thought Kohler.

'Both were some distance from the van, Chief Inspector, the one not among the herbs that are nearest to the ruins of the kitchen, but nearer the distant remains of the boundary wall and in what must once have been another herbal, the other in what little remains of the chapter house which is right next to what was once the sanctuary and main altar but has more walls.'

A mouthful, but Louis wasn't going to let him off.

'Father Adrien was summoned by yourself, was he?'

'That is correct. Whenever there is a death, I always summon him.'

'Now tell us why such a van would even have been here?'

'Robbery. Hijacked on the road from Reims to Laon. That bank regularly does collections from Reims to Laon, Soissons and Senlis before returning to Paris.'

'And is that all that Father Adrien told you?'

L'espèce de salaud! 'He said that it had to have been the Résistance from Reims, that they would have known the schedule far better even than the victims.'

And wouldn't you know it, thought Kohler. Reims instead of Laon which was much closer to Corbeny. The steaks were woody, the lard a trifle off and the tea as thin as usual.

Snapping his fingers, Hermann demanded the reserve cigarette, and carefully cutting it in half, lit both at the fire and passed one to the corporal before sharing the other with this partner of his.

It was Louis who told Rocheleau to keep the fire going and the tea warm. 'We'll have a look.'

When well away, it was Hermann who said, 'That was one of the old Lebel Modèle d'ordonnance 1886, eight millimetres.'

And the first to have used the 'new' smokeless powder and find itself in the Great War and then during the Blitzkrieg of this one. 'A museum piece, Hermann. The bolt sticks out like a sore thumb and catches on everything, and the spare rounds that have been patiently fed into the forestock's tubular magazine insist on taking their time.'

'That needle of a pig sticker's lance is a good fifty centimetres long.'

'He's hiding something. Me, I still don't know what it is but assume there's got to be more than meets the eye.'

'Another piece of canvas for starters. It was tucked behind the rubble he had leaned that beat-up old blue chariot against. If you'd been observant and using the cameras of the mind that you repeatedly insist on, you'd have seen it.'

'*Ah bon, mon vieux*, you *did* see it. Me, I'm gratified. The lessons I've been trying to teach you are finally coming home. Keep up the good work.'

'Laon may have lots of *réseaux*, Louis, but that priest of his was smart enough to point us in the opposite direction.'

'But was the poor box of his church alleviated?'

Since it was a bank van. 'Meaning that even priests might be tempted?'

'You said it, not myself. Me to find the bodies, you to look over the van. It'll be drier.'

'Then take this with you.'

'I'd no idea you were so light-fingered.'

'Stores at the rue des Saussaies would just have sold that flask on the *marché noir*, and you know that as well as I do.'

It even held an *eau de vie de poire*.

'The Williams pear, Louis, the same as what's called the Bartlett in America. Giselle got it for me. The bottle's in the boot but it doesn't have a label so it's just one of those from a travelling still that goes from farm to farm and holds a good deal back because of that same black market and in spite of all the red tape your Vichy food controllers have thrown up against such necessary things.'

Giselle being one of the two women Hermann cohabited with when he had time and was in Paris and not busy, the girl having returned to live with him, Oona also. 'Enjoy yourself.'

'Be sure to look for cartridge casings, Chief. Footprints will be out of the question. We'll let that ex-corporal stew in his own juice and then we'll pickle him for good measure.'

Adding a few twigs to the fire that siphoned gasoline from the van had started, Rocheleau heaved a grateful sigh. The 'steaks' had done their work. Those two from Paris had noticed nothing. They'd find the bodies and would have a look at the van and then they'd come back with their questions to receive the answers already given.

Taking another piece of sausage from his coat pocket, he skewered it onto the stick he would burn once the repast had been consumed. *Un saucisson fumé de Champagne* and with the fully ripened Brie de Meaux, a little taste from heaven and who would have thought such would be possible in a bank van? Even Father Adrien had been surprised. He had seen the bottles and had immediately shoved two into the deep pockets of that cassock of his and had clutched a third and given him the gospel. 'For the Mass,

Eugène. Say nothing, my son. What has happened here is not for us. Let the police from Paris deal with it.'

Fritz-haired when he had pulled off the Gestapo's storm hat, Herr Kohler was taller by far than that Sûreté turtle of his. And yes, a glistening scar caressed the left cheek from eye to chin, giving reminders of something Herr Kohler would definitely remember for the rest of his life should the end of this Occupation require a certain *garde champêtre* to point the finger of truth before the post was used, the one at least for that collabo partner of his.

Shrapnel scars from that other war had graced the storm-trooper countenance, the age, that of about fifty-five or fifty-six and maybe three years older than his little follower. Bulldog jowls had given the sad, rheumy faded-blue eyes a little more intensity, but they had held interest only in the rifle and its bayonet, and memories perhaps of that other war. The hands had been big, the touch of the fingers as he had held that cigarette, light.

The tortoise was, of course, still with that bland, broad and defiant holier-than-thou brow, the moustache much more than that of the German Führer he served, the thick and bushy eyebrows the same as before, the hair a dark brown but without the grey that had immediately overtaken his own after that battle. Medium in height, blocky across the shoulders, that one had changed so little he still terrified. But the bullet scars across the brow had been more recent, though it was a great pity some criminal had missed him. Here, as the battle had raged, the limestone had caused an infinity of rounds to ricochet until one from a sniper had slipped through to knock that *salaud* off his feet, causing St-Cyr to drop the rifle he had only just picked up, intending to thrust it back at himself and prevent such an act of cowardice.

Crossing himself, he said to no one but himself, Me, I thought he really was dead and that all my worries were over, but when I found that he wasn't, I thought to take up his Lebel Modèle 1873 and let him have one of those old eleven millimetres even if that revolver should misfire due to the years of the government's having stored them in dampness. Black powder too. But he opened his eyes and said, '*Ah bon, mon brave*, you've got your rifle again. Push on. Keep them from me.'

When everyone else was shitting themselves and wanting to run. Those two from Paris would find the victims for certain and food enough for the Action Courts, but could they be accused of stealing any of it for themselves?

Having crossed what little remained of the cloister and its court-yard, and now adjacent to the eastern end of the church itself, St-Cyr entered what had been the chapter house. This small, square room, with its arched and gaping doorway to what was left of the sanctuary and altar, had two openings that faced onto the eastern walk of the cloister. Light would have entered from the remains of the three windows in its outer wall, and it was here that the abbot and his monks would have met each morning after the first hour to go over any problems and the business of the day. A lectern would have stood facing the cloister openings, the abbot sitting behind it, the monks on two rows of benches before him.

But all of that was gone except for the broken-off stems of a couple of the columns that would have supported the vault above which now gaped at the sky.

'From just such a past do we poor mortals pass into the pres-ent,' he said to the victim as if by way of greeting, for no matter how hard one tried, the reverence of these ruins still intruded on the thoughts.

Caught among the squared-off blocks of medium-grey lime-stone with their encroaching dark-green moss, ivy and wild grape, the man lay under canvas as if in the Great War. Hermann would immediately have turned away and probably thrown up. Having lost his two sons at Stalingrad before the defeat of von Paulus and the Sixth Army there early last February, this impulse of his had become more intense with every new murder. The younger, the harder; the more innocent, the more terrible. 'My partner's really a very good detective and I've come to absolutely depend on him, while he himself has increasingly become the citizen of the world I've been encouraging.'

Pausing to let that sink in and the cameras of the mind to do their work, he gave the room the once over, noted the sodden grass and wildflowers that had gone to seed, lush as they both were, and the encroaching saplings of the forest. And finding one of the latter broken off some distance from the corpse, fingered it in doubt and said, '*Ah bon, mon ami*, what has gone on here?'

The grass could, or could not have been trampled more than

necessary. It was simply impossible to tell, but the room was small and all but a cul-de-sac. Had the victim been trying to hide? Had he heard the other one being shot, or had he been the first?

Gently pulling back the canvas, he had to pause, for before being killed, the victim had been holding a bloodied handkerchief to his forehead. 'Had you been hit by a stone, or did you fall and hit yourself? Is that why there was that broken sapling? Dazed, you would have stood, the killer then jamming that weapon of his tight against your chest.'

Surprise . . . Had that been it, that left hand up and near the head as if, in having been startled, he had just removed the handkerchief?

The bank's uniform jacket, vest, shirt and undershirt had all been torn by the bullet's entry, the muzzle having left its circle around the bullet hole. There would be powder burns. Joliot would also find the tiny tattoos the grains of that gunpowder would have left as they'd been driven into the skin.

'Had your clothing not been torn, I'd have thought the bullet had been fired from at least a metre away.'

Rigor had passed, but with the cold and dampness, decay would have been retarded. Hypostasis, the lividity due to the gravitational settling of the blood into its lowest parts, would have begun after about two hours, giving the slatey blue to reddish patches that were evident. The lips were that same blue, the eyes somewhat clouded, though of a deep brown, the face broad, strongly-boned and quite pale.

'Since on average rigor lasts for sixteen to twenty-four hours, *mon ami*, and begins from two to four after death, the time this could most recently have happened is yesterday and probably in the morning since it is now 1320 hours, but it could also have happened on the preceding day, perhaps in the afternoon. Joliot will be able to give a far more definite estimate since I've broken my thermometer, but when were you first found and who was it that reported the killings? Certainly not Rocheleau, and why, of course, did whoever it was happen to come upon you and that van in a place like this? It's not usual to walk here, nor to visit the ruins in weather like this.'

The victim had been unarmed, the Germans increasingly hesitant to even allow such a thing as pistols for bank guards. In age he was in his mid-thirties, but nowadays especially with Gauleiter Sauckel's demands for forced labour and the Vichy government's compulsory labour draft, the Service du Travail Obligatoire, papers would be needed detailing the absolute necessity of the Banque Nationale de Crédit et Commercial's having him. Such a necessity would also have meant that the third bank employee, the one who would normally have ridden in the back and assisted the second with the pickups and deliveries, had no longer been possible and they were having to deal with only two victims.

'Also, *mon ami*, and one has to ask this, why were you not a prisoner of war in the Reich, along with all the others? Had you been rejected by the military for health reasons, tuberculosis perhaps? *Bien sûr*, there could be any number of reasons, the eyesight among them, but still there has to be a reason, *n'est-ce pas?*'

The pockets had been turned out and emptied, the papers and everything else simply taken, even the small change that was so necessary now if one was to ride the *métro*, whose riders had gone from 2 million a day in the autumn of 1940 to nearly 4 million. And since German soldiers on leave were fond of being forgetful and continued to take their change home, the correct amount was now being demanded by the ticket collectors, causing utter chaos at times.

Unlike so many these days, however, this one had obviously been eating well enough. 'And married too. Have you children?' he asked.

When he found a wooden-handled Opinel, the peasant's standby, behind a stone, he wondered if the knife had been held in defiance. 'But not by yourself, *mon ami*. Not when found here. Was it torn from the hand that held it and thrown aside by yourself, eh? Is that why the rock that bashed your forehead left such a mark you had to pause to mop it?

'*Ah merde*, monsieur, was it a *third* victim we are now going to have to concern ourselves with, and while we're at it, why would your killer take the time to empty your pockets if your partner was still on the run, or was he the first?'

Deep in the grass and wildflowers to the right of where the killer would have stood, he found the cartridge casing and heaving a contented sigh, said, 'Now the investigation really begins, doesn't it? An altercation causes the forehead wound, that party then running from you, yourself to sit and mop the forehead only to then be confronted by the killer. Understandably I need more proof, of course, so for now we'll just say it's curious.'

The cartridge casing was from a nine-millimetre Parabellum round, common enough in a Luger or Walther P38, and certainly the Résistance, if the killer was of them, could have bought the weapon from among the Occupier.

'Automatically this casing was ejected, but Hermann will remind me that the Browning FN, the first truly automatic pistol, the one that the Belgians gave to the world of killing and adopted for their own army prior to this war, was also adopted by the Dutch, who called it the Pistool M25, No. 2. The Browning Hi-Power has a thirteen-round magazine and it's not a common Résistance gun, so it has to be telling us something else if that is what it really was. *Merde*, but the questions keep piling up, don't they? The Parabellum is a high-powered round. There will be markings on this cartridge—scratches from the breech and its ejector, the imprint of the firing pin as well. All of these can be compared with the next one I had better find because then, if they're the same, it will tell us that whoever killed you most probably went after your partner using the very same weapon.'

But clearly something else *had* happened here before that shot had been fired. 'It really does get deeper and deeper, doesn't it? Hermann would have said, "It's like swimming in gravy, Louis. The bottom's hard to find and the lumps just get in the way, but we always have the taste of it."'

Turning the body over, he found the slug and pocketed it. Hermann would be pleased.

It was a Purdey smooth bore, side-by-side 12-gauge, an absolutely gorgeous upland gun. Still in the cradle that had been made for it between the two seats in the van's cab, it certainly would have been a bit of a problem drawing it quickly, but there would have been no argument from anyone as the crew had collected deposits or made a delivery. Beautifully chased ducks on the wing in silver set off the gun-metal blue of the barrels and the straight-grained French walnut stock. Tightly incised, the crosshatching of the left hand's grip sparkled even with this lousy daylight and fitted that fist perfectly. And were the day not so miserable, Kohler knew he would have stepped out to flow through the motions of shooting imaginary birds on the wing.

'Louis, it's a honey,' he said, though Louis was elsewhere. 'I'll have to lock it up in the Citroën's boot so that no one steals the evidence.'

As to why the killer or killers had left it, and why the driver or his assistant hadn't at least tried to draw it, would have to remain questions for now, but back in the early autumn of 1940 guns like this had been confiscated unless smeared with cosmoline and buried, the penalty for doing such being far too onerous for most. There had been racks and racks of hunting rifles and shotguns, pistols and revolvers too. Those whose owners had held British passports, including, no doubt, the owner of this shotgun, had been arrested, the men sent to the internment camp in the former French Army barracks at Saint-Denis, just to the north of Paris. British women, and those with that passport who were French, had all been sent to the old military barracks atop the mesa over-looking Besançon, but so bad had the winter of 1940–1941 been, so appalling the conditions the French had imposed, that the Wehrmacht had insisted that those with children under the age of fifteen should be released and sent back to their homes in France, the rest to Vittel's Parc Thermal, an internationally famous spa and one that Louis and he knew only too well from last February.

Stamped and signed by the Kommandant von Gross-Paris and the Reich's chief supervisor of French banks, since such travel permission was required, the van's manifest on its clipboard was under a spill of shotgun shells he quickly pocketed. As he ran his gaze down the list, he muttered, 'Cash . . . cash . . . and more of it. Eighteen branch pickups, for a total of 42 bags and 65,250,000 francs.'

Even at the official exchange rates of 20 francs to the Reichs-kassenscheine the troops were given to spend, it was 3,262,500 of those, or when at 200 francs to the British pound, or 45 to the U.S. dollar, not the black bourse's 100 to 140, still 326,250 pounds or 1,450,000 dollars, a bigger than usual pickup.

All of the notes would have been sorted as to size and tied with that twisted paper string everyone had to use these days and hated, elastics being simply nonexistent. But once at the desig-nated entrance to the city, the Porte d'Aubervilliers, no one would have bothered to take any more than a glance at this manifest, not unless some of the Führer's finest had had a share in what else was in the back.

Squeezing round, he had a look through the armoured window. Cut open, the heavy grey bags had been scattered in haste, loose banknotes seemingly everywhere, the blue, green and white of the five-franc notes, brown of the tens and hundreds. But right on top of a wooden case whose straw packing had been scattered, was a round of what could only be Brie de Meaux. A bottle of Moët et Chandon had had its neck snapped off, the champagne downed in celebration probably, but why leave it standing upright near that cheese, why not throw it out the back since that door would have been open as it now was?

There was nothing for it but to have a closer look, and going round to the back, he climbed in and somehow found room enough to stand. 'Louis, what the hell has really gone on here? They didn't even go into lockdown."

Louis could take forever with a corpse and was still nowhere near. Two wedges of the Brie had been eaten and, since taking fingerprints was next to useless these days, as he cut into that velvety white surface, the aroma, when held closely, was magnificent, the taste like heaven. Yet case after case of the champagne had been left, six in all: two of the Moët et Chandon, two of the Taittinger and the same of the Mumm. And as if those were not enough, there were two open cases of a *vin rouge* and another two of a *blanc de blanc*, three bottles of the former having been taken.

Bought at 85 francs the litre, that wine would have sold in Paris for a good 500 francs, the champagne for 1,000, the bottle having been bought at 150 probably, and at 10 bottles to the case, a good 51,000 for the champagne, and 16,600 for the wine, for a total profit on these alone of 67,600 francs and not bad at all.

Certainly the two with the van hadn't just been augmenting their wages. If each trip had been like this, they must have been planning an early retirement. There were even bags of cooking onions, unheard of these days in Paris and most other large cities and towns. Smoked sausage was in coils atop hams from Reims, at least twenty of those, and beneath them all, as if they were not

---

* A lever that locks all the doors if the van is threatened.

enough, several sides of bacon, a good ten rabbits and two dozen fully plucked chickens. Obviously these boys had had deliveries to make as soon as they arrived back in the city and before returning to the bank's garage. That bacon would have brought at least 250 the kilo, the chickens from 150 to 200 each and the rabbits maybe 50 apiece since most who could raised their own in the cupboard or on the balcony or roof, the citizenry having turned Paris, with all its vegetable pots and plots, into the largest farming village in the world.

Garlic hung by the necklace and would bring at least 35 francs the bulb, whereas before this Occupation it would have cost 50 centimes at most, but when he uncovered black truffles, he really had to pause, for these were of the winter variety and would bring at least 5,000 a kilo, maybe even 7,500, the summer ones a hell of a lot less, but it all depended on who the customer was and how much was on offer; other things too, like friends and friends of friends.

Merde, but there were sardines in tins from as far away as Marseille. At eight-five to ninety the tin, they would originally have cost maybe three, if that, before the Occupation. Butter was now at 120 the kilo, and there were four crocks of it, another four of eggs submerged in water glass. The eggs, bought at sixty francs the ten, could bring twenty each if sold individually for something that would originally have cost from five to seven for the ten back in 1939, and with wages stagnant at generally 1,000 to 1,500 a month, or lots less, prices had simply climbed and climbed.*

There was even coffee, but had these boys had access to one of the warehouses of the Vichy food controllers? Coffee was like gold, the ersatz simply horrible, so at least 500 the half-kilo for the real.

'This has to suggest someone big, *mon vieux*,' he said, though Louis still hadn't shown up. Moving on, he came to the topic of bread. It was one of those few things that couldn't be bought on the *marché noir*, but flour could be and they had four fifty-kilo bags of that beautiful white stuff that would go for at least

---

* Tracking prices during the Occupation is exceedingly difficult, for they changed from year to year and place to place, hence best estimates for October 1943 are used.

seventy-five the kilo, since birthday cakes, brioches, croissants and other such things had been judged 'luxuries' by Vichy and banned back in the late autumn of 1940.

Yet not only had the killer or killers left all of the provisions behind, they had seemingly left the bundles of five thousands, one thousands and five hundreds and had taken what they could grab of the small bills, the hundreds, twenties, tens and fives.

Placed as it was a goodly distance from the ruins of the monastery's church and other buildings, and right near what had once been the two-metre high peripheral wall, with plenty of open land left inside, the second 'herbal,' felt St-Cyr, must have been a centuries-old throw bed and humus pile. Fully in sunshine, when available, its plants had flourished.

The other victim was lying face down and clearly visible from the ruins of the church, he having all but made it into the thickness of the encroaching forest, having run from the killer. Challenged from behind, he had thrown up his hands in surrender and had immediately been shot in the back of the neck. 'The *Genickschuss*,' St-Cyr heard himself saying with that certain sense of alarm since it was a favourite method among the Occupier no matter which country they were in, especially the SS and Gestapo, but the Wehrmacht also when *Banditen—résistants*—who had been caught were to be executed on the spot.

'My partner will immediately think, as I now must, that the pistol was most probably either a Walther P38 or Luger and the killer German. But that doesn't make much sense, does it, unless whoever fired that pistol was on the run and a deserter? We've had some of those coming through, now more since the Russian front is far from a picnic.'

In age this one was the younger, more strongly built and probably, at somewhere between twenty-five to twenty-eight, the assistant. Certainly all those background questions again needed to be asked, then, too. 'Were you also a father?' For killings like these always tended to hurt far too many.

As before, the pockets had been emptied. *'Bien sûr*, identity cards and all accompanying papers can be doctored, and there's a ready market for them, but why bother when you've a van loaded with cash?'

It made no sense, even though the price for used identity papers had gone from fifty francs in the autumn of 1940 to 250, the supporting documents extra.

'This inflation of ours is terrible, isn't it?' he said. 'Seventy percent since the autumn of 1940, with most wages frozen at prewar rates, my own included.'

Covering the victim, he added, 'And now for the challenge, eh, especially as I'm all but certain your killer was the same as that of your boss.'

Left to itself, fennel could grow in great profusion and here it was so tall and thick, the dill was threatened as was the recovery of that cartridge casing. Down on his hands and knees, forcing his way into the thicket, he said, 'There are limits to my patience, Hermann. Maybe you should be here instead of myself!'

Leaves, old stalks, the refuse of the forgotten years didn't make the task easy. Taking a break, he went to harvest a little dill. Letting that wonderful astringency and aroma come, he again went down on the hands and knees, was now soaked through and with no easy way of getting dry.

The ground wasn't just spongy. The knees sank in, the hands too. Sunlight, if God had granted it, would have made the job easier. In all it took an hour and by then he had, of course, repeatedly heard Hermann calling for him and at the last, a more vehement, '*Verdammt*, Louis, where the hell are you?'

Disregarding the summons, sheltering the 10x lens the years had given him, he scanned the two casings side by side. '*Ah bon*, there's little doubt. Similar scratches imply that it was the same gun, the killings done by a decisive individual who, for some reason, didn't hesitate to silence both of you.'

The pungent aromas of juniper and rosemary were here, the taste of those and of sage, thyme and oregano in scatterings, and had the day been different, he would have spent happy hours harvesting. 'There's even a stonemason's mark,' he said, tracing it out on a large rectangular block. Though several hundred years old, it was still as fresh as the day it had been cut. 'A circle with inwardly pointing arrowheads on the single horizontal line that cuts it exactly in half and is parallel to the bedding planes of the limestone. As to its meaning, *mon ami*, it's somewhat like a murder investigation. One should consider that the job must be compassed round and studied carefully from every angle. This one was a master builder. No names are ever in any of the history books, hardly a mention even, and yet . . . and yet they have left us so much.'

Hermann was now madly waving both arms, only to finally point toward the muddy lane they had taken to get the Citroën in as far as possible.

Top down, for the rain must have miraculously stopped, a Wehrmacht-camouflaged tourer flew drenched swastika penants. The one at the wheel had stood up to better see them and signal that they both should come near. No need, then, for anyone else to muddy their boots or shoes.

'*Merde*, visitors no one wants, and with no time for us to first talk things over.'

Apart from the silver skull and crossbones on the cap, and the braiding, the one in the back with the open topcoat looked like Rommel in the desert war that had finally been lost on 12 May of this year after so many successes, while the one in the dark-grey fedora with down-pulled brim and topcoat collar up who was sucking on a cigarette in the front seat beside the driver and polishing his steel-framed specs, looked the epitome of an aging Gestapo gumshoe.

'God always smiles when least expected, Hermann.'

'Why a Standartenführer, Louis?'

That, too, was a very good question: a colonel in the SD, the Sicherheitsdienst, the Secret Service of the SS and Nazi Party. 'Ours is but to ask, but let's keep things to ourselves. You to do the talking, me to play the conquered subordinate with Gestapo detective overseer.'

'Don't rub it in. Let me just tell you that things are definitely not right with what's happened here and that bastard under the grey sombrero who's still sucking on his breakfast teeth is someone we simply don't want meddling in our business.'

'*Ah mon Dieu, mon vieux*, it gets deeper and deeper, doesn't it?'

'You really do want the last word so I'll let you have it while that *garde champêtre* of yours cooks his own little goose and fails to show himself at such a time.'

Orders were orders. Taking up his position, Rocheleau stood guard with bayoneted rifle behind the van. If the rain didn't return, he would be all right, but these old boots . . . The wife *would* insist that he wear them to remind that *salaud* St-Cyr of the battle, but of course a person like that would make no mention of his having been *saved* by anyone, let alone a corporal he had apprehended. Indeed, getting a medic to attend to him had not been easy, nor without extreme danger. 'He would have died had I not done what I did, yet still he fails to thank me. Well we shall see, won't we, *Monsieur l'Inspecteur principal de la Sûreté Nationale*? When the end is near and all you collabos get what's coming to you in the purge, me I will rejoice! The blindfold, eh? The priest perhaps, but I don't think the Résistance in Reims or Laon or even in a little place like Corbeny will ever allow one. Rather it will be that the soul, it goes straight to hell.'

St-Cyr and that Gestapo partner of his were now standing in the mud beside the car that had arrived, but . . . *Ah merde*, Herr Kohler hadn't returned the Heil Hitler salute that the one in the back with the officer's cap had given.

There were no medals on the colonel. There didn't need to be, felt Kohler, for this one was a behind the scenes man, a non-entity, a shadow unless he, or his superior officers in Berlin, wanted it otherwise.

He was also, of course, one of Heinrich Himmler's 'Teutonic Knights.' And as for the ruffled dumpling in the nondescript fedora and years-old grey topcoat who was now sucking on a fresh fag, that one had the look of Hamburg and the age and experience of a pending retirement that simply wasn't going to happen, not with the war in rapid retreat.

The adjutant, knowing his place, sat down behind the wheel and said nothing, neither did the Gestapo. Mud had, however, splashed the right sleeve of the colonel's coat. Livid, that one's gaze leapt.

'Kohler, who did this, where are they, and why have you not apprehended them?'

Louis would be taking in everything while smiling at his partner's discomfort, but Berlin couldn't possibly have any interest in what had happened here. '*Ach*, Colonel, those are excellent questions, but might we have your name and those of the others, just for the record? And while you're at it, could you tell us who found the bodies and when? We'll assume they then reported the crime.'

'*Lieber Christus im Himmel, verdammter Schweinebulle*, are you to remain defiant of authority even when I am in charge?'

Pig-fuzz, was it?

'You fail to return my salute, Kohler? You give me no answers? Living with a Dutch widow whose husband was a Jew? Living also with a French whore who is young enough to have been your daughter? Well, we shall see. Now answer me, damn you.'

Louis would have urged caution, but an answer had been demanded. 'Definitely, Colonel, but let me clear the air. The widow lost her two children during the Blitzkrieg's exodus and still hasn't found them, and the husband was later rounded up and killed, she then needing help. The "whore," as you're calling her, is now lead model at a very fashionable shop on the *place* Vendôme— it's right near the Ritz and sells female undergarments, perfume, soap and other rare and very expensive unmentionables to generals and visiting dignitaries from the Reich. As to your questions, when my partner and I have the answers, we will be only too prepared to give them to you after first checking everything out with Gestapo Boemelburg, my superior, and Major Osias Pharand, my partner's. Now *liebe Zeit*, back off and tell us who found the bodies and when, and while you're at it, if you know something we should, then spit it out.'

This *Scheisskerl* wasn't going to like the answer to that simplest of his questions. 'Untersturmführer Ludwig Mohnke and Oberführer Wolfgang Thomsen, his senior officer. Brigadier Thomsen wanted to show the young man the Drachenhöhle, to go over tactics he had used here during the Great War.'

La Caverne du Dragon had been a quarry on the other side of the Chemin des Dames. Enlarged into a bunker, the Wehrmacht had then made rooms and rooms for the boys to sleep, relax and take their meals in until the French had finally mined their own way in and the two sides had bricked off each other while still shooting. It wasn't any more than a kilometre or two to the south of the ruins, but that second lieutenant was related to the SS Major General Wilhelm Mohnke, the commander of Heinrich Himmler's bodyguard.

'They came on here yesterday afternoon, Kohler, and found the van and the bodies at between 1430 and 1530 hours, reporting it to the General Hans von Boineburg-Lengsfeld directly on their return to Paris, since the van's head office is located in his city.'

Louis would be thinking, *Merde*, now they really were in it! That Kommandant von Gross-Paris had been a cavalry officer in the Great War and was a stickler for protocol, a dyed-in-the-wool Prussian of the old school just like his predecessor.

'Kriminalkommissar Ludin will be your liaise, Kohler. At 0800 hours tomorrow, you will present yourself at 84 avenue Foch. A full report.'

And never mind the Führer's having put France on Central European Time in June 1940 and recently having added an hour of daylight saving time in autumn and winter, making that 0800 really 0600 the old time. 'Not if we have to spend the night here, Colonel, and haven't finished our preliminary examination and are still awaiting Coroner Joliot and his clean-up crew.'

The first sprinklings of the next deluge had arrived. As if he had plenty of tobacco, this 'Ludin' passed his cigarette over.

'Contact me when you're ready, Kohler, but don't leave it too long. Full details, nothing left out, everything to myself.'

'Then be so good as to tell us why the hell you lot should even be interested?'

'That's for us to know, and not yourselves. Just do as I've said and we'll get along fine.'

Skidding in the mud, the tourer departed, and as they watched, that feeling of being alone against the world returned. In spite of the partnership's desperate need, Hermann crumbled the cigarette and let the deluge take it.

'*Merde alors*, Louis, what has Boemelburg dropped us into this time?'

'A fetid shell crater full of water and hidden by barbed wire. Let's deal with our *garde champêtre* while there's still some semblance of daylight. We'll visit his campfire, pick up the necessary, and let him stand guard while we question him from the shelter of the van.'

'Why hasn't the bank shown up?'

'A good question, but perhaps no one has thought to tell them or they simply got word of the other visitors and decided it would be better to wait. That *Kriminalrattenfänger* is trouble, Hermann. Didn't the RAF firebomb Hamburg on the night of 27 July last, and the USAAF during the day, the two then carrying on the visit for a few more nights and days?'

With winds said to have been at temperatures of up to 1000°C and speeds of 240 kph, there had been more than 40,000 dead, up to 100,000 injured and countless left homeless. And since *Kriminalkommissar* and *Kriminalrattenfänger* meant the same, the latter's shortened form of 'criminal rat-catcher' would do. 'Maybe that *Kriminalrat* is just out for blood, Louis, and feels we'll slake his thirst, but whoever killed those two didn't bother with the big bills and left virtually all of the food and wine, the champagne and black truffles.'

'But took time to empty the pockets and take the identity papers of the victims, even the small change? That doesn't make sense.'

'Not unless we're dealing with something very different.'

Rocheleau hadn't just stolen a few coils of sausage and several other items. His makeshift satchel, tucked as it had been behind yet further blocks of stone, betrayed something in the clutter they definitely didn't want to see. Sickened, Hermann said, 'Where the hell is she, Louis? Out there somewhere lying naked with her throat cut?'

A forearm was grabbed to steady him. 'It's only a pair of shoes. There could well have been a perfectly logical reason.'

'You're hedging. Me, I can always tell. High heels like those? Dark blue leather like it used to be? Hardly ever worn? Kept for good? Those were kicked off so that she could run when those bastards up front brought her here and she realized what they were going to do. They hadn't gone into lockdown. That back door would have been locked from the outside with the key they use when collecting cash or delivering it. She wouldn't have known what the hell to do to open it and they damned well wouldn't have told her, not with what they had in mind.'

Sometimes Hermann jumped to conclusions, but was that really the case, considering the forehead of the first victim and the Opinel that had been thrown aside? Yet there had been a robbery. 'She could have been a decoy.'

Must Louis examine everything from every angle? 'A plant who then found she had to run? Did those two grab her?'

'Or find her too fleet of foot, and then find a little something else? A nine millimetre in each, Hermann, the *Genickschuss* in the second, the chest up tight in the first.'

'Then why not empty that bloody van? Why take only the small bills, cut two wedges from a Brie, snap off the neck of a bottle of Moët et Chandon and drain but a mouthful?'

This definitely wasn't good. 'She can't have been a decoy unless the robbers and the killer intended to silence her too. We'll both have to search, you to the ruins, myself to where I think she might have headed, since its cover is somewhat better. Rocheleau is to remain on guard.'

'I'll take that bayonet and rifle and lock them in the van.'

'Not without its keys, Hermann. The killer must have taken them.'

'So as to break into something else?'

The bank's depot, garage, offices or vault? Had Hermann hit on it? 'Let's leave that one for now.'

Louis headed off toward the Chemin des Dames with determination. Young or old, corpse or no corpse, it was always the same, a detective through and through, felt Kohler. 'And an example to us all,' he muttered, 'but *lieber Gott, mon vieux*, is she lying up there in those woods, naked, splayed out, pegged down hard like the one I found in Munich on a Sunday, 6 May 1939 at 0540 hours?'

Ilse Grünwald had been fifteen, the throat cut so deeply, the head had all but been severed, the flashlight glinting from her eyes.

He paused. He had to, and when done, said, '*Verdammt*, I can't be throwing up anymore. I'm just going to have to press on like the chief, and he knows it too.'

When he found the ashes, though soaking wet, they lay in the tall grass but a couple of metres from the ruins and ten along from the van. Almost side by side were two arched doorways, the farthest with an empty ocular that gazed with suspicion, as rampart by rampart the ruins descended until almost shoulder height next to the ashes. Incompletely burned charcoal lay amid what had to be the ash of starter wood and charcoal, suggesting that the robbers had come in the usual: a *gazogène* with firebox well dampened to make the producer-gas with which to feed the engine instead of gasoline or diesel fuel.

When he saw what looked to be metal, he began to sift the ashes, and when the corners of identity photos came up and then some coins, he fortunately found the keys to the van and set them all aside in a cluster on the nearby wall, only to find a little something else too. It was just lying there, yet tobacco was in such short supply, most collected cigarette butts and thought nothing of picking them up in the streets and bars, and this just had to be the *mégot* tin of that firebox's feeder. On its lid was an enraptured, free-spirited *fin-de-siècle* nude lying back on a divan, sampling one of the honey-and-absinthe throat lozenges and declaring it perfect while admiring a diamond the size of a pigeon's egg on her finger.

An elongated puddle, parallel to the wall, lay in the grass. Deep, it indicated a heavy load, and when that truck had finally got going again, it had skidded several times, but had that girl of the shoes managed to escape, only to be caught by the killer or one of the others who must have been with him?

When he had gathered up the necessary, he glanced behind the wall and found the charred, soggy remains of what must have been a poultice.

2

Coming to a grove of beech, St-Cyr immediately began to gather a few of the nuts only to stop himself. He was now to the south of the ruins and much nearer to the Chemin des Dames. From its lower heights, he could look back out over the flat valley floor to see Hermann and then the van, the ruins running east-to-west to catch maximum sunlight whenever possible, for the Cistercians always built their abbeys this way and with plenty of water, forest and field. He could even follow the line of the hollow, now full of rainwater, that must mark the top of the once much deeper, timber-lined channel that would have conducted water from the Ailette to gristmill, forge, brewery, latrines and sawmill, and the ponds in which the monks would have raised the carp they ate instead of meat. But they would not have used that water for everything. He was, he realized, near the spring they would have visited daily for their drinking water and cooking. He could even hear it.

Uphill of him, the sodden ferns revealed cobbles in places that had once paved the former path, but had that girl known of the spring, had she run this way knowing there might be a grotto in which to hide from those two in the van?

Nothing was broken, nothing flattened. It was as if she had deliberately avoided leaving any such trace, and when he came to the spring, it poured readily over a flat, grey slab of limestone the monks could well have left in place.

Pausing to drink as he would have done in 1914 or 1917 had opportunity allowed, he rested a hand on the slab. Surprisingly, it moved ever so slightly, but . . .

'Did you even come this far?' he had to ask, and only then

saw that she must have slipped away to his left to enter somewhat denser forest uphill. But she wasn't there either. Instead, a good twenty metres from the spring, the single frond of very healthy fern among many had been hesitantly grasped and its top broken. No others had been damaged, but he was all but certain she had stood where he now was. Having heard the first of the shots, she had sought comfort in that touch and then, as the second shot had come, had instinctively snapped the frond and known exactly what must have happened.

Not until he returned to the edge of the encroaching forest, and with his back to the Chemin des Dames, did he find any further evidence.

She had stood here and waited, not knowing if she, too, would be killed.

Two healthy young saplings of hornbeam had been deliberately trampled. Of the two killings, the first he had examined had been the closer. The second had been all but across the ruins to the north and by that peripheral wall, which could only mean that she had run that way first and then had used that wall to hide her coming back and around the ruins to here and the spring. 'But why leave such a trace, mademoiselle, when you already knew the location?' Hermann had gone all but right around the ruins of the church and remains of its outbuildings, had even had a look at the bodies, for he was standing by the farthest, holding a corner of the tarp, had forced himself to do it. But if she hadn't been a decoy, then what better way for her to get through the controls and into Paris unnoticed than by riding in the back of a bank van? Unless he was very mistaken, she couldn't have known that it was going to be robbed, nor that those two would even think to turn on her.

Still feeling her former presence, he heard himself saying, '*Ah bon*, mademoiselle, Joliot and his crew have finally arrived. The two who are with him can start looking for you in earnest then come back tomorrow with others and the dogs if needed. But if the killer didn't shoot you, what then?'

Joliot's faded dark-blue 1933 Peugeot 301 two-door didn't have a firebox. Instead, having been fitted with a roof-top battery of fifteen-centimetre diameter metal tubes to hold the bottled producer-gas from the depot in Laon, it looked like a badly designed makeshift rocket launcher. One of the Russian 'organs' perhaps, their 'little Kate's' from the tender song of such a girl, the banefully howling Katyusha.

When Hermann caught up with him, he said, 'Yet another *gazogène*, Louis. That killer came in a heavily loaded one.'

More couldn't be said.

'*Mes amis,*' shouted Joliot, who looked like a rake handle in stiff black tweed and a detachable snap-on collar that had been yanked at so hard Kohler could see that it had come loose. '*Putain de merde*, Jean-Louis and Herr Kohler, the fart-gas that wretched old china vase of ours insists on gave the carburettor a hiccup and stopped me cold on the road. Me, I was patching a tire whose inner tube only Picasso would want for the variety and design of its innumerable patches. Profound apologies. Emergency repairs take time and these old hands, they can only do so much when that Victor of Verdun insists I pay the official eighty francs for a new inner tube that will be useless if I can get it, instead of the eight hundred of the *marché noir* where the availability and quality are almost, if not quite, as they used to be. What have you two for me this time, eh? More trouble?'

So many china vases had been made with Pétain's mug on them, the *maréchal* had acquired that epithet, thought Kohler, but it was Louis who said, 'Just the two for now, Théo. We need you to pin down the time, but there may also have been another. *Garde champêtre* Rocheleau will be only too willing to show you where the first two are, and while you're at it, Hermann and I will give the van another going over.'

'Rocheleau, *ah oui, oui,* that one, he has the wife who is twenty years the younger and has not only ambitions for him but for herself. Me, I don't envy him, even if she does have a figure fit for the gods and likes to display it. Father Adrien, their priest, simply lifts the eyes of despair and tosses the futile hand since the confessional, it is private and none of my business. No one comes here, Jean-Louis, yet suddenly there's a robbery and two murders and we must have tourists who visit the Caverne du Dragon yesterday and happen upon the bodies when looking at the ruins here? Order is required, Herr Kohler. Order is what the Kommandant of Laon and others are insisting upon because of the robbery. Apparently having our police look after things is no longer any good, and even Herr Oberg in Paris is demanding that Vichy allow him to bring in good German police to oversee the whole 150,000 of the force, not just the 30,000 in Paris. Me, I happen to think they're crazy but that the *maréchal* and those people he has with him in Vichy had better agree since there are bound to be further such incidents, and spring is coming, *n'est-ce pas?*'

Again the Allies and the invasion.

Boots, oilskin, hat, satchel and specs were adjusted, a hand lifted in salute as Rocheleau deferentially came to lead him away.

'Joliot's even wearing a two-franc Marianne, Louis, and the coins I've collected for you just aren't the same.'

Back in 1940, the wearing of all such badges and pins, political or not, had been forbidden, but lately the young especially had taken to making protest buttons of the discontinued small coinage of the Troisième République. 'Théo's six granddaughters know well enough that the head of Marianne and the cloth cap she wears are symbols of liberty. As one of the Occupier, Hermann, I expect you to say nothing beyond telling him that it brightens up such an atrocious suit.'

'*Ach*, no one but an idiot would ever challenge a coroner lest he find one looking over him.'

When they climbed into the back of the van, Hermann chose the bolted-down swivel chair she must have sat in and, opening the *mégot* tin, found the butts and matches dry. 'Junos from home, Louis, makhorka too.'

And taking out that last letter, dated 8 November 1942, from his Jurgen and Hans that had finally found its way to him two days ago, he read:

Vati, only the captains get tobacco made from the leaves. The others get the really strong stuff from the stems and because their clothing is so heavy and their boots often lined with felt, the scent clings and, though we can't hear them at night, we can smell them.

'Let's try it, shall we?' said Louis.

'We'd only choke, but it does tell us our firebox operator's been around. There are also Lucky Strikes and Camels from downed American aircrew, and Woodbines and Wills Goldflake from RAF aircrew. Dropped, probably, by Wehrmacht and picked up in bars frequented by those same boys.'

'We'll have to ask him.'

'If we ever find him, and we had better. Rocheleau's a problem, Louis. When a coroner even hints at something, we'd better listen.'

'He'll still have to pay the penalty, Hermann. We can't have him stealing evidence that is badly needed.'

'Maybe a warning. At least let's listen to him when he comes back.'

'Rocheleau will only lie and accuse us of having stolen things if confronted by that *Kriminalrat* colleague of yours from Hamburg.'

'Back off! His silence, even for a few days, might just give us the time we need. The bigger the issue, the lesser the other.'

It was an old argument, but perhaps the importance of something else should be emphasized. 'Although from 1910, your *mégot* tin is almost as if brand-new.'

'Bought from among the fleas of Saint-Ouen?'

'Hopefully it will lead us to the seller who can then lead us to the buyer.'

'There were also the keys to the van, and these.'

Coins and the charred corners of ID photos.

'And this.'

Singed at its edges, scorched on the underside, the poultice held a sachet between the two layers of cloth. 'Laid against a ragged tear in the skin, Hermann. Cloves, thyme too, and lavender, camomile as well probably. A temporary attempt until medical assistance, since a good deal of pus was leaking and the wound must have been badly inflamed. The cloves would have been for the pain, the thyme for its antibacterial, the camomile to readily soothe the inflamation and the lavender to offer both its stimulation and calming due to such a pleasant aroma.'

'You should have been a herbalist monk.'

Since they were in a place where there would have been successions of them. 'The sachet is first plunged into boiling water and then applied as hot as can be withstood.'

'But not made up here, Louis. It couldn't have been, not when in such a hurry, but did they bring her back to that truck and take her with them?'

'That we won't know for a while, but why the attempt to destroy it and the pocket contents of the others?'

'Evidence someone didn't want hanging around, not after the killings.'

'And who was that someone, Hermann, since those items must have been seized and flung into the firebox?'

Trust Louis to always look beyond the obvious. 'A boss who wasn't happy and in one hell of a hurry, hence a forgetful firebox handler, but a killer who should never have taken what he did.'

'But was she originally in the truck hitching a ride and then in the van?'

Merde, must Louis look beyond everything? 'If so, that *gazogène* could never have kept up with it.'

'*Ah bon, précisément*, since it had a gasoline-driven engine which would have put them at least an hour or more ahead of that truck.'

Scheisse! 'Which was heavily loaded, and since they damn well couldn't have known where that van would be taking her, did they happen to see it from the road to Laon, eh, since we went through a woods to get here?'

Apparently the small things did matter. 'But why is she so important Berlin are interested, Hermann, or is she the reason at all?'

Some questions simply didn't have ready answers.

'Ah, Rocheleau, these shoes,' said Louis. 'Come up, squeeze in and point out exactly where and how you found them. They may be important.'

This Sûreté was going to have him dismissed, thought Rocheleau. Lackey to his Gestapo partner, he had even spread the rest of the satchel's contents at that one's feet. 'The wife,' he heard himself blurt. 'Inspectors, you must . . .'

Already there were tears behind those Bakelite windows, thought Kohler, but the *salaud* would only blame Louis unless his partner took charge. 'Might I remind you that it's Chief Inspector St-Cyr and Herr Detektivinspektor Kohler of the Kriminalpolizei i.e., the Geheime Staatspolizei.'

'Hermann, *please*, these are difficult times. *Garde champêtre* Rocheleau, like far too many others, had his wages frozen in the autumn of 1940. The wife, Eugène?'

Was further humiliation now to be demanded? 'My Évangéline loves to dance and those, they are of her size or almost.'

Kohler couldn't resist. 'Isn't dancing considered an affront to those million-and-a-half of your boys in our prisoner-of-war camps and the others that have been buried? Dancing is in the Third Reich, as is kissing in public, and exactly the same as your *maréchal* has banned.'

'*Ah oui, oui, mais . . .*'

'But dances are held each week near Corbeny, are they, in someone's barn or forest clearing?'

'Hermann . . .'

'Louis, I can't believe it. A thief, and now a rural cop who allows dancing. Gestapo Boemelburg will be demanding the maximum.'

'Hermann, surely you know, as I do, that were *garde champêtre* Rocheleau to have arrested those involved, he would not only have been hated by everyone in his district, those who had information would be reticent to impart it. Eugène, please point out for us exactly where and how these shoes were found.'

Ten or even twenty years of hard labour, wondered Rocheleau. Is that what this Gestapo would demand? Squeezing past the boxes, the litter and all the rest, he laid the shoes on the rubber mat that was also under Herr Kohler's. 'She must have been sitting in this chair and quickly pried them off when the van came to a stop and she realized what those two were going to do. She then leaped between them when the door was unlocked and opened.'

'*Liebe Zeit*, Louis, we've got ourselves a detective.'

'Hermann, we could perhaps be missing something. Let's make allowances and overlook the indiscretions, but was there anything else, Eugène? A suitcase perhaps?'

'A handkerchief. This one. She tried to hide it under the mat. Me, I noticed a corner.'

Smudged, trod on yet bone dry, it had obviously been given up regrettably, and when smoothed out, revealed an embroidery of tulips, daffodils, crocuses and hyacinths. 'Perfect, Hermann. Done at the age of ten. Silk thread from the colonies. Java perhaps, but prior to this war since it's now under the Japanese.'

There was also a name, an Anna-Marie Vermeulen, but he wouldn't remind Rocheleau of it, felt St-Cyr.

'And yet he would have kept that knowledge from us to satisfy the urges of his wife, Louis?'

'Hermann, again I must insist these times, they are . . .'

'Not the best, eh? Then maybe I should ask him why he attempted to steal not just one of those bundles of one hundred of the 5,000-franc notes, but five of them for a total of 2.5 million? Obviously he's got someone he wants to impress but had better be careful when spending it, or was he going to stuff them all into a glass jar like most of your peasants? A man with a 2.5 million-franc jar, eh, and not just a 200-franc one or even a 1,000? Ten tins of sardines as well, two coils of smoked sausage, six half-kilos of the coffee that Évangéline of his must have a longing for like the rest of us. Two handfuls of the truffles for the omelettes those eggs would have made had he taken any. Not one but two rounds of the Brie de Meaux. Eight weeks in the curing, isn't that right, my fine one? Me, I did sample it but only to be certain it wasn't fake like so many that are flogged on the *marché noir* you French insist on having even though it's illegal. Detectives have to do things like that and you'd better not forget it.'

Such a storm probably wouldn't help but it had been good of Hermann not to mention the missing bottles of wine. 'Eugène, please return to your fire. Brew up some more of the tea. Coroner Joliot and the men who are with him will welcome it, as will we.'

Only when he had left, did Louis point out the impression inside each of the shoes. 'Monnier, Hermann, the rue du Faubourg Saint-Honoré. Made to measure, but definitely not to hers.'

And taking a small, packed-down wad of newspaper from each of the toes, unfolded these and said, *'Le Matin*, but dating from 20 August of last year.'

'And with a name like a Netherlander. A submarine?'

One without papers or with false ones.

'And no suitcase, Louis. Either she never took it with her when she went to that van, or they must have taken it back, but in their haste, forgot the shoes.'

It was Joliot who said, 'Both killed most probably between 1000 and 1600 or 1700 hours, Wednesday, 29 September. The one hit first on the forehead with this. There are even scraps of skin.'

Questions . . . It was a night for them, thought St-Cyr from behind the wheel of the van. Pitch-dark except for the regulation slits of the headlamps, it was taking forever to get to Paris. Basically they were sticking to the N2, but Hermann, in the Citroën which had no governor, would speed up only to realize he had gone too far and that the dim red twinkling of his taillights might be necessary on an otherwise empty road. And of course they were travelling through country that had been brutally fought over during the Great War, the Germans loving to shell things so much, Laon had all but been destroyed, Soissons's thirteenth-century cathedral having had its nave cut in half and tower obliterated.

Villers-Cotterêts, which they were now entering, had its all-but enclosing forest: oaks, beech and hornbeam but still, even seventy-five kilometres or so from Paris, there was virtually no sign of the Occupier, just an emptiness that made one feel as if the end of the Occupation had finally come. *Bien sûr*, there would then be a bloodbath as during the Revolution, old scores being brutally settled, neighbour against neighbour, brother against brother, former corporals against former sergeants who were not even of their own unit and had just come upon them abandoning their weapons. God having a bit of fun.

That bank had failed entirely to recover its van. Hours it had taken hunting for that girl, Hermann insisting that they keep on trying until Joliot had finally said, 'Enough. That's it, *mes amis*,' and he and the two with him had returned to Laon with the victims who would eventually be sent on to Paris.

Rocheleau had not been dismissed, but given a warning. He was not to discuss what had happened with anyone, wife or not. Father Adrien the same.

And Anna-Marie Vermeulen? 'Paris, 20 August of last year and a pair of shoes,' he said as if she was with him. 'Perhaps it is that you did have some prior knowledge of l'Abbaye de Vauclair, but why a handkerchief that would positively identify you if arrested, since that must have been why you tried to hide it?'

The lower slopes of the Chemin des Dames, the forest, path, ferns and spring all came to mind, the smell of the wet, autumn leaves, that of the water too, even its taste, and the sight of that broken fern and those trampled saplings.

'You must have willingly gone back to that truck. The poultice, having come loose and fallen, either earlier or later, was put into the firebox and then later, when that was cleared in a hurry, removed from the ashes and dropped behind that wall. But to live as a diver in Paris couldn't have been easy. Always there are snap controls. Even walking in the Jardin du Luxemburg or sitting with a "coffee" outside a café can lead to the same. The date on that newspaper gives us only a lesser limit to the length of your stay. Weeks, even months, could have been spent in Paris before you ever acquired those shoes. And you wouldn't have bought them on the *marché noir*, since the price alone would have drawn attention to you. Instead, you either found them, which seems unlikely, or were given them, and if so, by whom? A wealthy woman?

'And since you had managed to remain free for such a time, why did you then suddenly decide to leave, only to return, and where, of course, did you actually go? Back to the Netherlands, as suggested by that handkerchief? There has to have been a very pressing reason.'

Anise might help, since the pipe or even cigarettes were simply unavailable, that need so great, it had simply refused to go away.

'*Anise de l'Abbaye de Flavigny, mademoiselle. Bonbons à la menthe.* Me, I will also chew a couple for yourself, though I'm not sure at all that you would have used tobacco since women don't have the ration cards for it, and smoking does draw attention, especially since some men resent a woman's having cigarettes they themselves haven't. But, please, was the one who threw the contents of those pockets into the truck's firebox a *passeur*? I ask because there are such, though also a fee: 10,000 in the autumn of 1940, now 100,000 or even 200,000, the half down, the other half when safely delivered, and if so, are those three—that *passeur*, his firebox feeder and the killer—now continuing to take you on to Paris so as to get paid the other half, since that *passeur's* reputation would be at stake if he didn't?'

Is there such a law? she seemed to ask.

'Though many can, unfortunately, do otherwise and even turn you in for a much higher reward, this one wouldn't because he definitely doesn't want it known that they were involved in the killings.'

Again he thought of that empty road ahead. Again he spoke as if to her. 'It's as though the Occupier has suddenly left, mademoiselle. Russia is draining so many, the border between Belgium and France is now no longer being manned and one can drive straight through from Brussels to Paris. Certainly there may be the snap controls, and on the trains and in the railway stations there is always that, but did the Occupier have photos of you? Is that why you didn't use the trains? Even in the Netherlands there are now areas so poorly manned one can apparently cross those without too much trouble, if one has something to ride, even a bicycle, of course.'

When she didn't seem to want to reply, he took out the hand-kerchief to feel its softness and embroidery. 'Your mother would have looked very carefully at this while at that age you would, I believe, have bravely awaited the verdict. Excellent, of course, but were you an only child, and where, please, in the Netherlands did you live? Paris suggests a big city since in those, despite all the dangers, it's still much easier to live as a diver than in a little village or town where everyone notices what everyone else is up to and they all gossip. Oh for sure, some of Paris's streets and districts are still that way. Until last winter, Hermann's Giselle had regarded the Seine as a moat and had never been across it to the Right Bank. To her, the whole world was completely contained in the quartiers Saint-Germain-des-Prés, Sorbonne and Jardin des Plantes, with an occasional voyage a little to the south and west. She simply didn't know of the rest or care and had closed her mind until offered a job she couldn't refuse. The shop Enchantement on the *place* Vendôme and two old friends of mine whom I haven't seen in months and must. But Vermeulen is not a specifically Jewish name, yet those were often changed to erase the inevitable prejudice only to find that the Germans have lists and records going back at least five generations. France and Paris are suffering the same, so if you were one of those who managed to get away from the Netherlands, you would have had that extra burden, though Berlin would not have sent those two expressly for that reason, yet still you carry something that would identify you? Was it needed to identify you to that *passeur* or to someone else? We'll help in any case, and I know my partner will be thinking the same.'

A diver, a *Taucherin*, an *onderduiker*? wondered Kohler. Longing for a cigarette, he felt for the *mégot* tin only to tell himself he would have to write down the name of each of the butts used and, of course, he'd need Louis to roll the *verdammt* thing.

Not one for talking alone and aloud to himself, or to the victim and such like Louis, he said, 'Oona will want us to find out everything we can and help that girl if at all possible.'

From Rotterdam, Oona was special: gentle, beautiful, supremely intelligent and everything he would ever need in a life's companion. Louis had been absolutely right, but having lost both her husband and children, she had, he knew, times that were very hard. A voice, a photo in a magazine or child near a school, and the tears would start and she'd have to be held. 'And I'm not there enough. Giselle helps, that's for sure, but Johan would be nine now, Anna seven. Would they even recognize their mother?'

Six to eight million, maybe even ten, had been on the roads during the Blitzkrieg. The Stukas had come, and then the Messerschmitts, and she and Martin had been unable to find the children and ever since then she had maintained that a mother would know, that she felt they had been buried in unmarked graves beside that road. There *had* been those, he and Louis had discovered, but not their names. Constantly he placed advertisements in the newspapers, like lots of others still. 'And she always wants to know what's been going on at home.'

Back in February 1941, in Amsterdam, there had been an altercation at an ice-cream parlor and about four hundred young Jews had been arrested, some so badly beaten, fifty had soon died in the *Konzentrationslager* at Buchenwald, the rest being sent on to the KZ at Mauthausen. But being Dutch and not liking what had happened, the Netherlanders had gone on strike on the twenty-fifth of that month, circumstance putting a stop to it within about three days. Even so, by September 1941 every Jew in the country had been registered. All 140,000, of whom about 20,000 had been refugees, most of whom had fled the Reich before the war. And by April of this year, none had been allowed to live anywhere other than Amsterdam or in the internment camps of Vught and Westerbork, the latter being the main transit point.

'And now?' he asked himself, clenching a fist at the inhumanity, for it had been going on here too, and Louis and he had come up against it time and again. 'Only about 2,000 are left in the Netherlands. That *Le Matin* of 20 August 1942 dates to just a month after that first major round-up in Paris. What was happening here would have driven her crazy with worry.'

Slamming on the brakes, he got out to impatiently wait for Louis.

One would have thought him a sudden control, felt St-Cyr, for Hermann was a big man and the breath was billowing from under that fedora and into the frosty darkness that was lit from behind by the faintness of the Citroën's headlamps and then his own.

'Louis, she went home to find out what had happened to her parents. Oona's always wanting to for the same reason, and not just her own, but Martin's too. That's why that girl took such a chance with the embroidery. She brought it from home—it was all she could find. She couldn't stand not knowing what could well have happened and had finally forced herself to leave Paris.'

'Only to then find out and hitch a return with a *passeur?*'

'*Passeurs* don't drive trucks like that. They're usually loaners. They sit a few seats behind in the bus or railway carriage, not in heavily loaded trucks that can't even get up the speed of a gasoline engine.'

'Unless . . .'

Ah merde! 'Using the cover of hauling stuff to sell on the *marché noir.* I don't think there've ever been any *passeurs* caught doing that, but . . .'

'There's always a first time, Hermann, though it still doesn't explain Berlin's sending those two.'

'Then maybe there's an FTP connection.'

As Hermann and he both knew, the Francs-Tireurs et Partisans were the backbone of actively armed resistance and the cause, no doubt, of the recent death of Dr. Julius Ritter. 'What a happy thought.'

'It's a night for them. Now roll us one from these. Two Wills Goldflake and two Chesterfields.'

Though but a rumour like everything else they usually heard, von Rundstedt, commander of the army in the West, had recently sent the Führer a detailed report of the rapid increase in rail sabotage. In September alone there had been more than 500 serious actions, compared to a monthly average of 120 for the first half of the year. FTP *réseaux* were thought to be small, their security so tight none would even fart in public, but there would be Italians among them from the days of 1930s and Mussolini's hatred of the Communists, Armenians, too, from the Turkish troubles, and Poles, especially from just before and after 1 September 1939.

'And Austrians, Hermann, from before, during and right after the *Anschluss.* The Third Republic and Paris, in particular, offered home to many.'

'And most would likely have taken day jobs that fitted them right in, some even having gotten married and had families.'

Name changes too, and false papers, but was that girl connected to any of them? If so, then they really did have a problem on their hands.

Near Le Bourget, the giant Paris aerodrome, the fog the rain had brought was so thick at 0347 Berlin Time, St-Cyr knew Lufthansa's early-morning flight from Berlin through to Madrid and Lisbon would have been cancelled. That such could even exist in wartime was remarkable, but there were also once- or twice-weekly flights to Bristol by Pan-American Clipper and the Free Dutch KLM* from Sintra, which was about ninety kilometres to the west of Lisbon. 'Not that they're one hundred percent safe from being shot down, mademoiselle, but they do offer hope,' he said as if again to her.

The Luftwaffe's Luftflotte 3 squadron of bombers that had taken over the airfield in June 1940 would also have been grounded, and London and other cities and towns given a peaceful night, this district too.

'And to think that not so very long ago I stood waiting, along with 100,000 others, including my first wife, to cheer Lindbergh as he landed the *Spirit of Saint Louis* at twenty-two minutes past ten in the evening, 21 June 1927. It was memorable, mademoiselle. Agnès and myself wouldn't have missed it for all the world, but who would have thought we'd be in another tragic war by 1 September 1939?'

At the turn-off to Drancy, that transit point for Jews and Gypsies, there was only one tiny blue-washed light over the black-lettered arrow that had originally been put up by the Préfecture du Département de la Seine more than a year ago. An unfinished, U-shaped complex of low-income tenements, five of which were currently being lived in by legal citizens, the remaining unfinished four-storey had at first been run by French police but had been taken over by the SS in July of this year, though the perimeter was still guarded by Frenchmen—jobs, if nothing else. 'Yet it's only five kilometres (three miles) from Paris. Technically you're an illegal, mademoiselle, and by the Vichy statute of 24 October 1940, subject to immediate arrest and internment regardless of whether you are Jewish or not. Even without the Occupier's having requested such a thing, Vichy undertook to have everyone

---

* The Royal Dutch Aviation Company used Douglas aircraft, one of which was 'mistakenly' shot down by a Luftwaffe fighter over the Bay of Biscay in June 1943.

who had come here to evade the Nazis prior to 1 September 1939 and thereafter locked up.'

Aubervilliers was industrial, the stench of soot rank on the fog-ridden air. Ash heaps, incredibly poor housing, raw sewage and all such things marred *la zone*, the peripheral suburbs, and made them deplorable for far too many but . . . Hermann had stopped and had taken out his pistol.

'When the end comes, Louis, it'll start in places like this.˙ It's now all but impossible for the Wehrmacht to even patrol the streets here at night. Stay close. It's not often a bank van crawls through at 0420 hours.'

The curfew would end at 0500 hours, but because of its imposition, the farmers couldn't do the usual and arrive at Les Halles in the early hours, and the belly of Paris had become a mere shadow of its former self.

Given the lack of traffic, the control on the Porte d'Aubervilliers had far too many heavily armed men. Again Hermann had to pause, and when he came back, he was clearly unsettled. 'It can't be for us, Louis. It has to be for that *passsseur*'s *gazogène*. Kriminalrat Ludin's been waiting for hours to have a word. Oona's with him in the car and desperate. Stay up front in the van and use the lockdown so that no matter how hard the boys here try, they won't get in.'

Acorn water lay between them on the linoleum-topped table. Nicotine-stained, Ludin's thick fingers lit yet another, a Juno from home this time, that gaze of his behind those steel-rimmed specs unfeeling.

'Kohler, must I remind you that a few answers are necessary?'

This *eingefleischter* Nazi was even wearing the *Goldenes Parteiabzeichen*, given especially to the very early members. 'Maybe first, Kriminalrat, you'd tell me what you think you were doing by terrifying Oona and bringing her here or anywhere else at any hour?'

Trust Kohler to think of the well-being of such.

'*Ach*, when I called round to the flat and found she didn't know where you were, I thought to ease her mind both by telling her

---

* In early August 1944, eight German soldiers were ambushed in Aubervilliers and shot, the first such major incident in what was to become known as the Battle for Paris.

you'd be arriving soon—my mistake, of course—and that I would be only too glad of a little company en route. Unfortunately we soon had to follow a convoy on its way out to Drancy. A child, wanting to feel the air, kept parting the rear truck's canvas tarpaulin and shoving an arm out, which upset her greatly, and for this I apologize profusely, but that fog . . . *Liebe Zeit*, I even had to rip the blinkers off my headlamps. Is it always so thick in Paris?'

'Usually it rises from the Seine to smother everything, but this one is different.'

Like himself, was that it? Matches were as if of gold and when Kohler set the box aside and didn't return it, the thought was to see if he would really attempt to steal it. 'Tobacco and that first drag, eh? Already things begin to look a little better, so let's make a bit of peace between us. What did you find in such a godforsaken place?'

The rumpled, grey prewar suit with the egg-stained tie and handkerchief that definitely needed laundering had obviously seen everything far too many times, but still he'd have to try. 'Maybe first you'd tell me what you and that colonel were looking for, and while you're at it, give me his name. He does have one, doesn't he, or did his parents deliberately forget?'

Insubordination was one thing, and Kohler was certainly noted for it, ridicule something else. 'Please don't continue to be difficult. Just give me whatever evidence you managed to find.'

'Two bodies, both with a nine-millimetre Parabellum, the gun perhaps a Walther P38 or Luger and probably sold on the *schwarzer Markt* by one of our own. It happens all the time now, Kriminalrat. The Führer ought to pay our boys a little more.'

'And you've concluded the killer was French, have you?'

'Was he?'

Verdammt, did Kohler suspect otherwise? 'Money was taken, was it?'

'Plenty, but until we get that bank to go over everything, we won't know the exact amount.'

To this, the grizzled fleshy cheeks and sagging jowls were favoured before sucking on that cigarette until only the smallest of butts remained.

'And this cash, Kohler, was it carried away on a bicycle or in a farmer's cart?'

'Instead of a truck? Is that why this crowd of imbeciles in uniform is hanging around looking as if waiting for one?'

Kohler was never going to learn. 'All right, there was a truck, one of those that uses a firebox and the resulting charcoal or wood gas. It depends. They don't usually burn both together unless desperate since it can cause problems.'

'And you've been chasing it?'

But from where and for how long—was this what Kohler wanted? The Netherlands perhaps? 'Looking for it would be better.'

'Why? Because they've robbed someone else?'

Again Ludin found his cigarettes and lit another, but would this irritating pest swallow what would have to be said in order to get him to cough up the necessary yet keep him from the truth? 'Human trafficking, Kohler. The Reichssicherheitshauptamt are concerned and want it stopped.'

The SD's Security Office. Ernst Kaltenbrunner was head of it, a drunkard and a sadist, but sending one Standartenführer and an aging Gestapo after a single *passeur* didn't make sense. 'Have you and that colonel got similar reception committees stationed at every entrance to the city?'

The Höherer SS und Polizeiführer of France, Karl Oberg and his deputy, Helmut Knochen, had warned them of Kohler's penchant for honesty bordering on intransigence, but an answer would have to be given with the curtest of nods.

It was, felt Kohler, hard to believe that Berlin's SD knew so little of how things worked in Paris they would unwittingly broadcast their interest in such a way. 'And who was this still unnamed *Schmuggler* trafficking?'

Had Kohler and St-Cyr found evidence of that girl? 'That I can't reveal, but was there any evidence of someone other than the killer?'

Finally the chips were down, and with Oona waiting in the Citroën. 'None. Far too much rain. No tracks, not even a whisper of that *gazo* truck you've been chasing.'

'Did I not say, "looking for?" *Ach, mein Strudel* at last. Are you sure you wouldn't like half of this? Illegal for most others in France, of course, but my Hilda was a remarkable cook. Every morning, six days a week, and even seven far too many times, there would be a little extra in the briefcase for lunch. A slice of her marvellous strudel, Kohler—I'm partial to the apple-and-raisin. Though the latter are so difficult to find these days, she still managed somehow. A few of her *Lebkuchen* . . .'

The cakes of life. '*Meine Oma* used to make them.'

His grandmother! 'Spicy, Kohler, as life should be now and then, yet sweet as it always was before I was forced to identify the *Bombenbrandschrumpfleischen*.'

The heat-shrunken corpses the firestorm had left, but must that God of Louis's keep smiling at the partnership?

'The wife, Kohler, our eighteen-year-old house-daughter, Inge, too, and my Hilda's parents and their four dogs, the ones I always hated because they'd piss on my shoes and trousers if they could. Now I will have answers from you, *mein lieber Kamerad*, or that Netherlander out there in my car will end up exactly like them.'

And to think that 40,000 of these in the Reich could control a nation of 80 million at home largely through voluntary denunciations. 'Let me talk to my partner. Let us take that van to the bank and settle a few things. We can't interrupt a murder inquiry just to fuck about with something Berlin's SD might or might not even know, and if you question it, *mein Freund*, think of all the shouting that must be going on about the Résistance getting the better of us. Von Rundstedt, eh, and the Kommandant von Gross-Paris, to say nothing of the avenue Foch and Oberg and his deputy.'

'Then take the woman with you. Maybe she'll be reminder enough.'

Oona was silent. She didn't even respond when held in the partnership's Citroën. Instead, she pulled away from him, felt Kohler, and through the darkness between and around them said, 'First he told me that should I ever find my children, I must remember that they were half-and-halves, *Mischlinge*, crossbreeds, and that their fate would soon be decided, that Seyss-Inquart, the Austrian SS who runs my country, is determined to include them, as is Darquier de Pellepoix, Vichy's commissioner for Jewish affairs, but that Herr Kaltenbrunner and others in Berlin are still mulling the question over. But with myself, because of whom I had married, there would be no such problem. All of my hair would be shaved off and I would be deloused, and if fit for work, would be made to, if not, the furnace. Is that what those people would have done to my Martin, Hermann, and my Johan and Anna?'

The truth about the *Konzentrationslager* was never mentioned openly by any of the Occupier but had become very clear to Louis and himself at Natzweiler-Struthof in Alsace last February, but for Ludin to have said anything like that could only mean he and that colonel were desperate. And that could only mean that Kaltenbrunner had ordered them to find the truck, the killer and that girl and settle whatever it was, or else.

'And Giselle?' he asked, for he had to, and Oona would understand.

'The same.'

Again Hermann tried to hold her but having lain with him, having come to love and accept, and to befriend his Giselle like a sister, had she not done the most hateful of things, no matter his having put himself at terrible risk to rescue and look after her?

Pushing him away a second time, she said emptily, 'When he went to pull the blackout tape from the headlamps and talk to the men in those trucks, he used the pinch-the-cat* he had kept in a trouser pocket, but when he returned, he didn't put it back. He just tossed it onto the seat between us, and I heard it hit the little bottle he'd been using and then the tin of cigarettes, and every time those trucks made a turn, we did too, and it would roll toward me, only to roll away.'

'What little bottle?'

'Bitters for the stomach to help the digestion. Jägermeister.'

'And?'

'Beneath it and the tin of fifty Lucky Strike, was a large flat envelope. Brown, as it turned out, and of stiff paper. Manila, I think, though it must now be so rare, few would ever get to use it.'

'Sealed?'

Was Hermann beginning to understand? 'Red wax impressed with a swastika signet, the writing in black Gothic lettering, the seals broken.'

'Geheime Reichssache?'

Secret Reich business, but did this man whom she had come to love now understand how she must have felt and still did, that Kriminalrat Ludin, knowing she would look when he was away

---

* A pocket flashlight activated by pumping a thumb lever.

from the car, had silently dared her to? 'Me, I was alone, for he had gone to meet you in that café, but had he really? Wouldn't he wait to see what I did? Prisoner to him, I hung on for as long as I could.'

'And?'

What a brief and final word that was, but Herr Ludin must have wanted her to tell him. 'It had been sent from the Hague.'

'The SD's Central Archive for the Netherlands.'

'Is that not my country, Herr Kohler?'

'Oona, I'm your Hermann. Please just tell me.'

'Maybe I don't understand you anymore or myself. His following those trucks full of the deported to Drancy really upset me and he knew it. Two twenty-by-twenty prints of the same girl, the sliver of light I let escape reminding me of how I once looked at that age. Full of hope and joy, Hermann. She wasn't any more than twenty or twenty-one, the hair like mine. Very fine and fair and braided into a short rope for convenience, the other photo showing her with a page-boy cut dyed jet-black to hide her identity from those who would then have snapped her photo anyway.'

'Taken when?'

'When do you think?'

'Oona, please.'

'Will you marry me like you've said often enough?'

'Yes, and as soon as possible.'

Which, of course, would mean never. How could it be otherwise? 'Imagine then, me drawing those photos out of that envelope knowing that at any minute he might return from speaking to you. 25 February 1941.'

And stamped on the back. 'The general strike and snapped by . . .'

'An NSB* probably. That's all I really know.'

But working hand and glove with the Occupier, just as did the home-grown fascists in France. 'Did you get a look at the sheets the Hague would have sent?'

How anxious he was, all else now set aside, even such thoughts for the future. 'There were sheets and sheets of that grey office paper the war has given. Carbon copies so thin, I was terrified they would bunch up and betray me.'

And badly faded because when used over and over again, the

---

* The Dutch fascists, the Nationaal Socialistische Beweging.

carbon paper would also have been reversed, the bottom fed into the typewriter first, as per Goebbels, the Reichsminister of propaganda and public enlightenment. 'Six copies made and only one of them needed.'

'Who is she, this Anna-Marie Vermeulen who bears the first name of my daughter and is a *Mischlinge* as well? *Eine Halbjüdin* just like my own?'

'We don't know anything about her. This is all news.'

'Is it? Is it, really? Or are you lying to the woman you've just said you'll marry?'

'All right, I was only trying to protect you. She left a bit of embroidery with her name on it.'

'How very like myself at the age of ten. My Anna was looking forward to learning.'

'Was there anything else?'

'When I pulled the photos out, it fell to the floor, a piece of metal.'

Oona would have been desperate to recover it. Reaching for her, he heard her saying, 'Don't! I might scream because of what I've been allowing myself to do with you. I want to be certain.'

'You know that's not necessary.'

'It might be.'

'What was it then?'

'A rijksdaaler. Silver and minted early in 1940 and the last of those. Everything must now be of paper or zinc, and thin at that.'

A two-and-a-half guilder coin.

'When I carefully put it back into that envelope, I felt two others and these have made me ask if they were sent from the Hague or had that Gestapo found them somewhere? One is interesting. Three's a lot, especially when one of them was wrapped tightly in a small piece of white paper and still had earth on it, mud I couldn't replace because it had dried, Hermann.'

And Ludin had wanted her to have a look.

Though it would still be dark for ages, felt St-Cyr, the curfew had lifted and traffic had begun to enter the city but not yet themselves for they still had the van to deal with. Mostly there were the bicycles of those going to work, but all were subjected to a rigid checking of the papers, et cetera, and beside every Feldwebel

was his interpreter, and always there were the Vichy food controllers, the *flics* and black-market cops ready to pounce.

Emotionally and physically exhausted, Oona had instantly
fallen asleep behind them in the back seat of the Citroën, with
Hermann's coat over her. Hunger had had to be set aside, thirst
too, and the need for tobacco. 'Photos, Hermann. Typed sheets
from Hague Central.'

They would have to keep their voices down. 'Oona only managed to read that Anna-Marie was a half-and-half, but obviously
Ludin and that SD are after her.'

'A *Sonderkommando*?'

One of the specials. 'And that still doesn't make much sense,
does it, but Ludin threatened Oona with the furnaces, Louis, and
that has to definitely mean they're really under the gun. *Bien sûr*,
Kaltenbrunner is fond of dispatching such and ordering them not
to tell anyone anything. Even Oberg probably doesn't know why
the hell they're in the city.'

So great was the fear of reprisals, even having SD Head Office
papers or a letter from the same negated anyone asking anything.
'Yet Herr Ludin gives Oona a chance to look.'

'Since he's been ordered not to tell us the necessary, he technically hasn't and won't be blamed—Oona will—but obviously he
feels we need a little help, if we're to make life easier for himself
and that SD.'

'A Netherlander, Hermann. A protest marcher who dyes the
hair and changes its style only to unsuccessfully hide her identity.'

'Well, at least we now know why she didn't use the trains on
her way back to Paris.'

'Do we really?'

'*Ah merde*, don't be difficult at a time like this. Instead of those,
it's a *passeur* at heavy cost, a firebox feeder with an antique *mégot*
tin, and a killer who empties his victims' pockets only to have that
passeur—and it must have been him—toss everything into the fire.'

Hermann always liked to hurry. 'Shouldn't we ask ourselves
first, did someone warn her of the photos and even pay for the
trip? After all, this is a girl who can't have had a lot of money.'

'Agreed.'

'Now let's deal with that *passeur*, the firebox feeder and the
other one, but before he became the killer.'

'*Mein Gott,* must you?'

'I'm waiting. I need your help.'

'She would have been hidden in the back of that truck, would probably never have been allowed up front, but came to feel that something was terribly wrong, and when she saw a chance, left that *gazo* to walk ahead alongside the road to that van where she cajoled a lift. She's again a blonde, has blue eyes, was young, *et cetera et cetera*, so she took those shoes out of her suitcase and put them on to add further spice and give a bit of extra height.'

'*Ah bon, merci,* you've got all the answers, but wasn't she wearing a poultice, probably on the hand or forearm? Also, *mon vieux,* since when have we ever seen any woman in high heels walking alongside any of our roads for very far? France really doesn't have as many of the paved *Autobahnen* as the Organisation Todt built for the Reich in the 1930s and are still building.'

'That van and truck were relatively close. They'd have to have been.'

'*Bon,* now let's ask why they were close, and more importantly, Hermann, why had they stopped, since they must have.'

'A control.'

'Which would, I think, have worried both vehicles.'

'A long line-up, but not yet at any entrance to the city. Simply on one of the main access roads. Maybe the RD 380 to the east of Reims.'

'Perfect. Except for isolated lookouts and fortresses, it runs through dead-flat farmland, but what would have made her do such a desperate thing since she or someone else must have paid plenty to get her into Paris?'

'Oona said that one of those three rijksdaalers had earth on it and was wrapped in a bit of paper.'

'A note, Hermann?'

'Probably, but Oona was so terrified she'd be found out, she didn't try to read it.'

'But were those coins being left as a signal to Herr Ludin by someone with the *passeur,* someone that one and his firebox feeder didn't know everything about? Places that the killer and Ludin would have known of beforehand, and that Standartenführer also?'

'Since they'd been following because that killer would have told them of the route, and like crumbs in a fairy tale, had attached a note to one of the coins, telling them that she could well be onto him. *Ein Spitzel*, Louis?'

An informant. 'But one of those coins wouldn't have been left at l'Abbaye de Vauclair since that stop would not have been on the schedule.'

'And Ludin didn't even bother to get out of the tourer to have a look.'

'A traitor, Hermann, though maybe not a prisoner of war from the Dutch Army, but are we still missing something? Has it been too easy so far? Two vehicles, both heavily loaded with goods in part at least for the *marché noir*, the *passeur* using that as cover, the other simply to line the pockets or those of someone else.'

'And is that not why the killer did what he did?'

Good for Hermann. 'Because they couldn't be left alive, could they, but did that *passeur* agree beforehand and order the killings or come to accept the haste with which they were done but only afterward?'

Ach, mein Gott, trust Louis! 'The killer thus proving how reliable and loyal he was, but that girl would never have accepted it, would she, and must have kept quiet for fear he would kill her too.'

'And if so, Hermann, is now even more terrified.'

'They then staged the robbery to make it all look like that but failed because they took only what could never be used to identify them. And as for that *gazo* of theirs, they don't need to use this entrance to Paris and probably won't. They'll simply wait and let things cool down, then use one where they know there are those who will let them in for a price because they've done that lots of times. They must have.'

'And that, Hermann, is why I think Herr Ludin took it upon himself to break Herr Kaltenbrunner's strict order of silence. He and that SD colonel really are desperately in need of help, though the latter of them might not have sanctioned what the former wanted Oona to see.'

'Along with the constant cigarettes and repeated swigs of bitters.'

'Me, I just wish I felt more confident and that we weren't missing something vital.'

To the rue de Crimée in the 19th, in La Villette at 0532 hours, came the awakening of Paris as it dragged itself through the icy fog and darkness. So numerous were the streams of bicycles, their lamps were as fireflies. Ever-present were the shouts, curses, cries of alarm and urgent ringing of bells, some so close St-Cyr knew he could open the side window of the van, as he had to clear the rearview again, and touch a cyclist.

Pungently ersatz perfume, unwashed bodies and tobacco smoke, this last of dried leaves, herbs and the roasted carrot tops of desperation, rushed in on the air. The traffic was insane. With occasional trucks and far fewer city buses, there were well over 1.5 million bicycles and bicycle taxis in the city, to say nothing of the countless pedestrians who tended to ignore all rules since there were so few cars.

Finding Anna-Marie Vermeulen's Opinel in his coat pocket wasn't difficult. Opening it, he laid it on the seat. Unless he was very wrong, Ludin must have felt that the sooner she was arrested, the better, and that must be why, in spite of there being so few private cars, two of them were following the Citroën. He had better have a word.

'Hermann, I'll just deal with the car behind you.'

'And the one behind it, Louis.'

To the fog there was but the usual, the lack of soot and exhaust fumes evident. So thick, though, was the darkness, those in the first Peugeot four-door didn't acknowledge him until the driver's side window had been opened a crack.

'*Ah bon, merci.* Are we near the intersection with the rue de Flandre?' he asked.

There were four of them in the car, the escaping fug of Gauloises bleues but a reminder.

'*Fous-moi le camp, vache!*'

'What's that you're saying? "Bugger off, cow," when all I want is directions? Get out. Get out now! St-Cyr, Sûreté.'

'Suck lemons.'

'And difficult, too, is it? These days I would gladly if I could, but I'll ask the ones in the car behind, shall I, and then we'll settle the matter?'

There was no response, the window simply being closed, which meant of course that they were all armed and had egos to bolster. The next side window, however, was calmly rolled all the way down, the words and accent nonthreatening, at least for the present. 'What can we do for you, Inspector?'

'It's Chief Inspector, but are we near the intersection of the rue de Flandre?'

'If you already know, why ask?'

Such politeness had to have a reason. 'You wouldn't have a spare one of those, would you? Two, actually.'

'Shall I light them for you?'

'That would be much appreciated.'

All this time, bicycles streamed past, their bells sounding one crisis after another, along with urgent shouts for him to get out of the way, but there wasn't the sharply intent flame of the usual lighter fuel of gasoline. Instead, it was of the long-remembered, but one thing was for sure: that accent wasn't French. He had seen this one before, but where, and did that then mean that extra troops had been brought in?

'You're heading where?' asked the donor.

'The Banque Nationale de Crédit et Commercial. It's address is on . . .'

'We can read.'

'Who told you to follow?'

'All we know is that something big is coming to town and that you and that partner of yours have been brought in on it.'

'*Radio-trottoir?*'

Pavement radio. 'Our ears are constantly tuned. Aren't yours? Here, take the package. We've lots.'

Hermann would have advised leaving things as they were, but Hermann had Oona to think of and they had, of course, to first take care of her and not let these others know where.

'*Merci*, I'll continue to lead the way, shall I?'

'Of course. An entourage.'

'Excellent!'

Stepping quickly back and in among the oncoming cyclists, he did the unforgivable and shoved the first to come along against the car. Another and another gave cries of dismay, he driving the Opinel into both of that car's front tires, the altercation continuing with the opening of its doors as the headlamps were shattered by the butt of a Lebel 1873.

The front tires of the lead vehicle followed and then its headlamps.

'Now I'll deal with the *vélo-taxi* you missed,' said Hermann, taking a first and welcoming drag and handing the cigarette to Oona to hold for him.

'Later, *mon vieux*. Later. Let's give them a bit of distance, then you to the left, me to the right and we'll squeeze its driver between us and find out who they're working for.'

It didn't take long, and when Hermann finally found him waiting with the van in *place* Vendôme before the shop Enchantement, he took Oona from the Citroën to that door and, ringing its bell, got the lecture of his life from Giselle, who quickly pulled her inside and slammed the door in his face.

Alone again, they shared a cigarette even though they still had the extras.

'Rudy de Mérode,' said St-Cyr with evident dismay, for the so-called 'Neuilly Gestapo' was but one of at least ten major gangs of *gestapistes français* operating in and from Paris, Lyon and other cities and towns. Back in the summer and autumn of 1940, the Occupier had needed purchasing agencies as well as Frenchmen and women to watch the French. Deliberately, the Abwehr, the counterintelligence service of the German High Command, had let far too many gangsters and others out of jail and put them to work they enjoyed immensely. Given the directorships of some of those purchasing agencies, for the Reich had needed, and still did even more so now, vast quantities of nearly everything France could supply, they had done that as well as a lot of other things and continued to but with even more determination. And the unfortunate thing was that far too many of them had been put in prison by himself.

'Apparently, Hermann, word came through to those pavement listeners of a control on the RD 380 just to the east of Reims last Tuesday and Wednesday. A very determined SD colonel who wouldn't listen to anyone but himself. Every truck, car or wagon was ripped apart, no matter the lineup, even though it was at the start of the *vendage* and the grapes needed pressing. Every other entrance to Paris was also placed on the same alert.'

'Which still continues, and since de Mérode and his gang have been sniffing the air, we can assume the others have. *Merde*, this isn't good, Louis.'

'And they'll all want to hear the reason first from herself before turning over what's left of her to Kriminalrat Ludin who, with that colonel, must have been following her and that *gazo* and its crew since the Netherlands.'

'Just what the hell is she carrying that's so goddamned important Kaltenbrunner would demand absolute silence? A girl who's only in her early twenties?'

'We have to be missing something, Hermann, including the name of that last one I just met. I've heard and seen him before, but where?'

'It'll come to you. It always does.'

'The pseudo-robbery of a bank van whose driver and assistant willingly gave a lift to a complete stranger, no matter how vulnerable and tempting?'

'Did she know of them, Louis? Did they of her?'

The question of questions, for if so, it implied a whole lot more. 'And when both vehicles turned off the RD 380 to avoid that control, did she look back to gratefully see the distance between them steadily increase and think she had got safely away?'

Only to then discover something else. 'Monnier won't open until 0900 hours.'

3

French banks were nothing but trouble, felt Kohler. They opened when they wanted and closed soon afterward, this one at 1100 hours, with the customary two-hour lunch from 1230 to 1430. But they *all* even took the half-day holiday on Wednesday afternoons.

It was still dark. Fortunately a carriage entrance lay off the rue Volney, and having squeezed through it into the courtyard, van and Citroën were locked and left as they headed for the little blue wire-caged light above the tradesman's entrance.

'Me or you, Louis?'

'Both.'

All too soon a throaty voice rebelled. *'Merde alors, messieurs,* even the roosters on the roof haven't had time to crow! It's also a Saturday and since when did banks ever open on such days?'

'As of right now. Gestapo and Sûreté, my fine one. Just let us in,' shouted Hermann. 'We've brought your president a little present.'

Something would have to be said to stall them until contact could be made, felt Olivier Gaudin, concierge and of some importance to the Crédit et Commercial. 'Monsieur le Président Bolduc, he is away at the autumn pot-shoot with Hauptmann Reinecke and Leutnant Heiss, the overseers of the bank. *La Côte Sud des Landes. Les palombes, n'est-ce pas, et les ortolans.'*

'The coastal dunes back of the beaches to the south of Bordeaux, Louis. Wood pigeons and songbirds.'

The autumn migration and within the forbidden zone that bordered the Atlantic Ocean. 'Ortolans are caught in nets, Hermann. Monsieur le Concierge, we'll wait in his office for his second-in-command.'

'See that coffee is sent up,' said Kohler. 'Hot croissants, fried Reim's ham, omelettes, too, and wedges of Brie de Meaux for starters. Just the usual that president of yours must serve up to those bank overseers you mentioned.'

Merde! 'And where, please, am I to find such things, let alone pay for them?'

A tough one. 'Here's a 5,000 franc note that's not from the van. Use it and bring me the change and a receipt. Don't and you'll have to deal with me since like yourself, I'm not an early riser. Add four shots of cognac to the coffee. We'll wait in your president's office as the chief inspector here has suggested.'

'Not without his key. The boardroom will have to do.'

Under flashlight, the ghost of another and far better time appeared, felt St-Cyr, for the staircase to which they were led had been done by Hector Guimard of *métro*-entrance fame. Serpentine in seductively curved wrought iron, its banister led the way up as if to the gods. Equally of art nouveau and the belle epoque, enamel-and-bronze, sugar-cake elevator cages waited out of commission since the Occupation's all-out drive for tanks, trucks, aircraft engines and lots else had robbed them and most of such others of the needed electricity in June of 1940. But business had been so good and still was, taking the stairs would be no problem. There was even the taint of leftover cigar smoke, and among the bank's primary tenets to those with far less would be the admonishment of 'one mustn't grumble.'

But now a light switch was thrown. Variegated jade-green marble panels and mirrored glass lined the boardroom while fair-breasted bronze lamps revealed that money had simply been no object when the bank had moved in. Fortunately the blackout drapes were still drawn. Not only did the table seemingly go on and on under electric light, the two dozen straight-backed art nouveau chairs funneled the vision to one of Klimt's larger masterpieces. Jewels of light were replete with haunting female thoughts not just of carnal lust but of vengeance if not careful. Yet another was on the wall behind them and each was worth an absolute fortune.

'Bought at the Jeu de Paume, Louis?'

Where the confiscated art collections of the deported were placed on display to be auctioned off for the good of Vichy and others, especially the Reichsmarschall Göring and the Führer.

'Our Chairman Bolduc has taste, Hermann.'

Left to themselves, a mistake of course, they soon had the connecting door unlocked and were able to enter that sanctuary of sanctuaries, for Hermann had found a spare key tucked under that end of the table in case Monsieur le Président should forget his own or someone else should need to get in. Classed as degenerate art by the Nazis, paintings by the Czech artists Alphonse Mucha and František Kupka were entirely evident, as were several by the Yugoslavian Leon Koen, with glassware pieces by the Daum brothers and René Lalique and Émile Gallé, and bits of sculpture by Rodin and others.

'Exceptional investments, the Reich won't mind since they need the cash, but he also lacks taste,' said St-Cyr, for beneath some of the sketches, and even among Rodin's pieces atop a mahogany cabinet, were maquettes, but not the usual. These were not of plaster or papier-mâché but had been cast in bronze along with some of the statues they had led to, and at a time of war.

Big, muscular, virile examples of Germanic manhood were ranked side by side with the equally naked Valkyries of Arno Breker's Paris Exhibition of May 1942 in the Orangerie, much of its larger pieces done in plaster of course. But having lived and worked in Paris up to 1934, Breker had become known for the subtle and exquisite sensitivity of his sculptures, though all of that had changed and gone downhill when, just after signing the Armistice, Hitler had gotten the sculptor to give him a guided tour of the city he had just conquered. Breker had instantly become the Third Reich's chief sculptor and ever since then had given the Führer exactly what that one had wanted.

'Bolduc is well connected,' said Kohler, 'but if he has any sense, he had better be having these melted down or buried in the garden at home.'

Behind a spacious desk with Lalique dragonfly lampshade, was a wall map devoted to the pickups and deliveries of, in total, a fleet of eight vans. Virtually all of the Île de France and beyond was covered, the entrances assigned being not just those closest to their respective routes but definitely circled.

'Our van didn't just make those stops suggested by Rocheleau, Louis. It went to Meaux first, then east to Chalons-sur-Mer for the wine and champagne, northeast to the Ardennes, and only then would have gone to Reims before hitting Laon, Soissons and stopping also in Villers-Cotterêts, then Senlis and finally Paris with unrecorded side trips wherever necessary. If every one of these vans is gathering goods for sale on the *marché noir*, our Bolduc is deep into it and has all the gasoline allotment needed.'

Thanks to his overseers. 'And is one of the BOFs, eh?'

The *beurre, oeufs et fromage* boys. The big dealers. 'We'll have to ask him.'

Tidy files lay on the desk to the left of its chair. 'Vineyards and châteaux to the north of Bordeaux, in the Haut-Médoc, Louis, but promising resort areas to the south, along the beaches of the Côte d'Argent and Côte Sud des Landes and in the dunes behind. Wars can never last forever and bank presidents with extra cash on their hands have to plan for the future. He's already purchased some of these and has offers on others.'

Framed in art nouveau and complimented by a silver pen-and-ink stand with kneeling nude at the inkwell was a photo of the wife, two daughters, a villa in Neuilly, probably, and the family poodle.

'Messieurs . . . Messieurs, what is this? You invade the privacy of Chairman Bolduc's office without permission? You search but I do not have the necessary . . . *Vite, vite, immédiatement, s'il vous plaît* . . . The magistrate's warrant!'

This keeper of the spare key had even snapped her fingers. 'Deal with her in the boardroom, Chief Inspector, while I take a more thorough look at these files and that route map. There's got to be a garage to service those vans and a depot to store all that contraband. Ask her where it is. If she objects, tell her that the Action Courts will be interested.'

Objecting to being hustled out of the office, she refused to budge and sharply cast the early-morning's hastily made-up deep brown eyes at what Hermann was up to.

'Madame,' insisted this obstinate Sûreté to distract her and give that partner of his time to find out all he could, 'the names, please, of the driver and his assistant.'

He had even thumped his little black notebook on the desk in front of her and had taken the monsieur's pen and was now dipping it into the inkwell. 'The Action Courts, Inspector? What is this, please?'

Nothing but damage control was racing through her mind, felt St-Cyr, noting that beauty often came in various forms at the age of forty-four or forty-six and that dealing with trouble was paramount among such attributes. 'Items not usual for a bank van were found with what remained of the cash, madame.'

Merde! It had finally happened and she had let the pen betray her feelings. 'Though I still wear the wedding ring lest that reminder be cut off, Inspector, it's Mademoiselle Yvonne Roget and has been ever since I joined the bank in 1934. Murders of whom, please, and was our van robbed but not of all of its cash?'

'Only some of it.'

'That's not an adequate answer. What's this all about?'

'Two murders with subordinate charges.'

They could see that she had been badly shaken, felt Yvonne, the Sûreté drawing out a chair for her, the Gestapo having found what he had felt necessary and pouring her a stiff one.

'*Merci,*' she quavered, but had they really believed her? Flashing the Gestapo an anxiously fleeting smile, she would let the tears come and the lips quiver. 'Both the driver and his assistant? *Ah mon Dieu, mon Dieu, quel désastre, quelle tragédie!* Both have little children and big families. Why would anyone do such a thing?'

Offered the Sûreté's handkerchief, she found it clean and ironed well enough, though smelling of the stewed ivy-leaf-with-pine-needle water he had used instead of the soap most could never get these days. Dabbing at her eyes and hoping that he had shaken out all of the sand he would also have used, she tried not to smudge shadow, foundation, rouge and face powder, but heard again that one saying, 'Their names, Mademoiselle Roget? Please, it is necessary, and the addresses. And while you're at it, jot down those of Chairman Bolduc's mistress. One never knows when such information might be useful.'

This *salaud* was going to want everything! 'René Deniard was the driver, Raymond Paquette, the assistant. Both have been with the bank for some time, the first since 1938, the second since 1939. They were to have returned last Thursday, possibly late, but Chairman Bolduc, he felt we should give them a little more time.'

Three days of it. The cologne she had hastily applied before arriving had the lightest of citrus blends and a bouquet of lavender and rosemary that was *trés délicat et merveilleux.* 'That's Guerlain's Eau de Cologne Impériale.'

Ah bon, she would say it with a faint, sad smile 'A gift from my boss. He's always finding such things for myself, and for others too, of course.'

'And Deniard and Paquette were not called up in 1938 and '39? Why was this, please?'

'Are such not necessary to banks and those not necessary to wars?'

'That is not the answer needed.'

The worm. Well all right then, Chief Inspector, let's see how it turns! 'Deniard had bad eyesight; Paquette the same.'

How understanding of Bolduc, but neither had worn glasses, though those could, perhaps, have been thrown into that *gazo*'s firebox with the pocket contents and somehow failed to turn up in the ashes. 'And this van, mademoiselle, they had a lot of pick-ups, did they?' Hermann was now perusing the photos on the wall behind the desk, having just sorted through some other files.

'*Oui, je pense . . .*' she began, but must this one seize every opportunity to distract her so as to let the other find out everything?

'You knew, did you, exactly where those pickups were to be made and what was to be collected?'

Ah Sainte Mère! 'Inspector, I did not say that they had lots of pickups for stuff to sell on the *marché noir*. Me, I don't know anything about that business. How could I?'

'But you did know they were up to something other than for the bank. You must have. You've been personal secretary here since 1934.'

'*Pour l'amour du ciel*, I'm not his wife!'

Nor mistress, sad though that might well be. 'But you do keep the wheels well oiled. You must. Now be so good as to write down the address of the bank's garage and depot, and while you're at it, the name or names of those in charge.'

'And their addresses?'

Normally far from easily ruffled, felt St-Cyr, she had simply used that outburst to stop Hermann from looking at those photos too closely. Dropping those lovely eyes under Sûreté scrutiny, she swallowed tightly, deliberately touched the base of her throat, and took a deep breath before swiftly glancing up at Hermann who was again trying the desk drawers, but was she now wondering if he would demand the key or simply find the spare one she had hidden, just like the other one?

'Now please, Inspectors, I must notify Monsieur Grégoire, who is the operations manager but does not live in this building.'

'Like yourself?' asked the Sûreté.

But could that readily be admitted if a little something else was added? '*Oui*, the bank has always provided me with a flat here. Chairman Bolduc, he often works late and I am always on call because it is necessary.' A cosy little arrangement, was this what he was thinking? Well good, now she could hit him with it! 'Madame Bolduc is my sister. Me, I am aunt to her two darlings, Didi and Yvonne, ages ten and twelve.'

Hermann looked as if he was about to choke, but there was a more important matter. 'And your ex-husband, mademoiselle?'

Perhaps he should hear it since it wouldn't hurt. 'Sleeps in his coffin, thanks to the plane crash that took him from me in 1932. Me, I will telephone Monsieur Grégoire and instruct him to meet you at the garage, Inspector. He will know what is best. If he needs help, he can always call on one of the others.'

'Are they all PPF?' asked Hermann, leaning over the desk to give her glass a refill and touch the fingers that were still holding it.

Her look must be one of cold appraisal, felt Yvonne, for he had the definite appearance and touch of a womanizer. 'Members of the neofascist Parti Populaire Français? That I most certainly wouldn't know, Inspector. I'm simply a typist. I never go to that garage. Why should I, when I know nothing of engines and am kept busy here?'

Leaving the Citroën where it was, they got into the van with Louis again at the wheel. 'Old money, Hermann. For far too long, about 200 families have controlled our banks. While presently they will have German overseers, there will always be someone who watches things for the family. Having married that sister of hers, Bolduc will have got his hands on his wife's portion of the family's money, since that is how it is in France, but Yvonne Roget realized immediately that her boss wasn't the only one on thin ice and that if a sacrifice was to be made, it would be him and no one else. She won't just be contacting Grégoire, she'll be disturbing the sleep of that pot-shoot even though the Gestapo's listeners will hear her. She'll also, bearing those same listeners in mind but avoiding them at all costs, be on her way to see that sister of hers who obviously must know only too well that her husband has a mistress.'

Louis certainly had an understanding of things. 'Tolerated, eh, for the good of the family? Though in a hell of a rush, our Yvonne still took time out to brush that lovely auburn hair and do her lips and the rest before dashing off to throw a wrench into us if possible.'

'After lightly dabbing herself behind the ears with the Empress Eugénie's favourite, but is Bolduc a Royalist yearning for the days of even Napoléon III and his consort?'

Who had been banished to England in 1871, but the partnership had been up against those wanting the strong hand of royalty before, though there was something else Louis had better hear. 'Three of those vans use the Porte de Versailles as a designated entrance and we both know what it's close to because it's also Oberfeldwebel Werner Dillmann's beat.'

And the entrance used by the Tabac National. '*Ah bon*, but why bother to talk to the cat when you can talk to the tiger?'

An old saying from home, and also from Louis's childhood summers at an uncle's farm near Saarbrücken, but there was still more to come. 'Yvonne left that boss of hers a note, Louis. Apparently the PPF are due another donation.'

'Aren't Rudy de Mérode and the other gangs enough?'

'Easy, *mon vieux*. Easy.' But many of the big banks *were* funding the PPF, and always such donations were in cash to avoid a paper trail. Vehemently anti-Democratic, anti-Communist, anti-the Allies, de Gaulle, the Masons and the Jews, PPFs were especially anti-Résistance now and had their spies everywhere.

'And like a lot of the others, Hermann, they will have realized Herr Himmler's determination to destroy the Abwehr and absorb it into the Sicherheitsdienst, and will have switched sides.'

Leaving the Abwehr, which had originally done so much for all such types, right out in the cold. So bad had things become, Abwehr-West had forbidden its German and French staff to have any dealings with the SD and SS, but it was all too clearly a battle the Abwehr were fast losing. 'And that has to include Bolduc's two overseers, Louis. Hauptmann Reinecke and Leutnant Heiss must be Abwehr-West and will have been with that bank since July of 1940.'

'With lots of time to get to know and work with Bolduc. This investigation just gets deeper and deeper, doesn't it?'

Unfortunately, there was something else Louis had better hear. 'When he assigned us to this investigation, Boemelburg thought to tell me that the SD had just recruited a *Selbstschutz* from among the PPF. I know I should have told you, but . . .'

'News like that would be too upsetting, a self-defence hit squad to do what the SD themselves don't want to be associated with like taking care of outspoken detectives?'

'If I have to, I'll use the Purdey.'

The rue du Faubourg Saint-Antoine ran from *place* de la Bastille to *place* de la Nation. On either side, in the 11th and 12th arrondissements behind what must once have been elegant residences with wrought-iron balconies, shops and all the rest, were warrens of narrow *passages* and courtyards. Generations of cabinet and furniture makers still had their shops here and, in the past, had incorporated marquetry, gilding and bronze work and become known for it throughout Europe. 'Yet it's also an enclave of political troublemakers, Hermann. Repeatedly they have taken to the streets with their likes and dislikes.'

There were also produce shops, and the long lines of the Occupation had already been forming since the lifting of the curfew at 0500 hours. Some had even brought a stool or fold-up chair. Kids with runny noses and untied shoelaces seemed everywhere, baby carriages too, and even grandmothers wearing carpet slippers, all with the inevitable shopping bag, flowers pinned to their hats and the hopes of getting something more than the likelihood of a few radishes and carrots with tops for the rabbits if lucky.

The bank's garage was just to the east of the intersection with the rue de Charonne. Four- and five-storey tenements, all grey with prewar soot, had balconies whose livestock awaited the sunlight. Merely a slot in the wall, the entrance was labeled GARAGE in grey-blue tin metal with flanking notices for CITROËN, HOTCHKISS, PEUGEOT and RENAULT repairs too, but who had cars other than the chosen few?

Iron bars guarded the lower windows, and above and beyond those were curtains, some open, others perpetually drawn. The depot and repair bays were at the very back of the courtyard, the beams above them sagging. Ateliers of two and three storeys were to the left and right, while in the tenements above, the grey and flaking walls from which laundry hung definitely needed repairing.

'There's an iron gate that closes all this off at night, Hermann.'

'And a hive of industry with hardly a sound. Is it that we've been expected?'

Bicycles, well chained, were nearby. Rank on the damp air was the stench of the outdoor toilet, while from the cast-iron tap of another century, a constant stream dribbled as two Alsatians lapped at it, completely ignoring Hermann's, '*Ach, meine Schatzen*, you're lovely.' They barely tolerated his touch, but he was never one to give up easily and soon had these 'treasures' all over him.

'Guard dogs they may be, Louis, but a little scavenged smoked sausage does miracles.'

Beyond the bay for greasing and minor repairs, and the one for flat tires, the sliding door opened into the service centre, a warehouse that seemed, by contrast, huge. Four of the bank's eight vans were in a row, leaving three still out and probably soon on their way back to Paris, the mechanics and their assistants in *bleues de travail* and busy, though casting glances at them. But there were also a Vauxhall sedan, a Citroën coupé, a Ford Model C Ten and a forest-green, four-door Cadillac Series 60 limo that was absolutely beautiful. A 1938 or '39.

Daylight now entered the barred windows high above, while a gleaming black Renault Vivastella four-door, the 1939 and capable of 177 kph (110 mph), had beat them to it.

'The hood's still warm,' said Louis.

'Inspectors . . . Inspectors,' came a deeply resonant voice from on high, behind an iron walkway's railing at the back. The suit and tie were those of a banker, the gut and shoulders something else again. '*Mon Dieu*, but you've had a time of it, I gather. Hector Bolduc *à votre service*. Come up, come up. Back of this walkway is my office away from the bank. A little coffee and cognac to take the chill off? Two trusted bank employees murdered, was it, at l'Abbaye de Vauclair of all places? Their wives and children have been notified, have they? Funeral expenses will have to be found—the bank of course—and a little set aside to keep them all going.'

A hand was quickly extended, theirs taken by the grip of a wrestler. 'Here, I'll close the door to let the boys get on with their work. Grégoire will soon be here. You've left the van locked, have you? The keys then, for later.'

He, too, snapped his fingers just like Yvonne Roget. 'A few questions first, Chairman Bolduc,' began Louis. 'Nothing difficult you understand, since your return from the Côte Sud des Landes has been so remarkable, my partner and I are a little taken aback.'

And if that wasn't kindly, what was? wondered Kohler, for if damage control was intended, the set of this one's lips and arch of the fiercely bushy grey-black brows and the look in those deep-brown eyes said enough. Greying at the sides, thin and curly and almost bald on top, the hair would see a barber every other day at least, but the grizzled cheeks, chin and throat simply reinforced the appearance not just of toughness, but of a slum landlord about to toss out a family of ten.

The big hands gestured at the thought of his still being in Paris. 'Yvonne was only trying to give me time to get here. I'm not off until Thursday at 0500 hours. Hauptmann Reinecke and Leutnant Heiss, who are assigned to my bank, are to deliver the Dornier DO-24T flying boat we at the bank have donated to the Luftwaffe's Coastal Command. It's come straight off the line at the Potez-CAMS works at Sartrouville.* Very safe and reliable, it's the perfect reconnaissance aircraft. The Dutch are also producing them. Now please, a little refreshment since Yvonne has told me you hardly touched a thing she had ordered in for you.'

'A moment,' said Hermann. 'Are Reinecke and Heiss also attached to Abwehr-West?'

The Army's counterintelligence service and the usual for such. 'Would it matter?'

'It might.'

'Then that I wouldn't know, would I, otherwise it wouldn't be top secret.'

Seizing the coffeepot, he filled the mugs, then smoothly set three glasses in a row and gave them the Rémy Martin Vieille Réserve. 'It's a favourite,' he said. 'Fifteen years in the cask. Look at how deep the colour is, savour its aroma first. Warm it in the hand and only then brush the lips while breathing in the scent. It's magnificent.'

One could but try, thought St-Cyr. 'Monsieur, the back of that van of yours was loaded not just with cash, but items gathered along its route for sale on the *marché noir*. Brie, wine, champagne, bacon, ham, flour, eggs, truffles . . .'

---

* An industrial suburb in *la zone* to the northwest of Paris.

Confessions would be out of the question, felt Kohler, since the swiftness of a dark and challenging look had erupted into, 'What's this you're saying? That trusted employees of my bank would dare to do such a thing when half the city is starving and the other half entirely hungry? No milk for the newborns whose mothers have gone dry?'

'Apparently so,' went on Louis, 'but those employees of yours certainly got taken on the truffles. They're not of the winter variety. They're from last summer and, in a foolish attempt to increase their price, have been dyed with the juice from walnut husks.'

'And what, please, am I to say? That I'll cut the balls off the sellers, eh, since I knew absolutely nothing of this matter?'

Indicating that he should sit facing them both from across the table, this Sûreté even had the audacity to drag out a little notebook and a pair of ivory bones!

Kohler had already started in on the cognac and judging it perfect, had given him an appreciative nod and was now lathering one of the buttered, hot croissants with the jam, so one had best calm the voice. 'It's blue damson, Inspector, albeit from Poland, but from before those people started the hostilities that have taught them such a lesson. Word has it that the Crusaders brought the plum back to France from Syria, the Romans having grafted it.'

And a little like the walnut husks, but ancient history when needed, was it? wondered St-Cyr. 'Again, monsieur, I must remind you of the contents of that van of yours.'

Kohler had crammed his chair into the corner and was leaning it back against the wall, relaxing. 'Remind if you wish, but eat, please, since the croissants are fresh and sharing a meal always brings people together.'

He couldn't have known of *garde champêtre* Rocheleau's similar offering, felt St-Cyr, but there it was, his own comment to Hermann at that time as well.

'Me, I have the coffeepot on here at all times,' went on Bolduc gregariously while buttering himself a croissant and adding the jam. 'This is made with honey. Whenever time allows, and there's little of it these days, I love to work on my car. I also own the building, of course.'

'And those other cars—are you a collector?' asked Kohler.

A laugh, a grin, a smile would suit for they would probably

have already figured it out. 'All are being cleaned up for resale in the Reich by Hauptmann Reinecke and Leutnant Heiss who have that duty also. We here are simply doing the necessary, as we have now ever since the hostilities between our two nations ceased. Gasoline is in such short supply in France, few can afford to keep them, so the cars, they are unbelievable bargains, but what can one Frenchman do, eh? Object or simply repair them to at least take in that amount of cash?'

Bought at next to nothing, thought Kohler, they'd be sold for at least 8,000 marks or 160,000 francs for a tidy profit, especially if those bank overseers pocketed half the sale and said nothing about others they were selling on the side, since they'd be the ones to do all the necessary paperwork even if Abwehr. No doubt about it, Bolduc was in deeply, for he'd have a cut of that as well. 'Business has been good, has it?'

Refilling Hermann's glass, Bolduc then hunkered down with forearms on the table. 'Listen, you two, I can buy just about any-thing and everything I want. I knew absolutely nothing of what those two employees of mine were up to, so please don't try to attack my reputation and bring disgrace down on my bank.'

The cognac was excellent, felt St-Cyr, the jam and croissants perfect, the coffee that little added touch. Taking the worn pair of dice that had been with him since joining the Sûreté, he would begin the necessary by tossing a seven or an eleven. 'Monsieur, is it that you know so little of what goes on with your bank, you would ignore the news Oberführer Wolfgang Thomsen and Unterstrum-führer Ludwig Mohnke brought to Paris on Thursday after discov-ering the bodies? Two much valued employees, both with bad eye-sight but no glasses, which is a puzzle, is it not? Cash—how much was there on the manifest, Detektiv Inspektor Kohler? Remind me.'

'I didn't count what was left of it, Chief, but 65.25 million francs in 42 bags, for starters.'

These days everything was a gamble. 'First, I wasn't informed of the robbery and the killings by anyone, especially the two you've just mentioned. Secondly, as to that amount of cash, it was the end of the month and our friends like to pay in cash when they buy the champagne and other things we French are only too willing to sell, so is there a problem?'

Snake eyes had turned up far too early. Gathering the dice, Louis gave them another toss. 'When information is demanded, monsieur, it's necessary for you to answer completely and truthfully, especially since this is first and foremost a murder enquiry. Bad eyesight, was it?'

Yvonne must have told them. 'Both Deniard and Paquette were called up but rejected, and since the bank needed them, is there still a problem?'

Probably but . . . 'Charges will have to be laid regarding the black-market dealing, there's no question of it. It's only a matter of who gets them, the *lampistes* or the big dealers.'

Underlings were often convicted to soothe the press and the public, but the courts seldom touched others, it being too difficult, they knowing far too many who would speak for them. 'Kohler, you'd better caution this one. The Banque Nationale de Crédit et Commercial is not in the business of the *schwarzer Markt* and never has been. *Mein Gott*, you two, what's a few things? Deniard was probably thinking of his mother who is always bitching about how hard it is to get things. Paquette would simply have gone along with him. It's an isolated incident. Set it aside for the sake of the families. I'll have the boys here take whatever it is over to the Hôpital Quinze-Vingts for the blind. They'll be more than delighted and we'll let the whole affair lie.'

Yet another pair of snake eyes didn't help. 'Louis, I think he's got a point. Why lay more grief on the families when they've enough to handle?'

'It's a matter for the courts, Hermann.'

Had Kohler seen something he shouldn't? wondered Bolduc.

'Louis, he didn't have anything to do with it and we'd never be able to prove otherwise. Let me talk to Boemelburg. He'll clear it, no problem, then we can just deal with the murders.'

Merde alors, what was this? wondered Bolduc, refilling Kohler's glass. Cash was certainly not being hinted at, not with these two who were known for their honesty and the trouble they could cause, but perhaps Kohler had seen that he would simply go to the Höherer SS Oberg, since the bank did have its friends and Oberg was definitely *not* one of theirs. 'You should get yourself another pair of dice, Chief Inspector. Those are so worn you keep tossing the same things.'

A seven and then an eleven landed, but was Bolduc now willing to back off himself? 'Dice are far too scarce. Last year's *Aktion* for the Reichsmarschall Göring purchased thousands of pairs including, if I remember it correctly, 877,000 decks of playing cards.'

And all for German armaments workers to brighten their Christmases, thought Kohler, along with equal numbers of nail-files, clippers, combs, bottles of hair lotion, pipes and pocket knives, and good for Louis. Bolduc had been distracted.

'Monsieur,' said St-Cyr, 'we understand that the van was due back here on Thursday but that you felt the bank should give René Deniard and Raymond Paquette a little more time.'

And damn Yvonne for having said such a stupid thing. 'As I've already told you, Chief Inspector, it was an end-of-the-month pickup. Sometimes our branch managers need a little extra time simply because our major clients, all of them businesses, need it to tally the cash and get those deposits in.'

'Three days of it?' asked Kohler.

'It's a Saturday, is it not?'

'Two days then, assuming that they wouldn't have arrived back in Paris until just before midnight Thursday.'

These two were dangerous. 'I was very busy with other matters and might have tossed off the comment. Besides, such a responsibility is always delegated.'

And Yvonne Rouget was bound to hear of it a little later.

Out in the courtyard while waiting to be given a lift back to the bank, since Grégoire was to take care of listing everything in the van, including the cash that had been left, Hermann turned his back on the garage and, keeping a hand well out of sight of any chance watchers, opened it to what he had collected.

It was a mousetrap with a once healthy mouse, the cheese still firmly in its jaws. 'Let's hope he was convinced, Hermann, and that he doesn't empty the storeroom or rooms before we can have it done for him. His set-up is admirable and he must have all the dealers and underlings he needs, and certainly those three days of extra time suggest that he knew far more about that van than admitted, but for now, me to Monnier with the shoes and on foot, you to the Citroën and then to Oberfeldwebel Dillmann.'

Unlocking the back door of the van, Kohler simply said, 'I'll just take a few things and a little *Schmiergelder* to open that one up, but will write it all down.'

*   *   *

Shoe-saver, with the painted storm clouds and fork lightning, would do, felt St-Cyr of the *vélo-taxi* he would hire.

Plucked from the *place* de la Bastille's stand, Henri Vincent looked this one over, for Sûreté was written so clearly it would not have influenced the judgement had the *vache* been naked. 'Six francs the kilometre, ten if it's too far.'

The inevitable dead fag-end clung to that lower lip. 'Don't take to the streets at the least impulse like your forefathers must have. I'll agree to seven with a tip you won't forget.'

A *zéro* probably, but it was still early and the district was not inclined to hire anything if it could be avoided in these days of hyperinflation. 'Where to?'

'Not far at first. The Passage du Cheval-Blanc, but go back along the Faubourg Saint-Antoine then duck into the Cité Parchappe to find that passage and turn left on it. Having let me off, continue but go north on the rue de la Roquette.'

And all of it relatively close, so this one, he knew the city well enough, but he wasn't finished.

'Continue past the women's prison to the five stones where the widow-maker*—or the widower, in this case—used to stand as a reminder. Wait there five minutes then continue on to the boulevard des Capucines and Banque Nationale de Crédit et Commercial.'

Dieu merci and news of that bank-van robbery and murder everyone else at the taxi station had been talking about. 'How many are to be led astray?'

'As many as possible. I'll deal with the rest while following you in another taxi.'

This one might or might not do that. 'A hundred francs with a tip of fifty.'

Hermann would have said give him two hundred, but having grown accustomed to his ways, and having also flattened those tires earlier, which would but guarantee their being followed if possible, he had better say, 'One fifty it is.'

Taking the necessary from a wallet that was so mended with fishing line his mother must have given it to him, this Sûreté climbed

---

* The guillotine.

into the back and when he had judged it appropriate, vanished, but these days, felt Vincent, one could argue with the conscience, if one had one, and return to the stand having pocketed the cash. But then, too, there had obviously been a need for assistance and improving the criminal record by having helped could never hurt. Besides, he'd have lots to talk about and such would bring its stream of urging fags, though maybe silence would be the wiser.

Monnier was to the west of the avenue Matignon and on the south side of this oldest of faubourgs, felt St-Cyr, and near the corner of the rue Montaigne.* Here there were luxury-filled galleries, antique and jewellery shops, ladies' clothing, too, and men's. Just to the east were the *haute couture* and perfume houses, all still doing a roaring business. A pavement of the *bourgeoisie* and *bourgeoisie aisée*, the rue du Faubourg Saint-Honoré was like no other in Occupied Europe, it was said. Window shopping was, of course, the order of the day. Strolling Germans in uniform, many with their *petites amies*, seemed to be everywhere in Hitler's showplace to the world of what a German-occupied city could really be like. And as if that were not enough, October, which was truly Paris's loveliest, had let the sun enter to prove it, for many had already removed their coats. Made-over suits and skirts or blouses and sweaters some might be, but all were of quality, and with lines painted up the backs of the leg-wash to give the lie of silk stockings, the skirts were now cut to knee length. Handbags were of prewar leather, *les chapeaux* of autumn's snap-brim cut with more delicate touches of dried flowers, imitation fruit or feathers than in summer, and as for the sounds of the traffic, one was struck by the utter absence of blaring horns and squealing brakes. Even the cyclists were quiet, though the *agent de circulation* with white baton blew his whistle as shrilly as usual.

Shoes were tastefully displayed and exclaimed over by window-shoppers. While many pairs had the regulation wooden soles, or the evening's glass, and there were straps instead of full leather, others were being constantly pointed at. Of Parisian last and style, with the one strap, the high heels were very similar to the those that were tucked deeply in his coat pockets, yet

---

* Renamed the rue Jean Mermoz.

at 6,000 francs the pair, they were half the annual salary of a school teacher and 40 percent of this Sûreté's.

Entering the shop, the aroma of good, sound leather was all too present. Seemingly bound to constant motion, the dominant salesman was wearing a brand-new 'national' suit, those with the slimmed-down collars and loss of pocket flaps and turn-ups. Ersatz cloth, too, namely rayon, this one having paid the same on the *marché noir* as for those high heels or handed in the two old suits required along with the clothing tickets and the 350 francs of the officially controlled Vichy price, if one could but find such a suit. But had this salesman expectations of immediate promotion or those of ownership?

'Monsieur . . .'

'It's Manager Chartrand. Be so good as to speak to one of my sales people.'

And with the head in the air too? 'You'll do. St-Cyr, Sûreté, and before you say anything further, it's a murder inquiry. Where is Maurice Monnier who owns this shop and has always welcomed me?'

Merde, the day had begun badly with the fog and now could only get worse. 'Murder, Inspector? What have we to do with that?'

Chartrand even had a carefully groomed Hitler-like moustache. 'That's for me to determine and not before you have answered all of my questions truthfully.'

Customers were beginning to take notice, a colonel and his latest *horizontale*, felt Chartrand. 'Monsieur Trudelle, please attend to the colonel and his lovely companion. Nothing but the latest fashion, you understand? The boots for winter, the slippers for the fire, the high heels that will give height and do justice to the mademoiselle's beautifully magnificent *coiffure*.'

That hairstyle of piled-on waves and curls had already given her added height so as to be closer to that of the colonel. 'Now, *mon ami*, come down to earth and answer me.'

The shit! 'Still in the free zone that is no longer free.'

'But you've not heard from him since before 11 November last?'

When the Wehrmacht had moved south to occupy the free zone, too, the Italians increased their occupied zone of France as well, since the Allies, the Americans among them, had landed *en masse* in North Africa to take care of Rommel and his Afrika Korps. 'Inspector, what is it you . . .'

'It's chief inspector, and I'm the one who asks the questions. Drancy was it?'

And a train trip by cattle truck to those camps no one wanted to talk about. 'I believe so, yes.'

'So you've elevated yourself to manager. Is ownership in the offing?'

Why had he chosen to come here today of all days? 'My offer has been made to the proper authorities and I'm expecting a positive response today or on Monday. Those shoes you have were made by us but look as if they've not been treated as shoes from Monnier should. A very thorough cleaning, the application of replacement dye if we can but find it, and then . . .'

'Just tell me when they were made, since there are those here that are still being made in spite of the severe shortages and restrictions and we both know that to get leather like that you have to be buying it on the *marché noir.'*

'I'll have to get the register.'

'And I'll wait and empty the shop if you delay me much longer.'

'Friday, 14 August 1942, a rush order. Me, I remember it clearly because I made the delivery myself, as requested by . . .'

'By whom?'

'Inspector, it's a delicate matter.'

'Delicate or not, who ordered them?'

'Madame Nicole Bordeaux. She's been a client for years.'

Hermann would have instantly said, Uh-oh, Louis, she'll know all the *Bonzen und Oberbonzen*, but . . . 'The same as has the fine big house of the rue de la Boétie?'

Nearby and just around the corner from the rue des Saussaies, home of this one's fellows and the Gestapo. 'Certainly, but she didn't wish them to be sent there, Chief Inspector. The shoes they were to match a dress she had chosen for someone she was helping.'

This whole thing was only getting deeper and deeper. 'So you delivered them where?'

And now for the delicious part. 'An escort service, Les Amies françaises. Salle Pleyel, Studio 51, but please don't ask me why Madame Bordeaux would have given some young girl an expensive dress and all the underthings to go with it plus a pair of our finest shoes since those obviously did not fit her precisely.'

Nicole Bordeaux was of *les hautes* and held parties and gatherings at that house of hers that were the talk of Paris: splendid gatherings to promote artistic and cultural exchanges between Occupier and Occupied. Alice, the Swiss wife of Dr. Karl Epting, head of the Deutsches Institut, was a bosom friend, as was Suzanne Abetz, the French wife of the German ambassador. Anna-Marie Vermeulen could simply not have been that girl. 'Say nothing of this to anyone, Monsieur Chartrand. Get contrary and you will not only have to deal with me but with my partner, the Detektiv Inspektor Kohler of the Kriminalpolizei, the Kripo for short.'

The Tabac National was to the south of Paris and in the suburb of Issy-les-Moulineaux just on the other side of the 'wall,' the *enceintre* that encircled the city if one could find it. Drawing to the side of the road nearest that hive of industry, Kohler longed for a cigarette, for it was here that each of those Gauloises bleues began their little lives. At twenty to the soft packet and a ration of two of those per month plus one of the loose, it was no wonder there was a healthy trade in forged and stolen tobacco cards. Men only, too. Women simply hadn't been factored into Vichy's tobacco thoughts even though hundreds among the staff of 3,000 would be working here, especially when so many of their boys were locked up in POW camps in the Reich and not likely to ever get out as far as the Führer was concerned.

Coal smoke did issue from the chimneys but the parking lot of prewar days held only bicycles and a few of the delivery trucks. But when two of those last started out for the Porte de Versailles entrance, he followed. Turning to the right, onto the avenue Ernest Renan,* they drove past the factory and the Parc des Expositions where from 1925 until the defeat there had been trade fairs showcasing industry and technology. Directly to the west, and taken over by the Luftwaffe of course, was the Champ des Manoeuvres,** where the very first French aviator had learned to take off and land in 1905 and the Paris-Madrid

---

* Now Rue Ernest Renan.
** Now the Paris heliport.

air race of 21 May 1911 had been won by the only pilot to finish it, another Frenchman. Huge swastikas announced everything, the gates of the exposition dominating the eastern side of the entrance. Rent-controlled brick tenements, drab in their essence and built in the 1920s and '30s, clustered closely, for the 15th arrondissement, the Vaugirard, was industrial to its core. Long lines of traffic were impatiently waiting to enter the city for here, too, Ludin and that no-name colonel had still not lifted their high-priority. But tobacco trucks, like vans from the Banque de France of all things, could draw over to the western side and have it a lot easier. Well, some of them.

'*Ach, meine Herren,*' shouted the sergeant-major of this little detail, 'no one breaks the *gottverdammten* rules while I'm in charge. Corporals Mannstein, Weiss and Rath, do your duty!'

Flung open, the back door to that Bank of France's van let a third employee tumble out to face the trouble. 'Ducklings˙ among the banknotes and ready for the squeeze at the Tour d'Argent?' yelled Oberfeldwebel Dillmann. 'Sugar? Wine you've bought at 50 francs to sell at 800 the bottle? Butter . . . *Ach, mein Gott*, the charges. *Ihre Papiere. Papiere*, damn it. *Schnell!*'

Terrified, the three from the Bank of France collided while trying to find the necessary. Waving the papers, Dillmann who couldn't understand much more than *oui ou non*, and less of the latter, took time out. Meanwhile his boys carried the offending loot to a nearby Wehrmacht truck whose tailgate was down and canvas tarp pulled slightly aside.

'Now, *meine Freunden,*' he yelled. 'Take yourselves over to that batch of Vichy food controllers and those *flics* with their salad shaker˙˙ and wait for me there.

'*Liebe Zeit*, Corporal Weiss, that can't be milk, can it?'

Two of the grey metal containers were lifted out by Dillmann as if but featherweights. Deftly opened, indicating a former proficiency, they were tipped over, letting a flood of what most Parisians hadn't seen in years pour across the paving stones toward those very food controllers. But as for the two tobacco trucks ahead of himself, felt Kohler, there was merely a glance at each

---

* Pressed duck, a house specialty.

** A *panier à salade*, a Black Maria.

set of papers and a nod that could only mean, 'Do as agreed and I'll see you later. Don't, and you'll be in hell the next time.'

Big in the chest and lips, which Dillmann constantly seemed to be wetting, the left hand had somehow lost all but its forefinger and thumb, while that ample greenish-grey girth and chest, with its *Gott mitt Uns* belt buckle, sported the ribbon of the commemorative of the Spanish Revolution. A Wehrmacht volunteer against the Bolsheviks, few would know that Werner had had his reasons for leaving the Reich in a hurry in April 1937 to join the fight in Spain: namely one altercation in a Nazi *Bierkeller* that had gone terribly wrong. Having been dragooned into making an arrest, this Detektiv Inspektor had figured it at fifty-fifty and given much-needed advice: join up and bugger off or else.

Apart from the neck and facial scars shrapnel had left, there was other evidence of Dillmann's having been through things, for the right hand had lost its little and fourth fingers. But to the left and higher up on that bulwark chest was the Assault Badge, the *Infanterie Sturmabzeichen,* and beside it, the Polish medal and the one he had earned in that first winter in Russia, along with the frozen and now missing toes.

'Werner, mein Lieber . . .'

'Liebe Zeit, Hermann, is it really you and not a ghost those bastards in the SS, SD and Gestapo have sent me?'

'I need a fag and a word.'

Ice-blue and wary above a full and beautifully tapered moustache the Wehrmacht had somehow let him keep, that gaze instantly narrowed. '*Ach*, the first is easy, the second . . . Well you can see that the place is crawling with blowflies, yourself excluded, of course.'

The cigarette was lit, a welcome drag taken. 'They're the very reason I need a word.'

Lying on the seat beside Hermann was a bundle of 5,000-franc notes—a good one hundred of them—two rounds of Brie, some tins of sardines and two bottles of champagne, the Moët et Chandon.

Favouring his moustache, Dillmann wet his lips again and finally said, 'The horse abattoir. Follow those tobacco trucks. Tell them you're not about to make an arrest. Just let them leave what they have for me, then tuck the car out of sight, leaving room for my truck and others, and while you're at it, ask Hartmann, my latest recruit, to close the big doors and give you two packs, no more. I'll be there as soon as I can. Are you still working with that Frenchman?'

'Louis? We're still divvying up the work. I give him the harder tasks.'

'But he knows you've come here? Our little secret has been shared?'

'He'll be expecting you not to forget it.'

The Salle Pleyel wasn't far. Satisfied that he hadn't been followed, St-Cyr hurried, for that edifice of culture was simply far too visible, an escort service? At 252 rue du Faubourg Saint-Honoré and art deco in design, the concert hall had been built in 1927 by the Pleyel piano firm. Fire had consumed it but a few months later. Unable to rebuild, it had fallen into the hands of its major creditor, the Banque de Crédit Lyonnaise, a link perhaps. Bank to bank, Hermann would have said, but still . . .

In the years prior to the defeat, the Pleyel had featured all the greats, including France's pianist, Alfred Cortot, and yet again here next Saturday evening. The Schumann Concerto in A minor was his speciality and the same as he had performed in Berlin with the Philharmonic last year. Fully eighty percent of the audience here would also be German. An ardent *pétainiste* and feted by the Groupe Collaboration of wealthy industrialists and bankers, Cortot had been the first French artist to perform in the Reich after the defeat. Later, a subsequent tour had taken him back to Berlin and triumphantly on to Hamburg, Leipzig, Munich, Stuttgart and Frankfurt even though married to a wealthy Jewess eight years his senior. Now, of course, the bombing of such cities had caused him to cancel further concerts there, but music could, apparently, overcome the forbidden, though for a Dutch under-diver to hide here made absolutely no sense.

But neither had her *passeur*'s hiding behind the *marché noir* been the usual.

Completely avoiding the concierge's *loge*, he quickly went up and up, and then along corridor after corridor behind the concert hall, only to still feel it was far too exposed. Ballet, waltz, tango and the popular now went on all around him in the private studios in spite of the Führer's ban and that of Vichy, but finally a rippled glass door with Gothic lettering gave the necessary, indicating at least a year or two of existence.

LES AMIES FRANÇAISES
BUREAU D'HOSTESSES, JOUR OU SOIR ET VISITES TRÈS
MÉMORABLES
MADEMOISELLE JACQUELINE LEMAIRE
TÉLÉPHONE: CARNOT 33.72
DEUTSCHFREUNDLICH, DEUTSCH SPRECHEN

Soon after the defeat, a number of such establishments had sprung up. Some, like those on the Champs-Élysées, were merely fronts for expensive prostitutes, others but offering German businessmen that tantalizing possibility, but this . . . That name alone rang far too many bells.

Taking out the little black notebook all detectives should carry, he glanced at what Yvonne Rouget had written of Hector Bolduc's mistress.

The home address, though different, would overlook the Parc Monceau nearby. Money then, and lots of it, high society, too, and obviously a friend or associate of Madame Nicole Bordeaux, but a delicate matter not just because of the shoes, the dress and under-things that had been delivered here, but because, if approached, Mademoiselle Jacqueline Lemaire would immediately convey that news to Bolduc.

There was nothing for it. Bridges had to be crossed. Retreating to the concierge's *loge* next to the artists' entrance off the rue Daru, he ran a forefinger down the posted list of tenants until one name stood glaringly out to ring bells of its own.

MADEMOISELLE ANNETTE-MÉLANIE VEROCHE

False papers often did such things, allowing their owners to hide behind similar names so that if unexpectedly addressed, there would be no hesitation. But for that girl to be living here still made no sense, especially as the shoes had been made to fit someone else.

Or had they? Had the size simply been a mistake, Madame Bordeaux being a socialite bent on doing something she had dreamed up on impulse, or alternatively, had she thought that girl a possible candidate for Jacqueline Lemaire to groom as an escort?

Behind him a throat was cleared. 'Chief Inspector, you have caused me to hurry up all those stairs. These old legs, as you well know, don't relish such a task. What is it you want this time? Another dancer?'

A previous visit last January with Hermann had been completely forgotten. 'Monsieur Figeard, please overlook the haste. It's merely another dance studio, as you have mentioned, but only to refresh something that will then allow progress in yet another direction.'

'The usual, in other words.'

'Ah, perhaps I had better just run a finger down your list again.'

'Chief Inspector, surely you know these old ears have been dinned enough by those who occupy the studios?'

From the Auvergne, and a former deliverer of coal until the back and the legs had given out, Armand Figeard was in his mid-seventies yet still wore the black leather cap, dark grey shirt and sweater, black coveralls, boots and apron of the trade, right to the safety pin that had held fast the chest pocket where he had tucked his daily receipts.

Yet if asked if any of the tenants were away, that too would not be safe. 'I'll just have another look upstairs.'

'Not without me, Inspector. Me, I know the law as well as yourself.'

'But have unfortunately forgotten that it's not just "Inspector."'

'Mademoiselle Veroche is the only one who is away at present. She hasn't yet returned from Rethel. The mother again, the chest and pneumonia. Me, I sincerely hope it wasn't a funeral that has delayed her this time.'

'Had she been back to Rethel before?'

Such an interest could not be good. 'Early last December, from Tuesday the first until Thursday the tenth, but was certain her dear mother had recovered. Never have I seen one so relieved. She said a week or two more in hospital would do it. The doctors were all very happy with her mother's progress; Mademoiselle Veroche so pleased we even had a little celebration, just the two of us. Where she got that wine from the Haut-Médoc, I'll never know. The half of a Château Latour, warm yet full-bodied and as urgent as Rubens's *Portrait of Hélène Fourment* or Boucher's *L'Odalisque*.'

A concubine, but *ah mon Dieu*, wine from a region Hector Bolduc had a definite interest in.

'We had rabbit, too, which she helped to cook since she had fed and cared for it as much as myself. We've three, with two females that produce like clockwork, chickens too.'

Yet she hadn't stayed over in Rethel for Christmas. That city was, of course, about fifty kilometres to the northeast of Reims and had all but been destroyed during the Blitzkrieg, false papers using names from there and similar places since only the tombstones could be checked. 'And now again, Monsieur Figeard, another visit. When exactly?'

Why was there the need to also pin that down? 'Last month. She left on Sunday, 19 September, would be about a week, maybe a day or two more. It all depended on her mother's health.'

Was Figeard so gullible? The SS, the Gestapo and the *gestapistes français* wouldn't have hesitated. 'A student, you said?'

'*Oui.* Of medieval history, the role of the Benedictines, especially the Cistercians.'

She *had* known of that spring. 'The two of you actually raise rabbits and chickens on the roof?'

'And have a little garden. The bell jars now, if there's the threat of frost. Annette-Mélanie can't have done anything a person such as yourself would be interested in. She even has a part-time job here as an usherette at the concerts but also does the Friday afternoons and Saturdays at the German bookstore on the rue de Rivoli.'

The *Frontbuchhandlung** but this whole thing was simply going far too deep.

'She speaks German, does she?'

'Fluently. Otherwise she would not have been offered either position. None of the other usherettes speak it, though some are taking lessons.'

'And how long has she lived here?'

'Since June of 1941, the third week. Me, I . . . I offered to keep an eye on her bicycle so that she wouldn't have to walk it up to that room of hers where there's little enough space anyways, and those stairs . . . It's a good one, too, a Sparta, but heavy.'

---

* Formerly the British bookshop of W. H. Smith.

A Dutch bike, and if that wasn't taking a chance, what was? 'And kept where?'

'In the cellars, of course. She's beyond reproach, Chief Inspector. Me, I have seen her studying by candlelight, if a stub can be found. I once, on taking a little something up to her, teasingly asked if she, like others, had been borrowing them from the Église Saint-Philippe-du-Roule.'

At 154 rue du Faubourg Saint-Honoré.

'But she shook her head and told me with all earnestness that she had been given them by a subdeacon at the Cathédrale Alexandre Nevesky, a boy no older than herself, the one who mixes the incense, she said, and lights its little fires of charcoal before handing the censers to the priests. She liked, she said, to experience other religions. A good Catholic can have doubts, can't one?'

Especially since the accent of that second driver who'd been following them this morning had been Russian. 'Repeated visits, repeated candles?'

'That I . . . I wouldn't know, Chief Inspector.'

'But assume it's correct?'

Must he press so hard? 'Do the young not like to talk to the young, especially these days?'

A centre of the White Russian community and no friend of the Bolsheviks and Stalin, the cathedral was behind the Pleyel and faced on to the rue Daru and its intersection with the rue Pierre-le-Grand. Chez Kornilov, the Russian restaurant that was favoured by many of the Occupier and especially by its black-market dealers and sometimes, too, by the *gestapistes français*, was just across the street, but . . . 'You're absolutely correct. At times, I tend to question things far too much. She's obviously of no concern to myself and my partner.'

'Then you won't be needing my pass key?'

'Whatever for? I'll just walk back through by the concert hall and let myself out that way. My thanks for your patience. It's always good to refresh old acquaintances.'

Oberfeldwebel Dillmann had better have some answers for Hermann.

4

For one who loved horses and had, felt Kohler, used them often both on the farm and in the artillery of that other war, the Vaugirard horse abattoir was far from pleasant. Rotting offal, horses' hooves, bones, dung and scraps of hide—vestiges of these were everywhere under daylight until the big sliding doors had been closed by Schütze Hartmann.

Now under the faded light, the bloodstains at his feet appeared darker. The gobs and mounds of fat were still a greasy-yellow, but to everything came the constant dripping of leaky taps, while above him, and thrown into shadow as if waiting for some insane SD, SS or Gestapo to string the piano wire, a railing carried large metal hooks. Had there been any stock, each would have taken a horse, stunned, killed or still screaming, to the knives that would have swiftly disembowelled it, the butchers in full-length rubber being constantly showered by blood and offal. That girl, that Anna-Marie Vermeulen, really couldn't understand what those types could do to her. Under the SD decree of 12 July last year, 'reinforced' interrogations had been given the okay but had already been in use by Rudy de Mérode and the other gangs. Oona and Giselle could face the same if Louis and himself weren't careful, and yet . . . and yet they still didn't even know why Kaltenbrunner had sent those two, and Heinrich bloody Ludin would be out there somewhere waiting for him to cough up everything or else!

Mein Gott, but he needed a cigarette. Butchering hadn't gone on here that long. In 1894, the hog abattoirs, which faced inward from the rue de Dantzig to the west, had been the first, those for cattle in 1897, and finally this one in 1904 and backing onto the rue

Brancion. Since the abattoirs were serviced by rail on their southern boundary—the Chemin de Fer de l'Ouest—those two tobacco trucks he had followed had taken the rue de Dantzig north to the rue des Morillons, and then had gone east on it to the entrance. Otherwise there was fencing around the area and only limited foot traffic in and out, but here an ordinary door must lead to the rue Brancion. Directly across from it would be a *boucherie chevaline* whose golden horse heads advertised the steaks, roasts, sausage, et cetera had the stock not been shipped on the hoof to the Reich. But would that girl know the Vaugirard? Had she hidden in this arrondissement? Wax-works, leather tanning, machinery, pharmaceutics, even the bleach that had given the Quai de Javel its name and every skylight its blackout coat of laundry bluing, dominated the 15th. The Citroën factories were on the Allée des Cygnes in the Seine. Like the 11th and 12th, the Vaugirard was also a warren of narrow streets and pas-sages, low-rental tenements, houses, small garden plots and ateliers and such that would have made it perfect if she could have settled in, especially as it was an area seldom visited by the Occupier unless well armed and in a rush. Even Dillmann would have had to make arrangements with the local BOFs and the *pègre*.

Pay off the one to pay off the other, and business as usual.

From a farm and fishing family in the old town of Schleswig, Schütze Hartmann couldn't have been in Paris for more than six or seven months, the Wehrmacht but a few more. Though he had the look of Viking ancestors, the steel-rimmed specs made him appear far from that. Hovering over the four cases of cigarettes that had been dropped off by those tobacco trucks, he was armed with a Schmeisser he might be able to use, though that gave little comfort since ill-experienced trigger fingers could be dangerous.

A teenager whose bad eyesight said a lot about the Führer's latest recruits, the boy finally opened one of the boxes and asked, 'Two packets, was it, Herr Detektiv?'

'Cigarette currency, eh?' replied Kohler, indicating the loot. 'And since your pay and that of the average regular is two Reichs-kassenscheine per day, and equivalent to forty francs, even at one-hundred francs the packet, those four cases hold a fortune.'

This was something he could talk about, felt Hartmann. '*Ach, ja.* Ten to fifteen packets will get you the full night with a really beautiful girl on the Champs-Élysées, but in Pigalle from three to five cigarettes are enough. Most are so desperate, they'll do it up against a wall, but if you have eight francs for the room in one of those walk-in hotels the French use, no questions are ever asked, no papers demanded, and she'll do anything you want again and again, and if you give her a few more, you can keep her all night.'

And no wonder the Oberkommando der Wehrmacht were constantly worried about the health not only of the men but especially of those street girls. 'You boys get time off do you?'

'Only when the Oberfeldwebel feels we need a break. He treats us well, though, and we're lucky to have him, that's for sure.'

And Dillmann, being Dillmann, had made certain of their loyalty. 'How long has he been using this abattoir?'

'Not long. For a while it was the sheet-iron horse auction, but when this place was temporarily closed, the Oberfeldwebel felt it would be better since it's out of the way a little more, but with that high-alert at the Versailles entrance, he had to keep the truck there.'

'But usually those with things they're bringing into Paris momentarily tuck the trucks out of sight here and wait for him?'

'*Ach, ja.* They give us half the load they're carrying, and we give them the motor oil, grease and gasoline or diesel fuel they need to get home, collect more stuff and come back.'

'And that truck of Dillmann's is also loaded with jerry cans of fuel?'

'For a *Detektiv* you ask a lot of questions.'

'Here, have one of these and give us a light.'

'Shit, they must have forgotten to drop off the matches. Now I'll catch hell for not having demanded them.'

Since the Tabac National also made those, but fortunately the boy had matches of his own.

'Why the muscle at that entrance to the city, Inspector?'

'I was hoping Werner could tell me.'

'All we know is that they're looking for a *gazo* that's hauling stuff for the *schwarzer Markt*. We don't even know when they'll lift the search. It could be days.'

'And that's not good, is it?'

'People like us already have enough to worry about.'

'Here, let me give you a little something to take the chill off.'

Opening the Citroën's trunk, Kohler found the bottle and handed it to Hartmann. 'That's the shotgun from the bank van that was robbed. Beautiful, isn't it? Feel how light it is and well balanced, yet how solid is the forehand's grip. Be careful. It's still loaded.'

Two men had died, they not having used it, thought Hartmann. 'We always get vans from that bank coming through. How much cash was taken?'

The things one learned. 'Lots, but they were also hauling things for the *schwarzer Markt.*'

'And people, too, like the other vans from that same bank?'

Ach, how lovely. 'Maybe. That's something else I wanted to ask your Oberfeldwebel.'

'This is good,' said Hartmann of the pear brandy.

'Then have some more and another of these. My partner won't mind. He's French and he does what I tell him because he has to, but he's cut himself rather badly. If you could lose that first-aid kit on your belt, would one of these five-thousand notes help you to get another?'

A five-thousand note, when two hundred was more than enough!

Listening to the sounds, distant now from the escort service and dance studios, St-Cyr paused in this last of corridors. He was, he knew, well above the avenue Beaucour, which, with its cul-de-sac, bordered the Salle Pleyel on the east. There were no immediate neighbours, no elevator next to the room, just a nearby back staircase that would have offered another route down to street level if needed. But beyond the room, there was something else: a short flight of stairs that would have taken her to the roofs. As a diver, she would have kept both in mind, for the roofs here would continue well along the avenue Beaucour.

Finding the Sûreté's pass keys the early 1930s had given him as a chief inspector, he began to try them, conscious always that Concierge Figeard might indeed have thought to check, and when the lock gave, whispered, *'Dieu merci,'* and softly let himself in, closing, and locking it behind himself.

A maid's garret, *une chambre de bonne*, the room was so bare he had to wonder at her having lived here since that third week of August 1941. Seemingly alone on the makeshift 1920s counter of the opposite wall, the washbasin was but one of those badly chipped enamel flea-market things. So small was the cube of the grey national, one could fail to notice it. Slaked lime, sand and ground horse chestnuts, it was not only gritty but likely to burn and leave a rash. But a wash every day, no matter how cold the room.

There was no heat, of course. Well to his left, tidily against the wall and in a corner, was a single-burner electric hotplate, the frayed cord well-taped. Half a box of Viandox cubes* was with two tins of sardines and one of peas. A chipped porcelain pitcher served as water carrier and source. Plate, cup and saucer, bowl, spoon, fork and knife were with a small aluminium pot and a cast-iron frying pan.

The walls were neither white nor pale grey and absolutely blank. The armoire, one rescued no doubt from the cellars, revealed equally little: two skirts, three summer dresses, a few blouses, and a light sweater. Separated from these, the dress she had been given was of a very fine and soft, dark-blue wool that matched the shoes he still had in his coat pockets. White Chantilly lace fringed the accompanying slip, brassiere and underpants and must have come from just such a shop. Enchantement? he had to ask. Would Chantal and Muriel have seen to Madame Nicole Bordeaux's order? Not personally, of course. One of their girls would have, though they would have gone over everything carefully, but why, of course, the very expensive and equally rare lingerie?

'I'll have to ask them and that, mademoiselle, is bound to take us even deeper, so maybe I had better not ask.'

The silk stockings, those rarest of things, had been very carefully smoothed and were on yet another hanger, the garter belt with them. Three plain pairs of repeatedly and beautifully mended step-ins, another blouse and sweater were in a drawer with two pairs of worn-out tennis shoes, and another of walking shoes whose heels would definitely have to be replaced when money allowed. 'But for a girl who has gone home once before, mademoiselle, there is as yet no evidence of that earlier trip. Such a spartan behaviour demands answers in itself.'

When he opened the small cardboard suitcase that was under the military cot from the Great War, he realized what she had done, for here there were three berets, one black, another crimson, the third a medium brown, also two very colourful shopping bags, both reversible but instantly giving the drab and functional. A selection of scarves that could be quickly switched was evident, also

---

* The Bovril of France.

another dress, a pair of woollen slacks, shirt-blouse, warm sweater, even a spare toothbrush, step-ins, brassiere, flannelette pajamas, face cloth, towel and sanitary pads. She had put all that she would absolutely need here so that if driven to, she could quickly leave with the suitcase, and that, of course, had to mean that she would have laid out at least two routes of escape across those roofs. She had even chosen one of the Occupation's suitcases so that if necessary she could leave it tucked in with others at a railway or bus terminal checkpoint and simply walk through with papers only. Even her jacket was reversible, and from the look of it and by hand-spanning both waist and slack-length, came the estimates: Height: 173 centimetres, weight: 50 kilos, though some of that would definitely have been lost due to the constant shortages.

'Hair, a very light blonde, mademoiselle, but you should be more careful, since these days someone other than myself might take interest.'

Carefully coiling the strand, he tucked it away in his wallet. There were no snapshots, no mementos from home, no bottle even of black hair dye. 'No past, no future, just the present, eh?' he demanded, and returning the suitcase, looked carefully under the bed and found a little something else. But why hide it unless when helping with the rabbits and such, she had been forced to return the original every time and would need her own, especially if to escape?

She had had it made, and that could only have meant a block of wax, an impression, and a little help from someone else. 'But now, of course, you have forced me to use and return it, but first I must have a further look here.'

Tidily arranged on the small table she used as a desk were her notes. It was indeed a dissertation on the Benedictines and their place in the medieval history of France, with an emphasis on the Cistercians. Everything had been carefully referenced. She must have been working on a history degree. Only frequent visits to the reading room of the Bibliothèque Nationale could have produced this. Diagrams gave the layouts of abbey after abbey, among them l'Abbaye de Vauclair but also l'Abbaye d'Orval to the east of the Ardennes, in the heart of the Gaume forest and all but on the frontier between Belgium and France. Torched in 1637, that one had been rebuilt in 1680, she had noted. Demolished in 1793, sold off as a quarry in 1797, it had been, again she had noted, rebuilt in 1926 and finally reopened in 1938 only to find itself all but in the path of the Blitzkrieg.

Down through the centuries, travellers have always been offered three days refuge, food, water and shelter.

Ah merde, she could well have told that *passeur* of hers where they could stop over en route to France, but had that poultice come from there? Had a herbalist monk attended to her and given warnings of septicaemia?

She had definitely known of the spring at l'Abbaye de Vauclair. A diagram, neat and perfect, even with the distances noted, gave its location, along with the notation '*L'eau potable.*'

She hadn't just been studying for the sake of a licence. She had been plotting the use of these abbeys as way-stops en route to and from France. 'Pilgrims, was it, mademoiselle? Is that why you found yourself in that van at those ruins? Did you also tell those two of it when you bummed a lift? And what of the others, please? Did they, too, know of it and is that why they then followed? Are we even wrong to have assumed that you bummed a lift? Is there another reason for your walking ahead to that van? Did your *passeur* know of those two and tell you to leave the truck while you had a chance? *Merde*, but you engender questions!'

At the last of her notes there was a line that she must have written just before leaving. Though from the Rule of Saint Benedict, she hadn't quoted directly but had done as Benedict himself, and had gone right back to the primary source, the first epistle to Saint Paul, 1 Corinthians 15:10: 'But by the grace of God I am what I am.'*

Leaving everything but the key exactly as he had found it, he gave the room a final once-over, noticing only that he had missed the cork from a bottle of Moët et Chandon. It was on the little bedside table and behind the glass she had emptied, rinsed out, dried and left upside down until her return.

Up on the roof, the wind was from the east, the air so clear he paused to draw in a few deep breaths. To the forest of chimney pots he now faced, there was not a single trail of smoke. Beyond the entrance to the stairwell was an apron of flat roof that allowed for rabbit and chicken hutches and rows of bell jars and pots of earth. Leeks, celery, Belgian endive, chicory, lettuces, green on-

---

* The King James version of the Bible.

ions, chives, basil, too, and marjoram, rosemary, thyme and sage, she had them all. Sampling a few, he fed the rabbits a little, they eagerly expecting more.

'Two visits home,' he asked, 'and all you bring back is a piece of embroidery? The house of your parents, mademoiselle—the home you grew up in and would have come to love. Surely you must have brought something from that first visit. Additionally, you would have hidden it where easily retrievable.'

Wedged by two slats, and up under the roof of the last of the chickens, was a tin box, some twenty-four by twenty and eight centimetres in depth, the irony total. '"Chabert et Guillot," mademoiselle? When I was but a boy of four and behaving myself for a change, Grand-mère decided a reward was necessary. "They make the finest nougat in the whole wide world," she told me. "Even Napoleon had a passion for it. Lavender honey and grape sugar, and no others but those are first heated. Egg whites are then beaten and stirred in until the consistency is such that you can dip a finger and draw out nothing but the most perfect of trails. Only then are the pistachios, almonds and dried fruit added, the whole beaten until ready to be smoothed out on special paper and cut into squares and cubes."

'Until the age of ten it, too, was my passion, but on 3 December 1900, my birthday, I received a tin just such as this and was of course, overwhelmed and warned not to chew too many at a time. Yanking a filling, no fault I assure you of the quality of the nougat and its perfect softness, I lost my passion and found another: the fierce and unbridled terror of dentists that I still harbour, especially since these days, no anaesthetics are available.'

Tucked out of sight behind the rabbits, he opened the box and immediately said, '*Ah merde*, you poor unfortunate.'

It wasn't a treasure trove, not that he could see. It was, instead, one of utter despair, for the house must have been ransacked, the parents arrested and deported, the neighbours or the Occupier or both having helped themselves, even to smashing up the furniture for badly needed firewood. 'Exactly the same is happening here,' he said. 'Much to our shame, necessity negates decency.'

Trampled, stained and crumpled snapshots gave views of the mother and father. In one, probably taken just after the general strike, the mother, aged forty perhaps, was pensively looking out a window. Tall, willowy and obviously very fair, her lips were tightly drawn at a future she did not want to contemplate, her left hand twisting the pearls about her neck.

Scattered, there were about six of those that Anna-Marie must have gathered.

Another snapshot was of herself at the age of ten at one of the Sunday afternoon antiques fairs in the Nieumarkt, for the Waag, that lovely many-towered building that had been built in 1488 as the southern gateway to Amsterdam, was behind her. She had a teacup she had just found to surprise her mother, the shadow of the father falling just to her right. In yet another, but at the age of twelve, she was with the brand-new Sparta her birthday must have brought. Anticipation of that newfound freedom, love, too, for her parents and that father in particular, simply emanated from her, the bike, though, one that she could never have forced herself to leave behind. Yet another snapshot showed her at the age of nineteen or twenty with the young man who must have become her fiancé, for there was an open bottle of champagne in the dune sand behind the couple.

'Hand in hand, mademoiselle. Those are, I believe, the dunes at Zandvoort on the Noordsee. It's only about thirty-five kilometres from Amsterdam and a favourite resort to which I once took my Agnès, but you and that boy would not have stayed over. You wouldn't have wanted to disappoint your parents, not you.'

The crystal stopper of a perfume phial had been recovered, a wooden kitchen spoon and several loose-leaf, handwritten pages from the mother's recipe book. '"*Stroop pannekoek,* pancakes with syrup; *gember pannekoek,* those with ginger, and *speculaas,* especially *janhagel,* the spiced almond cookies."'

She had even managed to find one of the wooden moulds she would have helped to fill at a very early age, that of Saint Nicholas.

Again he took up the photo of her and that boy but this time found the cork he had taken from the shattered neck of that bottle in the van. 'A Moët et Chandon as well, Mademoiselle Annette-Mélanie Veroche, lest I forget the name you're now using, but a bottle that matches exactly the one in this photo and the cork you kept beside your bed so that, instead of one of these photos, you could touch it every night before sleep. Did our killer know that you were engaged? Did he mock you and take that drink when you had finally returned to that *passseur*'s truck? An informant, mademoiselle?'

Below these there was a gold pocket watch, its chain with a cat's-eye fob. Obviously the father had had a hiding place she had known of. In Dutch, the inscription read, *To Jonas Vermeulen for 25 years of steadfast loyalty and exemplary service, Diamant Meyerhof, Amsterdam 7 June 1932.*

Even at the height of the Great Depression, the firm had done this.

Beneath everything were two flattened white cotton bags with ties. Feeling their contents brought only despair, for in the one, all the particles were essentially of the same shape and size until at last, he having opened it, he heard himself saying, 'Congo cubes, mademoiselle? Who else knows of these and if so, why on earth are they still here?'

Brown, dark grey, clear or yellowish, and even an off-green, all were typically dimpled completely on each surface and cubic in shape, and were of from one to two millimetres to a side. 'Boart, is collectively diamond that when crushed and ground, and separated as to size by settling in oils of differing specific gravity, yields the gradations of grinding powders modern industry simply can't do without. Mining for these cubes really only began in earnest in 1939, but by 10 May 1940 and the Blitzkrieg, the Congo was supplying the world with nearly seventy percent of the boart and other industrials needed, those for metal-cutting, wire-drawing, trimming, shaping glass, drilling, too, and cutting slabs of rock, but you've a terrible problem on your hands, haven't you? You've a fortune in these alone if sold on the *marché noir*, but can't have told a soul, not if planning to get that boy to you via those abbeys.'

Only then did he hesitantly open the other sack, carefully setting its tie aside and spilling a little into a hand.

Clear white to off-white, and among them the exceedingly rare coloured diamonds, there were stones of every description and size up to and including those of two carats. 'Mine and river rough,' he managed, still stricken. Many of the crystals were octahedral, others dodecahedral, cubic, modified cubes and even hexoctahedral, but there were still others of a flattened triangular shape that, with their natural facets and colour, looked ready for setting in jewellery but could well have been used as industrials too.

As with all of them, sunlight flashed, giving myriad telltale glints. However, from himself there was only despair. Oona, Giselle, Gabi and her son were all at risk, but how had this girl come by them, only to then make a repeat journey, and what, please, had she intended?

'*Un mouchard*, mademoiselle. One your *passeur* and his fire-box feeder didn't know about but you finally did, causing him to leave his operatives a note wrapped around a rijksdaaler? Since they didn't stop that truck from leaving Amsterdam, there has to be something that *Sonderkommando* desperately need you to do and that can only mean Hermann and myself are being dragged deeper and deeper into it.'

Through the silence of the abattoir came the constant dripping of those *verdammte* taps and the muffled coughing of that boy. Too many smokes and a complete loss of nerves had put Hartmann right on edge, the stench here rank enough to permeate the skin. It was now 16.32 and Dillmann hadn't arrived. To stay any longer was crazy. Louis would have said, Hermann, get the hell out of there while you can. Dillmann can't be trusted anyway. If Heinrich Ludin has his hands on him, he'll readily sing whatever tune is necessary.

Flinging the empty cigarette package away, his second, Kohler found the boy sitting on those boxes of fags into which he'd been dipping. 'Give me one of those and don't argue. Light it first.'

'They've all been arrested. It's Russia for sure. My mother warned me. She said they'd do that to me if I ever got in trouble. *Ach, Scheisse*, I would drop your cigarette. Why isn't the Oberfeldwebel here?'

'Hang on. We'll wait another five minutes.'

'Not me. I'm going, but where? With these eyes of mine, I haven't got a chance.'

'Steady. Here, take a couple of breaths and leave the fags alone. You've got too much nicotine in you. Now go and stick your head out between those doors and have a look. Maybe that's a truck I heard.'

Actually, there were three of them, two from farms and one from the Wehrmacht, but all drove in as if it were the end of the world, to slam on the brakes and leave engines running.

As Hartmann closed the big doors, men piled out and went to work, the tarp's being flung back. '*Bonzen* shrieking at *Bonzen* held us up, Kohler,' shouted Dillmann, tossing his cigarette away. '*Einen Moment, bitte.*'

Suckling piglets ready for the spit were chased by whole sides of beef and pork. Cages of chickens were noisy, those of ducklings too. Squash, carrots, cabbages and potatoes followed—*liebe Zeit*, were there no shortages? Onions by the sack came next, beets, too, for that much-loved borscht, sugar also and pears, apples, eggs, cheeses, grapes by the box but wine by the barrel this time.

All of it was swallowed up in exchange for the grease, oil and gasoline needed, the thumbs-up given and a 'beat it' until next time.

'Everything is organized because it has to be,' went on Dillmann, taking a breath and grinning from ear to ear before breaking out the cigars, even to lighting them. 'Within the hour, their half will be sold on the streets or to the shops, restaurants and hotels, our half as well.'

'Since it only takes about ten minutes to drive from one side of the city to the other, eh?'

'Maxim's, the Ritz, the Hotel George V, the Boeuf sur le Toit and the Grand Vévour for us, the Druant, too, others also, of course.'

'Chez Rudi's?'

'*Ach*, you're not here to find out about my travels, but that place too, since it's right across the Champs-Élysées from the Lido and Rudi's a valued customer as is the Lido. But rumours are flying, my Hermann. A *gazo*, a *Schmuggler*, and a person who a Standartenführer and a Kriminalrat want so desperately they would hold up traffic for hours and hours? Kaltenbrunner must have told them not to say a thing to anybody, so let me hear from yourself what you've thought to involve me and my men in without first asking.'

Everything was rumour these days, *Mundfunk** its primary source. 'We simply don't know, that's why I've come to the fountain.'

Rudi was that and everyone knew it. 'Flattery I don't need, not when that truck of mine should be leaving.'

'Then if you were a *Schmuggler* using a *gazo* they wanted what would you do?'

---

* Word of mouth. Literally, 'mouth radio.'

'Stop and change trucks. Use one that burned diesel or gasoline, or take the time out to change over the original.'

'And get you to let them in?'

A dark look should be given but there wasn't time. 'Or someone as capable. I'm not the only one, Hermann. Surely you know this?'

'That package has a cut on the hand or forearm.'

'That why you wanted Schütze Hartmann's first-aid kit, the one he was wearing on his belt when I dropped him off here and told him to obey me and no one else?'

'That package may need it's antibacterial.'

'And big words, is it? Such a concern tells me that package is a skirt but is she *eine Jüdin*, Hermann?'

'*Eine Halbjüdin*, we think.'

'From the Netherlands, is it?'

'That too.'

'And have they a *Spitzel* aboard?'

'We think so.'

'You think a lot, but that must be why they haven't posted photos of her.'

'Probably.'

'Not probably, *mein Lieber*. For Herr Kaltenbrunner to send a *Sonderkommando* after a skirt, she has to be carrying something really big or about to lead them to it, since silence is the order of the day.'

'Just don't ask me what it is, for we haven't a clue, but don't broadcast what you've found out either. Let us find her first. Look for that cut and let me know if they come in through that entrance of yours or any of the others you might hear about.'

And a deal, was it? 'A blonde and a perfect Nazi breeding ground if they were to overlook that other half?'

'Just leave a message with Rudi. Tell him where we can meet up.'

'You and that partner of yours go there often, do you?'

'Louis has to eat and so do I.'

Hermann could have him by the balls any time he wanted, but it was also good to know where he could be found. 'I'll have to tell Herr Sturmbacher there's something in it for himself. For myself and my men, of course, the half of what that girl is carrying or leading the others to, yourself to pay Rudi out of your share, not ours.'

The son of a bitch, but it would have to be said. 'Agreed. Now tell me about those vans the Banque Nationale de Crédit et Commercial sends through yourself and your boys.'

Hartmann must have said something. 'Bankers are like whores, Hermann. Questions only make them curious. Both are dishonest.'

'Each driver hands you the envelope, does he?'

'No questions are asked, no answers given.'

'But I'm still the one who's asking and now I'm telling.'

He would do that too. '*Ach*, that bank brings people in as well as stuff for the *schwarzer Markt*. Since its Chairman Bolduc is far better organized even than myself and has far too many friends in high places, and others as well, I tend to look the other way. Now give me that bundle of 5,000-franc notes you're still clutching. I'll get the one note from Hartmann so that there'll be nothing missing from it and no further misunderstanding.'

'There are still the sardines, the champagne and . . .'

'For yourself. We haven't time.'

At a shout, the big doors were again shoved open by Hartmann, the truck backing out, Dillmann leaving him with, '*Ja, mein lieber* Hermann, Chez Rudi's it is,' so that the words hung on the air like a horse about to be slaughtered.

Louis had better have found out something.

There was still no sign of Hermann. Though the war was going badly for the Reich, and some day soon this Occupation would end, here at Chez Rudi's during the Saturday *cinq à sept*, most would never have known it. Beer-hall big and full of uniforms, everywhere there was boisterous talk and bustling waitresses, but at this table, having drained the last of a bottle of Jägermeister, an uninvited Heinrich Ludin fought off another stomach spasm to light yet another cigarette, offering none and waiting impatiently for that empty chair to be filled.

Having ordered a plate of crackling, the Gestapo chose a piece, but found that the teeth and stomach rebelled. '*Verfluchte Franzose*, don't you dare fuck with me! I want everything you and that disloyal Kripo know, since he has apparently forgotten he was to meet you here.'

Hermann must have seen him, but to ask who had informed on their meeting here would not be wise.

'Just cut the *Quatsch* and tell me where the hell he went after that bank's garage.'

'I have absolutely no idea. Hermann and I often work independently, only to meet up in places like this.'

'And yourself, where did you go?' Another spasm led to the cigarette's falling to the floor where it couldn't be recovered.

'Myself? *Ach*, here, there, and forced to discover how the city's bus fleet has again been cut. With every second *métro* station closed to save power, time means nothing, even if in a bicycle taxi.'

'Did I not say don't bugger about with me?'

'Then let me remind you that this is a murder inquiry and that if you have needed information, by law in France, you are required to impart it.'

The avenue Foch had said that neither Kohler nor St-Cyr would cooperate unless a lot of squeeze was applied. '*Lieber Gott, Schweinebulle*, have you not realized what I can have done to that Russian songbird of yours?'

Stage name, Gabrielle Arcuri; maiden name Natalya Kulakov-Myshkin until she'd become Madame Thériault and a war widow first encountered in December last. 'Are you threatening me as you did Hermann?'

'We'll include those two old lesbians at the shop Enchantment that Kohler's got looking after his women. The KZ at Dachau or the one at Mauthausen would suit, and if not those, then the furnaces at Auschwitz since the Führer has absolutely no regard for such filth nor do I. And as for that songbird, not all White Russians are above reproach. Cough up or she'll become just like one of these.'

Breaking a crackling in half, grimacing due to the stomach, Ludin set the pieces in front of him. Golden brown, crisp and well salted, they were to have gone with the untouched steins of Dortmunder that Rudi had sent to the table, the beer flown in on yesterday morning's Lufthansa's early flight from Berlin since today it had been far too foggy.

'Don't continue to be troublesome,' said Ludin. 'Gestapo Paris's Watchers have an impressive dossier on that songbird, even to the infrequency of the two of you getting together. All I have to do is indicate to Gestapo Boemelburg that it can no longer be overlooked even if our boys love to listen to her as do others in the Reich and at the front, thanks to Radio Paris and Radio Berlin.'

Something would have to be yielded. 'I went to Saint-Ouen, to the flea market with this.'

A flat metal tin was slid across the table, the nude on its lid clear enough. 'The *Kippenzinn* of whom?' asked Ludin.

'That is what I was hoping to determine. You see, Kriminalrat, we found it at l'Abbaye de Vauclair.'

And Kohler, being Kohler, had said nothing of it! 'And?'

'Several of the dealers gave me names and possible addresses of its buyer and the price paid, and of course each wanted to buy it back since they immediately realized I was a Sûreté.'

Opening the box, probing the butts with a nicotine-stained forefinger, Ludin said, 'A traveller.'

'A firebox feeder, we think, but not the killer.'

Touching the butts brought him so close to what must be the end of this nightmare, felt Ludin, the ulcer was momentarily calmed, for it had to be the box of Arie Beekhuis, the alias of Hans van Loos, age twenty-eight from Rotterdam. A former engine-room operator on a tanker, the Stukas had changed his mind 14 May 1940 when they had wiped out nearly a thousand in that city, putting an end to the young wife and their brand-new baby.

'Everything, *mein Lieber*, or I'll let you listen to that songbird's screams.'

No doubt he would. 'Then start by pulling the canvas from those two corpses. Tell us who their killer was. *Ein Spitzel*, Kriminalrat? You've been following that truck since it left Amsterdam. At each stop he's told you of, your informant leaves a rijksdaaler in a designated place unless, and I must emphasize this, things are not going well. Then, and only then, is a note added and with it a bit of mud to secure the paper. What's so important that Herr Kaltenbrunner would demand total secrecy from you and that colonel even though you, yourself, now desperately need our help and are insisting on it?'

'An order is an order.'

'Why is it then that you have failed to distribute copies of those photos of that girl to every Commissariat de Police for posting? What does she know or carry that is so vital you can't even let Rudy de Mérode and his gang or any of the others know of it or of her? Instead, they attempt to follow us knowing only that there's something big in the air because you and that SD colonel have virtually locked down every entrance to the city.'

Gut, that Dutch whore of Kohler's had found the photos and the three coins and this one had finally realized he would have to yield what little that partnership of theirs now knew. 'Keep the tin and enjoy the beer and crackling. Tell Kohler he has two days but that he is definitely to drag that sorry ass of his over to 84 avenue Foch first thing tomorrow morning, Sunday or no Sunday, or I will have those women prove it to you both that you will cooperate fully or else.'

Rudi Sturmbacher was swift. No sooner had Hermann taken a chair, then that booming voice and mountain of aproned flesh had descended on them, flour up to the elbows. 'Helga, my beautiful young sister, the roast pork, the potato dumplings and spiced red cabbage for these two and a bottle of—*ach*, make it two—of the Schloss Johannisberg. Founded by Benedictines in the year 1100, damaged thoughtlessly by those shits in the RAF last year, that Schloss is still thumbing its nose at the British and providing us with pure magic.'

Grabbing the recently vacated chair, heaving himself into it, Rudi sat down, reached for the crackling and leaning forward over the whole table, dropped his voice to a whisper.

'What's going on, my Hermann? People like the one who just left come bearing papers from the Reichssicherheitshauptamt? You know as well as I that those people are untouchable. One glance at such papers is enough. No questions are ever asked. Everything wanted is done immediately.'

Pink-rimmed and small under flaxen brows, the pale blue eyes narrowed fiercely as this Bavarian with the round and florid cheeks doubled fists as big as hams.

'Why here, why this one, Hermann, why yourself and why my restaurant for which I have slaved the whole of my life?'

Emotional enough, Helga must have been in tears. '*Ach*, it's nothing, Rudi. Just some cock-up notion of Kaltenbrunner's. Girls from Bucharest, Prague and Budapest, I think.'

'*Mädchenhandel?*'

White-slave traffic. 'Why else the acid in that Kriminalrat's stomach when he's used to hunting far bigger fish?'

Hermann was just ragging him. 'It has to be because of what happened to our dear Doktor Ritter. Assassinated in our very own streets even though those *verfluchte Banditen* are being smashed all over France. Don't those people know there is no hope for them? In June, over sixty terrorist cells from the Sedan through to Paris and on down the Loire to Nantes taken. More than five hundred tonnes of illegally parachuted explosives and weapons from the British recovered. Then in late August and early September another three hundred more arrests all the way down the Biscay Coast to the foothills of the Pyrenees and now yet another bunch of railway dynamiters in Brittany and more arrests. Wireless sets, guns and explosives.* Why must they ignore the fact that the Führer will never lose this war, not when he has . . .'

Heads were urgently motioned closer. *'Wunderwaffen.'*

Miracle weapons.

'Flying bombs.'**

A veteran of the Munich Putsch, a Brownshirt survivor and dyed-in-the-wool Nazi whose hair was cut short and worn in SS and Wehrmacht style, Rudi reached for the stein a still upset Helga had quickly set before him only for her to then rush away.

Draining it, he wiped his lips on a forearm and said darkly, 'If not the *Banditen*, my Hermann, then why did Herr Ludin threaten this one enough to cause him to slide the *Kippenzinn* of someone else across the table?'

'And while you're at it, Hermann, enlighten us as to who informed him that we would be meeting here?'

'A private with bad eyesight.'

Or Dillmann himself. 'Can no one be trusted?'

'That little problem will be dealt with since a deal is a deal when cut.'

Fortunately Rudi was called away by a late delivery from a person named none other than Werner, Helga having brought their dinners and still unable to calm the tears. 'My Hermann,' she said, flooding him with those milkmaid-blue eyes. 'Why us,

---

* The Prosper, Scientist and Donkeyman networks were among those that had been in wireless touch with the British Special Operations Executive in London.
** The V-1 and V-2 rocket bombs, the first V-1s being launched against London on 13 June 1944.

why now when Rudi's little Julie is about to give birth and his Yvette won't even speak to him?'

'Trouble always comes in threes, Helga. Don't worry, everything will be fine. Just bring Louis a bottle of that red stuff Rudi uses to marinate the schnitzel and the liver.'

'The Château Margaux or the Château Lafite?'

'Either. Now let me dry those tears. Louis and I would never let anything bad happen to you and Rudi.'

Hesitant, the kiss became warmer when Hermann's hands slipped down that blue work dress to those chunky hips.

Everyone took to cheering because Helga had been after Hermann ever since they'd started occasionally eating here back in the autumn of 1940. . . .

'You're a saint,' said St-Cyr when she had left them. 'Me, I'm impressed.'

'Werner wouldn't have told anyone anything, but his Schütze Hartmann, who sold me this first-aid kit, might have since he must have overheard that one mention Rudi's name.'

'And what, exactly, is this deal?'

'Nothing, really. Werner will keep an eye out and let us know when and if anything turns up.'

'Through Rudi?'

'*Ach*, I had to tell him something and there wasn't time to think about possible repercussions.'

They had eaten as few would in a city where far too many had to get by on less than 1,500 calories a day and the schools had cancelled all physical education. Helga, having brought second helpings of a magnificent *Schwarzwälder Kirschtorte*, now refreshed their coffee with another packet of cigarettes and a plate of *Lebkuchen*. A film, a dinner out would be racing through her mind, Hermann kissing the back of her hand, she rushing off with thoughts of the future.

'Your "treasure," Hermann? Did you have to say that to her? Haven't we enough trouble?'

'We may need Rudi's help and that might just cement it. Bolduc's vans are also moving people.'

'Into and out of Paris? The PPF?'

'*Miliciens*, too, probably, since the High Command are still reluctant to let those bastards leave the former free zone.'

Some *had* gotten in before and they had had a run-in with them, but this was terrible news for it had to mean Hector Bolduc and others of the far right must feel those types were desperately needed. A paramilitary force, the Milice française had only just been given a scattering of weapons, mainly captured British materiel that had been dropped to the Résistance. Violently anti-Communist, anti-de Gaulle, the Résistance, the Masons, Jews, Gypsies and others, they had quickly become known and hated for the savagery of their reprisals. 'Perhaps that's why Bolduc didn't particularly care that one of his vans hadn't arrived last Thursday and told Yvonne Rouget to give them another few days.'

'But did our Anna-Marie know of what those bank vans were really up to, Louis? Is that not why, on seeing one at the side of the road ahead of them on the RD 380 to the east of Reims, she felt it would be a way of escaping the others and getting through the control?'

'Or did they also know of her, Hermann?'

'You'd better tell me what you've found.'

'It's where to begin that's troubling me. Not only have I encountered a minefield, it's bound to take us if we're not careful.'

Breaking a couple of the cookies, Louis reminded himself of the aromas of nutmeg and cloves, and of allspice and ginger. Around them the earnest forgetfulness of the crowd hadn't abated, more having arrived and waiting to be seated.

'Those shoes, Hermann, were meant for her. *Bien sûr*, they didn't quite fit. Not wanting to be so visible, she probably made up some excuse for not being able to go to Monnier herself in mid-August of last year and must have given Nicole Bordeaux her size and other details.'

'That consumptive?'

'That socialite who has made it her life's role to bring Occupier and Occupied together so as to foster collaboration and country-to-country tours for musicians like Cortot or singers like Maurice Chevalier, artists as well, and writers, actresses and actors. Gatherings, Hermann, every two weeks at her mansion on the rue de La Boétie.'

Right in the heart of where the Occupier felt safest. Not two blocks from Gestapo and Sûreté headquarters and but a pleasant stroll or drive from the SD and SS on the avenue Foch.

Good, Hermann was beginning to see the gravity of things. 'The shoes were to have gone with the dress, the slip and all the rest that Madame Bordeaux had chosen for her. Everything—now get this, please—was delivered a good fourteen months ago to Studio 51, Salle Pleyel, home of Les Amies françaises.'

'An escort service?'

Disbelief had registered in Hermann's expression. 'Me, I think you should be asking whose.'

'And I'm waiting. Everything we know so far counters what you've just said. An *onderduiker, eine Mischlinge?*'

'Mademoiselle Jacqueline Lemaire.'

'Mistress of Hector Bolduc? That girl can't be selling herself to the Occupier. Not our Anna-Marie.'

'But she is fluent in *Deutsch,* Hermann, and she *does* need to hide, so she becomes an usherette at the concerts and finds herself a part-time job in the Frontbuchhandlung.'

'The what?'

'You heard me.'

'Where she's in one-on-one direct contact with the Occupier? Christ, has she nerves of bloody steel?'

'Or simply those of utter commitment, having lost her family, the house she grew up in, and no doubt more recently the boy she was engaged to. Oh for sure, she could have negotiated a set of false papers herself, but acquiring those requires a certain finesse, otherwise one gets taken and/or betrayed.'

'And if help is given, help is then demanded, eh? That one-on-one contact would have allowed her to listen closely and relay whatever she found out to whomever has been helping her.'

'Precisely, for I also found the key she had had made to the roofs and the little farm she and Concierge Figeard tend. The farming she probably took up shortly after having moved in during the third week of June 1941, but that key, *mon vieux,* would have needed a wax impression.'

Trust Louis to have found it. 'An FTP *équipe?*'

'Or one of the others. Help certainly. Nicole Bordeaux could well have encountered her at the concerts and in that bookshop. Repeated sightings would engender questions about her and, satisfied with such an unofficial security clearance, Madame Bordeaux would finally have spoken to her.'

'She then ordering up the shoes and all the rest to be delivered last August, since interpreters are always desperately needed at such cultural gatherings and pretty girls had better be properly dressed, even if it was only one outfit and not a dozen.'

French parsimony, but Hermann held a finger up to signal a pause as he lit them both further cigarettes.

'Girls with virtually no money, Louis.'

'Students at the Sorbonne, Hermann. You see, our girl has avidly been working on a dissertation about the place of the Benedictine in medieval France.'

'She knew of l'Abbaye de Vauclair?'

'Didn't I tell you it was a minefield? In that all but barren room of hers were drawings, plans and details of monasteries from here to Amsterdam and return, way-stops for that fiancé to have used, only he failed to arrive.'

'So she had to make another trip. She's a skirt, she's young, she's pretty and fluent in what's needed in certain circles but vulnerable as well, so a little help given at the right moment might bring its later reward. Did Hector Bolduc offer it and the use of one of those bank vans of his? Is that why she left the one to walk ahead to the other, she realizing freedom was at hand and she had better leave while she could?'

'Or was that arrangement laid on, Hermann? You see, Figeard, her concierge, mentioned that when she returned from her first trip last December, they shared a dinner to which she brought the half of a bottle of Château Latour.'

'From the Haut-Médoc where a certain banker has been avidly buying up vineyards and châteaux.'

'We absolutely have to pin down why and how that truck she was in met up with that van.'

'And why they were then able to follow it to l'Abbaye de Vauclair.'

Helga, obviously now believing she had finally landed Hermann as a potential husband, interrupted things with a bottle of Danziger Goldwasser whose tiny flecks seemed to dance in its delightful concoction of orange peal, anise, herbs and eighty proof.

'That gold's real, Louis. Even the Führer has overlooked recovering it but obviously Rudi is on our side.'

'But only for the moment, so don't compound our troubles. Let your mind dwell on these instead, for I've saved the worst news for the last.'

Tightly wrapped in a small twist of the newspaper Louis always used when saving bullet slugs and other evidence, were a good dozen tiny crystals. As his hand quickly closed over them to keep from prying eyes, Kohler heard himself saying, '*Lieber Gott*, why us, why now when this goddamned war and Occupation have to be grinding down?'

'God never questions what might or might not happen to people like us, Hermann, but our Anna-Marie can't have told anyone of the kilo of these she has in the tin box I found. They've been there since at least that first visit home last December.'

'Even though it's only boart, and the cheapest of the cheapest, that kilo must be worth an absolute fortune especially on the *marché noir*. Any FTP *équipe* worth its salt would have promptly sold the lot if they'd known of them.'

'Precisely, but as the inscription in his pocket watch indicated, the father was a much-valued and trusted employee and would have hidden them in a place he and Anna-Marie knew of, the mother also, probably, but the diamonds didn't belong to him, and that girl would have known this. They must have been hidden just as the Blitzkrieg was upon them. Perhaps it is that his employer, Diamant Meyerhof, asked him and other employees to do just such a thing.'

'Maybe there's far more, then, that we don't yet know of.'

For now, felt St-Cyr, he wouldn't tell Hermann of the others, but would simply say, 'And that is why we must return to those ruins. You see, when I was looking for her at that spring, I found virtually no trace of her having even run that way. Instead, there was simply a fern, one of whose fronds had been instinctively snapped, probably as she had heard that second shot. She then took care to leave no further trace as she returned to the edge of the clearing at the ruins, but deliberately flattened two saplings, tramping them until hidden by the tall grass and brush.'

'To mark the spot?'

'But not for herself, for others probably, since she already knew where the spring would be and the path that still exists.'

'Did she hide something?'

'Given what we've uncovered, I think she must have.'

'Anything else?'

'Deniard and Paquette both suffered from "poor" eyesight.'

'Yet were given a shotgun and a hell of a lot of responsibility.'

'Also Herr Ludin has asked to see you first thing tomorrow at number eighty-four.'

'Where I won't be telling him anything because we can't, but you'd better let me know what you did tell him when you shoved that *mégot* tin at him here.'

Good, Hermann *had* been watching the two of them earlier. 'Having also threatened Gabrielle, I had to tell him something.'

'And?'

'He knows you failed to tell him of it and that we feel it's not the killer's, but that one of those with the truck is an informant who has been leaving coins for them to find and follow.'

'That *Spitzel* won't have killed her, Louis. He can't have because he can't fail his masters.'

'But did she tell that *passeur* and his assistant of her doubts about him, Hermann? That is the question.'

'She can't have because she would have known only too well that he would then have killed them too. Instead, she's biding her time and hoping against hope that they get into Paris where she can then escape and call on those who have helped her in the past before that *Spitzel* rats on the *passeur*, the firebox feeder and herself.'

A pleasant thought. 'Now me to Gabrielle, for I absolutely have to warn her.'

'And me to Oona and Giselle.'

Forbidden at 2147 hours, or at any other time after dark, lights blazed from the shop Enchantement. Sickened by the sight from across the *place* Vendôme, Kohler hit the brakes. Oona and Giselle had been taken. Heinrich Ludin hadn't hesitated. That son of a bitch must have been waiting outside Chez Rudi's and had seen him duck in to sit down with Louis. Those sadists of the blackout control were everywhere, *flics* too, and generals and other higher-ups, for these last must have poured from the Ritz, their dinner napkins dangling.

In a rage, one of them nearly tore the car door off as the Citroën pulled up. 'KOHLER, WHY HAVE YOU AND THAT . . . THAT FRENCHMAN NOT STOPPED THIS? *BANDITEN*, I TELL YOU, KOHLER. *TERRORISTEN!*'

Ach, mein Gott, it was the Kommandant von Gross-Paris. 'Just leave it to me, General. Go back to your dinner.'

'*Back?* When those dear ladies need to be calmed and that entrance replaced and the door upstairs to the flat?'

Only a Prussian could have overlooked the tragedy of what had really happened. 'I'll just go and speak to them, General. Maybe they can be more specific.'

'Specific, is it? Did I not say *Banditen?*'

A fortune in lingerie and lace had been trampled or stolen. Broken glass was everywhere. Aphrodite's alabaster breasts no longer beckoned, nor did Diana's, she having lost her bow and arrow, and as for the flimsily clad, limbless, headless mannequins, the wrecking bar had done its worst.

Dense, a cloud of unleashed perfume filled the air. Crystal phials lay among the ruin, scattered cosmetics, too, and bath salts, soaps, powders, garter belts, silk stockings and lace-trimmed stepins. Ducking past the cluttered office, he came at last to the stairs only to stop at the sight of Giselle's pom-pom slippers. She had tried to fight the attackers off and had been thrown down the stairs. Blood was flecked here, there, everywhere, Oona's white ribbon—the one she always used to tie back her hair before bed—was dangling from the railing.

Diminutive—never anything but vivacious and always perfectly turned out and looking years younger than she really was—Chantal Grenier, that beautiful blonde-haired dove from yesteryear, clutched a torn nightdress to her bare bosom while stern-eyed Muriel Barteaux, far taller, bigger, stronger, tougher and still wearing the usual broad-lapelled iron-grey pinstripe and dark-blue tie, tried to comfort her lifelong companion and business partner.

The voice was of gravel. 'Chantal . . . Chantal, *mon ange*, it's Hermann. He and Jean-Louis will bring them back.'

'Louis isn't . . .' began Kohler.

'*Raped*, Monsieur Hermann,' shrilled Chantal. 'Defiled, I tell you! The throat of the one slashed while the other has tried to stop them. They'll be violated, my Muriel! Mutilated, the one forced to watch as the other is . . . *Ah Sainte Mère, Sainte Mère*, they will scream but it will be of no use. None, I tell you!'

'Chantal . . . Chantal . . .'

'Easy, little one. Easy,' urged Kohler, wrapping his arms about the two of them. 'Louis isn't with me but as soon as he is, we'll find them and take care of things. Make her down a stiff cognac, Muriel, and then sip another. Find her something to nibble on. A biscuit, a crust—anything so long as it settles her.'

He looked as if in tears himself, thought Muriel, and though it was very dangerous to say such a thing, she could with Hermann and had better. 'They threatened to expose us. They said that since the Nazis would love to burn us at the stake, they would, and that as soon as they had finished what they had to do, they were going to torch the shop and make sure we never left it.'

'Frenchmen, Monsieur Hermann, in two big cars. Two, I tell you, and ten of them. Ten! *Résistants. La Croix de Lorraine!*'

'Nonsense,' said Muriel, her expression enough to shatter the thought. 'I already pay those people far too much to leave us alone.'

'PPF, then, a hit squad of them?' asked Kohler.

Ah, mon Dieu, what was this? 'One did shout to the others . . .'

'Let me, my Muriel. "The corner of the boul' Victor Hugo and rue de Rouvray."'

And in Neuilly-sur-Seine, the villa Gestapo Boemelburg used for those whose countries of origin, passports, politics, finances and such were suspect but who required far gentler treatment than usual. It would be blackmail for sure from that Hamburg Kriminalrat, but Louis would be the first to ask, Now what are you going to do about it? Submit or tell him absolutely nothing?

Muriel was using a sleeve to gently wipe Chantal's eyes. 'Look, I'll see that this is paid for in cash and otherwise. Louis will too.'

Would it break his heart all the more if she were to tell him? wondered Muriel.

Intuitively Chantal understood and, wrapping her arms more firmly about her, lifted herself up to whisper, 'You must, *ma chère.*'

'One of the others shouted that they should drive by Rudy's place to show him what he was missing, Hermann, that Jean-Louis had this morning not only been unkind to their tires and headlamps, but insulting.'

That Rudy being Rudy de Mérode, not Rudi of Chez Rudi's.

Alone, felt St-Cyr, and as if left out for him on her dressing table at the Club Mirage on the rue Delambre in Montparnasse was the crystal phial of scent that would immediately invoke its memories. 'Exquisite,' he said, as when first encountered early last December, Muriel Barteaux having designed it especially for Gabi and named it after the club. 'Mirage,' he went on, 'those three initials on this cigarette case being N. K. M.: Natalya Kulakov-Myshkin and a Russian who had escaped from the revolution in 1917, losing her family en route and having arrived alone in Paris at the age of fourteen, a survivor, a chanteuse.'

Seemingly, he still hadn't realized that her last number had come to its end, the club packed as always with the Occupier, they all shouting for her to return. 'Jean-Louis . . .'

Replacing the stopper, he didn't look up to see her sheathed as she was in shimmering sky-blue silk, felt Gabrielle. Perhaps he was remembering the brown whipcord jodhpurs she had worn at the mill on the Loire, or was it the open hacking jacket?

No lipstick or makeup as now, thought St-Cyr, her hair tied back with a bit of brown velvet and not blonde at all, as first thought, but the shade of a very fine brandy, her eyes of a violet matched only by those of Hermann's Giselle.

'Every time I hear you sing, Gabrielle, I'm exactly like all of those out there, and Muriel too, filled and lifted entirely out of myself and present difficulties. You know, of course, that there are those who will never forgive you for having sung for the Occupier. Isn't it time you thought of stopping, or is it that you feel the Führer, with all his wisdom, will turn this conflict around and defeat the Russians, and the Allies who are now mercilessly bombing his cities?'

'Those boys out there and along the front need me as do soldiers everywhere, no matter which side they're on. Even Charles Maurice would have wanted me to continue.'

A lie, of course, for Captain Thériault, the dead husband, had prevented her from singing and had insisted, as most Frenchmen would, and had the right, that she stay home with their son, an absence Muriel had lamented, only to then find Gabi after the defeat and at the Mirage.

Though it would do no good to say it, and she was very much of the Résistance herself, he had better. 'The *Banditen* will never forgive you. Why skate so close to the edge when you don't have to?'

'Is it that you think my René Yvon-Paul needs me?'

René was now eleven and lived with his grandmother, the countess, at the Château Thériault near Vouvray.

'Me, I sing because for me, I have to, Jean-Louis. But why, please, when you must know this dressing room of mine could well have ears, is it that you should say such things so loudly?'

'Because we never whisper and they need to hear it from yourself.'

The Gestapo's Listeners—their Watchers too, the ones who had deliberately left that Résistance bomb on his doorstep early last December, tragically killing his second wife and little son instead. 'I think I need a cigarette.'

Seldom did she use those, but always they were Russian but not from the stems of the plant. 'Of course. Forgive me. Here . . . here, sit, please, at your dressing table. Rest. You put so much of yourself into every song, you must be exhausted.'

'Then light it for me.'

She was trembling, he was, too. *Ah merde*, what the hell was happening to them?

He held her. They did not kiss, they clung, and when at last he had relaxed his hold, it was herself who whispered, '*Merci, mon amour*, I didn't know for sure and now do.'

Only then did they kiss, something Hermann was never going to hear of for fear he would never shut up about it.

Taking out his little notebook, Jean-Louis found a blank page and wrote: *Sonderkommando. An informant. A submarine they want who knows something Berlin must absolutely have. A Kriminalrat who has threatened Oona and Giselle, yourself as well.*

Was it the end for them? Taking his pen, she wrote: *And what, please, of my René Yvon-Paul, the countess and the Château Thériault and its contents, lands and vineyards?*

A practical woman. *Everything, so please take precautions. We may all be lost, but for now Hermann and me know far more about that submarine than does this Heinrich Ludin and his SD colonel who has yet to even have a name.*

Silently she would tear the page free, felt Gabrielle, and lighting it with the end of her cigarette, watched the flames until done.

Crumbling the ashes to dust, she carefully blew them away.

Hermann didn't wait. Hermann just roared into the back courtyard leaning on the horn and then pounded on the back door. 'Louis . . . Louis . . .'

Ah merde, he was in tears. 'Here, take a few drags of this but remember it's Russian.'

'Take these too,' said Gabrielle, removing others from that cigarette case Jean-Louis would never forget and receiving a last touch of his fingers—was it that?

'Matches,' blurted Hermann. 'We've run out.'

Those, too, were handed over, Jean-Louis momentarily giving her fingertips a final squeeze.

'*Ach, verdammt*, Louis, don't dawdle. I'll drive. We'll never get there otherwise.'

'Where?'

'Neuilly. Boemelburg's villa but first Rudy de Mérode's little nest.'

'You can't be serious.'

'Unfortunately I am.'

5

Cloaked in that same darkness, and with but one tiny blue and legal light announcing its entrance, 70 boulevard Maurice-Barrès, a sumptuous hotel before the defeat, overlooked the Bois de Boulogne and its Jardin d'Acclimatation. Six cars were out front under the spreading dark limbs of the chestnut trees that were revered by the *haute bourgeoisie* of this most wealthy of suburbs.

'Two with engines still running, Louis, and no drivers.'

Had Hermann downed too many of those damned pills? 'Patience, *mon vieux*. Patience.'

'The time for that is over.'

It had been a harrowing drive through the late-evening traffic. Smashed side-mirrors, crumpled fenders . . . how were they to be replaced?

Switching off the still blinkered headlights and engine, Hermann locked the doors and, taking the Purdey from the boot, checked to see that it was still loaded.

'Cover my back, and that's an order.'

Celebrating with champagne, cigarettes, cigars, canapés and all the rest, the crowd was in what had once been an opulent dining room. The fleurs-de-lis sconces with their crystal globes were still giving light from the fluted pilasters, the chandeliers still throwing plenty of it from electric candles, but no longer were there the Longchamp racecourse paintings of winner after winner. Instead, there was the degenerate art of the Führer's Third Reich—magnificent Gaugins, Van Goghs, Picassos, Braques . . . *Ah mon Dieu*, Monets, Bonnards, Cézannes and Matisses, Degas, too, and others like those they had found in Hector Bolduc's office, all as if shoved aside to await trucking to whatever depot. With them were the antique furniture of the latest acquisitions along with the bulging leather suitcases and wardrobe trunks of the desperate, the arrested, deported and robbed.

Perhaps twenty or so men and ten or so females were in attendance. All had been toasting the evening's little entertainment, yet were now watchfully silent. Cigarettes clung to lower lips or, like the cigars and cigarettes in holders, had paused, the fingernails of one vermillion, a canapé being crushed under that spike-heeled foot. And among them all, and looking entirely like the successful businessman he wasn't, but in a deep-blue pinstripe with illegal pocket flaps and broad lapels, was the leader of this mob.

The handkerchief pocket sported silk and four gold fountain pens, and above it was one of the phosphorescent red swastika buttons favoured by the Occupier for those little walks in the utter darkness of the streets.

'Rudy de Mérode, alias Frédéric Martin,' sang out Hermann. 'Born 1905 in the Moselle, Louis. Abwehr agent since 1928, arrested for selling plans and secrets of the Maginot Line in 1936 and given . . . What was it?'

Ah merde, he'd taken far too much of that stuff the Luftwaffe's night-fighters needed to stay awake. 'Ten years, Herr Inspektor.'

'In Fresnes or the Santé?'

'Hermann . . .'

'Louis, you really *are* going to have to leave this to me.'

Released from the Santé by the Abwehr just after the defeat, Rudy had been given a 'purchasing agency' and put to work recruiting helpers from among his prison acquaintances and even those he still had contact with among the police and fire departments. But soon his *équipe,* his *groupe,* was handling all the security for the warehouses and transport of materials, not only for the Central Purchasing Agency, the Bureau Otto, but for the Einsatzstab Reichsleiter Rosenberg.

Progressing beyond that mission, he had been assigned the collecting of gold bullion and coins from those same victims and others, now in total, it was said, more than four tonnes. And since rampant inflation and the food shortages drove people to illegally sell valuables on the *marché noir,* Rudy and his men frequented the bars, clubs and restaurants, posing as buyers, and even kept an eye on the *monts-de-piété*, the state-owned, municipal pawn shops to see who was unloading what. But if a seller objected to being robbed, an invitation would be extended and the 'client' brought here and taken upstairs for a little persuasion.

'And a bath if necessary, Louis.'

To be held under. 'Anti-terrorism and the hunting down of *résistants* are now a further task, Hermann.'

'Just let me deal with those who wrecked that shop and man-handled Muriel and Chantal while abducting Oona and Giselle.'

Something would have to be said to break the impasse, felt Rudy. '*Ah bon, mes amis,* me I'm glad you've got that off your chests, but *un fusil de chasse,* Herr Kohler? *Un douze à deux coups?*'

'*Et un Lebel Modèle d'ordonnance,* Rudy, the 1873 with those black-powder cartridges no one but a fool would want,' said the one who, unseen until now, had moved to stand at his side: the hair a pale, washed-out blond, the jacket and vest of a heavy beige twill, the trousers of corduroy, and the tie subdued, but once a po-liceman, even if under the czar at first and then under the Préfet de Paris, always one, no matter what.

'*Ah bon,* Hermann, the well-spoken one from the second car to have followed us this morning.'

'Serge de Lenz *à votre service,* Inspector.'

'It's chief inspector, and it's Sergei Lebeznikov, Hermann. Ex-inspector of the Paris Police, dismissed and sent to prison in dis-grace in 1934. Me, I knew I had seen him before. The newspapers, of course. A good photo since it left an indelible impression.'

'And the crime, *mon vieux?*'

No guns or weapons of any other kind had yet been drawn, Rudy having slightly raised a hand to still any such outburst. 'Morphine and cocaine from Marseille. There was simply far too much of both for temptation to ignore, which is why some was unaccounted, but me, I unfortunately had absolutely no part in the subsequent investigation and arrest and still remain envious of those who had the courage to overcome his superior officer's objections and put them both away.'

'My girlfriend got careless,' snorted Lenz.

'Which can only have meant yourself,' countered Hermann. 'Now before anything further happens, Rudy, take one of those fountain pens of yours and write down the names of all ten here who felt they could do such a thing as to manhandle two lovely old ladies and my Oona and Giselle.'

Kohler didn't just have both barrels. He had extras clutched in his left hand and would likely reload so quickly, the effort of stopping him would just not be worth the trouble.

The pink tie with nesting stork that Mérode was wearing was hardly suitable for a suit like that, felt Kohler, the side whiskers a bit too long, that jet-black hair so well greased and tightly combed back, the light was reflecting from it.

To be edgy with a shotgun was not wise. 'Lulu, *ma chère*,' said Mérode, 'be so good as to offer our friends a cognac. Nothing but the best, *chérie*, and straight from its little trolley.'

'The Rémy Martin Vieille Réserve, and for yourself, *mon tigre?*' asked the blue-eyed, beautifully made-up blonde in the fabulous emerald-green Dior piqué dress with matching drop-earrings and bracelets from Cartier.

'Rudy, *mon étalion*, let me,' pleaded the one in the superb black crepe, off-the-shoulder from Paul Poiret, her jet black hair and dark-grey eyes perfect, the Chanel No. 5 maybe a bit too much, but the rest sensational, and so much for the same cognac as a certain banker had offered early this morning.

'*Mes amis*, relax, eh?' said Rudy. 'Certainly, Kohler, those boys from the PPF got a little carried away, but they were under orders.'

'From Heinrich Ludin and that SD colonel who's with him?'

'*Ah oui, oui, mon ami*, but we still haven't a name for that one.'

'Your girls were quickly covered, Kohler,' interjected Lenz. 'I draped each of them in a blanket. Rudy's Lulu and Suzette found slippers for them.'

'And bandages, eh?'

It was St-Cyr who said, 'He means, were they raped?'

'*Ah, mon Dieu,* of course not,' insisted Rudy. 'That wasn't ordered.'

'Those PPF boys were only to have a look,' said Lenz. 'Surely, that would have been natural, refreshing, even?'

The son of a bitch!

'Hermann, don't!'

'The names, then, Louis, of this little hit squad.'

'Why not be reasonable since no further harm has come to them?' went on Rudy, gesturing open-handedly. 'Me, I will personally see to the needed repairs and losses. Could we not . . .'

'Hermann, *please!*'

'Louis, I told you to leave this to me.'

Lingerie was dangling from the stuffed coat pockets of some, and it was to one of them that Hermann now went, having borrowed a pen from Rudy. 'Write down the names of your little squad in my notebook, *mon ami.* Spell everything carefully and truthfully, and when, after you've added your own, sign and dot it, and then gather up the papers of each of them, so that I can check your honesty.'

'And if I don't?'

A smart-ass. 'You won't even hear the sound this makes.'

'Unfortunately, *mes amis,* my partner really does mean it. Never have I seen him so angry.'

'Flat tires, smashed headlights and now this, Rudy?' objected Lenz.

It was Lulu who wheeled the cognac in, but Hermann who let its spigot constantly empty onto the floor as he said, 'Now, you little plaything, I'm going to borrow your cigarette lighter—yes, that's the very one, Herr Lebeznikov, and if I don't get the answers I need, this place and all that's in it, is going to go up.'

'Give him the names and the I.D. papers,' sighed Rudy. 'It won't matter. Not with these two. Not when Karl Oberg is through with them.'

'That's a threat we've had lots of times,' said Hermann, using the Purdey's muzzle to lift Rudy's chin, having moved so swiftly even Mérode had been caught off guard. 'There's gasoline in those jerry cans out in the foyer, Louis. Get two of them and we'll show him I really do mean business.'

'The list,' snapped Rudy, and when he had run his gaze over it, he handed it and the identity papers to Kohler. 'Now maybe, *mon ami,* you would tell us what this whole thing is about. A girl with a badly festering wound perhaps on the back of a hand or forearm and desperately needing a Wehrmacht first-aid kit with its sulphanilamide antibacterial powder, a *gazogène* truck hauling goods to sell on the *marché noir* and a *Sonderkommando* only Kaltenbrunner could have sent? What the hell does she know that we don't and they need?'

And so much for the silence of a certain Oberfeldwebel Werner Dillmann who should have known better. 'That Kriminalrat from Hamburg is just crazy. We don't know damn all yet but when we do, you and this lot had better not be involved. Now these, *mes amis*,' he lifted the papers, 'you can collect from the Kommandant von Gross-Paris himself.'

'Kohler . . .'

'Don't even say it, Rudy.'

It wasn't until they had withdrawn that Hermann emptied both barrels into the PPF engines and then, reloading, into the windscreen of the other cars.

'You're really good at making friends, aren't you?'

'You haven't seen anything yet.'

The villa was surrounded by a tall, wrought-iron fence under cloud-shadowed moonlight. Trees, bushes and shrubs all but hid the place. Access was by a walkway gate with lock and interconnecting speaker off the boulevard Victor Hugo; the one for the cars, Black Marias, and delivery vans being around the corner on the rue de Rouvray. But at 2310 hours, it was ominously quiet, even though more than 4,000 of the Occupier lived in Neuilly, having taken over the flats and houses of the deported or otherwise absent, and requisitioning still others.

'Hermann . . .'

'Louis, the "guests" in this place of Boemelburg's aren't even allowed to see or speak to one another. Oona needs Giselle. She'll hang herself or do something equally crazy if I don't go in there to see that she's not left alone.'

A man no longer in doubt and convinced that Oona was the one for him, but . . . 'Those who guard this prison of Walter's will have been forewarned of our imminent arrival.'

'Good!'

'I've Gabrielle and her son to think of. If we can convince those guards to let Giselle and Oona share a room, should we not also consider that the heat has momentarily been turned down a little?'

'Back off—that it?'

'How many more of those pills of Benzedrine have you taken?'

'Four.'

'*Ah mon Dieu, mon vieux*, that's twenty milligrams. Did you not think of your blood pressure? It'll be sky-high and will bring on the heart attack I've been dreading.'

Such concern deserved an answer. 'Look, I know you mean well, but sometimes you can sound like a mother hen.'

'Perhaps, but me, I'm not laying the eggs, am I? I'm just along for the clean-up.'

'I'll be sure not to let you forget it.'

The speaker gave the surprise of surprises, a gruff and throaty female voice of the streets and backwaters, the two halves of the driveway's gate automatically opening, the Citroën advancing only to be locked in.

'Messieurs . . . Inspectors, I am Aurore Décour. My youngest daughter, Bijou, and myself do the kitchen here, the beds, the tidying and laundry.'

There couldn't be just the two of them, felt Kohler. Under light from the foyer, she had the face and expression only time and experience could give: round, watchful and empty of all feeling, the knitted cardigan of rescued wool from unravelled cast-offs, the hips wide, hands big and apron that of a cook who was often too busy to think of anything else.

'What is it you wish?'

And so much for the sight of the Purdey, its extra cartridges and Louis. 'Giselle and Oona.'

'The mademoiselles, *ah oui, oui, mais certainement.* Captain Oster, he has said that I am to take you right up, while the other one, he is to wait in the kitchens for me to make him some cocoa.'

'Divide and conquer, Hermann. Avoid any trouble since the other guests will have retired for the night.'

'Is Oster a Haupsturmführer, madame?'

An SS, but had this one with the terrible scar from left eye to chin realized he was being watched by the captain and the others? 'Me, I always address him as captain. It's easier since I never went to school and the tongue finds it difficult to twist itself around such words.'

It was good that Louis had heard that. 'But they've all gone to bed, have they?'

Would he finally believe her if she said it again? '*Oui.* I can wake them if you wish.'

That gaze of hers now found the toes of the felt slippers she must have been given when that last daughter of hers had been born. 'I'll just leave this and my pistol with my partner, shall I?'

'That would, I think, be very wise, and in turn, if he is as un-derstanding, why he could leave all such weapons on the foyer's table. No one will touch them, since everyone else is in their re-spective rooms.'

Sleep and sleep, and even such a big word as that second-to-last one. 'Who else is here?'

'A Romanian countess, or so she constantly claims, who speaks many languages including that one and has the passports to prove it; a Portugese seller of wolframite, the principal ore mineral of tungsten, *n'est-ce pas,* but who has yet to produce the promised shipment; and an Argentine seller of beef and diesel fuel to the submarines of the German leader but one who speaks English fluently and apparently knows nothing of gauchos.'

Liebe Zeit, and she'd never been to school! 'A full house, eh?'

Why did he need to know such a thing unless still wondering if those who guarded the house had really retired and were not watching with their weapons at the ready? '*Oui,* now perhaps if the questions, they are finished, I could . . .'

'Bring them down. Just Oona and Giselle.'

This one slept with both, though never at the same time, or so she had overheard the captain saying to the others. 'Me, I am to take you to them, Inspector, but must ask that you first remove the shoes, the same for the one who is with you.'

'Louis . . .'

'Hermann, do it. Though there aren't any dogs unless they are highly obedient, the security here is still far too tight for us to do anything but what Madame Décour has kindly said.'

But a little look around might still be useful, felt St-Cyr. The living room was truly magnificent. Built in the early 1930s, when labour was desperately cheap and money scarce except for a few, it was spaciously welcoming yet now probably seldom if ever used. A high, floor-to-ceiling doorway, a gleaming parquet floor and soft beige walls funnelled the vision beyond soft brown, leather-covered art deco armchairs, coffee table and woven rug to an ad-jacent room replete with desk and Venetian chandelier circa the late 1920s, that entrance being flanked by two stunning paintings: a seated Modigliani nude to the left and a Kandinsky improvisa-tion to the right. More 'degenerate' art for sure, and certainly the property of the former owner.

A grand piano nestled in that corner, paradise palms in the other and all but hiding an oil on canvas by August Macke who, with Franz Marc, Wassily Kandinsky and Paul Klee, had founded the Blaue Reiter, the Blue Horsemen group. A Rhinelander whose paintings Hitler would, no doubt, joyously burn, Macke's were gorgeous to look at, for his use of light, when broken into its fundamental parts, transcended material objects. Here a tall, slender and obviously very interested woman in a wide-brimmed, feathered chapeau, black fur-collared, powder-blue overcoat, her cream-coloured dress coming well below the coat to hide her shoes, gazed raptly into a lighted shop window after hours. But what sort of a shop—was it not *all* such windows, *all* such rooms as these two, the shading and shapes suggesting things beyond their evident reality, a merging of the natural and human worlds? Drawn more and more deeply into the painting, the viewer was encouraged by Macke to look beyond the usual and deeply into the abstract for what it could tell us about life and all that was around us.

'Hey, you.'

'Me? But of course, the cocoa. I'll wait in the kitchen as Madame Décour has suggested.'

'*Ah bon*, this one has seen the wisdom of behaving himself, Maurice. Let's hope Kohler is as sensible.'

Very quickly Kohler began to feel that this had to be the longest staircase ever, for how were he and Louis to get Oona and Giselle out of a place like this, to say nothing of themselves? As prisons go, it was beautiful, fantastic, warm, comfortable, superb in every way but one.

Life-size, there were two art deco, white marble nudes on the first-storey landing, madame laying a restraining hand on him while she paused to catch a breath. The sculpture in the far left corner was standing with legs together, arms at the sides and palms turned toward him as if in welcome and just like Oona would after she'd dropped her nightgown. But the sculpture in that other far corner was not on her hands and knees as Giselle sometimes wanted almost desperately, but flat on her back, knees up and wide as usual, her invitation not only determined but anticipating every moment to come.

Bevelled wall-mirrors flung these two reminders at him and at themselves, madame having finally lifted tired brown eyes to study his every reaction. 'Like those, Inspector, your ladies are very interesting, but to see them, we must climb yet another flight of these stairs, and me, I must unfortunately take my time.'

She even crossed herself. 'Apart from the Captain Oster, your youngest daughter and yourself, how many others look after this place?'

Had he thoughts he should not have? 'There are three others. One does errands, chauffeuring and the marketing when I give him the lists. Another handles the maintenance—the furnace, the boiler, plumbing and radiators—and the last who also helps that one, does the garden.'

There would at least be one revolver among those three, an old Lebel probably, and that SD would have his regulation Walther PPK with seven-rounds in its magazine.

'Please, you are not to worry, Inspector. Gestapo Boemelburg himself has telephoned, you understand. Mademoiselle le Roy and Madame van der Lynn are to be allowed to share a room and to take their meals and walks in the garden together. Also, clothing is to be brought from where they were living and whatever other items they request.'

Boemelburg, having had to sanction housing them here, had offered a sweetener: cooperate with Heinrich Ludin and tell him everything he wants, or else.

Again, a Venetian art deco chandelier gave light but on the second storey's landing, the view was not nude-clouded but simply across parquet and rug to the wide-open doorway of that room. Wearing the white silk pajamas of the former owner's wife, mistress or daughter, Giselle and Oona sat side by side on the single black, iron-framed bed they would have to share. But it was Oona who was comforting Giselle and not the reverse as usual.

'Me, I will leave you now, Inspector. Let us agree on fifteen minutes, since that is what I have been told to tell you.'

Those walls and ceiling would have eyes and ears there simply wasn't the time to find, felt Kohler, but would it be their last few moments together?

Giselle's bruises, scrapes, cuts, blackened left eye and swollen nose must be hurting her like hell, but so, too, would be the thought, not just of losing those looks Muriel and Chantal had felt so useful, but of never again being their lead mannequin.

The tears were hot, but Oona . . . Oona was very gently urging him to kiss Giselle's every bruise and cut, that one to blurt, 'Those stairs . . . I thought those guys were going to *kill* me, Hermann. They were like animals, I tell you. Animals! Chantal's heart will have given up. Muriel . . . *Ah mon Dieu, mon Dieu,* Oona, she will be in despair without Chantal. Muriel, my Hermann. Never have I seen such a love for another.'

Merde, but this wasn't going to be easy. '*Chérie*, they're fine. Everything in the shop will be fixed and replaced. Louis and I have already nailed those guys and are busy teaching them a lesson they'll never forget, so please don't worry anymore. Just rest and get better.'

Decisively Oona drew him away, and wrapping her arms about his neck, whispered earnestly, 'She needs us, Hermann. Until now, I hadn't known how terrified she was of what might happen to her when this Occupation ends. She keeps saying they'll hack off her hair and bare those lovely breasts of hers and maybe all the rest as they parade her through the streets so that everyone can spit and yell at her, or punch and throw things.'

For having slept with him. 'Oona . . .'

'*Sh*. I do love you very much, Hermann, especially for the inherent goodness that is in you, but for now we must keep our little secret.'

The wedding.

'We have both agreed that you and Jean-Louis are to see that Anna-Marie Vermeulen is helped, even if it means that you have to leave us to be deported. When the end comes, as it surely must, it will be brutal and Giselle and I, we both know you and Jean-Louis will need all the friends you can get, not us. We'll just be extra baggage and a definite hindrance.'

Scheisse, had it come to this? 'Are you okay yourself?'

'A kiss would help. Giselle will expect it. Me first and tenderly, of course, and with passion and then herself, since she'll be expecting that too.'

Louis hadn't even touched the hot chocolate.

Small and once very much a symbol of the upper class, the Hôtel Raphael, at 17 avenue Kléber, was lovely in daylight as a reminder of how things once were for some. But at 0147 hours, Sunday,

3 October, it was just damned forbidding, as was the massive Hôtel Majestic at number nineteen whose rooms and suites had been cut up into the 1,100 offices the Headquarters of the Military Administration now felt they needed. 'Hermann, hadn't we better think this over?'

That early-morning meeting with Ludin was but a few hours and a stone's throw away. 'We haven't any other choice, Louis. Besides, it might just work.'

'Have I not heard that one before?'

'*Lieber Gott,* must you argue at a time like this? Walter's quietly telling me I have no choice but to behave. Oona's said a definite no to any thoughts of a wedding because Giselle's the one who's now desperately needing comforting, not her. It's not the usual, Louis.'

Ah merde. 'How many more of those pills have you taken?'

'None. I've run out.'

'Good. Then I'll let you summon Le Roc, the maître d'. They say that he was bullied as a boy, but only once and thereafter took care of himself.'

It took forever, even with Hermann using his Gestapo clout, but finally they were allowed to doss down in the lounge. Awakened at 0600 hours Berlin time, razors and such were brought from the Citroën and they managed to make themselves somewhat presentable.

Generals being what they were, the new Kommandant von Gross-Paris had taken but a modest bed-sitter here and that, of course, felt St-Cyr, should definitely be telling them something about him.

Shown into the small but elegant dining room, they found Baron von Boineburg-Lengsfeld alone and waiting. Severe in uniform, *das Eiserne Kreuz* at the throat and full medal bar from the Great War, this former cavalry general looked as if having just received unsettling news.

'Gentlemen,' he abruptly gestured, 'I've taken the liberty of ordering full breakfasts. The sweet apple cider first, Kohler, and none of that *Rhabarbersaft* Reichsminister Goebbels is foisting off on us Germans at home.'

Rhubarb juice. *Apfelsaft* was, of course, the favourite nonalcoholic beverage but in far too short a supply for any number of reasons. 'Things are getting tough, General.'

A wary response, so good. *Ja, gut!* 'Are they? That new war-bread of wholemeal and barley is not enough? Baked twice as long as a regular loaf, it's ten times as heavy and black too, but we Germans are to muscle our teeth around it because it's far healthier than the other? One-pot meals on Sundays to conserve food and energy, but everyone terrified of a visit from those zealots in the Sturmabteilung?'

The Storm Troopers did have the right to barge in and check any kitchen they wanted, but those one-pots were really only once a month, so what had brought on the outburst?

'And in Berlin, Kohler, what is it they're now saying of the initials LSR?'

Which were on the signs and arrows of the air raid shelters, as they were in Paris, too, the *Luftschutzraum.*

'Well?'

Had the walls no ears? '*Lernt schnell Russich,* General.'

'*Ach,* perhaps it's advice Berlin should hear since the Soviets have just driven a bridgehead across the Dneiper near Pereyaslav. Even two Panzer divisions couldn't stop them. Two, Kohler, considering that the Führer, having now reduced divisional strengths from 17,500 to 10,708, has allowed those to include, if I may say so, 2,000 Russian prisoners of war if they volunteer for combat duty.'

And with others from Occupied territories, dubbed the '*Hiwis,*' the *Hilfwilliger,* the willing help, but again what had set him off? The silvery-grey hair was immaculate in its military trim, the eyes of the deepest, most watchful blue, the whole of him polished to the nth degree and probably beginning at 0500 hours.

'Gentlemen, as a young student, I studied ornithology in my spare time and came to love and admire the eagle. But I was always torn when prey was being carried back to the nest. You see, eagles will attack one another and I would never know until the very last moment if the meal would be dropped or stolen and the young go hungry.'

Fortunately there was still no one else in the room, felt St-Cyr, and the general had even had the maître d's bell placed on the table in front of himself and had had the doors closed, but that eagle on his tunic was clutching a swastika and the analogy plainly evident.

'Yesterday at dawn, gentlemen, British commandos landed at Termoli and are presently hastening to link up with the American Eighth Army. On the twenty-eighth of last month, the Italians signed their final surrender effectively denying the Führer his staunchest ally. "Traitors," he's now calling them, and of course the Allies are not going to go away. The port of Naples is already in British hands, and they are rapidly repairing it so as to bring in the much needed materiel yet the Führer, for all his apparent wisdom, remains confident of a final victory, as do, indeed, the Japanese, another of his allies.'

There was likely more to come, and it would be wisest for them to stay out of it. 'Hermann, give him the list.'

'General, these are the names of the ten who forced their way into that shop to terrify those dear ladies.'

'And take your two as hostage, Kohler. I'm not without my sources but had no idea of the utter gravity of the matter when I spoke so harshly to you.'

Liebe Zeit! 'They were a hit squad of PPF.'

'Ordered at the request of Kriminalrat Ludin,' interjected Louis. 'Apparently he felt a little squeeze necessary, General. You see Hermann and I, we were called in to investigate the murder of . . .'

'Yes, yes, Untersturmführer Mohnke and Oberführer Thomsen reported the killings to myself. Some ruins, I gather. The Chemin des Dames, Kohler, and Falkenhyan's line. The Drachenhöhle. Reims, of course, and the shelling we gave it from those hills seven or so kilometres to the east, eh?'

'The fortress of Witry-lès-Reims, Hermann, and the one at Nogent-l'Abbesse, and the forest lookout and battery that is just beyond Cerney-lès-Reims.'

'Yes, yes. The 10.5 centimetre FH16 Leichte Feldhaubitze, Kohler, and the 7.5 FK16 Feldkanone. Our light howitzer was called the whizz-bangs by the British, the tempest of fire, by the French, eh, and by our boys, the drumfire. How it all comes back. Immediately.'

Even including, as Louis well knew, those thirteen-centimetre high-velocity guns whose key feature was that no one would even hear the shot until the bloody-damn shell had arrived. 'Kriminalrat Ludin and the Standartenführer who is with him have been following the truck, General, in which was the murderer. This we have established.'

'But they weren't after him,' said St-Cyr. 'They were chasing a Dutch girl that *Spitzel* of theirs was watching and leaving coins as reminders, but Herr Ludin refuses to tell us who she is and why their *Sonderkommando* want her, nor will he even give us the name of the killer, though they obviously must know it.'

Thwarting the course of justice. '*Ein Spitzel*, you say?'

'Their *Sonderkommando* is from the Reichssicherheitshauptamt, General, and under a security so tight no one is even to know why Herr Ludin and his colonel are in Paris.'

Kaltenbrunner again, was it? said Boineburg-Lengsfeld to himself. He'd show that sadistic, chain-smoking incompetent alcoholic Himmler had put in charge of the SD a thing or two. 'A mere girl requires such an effort, does she? What would you like me to do with those PPF, Kohler?'

'General, here are their identity papers. The Organisation Todt is always needing labour, especially with the Atlantic Wall still not finished. Have them assigned to breaking rock and shovelling gravel and cement on the Channel Islands. Get them to do a little honest work for a change.'

'And this Ludin, how can I help?'

They'd better keep it simple. 'Louis and I need to take another look at those ruins where the killings happened. You see, en route, that girl switched horses because she must have realized they had a *Spitzel* among the group she was with.'

'Leaving it, she went ahead, we believe, to ask for a lift in the bank van, General.'

'And they saw that she was pretty,' said Kohler, 'but that plain around Reims is so flat, we have to take a look at those 1914–1918 gun emplacements to see how those in that truck with its *gazo* could not only have seen the van but followed and finally caught up with it.'

'Did they take her back?'

'We think they must have,' said Hermann.

'And if I were to keep all of this in confidence yet call Höherer SS und Polizeiführer Karl Oberg, to tell him of the necessity of your request to delay this meeting with the Kriminalrat, where would you like it to be held and when?'

Good generals were rare but often thorough, thought Kohler, and of course among them, those who were dyed-in-the-wool Prussians most often had utterly no use for the SD and SS. 'The Boeuf sur le Toit and this evening at around 2100 hours.'

'An excellent choice since it will, of necessity, have to go in my duty report, but I'll also forward a copy to the Reichssicherheitshauptamt, another to the Führer and a third to the OKW.'

The High Command, but of course the Boeuf sur le Toit, being a favourite of the SD, SS and Gestapo, had been shut down and forbidden by the Führer last March to rid Paris of its slackers, felt Kohler, only to reopen illegally in a wing of the Hôtel George V and be but a nice stroll from its former location on the rue du Colisée, which had been much closer to Gestapo and Sûreté headquarters.

But there was still more to come, and Louis looked as if he knew it too.

Unpinning his Iron Cross First Class from the Great War, Boineburg-Lengsfeld ran the thumb of memory over it. 'This, as I'm sure you must know, Kohler, dates back to the Napoleonic Wars when on 10 March 1813, Friedrich Wilhelm III of Prussia inaugurated it. Like mine still does, they originally had the imperial crown at the centre. Now, of course, it's the swastika, but that hasn't been enough, has it? Nothing ever is with those people in Berlin. Were it the Abwehr you were dealing with, you would immediately have been told everything needed, but with Kaltenbrunner and the SD things are, unfortunately, insidiously different. Today I received final word from those who respect and revere it, that our world-renowned counterintelligence service, founded on 25 March 1866 by Count von Moltke, chief of the general staff, will cease to exist by the end of the year. Instead, it will be taken over and "absorbed" completely by the Sicherheitsdienst. For men such as myself, and I've been a soldier all my life, it's incomprehensible. According to Reichsführer Himmler's latest directive, all mention of the Abwehr is to be expunged from the history textbooks by next June at the latest.'

Taking not a second longer, he brought the palm of his right hand down firmly on the bell.

'Now, please, here are our breakfasts. Enjoy and I will see that a full lunch hamper is made up for you both.'

'Gasoline, General.'

'Of course. Two jerry cans and a full tank. You've only to call round to the Abwehr's garage since it still exists. I'll give you an order for them and a blanket *ausweise* for the journey.'

Two smoked herring, sausages, eggs and ham were set before Louis who had, Kohler knew, been looking forward to more illegal croissants, butter and jam but would now have to eat the lot as if enjoying it all.

Having come out here to the east of Reims about eight kilometres in an attempt to pick up the trail of that van and *gazogène*, they had taken a short detour to the north of the RD 380 to the base of what had to be one of the most massively ugly, pentagonal fortresses, felt Kohler. Smashed grey-stone walls rose to gun emplacements in tiers, reminding them both of the stupidity of all such wars, but here the maximum elevation was only 175 metres. Farms crowded the lowermost slopes and were spread out over the plain of Champagne. Sugar beets, rutabagas, cabbages, turnips, onions and potatoes, hay, wheat, barley and corn all seemed to flourish in that chalky soil in spite of the shortages of manure. Kids, mothers, grandmothers, wagons, handcarts, plow horses, bullocks, old men, too, and the disabled from that other war were at the harvest. And to the south of Reims, on the slopes of the Montagne de Reims, which wasn't a mountain at all but an escarpment and plateau of about 275 metres at its highest, the leaves would be turning and the *vendage* in progress: champagne and those roads toward Reims busy as hell, so you don't stop traffic, otherwise folks get very angry and shout their heads off.

Built between 1875 and 1878, the fortress of Witry-lès-Reims, named Loewendal by the Wehrmacht in 1914, had been but a part of the defensive chain of fortresses and batteries the Third Republic had thrown up after the Franco-Prussian War. Universal conscription had been introduced. Never again would *la patrie* suffer such a humiliating defeat, yet they had prepared for a style

---

* On the evening of 20 July 1944, believing that the Führer has been assassinated, Boineburg-Lengsfeld ordered his second-in-command to see that Karl Oberg and other leading SS in Paris were arrested. But the bomb had failed to do what it was supposed to. Recalled to Berlin and arrested but found guilty only of having obeyed General Heinrich von Stulpnägel's command to have them arrested, Boineburg-Lengsfeld was dismissed but not executed as others were.

of warfare that would no longer be in vogue, and had done the same damned thing in this one with the Maginot Line.

'In 1914, at the start of it in August, Hermann, there was a garrison of three hundred and seventy-seven. *Bien sûr,* the magazine alone held 85,000 kilos of artillery shells for the thirty-one heavy guns above, a cavern so huge it defied reason. Tunnels and tunnels, and even a bread oven that could bake three hundred and fifty loaves a day. Czar Nicholas II was very impressed when he attended the *grandes manoeuvres de l'Est* on September 1901, same garrison size, same bread oven.'

Yet it, and other such forts, and there had been a lot of them taken, had only been turned against the French in the 1914–1918 war. 'And assuming that my side would have rightly used those guns every day for 1,051 of them, we sent shell after French shell into Reims, a few of our own as well.'

'Levelling more than 12,000 of its 14,000 houses, virtually all of the public buildings and enough of the cathedral, its repairs lasted all but to the start of the present hostilities.'

But entry here was absolutely forbidden, the road up and into it all having been closed off by a mountain of rubble.

'Hidden in the back of that truck, Louis, our Anna-Marie wouldn't have seen a thing in any case and would have only wondered what the hell was going on.'

Knowing as she must have, that there was an informant amongst them. 'But they would have sought the heights elsewhere, Hermann, since those leaving the city and travelling east on the RD 380 would have told them of why there was such a traffic hold-up going west.'

'Every incoming vehicle being torn apart in a desperate attempt to find her by a Standartenführer and a Kriminalrat who should have known better than to broadcast what they were after.'

'Though it will now be overgrown by forest, the lookout at Berru might be better. It's about 7.5 kilometres from Reims and at an altitude of about 270 metres. Those comrades of yours also shelled the city from there.'

'And with French guns, was it?'

'There's a magazine that would have held 65,000 kilos of shells and a bread oven that would have produced three hundred loaves a day.'

Dented, speckled by bird shot and rusting, the sign wasn't any more than twenty-four years old, yet clear enough:

BERRU LOOKOUT AND BATTERY,
CONSTRUCTED BETWEEN 1876 AND 1881.
THIS WOODS AND ITS DEFENSIVE WORKS
ARE ALL PRIVATE PROPERTY
AND EXTREMELY DANGEROUS.
HUNTING AND TRESPASSING ARE STRICTLY FORBIDDEN.

'Messieurs . . . Messieurs, écoutez-moi, s'il vous plaît. Les bombardements de la Grande Guerre, n'est-ce pas? Les obus explosifs et des mortiers aux perforants.'

'The armour-piercing ones, Louis, but he's forgotten to include the grenades and land mines.'

'Leave him to me, Hermann. We don't have time to argue.'

Oaks, beeches, chestnut and pine, none probably more than twenty-five years old, grew in profusion, and through these and the underlying brush, a stone-laid trudge path brought instant memories of men slugging shells uphill and wounded down.

A stone lookout that no one had bothered to repair, and why should they have, nestled on high and might well have given a clear enough view and been used by that *passeur*, but Louis had gone back along the road a little.

The resident retainer's house was on a postage stamp of a clearing, with woodpile, drive-shed, chickens, cow, goat, and he with one arm, the left. But the frayed bit of ribbon with its red-lined green moiré and bronze palm on this bantam's chest indicated a Croix de Guerre. Less than the five mentions a silver would have brought, but no matter since one was quite enough.

Full and broad, and not unlike Werner Dillmann's, the grey and mercilessly tended moustache was given a decisive knuckle brush. 'Me, Horace Rivet and former corporal in an army that was an army and didn't run like those in this war, cannot let you pass, Inspectors. The wife will insist. She's a Jouvand. Her father and mother are far worse.'

'Are there others who would watch and report our trespassing if you did allow us to have a look?' asked Louis, pleasantly enough.

'They are all too busy at the harvest but will have seen that car of yours taking to this hill.'

'It's urgent. A murder inquiry. Your assistance is not only necessary, Corporal, it's demanded under the law.'

Ah bon, firmness would be necessary. 'Arrest me, then. If my boys were here, and not in the prisoner-of-war camps of that one, and let me tell you they and the others with them fought bravely, I would simply stand back and have them deal with you. It's far too dangerous as the sign plainly states, or is it that you can't or refuse to read?'

God *would* use the stubborn ones. 'Like yourself, we were both soldiers and know well enough what to watch out for.'

'Then you will understand perfectly that buried materiel can choose its moment even after the years of waiting.'

Which was absolutely true, given the recurring news reports of unfortunate farmers inadvertently hitting something or trying to dig it up. 'That partner of mine is a Gestapo.'

He would toss the hand at such muscle, felt Rivet. 'Even if he were that one's Führer, access would still be forbidden.'

Cheapness would allow Hermann to shine. 'Would fifty francs help?'

'*Merde alors*, what is this I am hearing from a Sûreté? The badge, Inspector. The number?'

A sigh had best be given, a hand tossed as well. 'He's one of Franchet d'Espèrey's men, Hermann. The Fourth Corps, but then the Third and Tenth joining them. The Battle of Guise, to Frenchmen; to yourselves, that of Saint-Quentin. Demoralized and discouraged, men like Corporal Rivet found in that new commander of theirs the necessary and fought bravely with both impressive courage and decisiveness.'

'Dawn, 29 August 1914,' said Rivet, 'and the mist as thick as porridge. Nothing but fear in our hearts, the battle wearing on and on until, at about 1800 hours, the miracle. There he was riding that chestnut charger of his out in front and waving us on. The whole of the German line gave way as we drove them back.'

'The British calling him "Desperate Frankie," Hermann; his men, "the fire-eater."'

'Our right flank then digging in atop the Chemin des Dames,

eh, Louis, to begin that terrible trench warfare you've been telling me about. Quit being so cheap. Here's a thousand, Corporal.'

'I'll say I was in the shithouse.'

'And the wife?' hazarded St-Cyr.

'No artichokes from Laon for four years if not eight, she'd tell you because of what those damned people from the Rhine and to the east of it had done to that beautiful city. No asparagus and strawberries from Chenay because of the battery there that was like this one? Had I not been in those "trenches" myself, I'd have wept like her and her parents, God rest them all.'

'Give him 2,000 francs, Hermann.'

These two must really be determined. 'No one comes here. Indeed, why should they, and yet suddenly there are others and then yourselves?'

Ah mon Dieu! 'What others, Corporal?'

'Perhaps a further . . .'

'Here's a 5,000-franc note,' said the partnership's banker.

'A van from the Banque Nationale de Crédit et Commercial early last Wednesday and then, an hour or so later, a heavily laden truck, a *gazogène*.'

Uh-oh, now here it comes, felt Kohler. 'Both to have a look at what was holding up traffic on the RD 380 to Reims?'

Since the forest that had been cleared by such in 1914 had obviously grown back in, and the lookout in total disrepair, one would have thought these two might have noticed, but one had better tell them anyway. 'Me, I have to think it had more to do with avoiding a little something else.'

That hand was extended, Hermann pulling out the bankroll to ask, 'What?'

Another 1,000-franc note was found. 'One of those little sand-coloured aircraft with the Maltese Cross on its wings and fuselage, the *croix gammée* on the tail, and from the desert war that was, apparently, lost.'

'Hermann, there's a Luftwaffe airfield just to the north of Reims. I should have remembered.'

'Me, too, so what else, Corporal?'

'The van, when it arrived, immediately sought cover under my chestnut trees, the truck the same. Both were, of course, told to leave but . . .'

'They paid you,' sighed Louis.

'Inspector, I did not say that!'

'Good. The ham, eggs, cheese or whatever, suited, Louis. And the girl?'

Merde, that 5,000-franc note was being teased away. 'What girl, Inspectors?'

'Just tell us,' said the other one.

They must be after her, felt Rivet, but had she been violated by those two in the van, the throat slit? 'At first, there was no sign of her and then the more robust of the three with the truck insisted on opening its back and getting inside to open something else, and finally she appeared, blinking at the unaccustomed light. A blonde, a looker *peut-être,* but I didn't think so at the time because she was very pale and obviously worried. Saying nothing, she remained apart by the truck, even though the one who had freed her asked me for water for her and I brought it, she then thanking me but in the faintest of voices as she looked questioningly at those from the van and the other two that had come with the truck. Me, I think her heart fell when she saw that van.'

'Why?' asked Louis.

'*Merde alors,* how am I to know such a thing? Maybe she knew of the bank.'

'Or of the driver and his assistant. Did they recognize her?' asked St-Cyr.

This Sûreté was determined to have the answer he and the Gestapo wanted.'Those with the van grinned at one another, but as to herself, me I think she was terrified of them. Did those two make mischief with her?'

'That's not for you to know.'

'That spotter plane could easily have reported them, Louis.'

'But couldn't have, Hermann. Instead, our *passeur* made a hasty decision just as he must have done with the contents of those pockets: she to the van, since of the two vehicles, it was by far the lesser to be stopped and searched.'

Ah bon, she was definitely the one of interest and that 5,000-franc note could now be demanded back. 'One of the two Dutchmen with the truck didn't want her to go in the van and claimed it would be far too dangerous, that they should wait it out here and then go well to the east before turning south to go around the Montagne de Reims to Epernay, that the forest there would hide them well. The other two talked it over and finally the French one went to speak to the two with the van and they shook hands.'

'A moment, please, Corporal,' said the Sûreté. 'Two Dutchmen and then a Frenchman?'

'*Oui.* One of the Dutchmen was the mechanic and driver of the truck, for when they first arrived, it was he who immediately dampened the truck's little fire to stop any smoke from giving them away.'

'Age, name—any such details?' asked Louis.

'Age, about twenty-eight or thirty; name, Arie; the other one, the complainer, lighter, taller, younger and far less robust. It's in the hands, *n'est-ce pas*? One always looks at them. This one hadn't done a lot of physical work. The mechanic and the . . . Was it a *passeur*, you called the Frenchman, Inspector?'

'Never mind. Just tell us this other Dutchman's age and name.'

Had that one done something to the girl? 'Maybe twenty-four, maybe younger by a year or two. Name, Frans. The girl was far more wary of that one than of the mechanic, who seemed to like her. She was easier with him, too, and even smiled faintly when he asked me to bring her some water. It was as though she had expected him to do that and was pleased to find her thoughts had been correct.'

'Arie. And that third one, the Frenchman?' asked Louis.

'Étienne. About thirty-four. Always intent. Never for a moment did he stop assessing everything, even the girl who steadily looked right back at him when he looked questioningly at her, she keeping her distance and her thoughts about the two with the van to herself.'

'Now tell us what they agreed,' said Hermann, fingering another 1,000-franc note.

'At first, the driver of the van said he would wait with her at the side of the road to the south of Laon, in the village of Corbeny, but when she overheard this, the girl said that would be far too conspicuous and that they should meet up at L'Abbaye de Vauclair, that she had once read of some ruins there. She was then locked into the back of the van and when the spotter plane had returned to the air base and they could no longer hear it, they started out, the truck following the other once its little fire had got going well enough.'

'The distance between them increasing, Louis.'

'They never knowing if that aircraft would take off and start searching for them again, Hermann.'

'Inspectors, they decided to go east and away from Reims toward Rethel, then cut overland toward Berry-au-Bac and the road to Laon.'

'And at Corbeny, would turn west,' said the Sûreté. 'Did she take her suitcase with her, Corporal?'

'That wouldn't have been necessary, since they were to collect her at those ruins.'

Good for him. Logic was everything to the French, but Louis had forced Rivet to say what he had anyway and now asked, 'Her shoes, Corporal?'

The smile was immediate. 'Those must have been very expensive. She hated to have to wear them, but her other ones had become impossible—a split seam, a loose sole and nothing but broken laces. The mechanic got the good ones for her, but she didn't put them on when she got into the back of the van.'

'Since she had to climb over everything, Louis.'

'And now for the cut on her hand or forearm, Corporal?' asked that one.

Another 500-franc note was found. 'It was festering badly and ran from the back of her left hand between thumb and forefinger, round and across the heel of her palm where it was deepest. Barbed wire, I'm certain. Me, I've seen lots of the damage that stuff can do, but didn't ask. Her fist was hurting like hell, that's for sure. She had pried off its bandage to have a look. Jagged, swollen and full of pus. Me, I told her she should squeeze it hard after first soaking in hot, salted water. I offered an ointment my wife used to make, but that *passeur* said there wasn't time. Is she still alive, Inspectors?'

'And that, *mon ami*,' said Hermann, 'we only wish we knew.'

Three stitches had been needed to close the deeper wound across the heel of her palm. Yet it was odd—fortuitous perhaps—felt Anna-Marie, that the object which had caused it, and the cut itself, should now have given her the final answer.

The coin was of silver and from among the last to have been minted. The rijksdaaler she had known, when but a child of five, had been 37 millimetres in diameter, 2.6 in thickness and had weighed, after very carefully having been placed on the special scales at Papa's work, a whole 25 grams. Even now, especially now, it felt as money should: good money, real money. Something a person could trust absolutely and be immensely proud of as she had been when Papa had pressed that first one into her hand and had said, 'Oh by the way, my dear miss, did you happen to lose one of these?'

She hadn't dared leave it in a pocket for fear Frans Oenen, the killer of those two from the van, would drag the chair away from the bathtub and search through her things. He must know that she had not only found and taken it from under that nest of barbed wire where he had secreted it on a wooden post at that frontier crossing into Belgium, but that she had finally realized who he really was. No alias anymore. One careless comment had revealed it. 'Collodion,' he had said not an hour ago to Étienne Labrie, her *passeur* and his boss. 'She can hide that cut easily with that.'

Étienne hadn't known what the stuff was—she had been certain of this. With his usual impatience, he had swiftly said, 'But only when the stitches have been pulled. Damn it, Frans, we can't wait that long. She *would* tear her hand on that wire we had to clear away at the crossing to the south of Reusel. They'll have brought in the dogs. They'll not have missed a chance like that.'

After Madame de Belleveau, his 'housekeeper,' had soaked the wound in very hot water and salt and had nursed the poison out on their arrival, that good woman had opened the cut and cleansed it throughly while speaking voluminously of the value of bruised sage leaves boiled in vinegar. 'The Romans and their legions, they swore of such and brought the plant into Gaul where Vercingetorix . . . *Ah mon Dieu*, mademoiselle, listen to me, please. That one, he had gathered the tribes at Alesia in 52 B.C., you understand, to take on the challenge of their lives since Julius Caesar, that one, he had surrounded their hill fort and put them all to siege.

'A terrible time. Rape, slaughter and all the rest,' she had added with a toss of her head, and had promptly bathed the cut with creosote, the shock of which, cognac or no cognac, had caused her to pass out.

Inadvertently she must have blurted something—her increasing doubts about Frans Oenen's loyalties. And now his mention of collodion: used by actors, showgirls and others to hide such telltale marks.

The theatre, the Hollandsche Schouwburg, was on the Plantage Middenlaan in Amsterdam.

Renamed the Joodsche Schouwburg by the Occupier in October 1941, it had been used ever since as a holding place for Jews in transit, her father among them, her mother having gone with him.

Salome, a play of Oscar Wilde's, and the part of Herod Antipas, tetrarch of Judaea, 15 February 1939, a Wednesday evening performance and her eighteenth birthday. Paul Klemper, now using the alias of Frans Oenen, had played the part of Herod so well, the ovation had gone on and on. And now, she asked, what now? Acting still, and perhaps the hardest part ever, that of a traitor and the only one to have a pistol. 'A Dutch Army Pistol M25,' he had quipped when showing it to her right after those killings. 'Very effective in hands like these.' His own.

He hadn't looked or acted at all as if Jewish in the restaurant with a crowd of his followers after that performance. He had been as Aryan as now needed, but the Occupier had known the truth and must have let him escape from that holding place with the promise of giving them exactly what they wanted. Herself—and not only what she had been carrying, but what she still knew.

The water was perfect. She would have to do it. Defenceless behind a makeshift curtain in the kitchen, her things on that chair, she gingerly stepped into the copper tub. They had arrived at this house in the country, this *maison de compagne*, in darkness four days ago and they would leave it in darkness tomorrow at 0500 hours, Monday, 4 October 1943. The truck's engine had now been changed over to burn gasoline but would they be arrested as soon as they got to whatever entrance Étienne might choose? They were, she now knew, just to the west of Sézanne and to the south-southeast of Retourneloupe and the western edge of the Forêt de la Traconne and among the hills that formed the cliff of the Île de France. They were about 100 kilometres to the east of the Bois de Vincennes and that entrance to Paris.

Behind its rutted single lane and scattering of beech and oak, the house, of stone and stucco, would normally have intrigued and delighted, for there was, she had discovered, an enviable *potager*. Attic dormers, shutter-flanked windows, faded green trim and white walls still gave, with the turning of the leaves, that wonderful sense of a country retreat. There had been no lights on when they had arrived—the blackout even here, of course—and Arie's flashlight had soon found the key beneath a stone.

'Martine, when I awaken her, will know what to do with that cut,' Étienne had quietly said when she had climbed out and down from the back of the truck. 'Just don't let her curiosity about how well you react to pain bother you. Just smile softly when she glances up from the needle, and don't mind her smoking good tobacco in that pipe of hers.'

'Martine?' she had asked.

'Madame de Belleveau, my Jeanne d'Arc, and the person I am fortunate enough to have known all my life. Now stop worrying about my selling you out to the Boche. Stop thinking Arie or Frans might. Just because we don't tell our packages any more than is absolutely necessary, doesn't mean we're up to mischief. Martine knows little of what we do and asks nothing of it, nor do we come here often because we mustn't. But she's been here since the Great War when her husband and my father were both killed on 7 September 1914, during the First Battle of the Marne. Martine has raised me since I was seven, my mother, having felt the job too much, had taken up with one of the enemy. He'd moved in, and really I mustn't blame her too much. Martine still insists. "Compassion," she always says. "Who knows what one might do under similar circumstances."'

He had let that sink in, and then had said, 'Now I really have told you too much, Anna-Marie Vermeulen, but only so that you will know exactly what I think of them. Arie, too, since his wife and their brand-new baby, the one he hadn't even seen alive, were both killed when they bombed Rotterdam.'

Arie. 'Look, I'm sorry I suggested they take me to those ruins, but Corbeny is a very small village and everyone would have seen us.'

'Be grateful Frans took care of the problem. I wouldn't have. I'd have let them off with a warning. Tell yourself, as I still am, that it was necessary.'

Frans Oenen—Paul Klemper. She still didn't know Étienne's and Arie's real names, they knowing her only as Anna-Marie Vermeulen because that had been the name Étienne had been given along with that childhood handkerchief by the one who had hired him, she then mentioning it to identify herself when they had met in Amsterdam near the diamond bourse in total darkness, Étienne handing it to her.

It had been Arie who had carted in the firewood to heat the water, Martine who had tested it and had raised a forefinger in pause when he had asked if there was any soap.

A cherished sliver from Provence had been found in a kitchen drawer and still had that lovely smell of lavender and feel of olive oil.

Secreting the coin under herself, letting the warmth envelope her, she reached for the dipper and with that good hand, began to wash her hair. No one could fault her for having done what she had at those ruins. It had been by far the only possible thing.

Nor could she really tell the others about Frans, and he had definitely known this, he must have, because he would then have had to tell them not only what she had been carrying but also what she knew, and of course he had the only gun.

The Sicherheitsdienst who were using him would not have told him everything, but he'd have figured it all out.

Anna-Marie Vermeulen = trainee borderline sorter, Diamant Meyerhof.

6

'A kilo of *what*, Louis, in addition to the one of boart you condescended to tell me of at Chez Rudi's?'

'Don't get huffy.'

They had arrived in Corbeny and had stopped near the ruins of its medieval abbey and tiny museum only because Louis, being Louis, had insisted. 'Just tell me.'

'*Bien sûr, certainement.* Virtually all of the kings of France came here the day after their consecration in Reims cathedral. Even Jeanne d'Arc on her white charger, no doubt. You see, *mon vieux,* the relics of Saint Marcou were here and venerated for his having had the power to cure scrofula, the "king's evil."'

'And what the hell is that?'

'Tuberculosis of the lymphatic glands. A sore neck.'

'And I think I've already asked you a far more pertinent question. Ludin won't have been happy with our having buggered off. He'll retaliate. It's in the Hamburg psyche. Those people are even moving back into the heart of their dead city. Never mind the stench of the countless corpses that still have to be found and removed. Never mind the smoke, the rubble, the living in some cellar, if possible, or even the signs that tell them it's absolutely forbidden to enter that area without a special pass.'

Almost a million had been evacuated from that city, thus spreading the terror throughout the Reich, but unfortunately it was no time to broaden Hermann's understanding of French history. 'About a kilo of mixed stones of up to a carat or two, but often less, and all useful either in jewellery or as industrials.'

'Borderlines are what you want to call them, *mein lieber Fran-*

zösischer Oberdetektiv. Of equal value *either* as one or the other. They require sorting too.'

'And were probably swept off that table and into their little bag even as the Blitzkrieg descended on the city.'

'Of Amsterdam.'

'Her father may not have been the only one in the family to have been employed by Diamant Meyerhof, Hermann.'

'That the one who insisted on her using a *passeur* and paying for it?'

Merde, and still huffy. 'Unless we meet her, we may never know.'

Fortunately Hermann was able to find a much crumpled emergency cigarette. Impatiently straightening and lighting it, he took two deep drags before handing it over.

'An informant, Louis, a spotter plane, a control that causes far too much trouble for far too many, a *Sonderkommando,* a wrecked lingerie shop, two hostages taken so as to threaten the hell out of me, and now two kilos of what the Reich most desperately need. What else is Anna-Marie Vermeulen carrying?'

'I really did try to tell you it was a minefield.'

'And I've just let you know of that Kriminalrat's psyche.'

Hermann hadn't even noticed the emptiness of the village. Oh for sure, there were the farms and the harvest to consider, yet still there should have been someone about. 'With a population of around 350, *mon vieux,* they are all, apparently, out in the fields.'

'Having heard and seen the car, just like our Anna-Marie would have noted, they've buggered off to stay in the fields with the others, but have now turned their backs on us, even the kids.'

A bad sign.

'Let's go and say hello to a certain *garde champêtre* and his wife, Louis. Maybe they can shed a little light on things. Évangéline was her name.'

The *tabac,* the general store, PTT and café-bar were all in one room, with no one even behind the wicket of the Poste, Télégraphe et Téléphone.

Hitting the bell didn't awaken anyone. Hitting it again finally brought the curves, the long and shaken-loose auburn hair, the deep-brown, made-up eyes and the slip with its plunging neckline and off-the-shoulder strap, the rabbit-fur slippers and the generous smile.

'*Messieurs,*' she asked, a hand now to her thirty-three-year-old throat, '*qu'est-ce que vous désirez?* A glass of wine, a cup of coffee or a little something else?'

The chalkboard even gave the additional business of '*poulets, lapins, oeufs,*' but Hermann would be putty in her hands. 'Your husband, madame. St-Cyr of the Sûreté, Kohler of the Kripo.'

So this was the one Eugène had saved on the battlefield. This was the one whose second wife, it was said, had made the grand cuckold of him, he having forgiven her. 'Father Adrien will know where he is. Me, I think you will find that one in his church and down on his knees before God, seeing as he's been a thief and fears that other Gestapo is going to come back for him.'

'What other Gestapo?' demanded Hermann.

Ah bon, that had got them interested. 'The one who drives a car like yours but drinks from little bottles like this.'

'Ah Christ, Louis, stomach bitters.'

Father Adrien was indeed on his knees, bare of back and applying the willow switch. Beside him were three upright bottles of the *vin rouge*, one of which was empty, one half-full and the other still sealed. And beside these, were two bundles of 5,000-franc notes from a hastily emptied poor box.

'Let's leave him, Louis. Let's let God handle it.'

The hour of decision. The Church could be mighty. 'Agreed.'

Again, and then again, Hermann rang the bell, Évangéline Rocheleau appearing in a sleeveless hip-clinging, made-over woollen dress of the latest Paris design, its hem at just above the knees, but obviously there hadn't been time to sew in a zipper or the more usual buttons.

'Me, I thought you would come back,' she said breathlessly. 'I wanted to go to Paris too. Maman, she owns the shop, helps with the PTT and lives with us, so there wouldn't have been any problem, but that other one with the car, his stomach was too acid. "An important meeting," he yelled, or something like that in his language. "A confrontation," *peut-être.*'

The weather had been perfect, felt St-Cyr, the day like a pleasurable journey into the countryside until now. 'God always has to pull out all the stops, Hermann. It's in *his* nature.'

'Finish the dress, madame. Pack a few things. This partner of mine and I will pick you up when we've done what we have to. Let's give that husband of yours a nice surprise.'

The image of lost lives and causes was all too apparent in the ruins of l'Abbaye de Vauclair, and when they had reached the spring, the falling leaves were caught in the water and rushed along. Ferns threw shadows over the grey flagstone that girl had lifted, Hermann finally breaking the silence that had suddenly overwhelmed them. 'She was on the run and terrified, Louis, would have had only one good hand yet had the sense not only to find the perfect place but to leave no trace of herself.'

'Is remarkable. You or me?'

'Both. Let's leave nothing for that Kriminalrat to find.'

In unison, the slab was tilted, letting the water well up behind it and over what she had hidden, Louis sucking in a troubled breath and saying, 'The Ashkenazim, Hermann.'

'The generations of one family, starting way back when?'

'Maybe in the 1700s, maybe earlier.'

'Yet kept hidden always, even from those of their own because only then would the "life" they held be secure.'

Creased and worn, wrinkled and old yet methodically oiled over the years, the plain and simple black leather bag, not quite the size of a clenched fist, had a braided tie of the same with two worn wooden pegs at the ends.

Under it there was a small, folded white paper packet, thoroughly wet but tied round with a bit of brown wool, something hastily pulled from something else and of the moment.

'Hochfeines Weiss,' said Louis, having carefully cradled the bag while opening the packet.

'A dozen beautifully cut and flawless brilliants, each of about two carats and maybe eight millimetres in diameter. Just how the hell did Josef Meyerhof, and it must have been him, keep these from the Third and Glorious Reich?'

A good question, but Hermann still needed calming. 'Maybe she'll tell us.'

'Those shoes are a problem, Louis. We can't have that bastard Ludin finding her.'

To open the bag, they would have to move away to a spot

among the rocks uphill a little where Louis first spread a hand-kerchief. Suddenly, sunlight was trapped, caught, reflected back and forth until finally releasing itself in flashes of fire. 'Six for a necklace that needed eight, *mon vieux.*'

And nothing but *big* trouble, felt Kohler. 'Meyerhof's great-great-grandfather beginning the search, the next keeping clarity, colour and size fully in mind while viewing thousands of others.'

'And so on up the ancestral line to the present, Meyerhof having carried on that search even with the Great War raging elsewhere and after it, the Great Depression.'

'When things were so tough, De Beers and the central selling organization in London found they had to buy up the overhang.'

The old diamonds that had flooded onto the market, forcing prices down, but Hermann had been right to be concerned. A rainbow of colours was before them, a sky-blue like no other, a canary-yellow, too, but clearer than clear, others of the softest, most memorable rose or deepest emerald green, others still, of a cocoa-brown. Some had been cut and polished, but were without their mountings, others still in the rough.

'And those are but the "fancies," the rarest of all,' said St-Cyr. 'The rest are exceptional whites of five, ten, even fifteen or twenty carats, lesser sizes too.'

A spread of maybe sixty to forty percent whites to fancies, but it would have to be said, and Louis had known it too. 'The "sight" of "sights," and not at all usual for the "life" diamonds most would have squirreled away to tide the family over the hardest of times. These are more than enough to have not only reminded their inheritor of the family but to have started up the business again and elsewhere.'

Good for Hermann. 'An absolute fortune on the *marché noir.* No wonder she felt she had to hide them.'

'And be very quiet about them, Louis, since greed can be everything to far too many. That bag would have been flattened and bound tightly against her middle, probably with a band of linen.'

'She'd have made sure there wasn't any unevenness in her clothing.'

'And will have hidden the linen elsewhere. Under a root, or maybe in a knothole.'

'A half-and-half.'

'A submarine.'

'A pair of shoes.'

'And a hell of a lot of trouble not just for ourselves, but for her, too, Louis. *Her.*'

It was Étienne who had cornered her, Étienne whose forehead and pointed chin emphasized the piercing intensity of his gaze. He had come up to this room she had been given in this house he seldom used, a room Frans Oenen had told her to stay in or else. Softly closing the door, he listened to the house while noting everything he could about her, the way she stood to one side of this window so as not to be seen by anyone chancing to arrive or pass by, the clogs she now had to wear, the leather belt and Norwegian trousers in whose right pocket was that coin. Or was he simply noting the frayed left cuff of her sweater from which she had managed to tear a desperately needed bit of thread with her teeth?

Grabbing a chair, he pointed to it and found one for himself, their knees all but touching. 'Whether you like it or not, you're far too noticeable. Blue eyes, blonde hair, and a complexion so perfect even with the lack of food and milk and all the rest, Martine still can't stop going on about it, yet you bring out the desperate in all of us. Myself, because you'll not have been forgotten with that hand, and I must choose a safe way into Paris. Arie, because, though I've yet to tell him, he knows you'll be the last we deliver. Thanks to you, it has simply become far too risky—insanely so, if you ask me—and we've done what we had to anyway.'

'Make a fortune?'

'Please don't be disappointing. We've put our lives on the line for far more important packages than yourself, and many of those have been from the Reich and all of them hunted.'

'And Frans, what does he say about it?'

'That you doubt his loyalty and will do some dumb thing that'll get us all arrested. So now you'll tell me why Josef Meyerhof would have given me these to get you out of the clutches of the Boche?'

It was a belt of louis d'or, something a businessman who travelled a lot would wear under his clothing. 'I can't for a moment imagine how he could possibly have given you anything like that, seeing as he must be under constant surveillance if still in Amsterdam and in the Jewish district behind that horrible fence with all its forbidden-to-enter signs and its barbed wire.'

Perhaps she didn't know. 'He was among the last of them and is probably gone by now."

'To Vught or Westerbork and on,' she said. 'Mijnheer Meyerhof was my father's employer.'

'Your own as well?'

She would shake her head because he couldn't possibly know the truth. Mijnheer Meyerhof wouldn't have let him know, nor would the contact he had used, and that left only Frans who wouldn't have either even if the Boche had told him. Besides, very few women were involved in that business and far fewer girls. 'I met Mijnheer Meyerhof once when I was five and my father took me to his place of work. He wouldn't even know what I look like now, and I could never have gone up to that wire to speak to him in any case. Indeed, why would I, seeing as I am what I am?'

And fierce about it. 'Yet he pays me the whole of my fee up front?'

In May of 1940, those louis d'or would each have been worth about 1,000 francs but now a good 10,000, and there were at least twenty of them. 'He can't have kept those hidden in that ghetto. Someone must have given them to whomever handed them to you. Have you thought of that?'

'He'd have bought his way out and not yours, would he? Instead, early last year he sends his son and that one's wife and their four children to France and tells them to head for the *zone libre*.'

Into which the Germans moved on 11 November 1942 in response to the Allied landings in North Africa, the Italians immediately extending their occupied zone west and all but to the Rhône, making the city of Nice a much preferred refuge.

'Arie and I took them in two trips.'

'With Frans?'

There it was again, that distrust. 'He didn't join us until February of this year.'

'The tenth, was it? Wasn't that the first time he saved yours and Arie's lives by running into that café to shout out a warning that company was on its way?'

---

* On 29 September 1943, all but about 50 of the remaining 2,000 were taken.

The Boche—the *Moffen* to the Dutch—but she hadn't hesitated. 'Frans should never have told you that.'

'Nor should you have told me of those louis d'or.'

Why was she after Frans so hard? 'He was on the run and had been hit in the arm.'

'The perfect submarine, a *résistant*, eh, a bullet graze that missed the heart?'

'You don't like him, do you?'

The urge to show him the rijksdaaler and to tell him where she had found it was almost more than she could bear, but if she did, Frans would be forced to defend himself and use that gun. 'He's too flippant. He presumes far too much. His toasting the killing of those two men was not just upsetting. It was sickening even though I certainly knew what they had intended. And as for any kind of relationship, I haven't the least interest in taking up with anyone, let alone a person like him, and it's equally sickening of him to have suggested it.'

'I'll speak to him. Arie and I are both sorry your fiancé was killed. We do know that he was found hiding in the red-light district on 20 July and that he deliberately ran from the Boche knowing, probably, that if he didn't, he might have given away the alias you've been using in Paris.'

'Josef wouldn't have told you that.'

Not Mijnheer Meyerhof. 'Or that Henk Vandenberg's body lay in the Oudezijds Achterburgwal for the rest of that day and night until two of the Grüne Politei threw him into the canal?'

The 'green police' due to the grey-green colour of their uniforms, the Feldgendarme, the military police. 'Who told you all of this? Frans? And if so, how, please, did he find out?'

Again the urge to show him the coin was there but if she did, he would then find out what Mijnheer Meyerhof had asked her to do.

This package of theirs was tough, felt Labrie, but maybe a little softening up would help. 'Meyerhof's son, daughter-in-law and grandchildren were among those arrested and deported on 11 September. The reason we know is because, during his subsequent interrogation, the son was so badly beaten, he didn't survive, but of course they couldn't resist showing the father a photo of him, for "identification purposes."'

And *that* must be why Mijnheer Meyerhof, on seeing her unexpectedly turn up to walk by the ghetto, had called out to her
and then had asked what he had, but that dear man hadn't said
a word of this. It had been a terrible round-up in Nice, far worse
even than that of the *grande rafle* in Paris on July 16 and 17 of last
year. In Nice and elsewhere in that Italian zone, more than 30,000
had been very quickly arrested and deported.

'Now I'll ask you once more, Anna-Marie, because I really do
need to know exactly why the Boche are after you so hard.'

She couldn't tell him about the diamonds she had been carrying, but something would have to be yielded. 'Josef Meyerhof was
the director of the Amsterdam protection committee that policed
the trade and had drawn up a blacklist of all those dealers who
were selling to the Reich. For years London has been the trad-
ing and distribution centre for rough stones, especially those for
jewellery, which were then sent across the Channel to the cutting
works in Amsterdam and Antwerp, where we also did the industrials for them and others. In turn, we then sent finished stones
back, but never once did the British think to establish their own
works since that would have meant bringing in the skilled Jewish
workmen we had. Finally the cutting tables and other equipment
were got ready for shipment and sent to Rotterdam but at the last
moment, during the Blitzkrieg, the city was hit and they were
never sent. Mijnheer Meyerhof will have that list.'

'But did he give it to you?'

Though a lie, her nod would be brief, her right hand firmly
extended, that fist still clenched with its coin. 'I don't trust Frans
Oenen. I can't. You see, I think I've seen him before.'

'Where?'

'The Hollandsche Schouwburg.'

'He escaped from there and we know that.'

'When?'

And still suspicious. 'When the Boche renamed it in October
1941, they weren't too careful at first and left its stage doors and
fire escape unguarded. Several escaped and were soon rounded up
or shot, but Paul Klemper has been on the run ever since and we
were able to verify this. He's good at it, Anna-Marie. He has had
to be and has helped us several times because he can act the part
of anyone he wants and is an absolute natural.'

Withdrawing her fist, she would shove that coin back into her trouser pocket and tell him only, 'I'm sorry I mistrusted him. It's been hard living like this, and I'm still trying to get over finding out that my Henki was betrayed. He was goodness itself and I loved him dearly. Those shoes I left in that van were to have been worn at our wedding, brief as that would have been.'

'Those shoes really are a problem, Louis.'

'I'm sure you'll think of something.'

No one had bothered them at l'Abbaye de Vauclair, felt Kohler. They'd had the place entirely to themselves and still did. Having found a suitable spot among the ruins, Louis had arranged, on a low and remnant wall, the bits and pieces of this investigation so that they could have a look at everything. Side by side were the shoes. Next came that single blonde hair tucked safely into one of them, then the champagne cork from that snapped-off bottle in the van, it being a clear reminder of the one he had found on her bedside table.

The white paper packet with its woollen thread followed, and then that little black leather bag, and only after those, the cartridge casings, slugs, poultice, *mégot* tin, coins, charred bits of identity papers and finally the Opinel that had been found near the first victim, the one she had hit with a rock. And if *that* didn't say something about her, what did?

Adding a scattering of small banknotes to represent what had been stolen from the van, Kohler laid out the white linen waistband he had found secreted in a knothole not far from the spring. Refilling their glasses, he said, '*Salut, mon vieux*. She's really something, isn't she?'

The wine was magnificent. 'A treasure in itself, Hermann, and not unlike what must have been in the half of the Château Latour she shared with Armand Figeard, her concierge after her first trip "home." Delicate yet full-bodied, elegant yet of great finesse and always delightfully giving those lingering touches of mystery. The Kommandant von Gross-Paris has done us proud. The vineyard this came from was first laid out in the reign of Louis XV.'

There were two bottles of the Château Margaux *premier grand cru*, the 1913. 'If I didn't know better, Louis, I'd say Boineburg-Lengsfeld knew of Hector Bolduc's penchant for buying land in the Haut-Médoc, Côte d'Argent and Côte Sud des Landes.'

'Since the Kommandant von Gross-Paris must know of the Banque Nationale de Crédit et Commercial and its president, he might at that, but me I'm inclined to think he simply wanted to remind us of the Abwehr's past and to encourage us to work together in defiance of Kaltenbrunner and the SD.'

They'd eat in a few moments, felt Kohler: a *pâté en croute* to be followed by the *soupe de Puy*, a purée of green lentils, with potatoes, leeks, carrots, cabbage, and afterward, a casserole of haricot beans with thinly sliced, tightly rolled pork that, with the baguettes, would, in itself, be magnificent. A *salade lyonnaise, tarte aux prunes*, Calvados and real coffee were to finish things off, but sadly no extra tobacco, only two cigars. 'Maybe he really is on our side, but we'd better not presume too much.'

Wise words. 'But is it that Kaltenbrunner's *Sonderkommando* knew of the life diamonds, Hermann? Is it that they *allowed* her to take them?'

'Hence the worried stomach, the bitters and a no-name boss, but a rather dangerous thing to have done if the outcome isn't successful. That *Spitzel* of theirs must have been told to let her run and lead them to something far, far bigger.'

'The so-called "black" diamonds, are those what this is all about?'

The rumors, the whispers, the voracious claims had all been written off as utter nonsense by most. That the Dutch and Belgian dealers could have hidden huge stashes of diamonds seemed impossible, given that virtually all, if not all of them and their families had been arrested, interrogated and then deported, they and their suitcases and homes and factories having been thoroughly searched, even to ripping up the floors and going through the clothing they had worn.

'*Geheime Reichssache*, Louis.'

'And three rijksdaaler.'

'One with a note probably telling them, "I think she's onto me."'

'But is it that they still don't know the alias she's using? Is it that her use of the name Annette-Mélanie Veroche is still secure?'

'Who really knows, not even herself probably, though she'll be thinking those shoes could well give her away.'

'Those diamonds and the boart that she had already hidden should also be included in what is now before us.'

'But do they know of those as well? Did they beat that out of Meyerhof—and beat him they will have, and she'll have figured that out too.'

Frans had trapped her, felt Anna-Marie: Frans had known that after Étienne's little visit she would wait and then try to quietly leave the house to speak to Arie who would be in the barn with the truck.

'There are coins and then there are coins,' he said. 'Is that what you told our *passeur*? Gold louis, eh, or was it of others that are so heavy they refuse to ring when flipped in the air or tossed onto the table in payment for a night of whatever it is you have to offer?'

'How dare you?'

Instantly, she tried to get away, but he would grab that bandaged hand and hold it tightly.

Wincing, she defiantly waited, steadfastness and loyalty even to a dead lover still registering, but he'd simply say, 'I don't dare. I merely ask.'

'Then let go of me.'

So close was he still, the thyme, used dry tea leaves, carrot tops and whatever else he'd been smoking with tobacco, were on each breath, and when he smiled, she could see the way his features changed as if he knew exactly the expression he wanted and had absolute control over himself.

Blue-eyed, fair of skin and hair, the cut that of the military for he would have needed it that way, he was not overly handsome but now knew beyond doubt that she was afraid of him. 'I don't know to what you're referring unless it is that there are two louis d'or. The first dates from 1640 and was minted during the reign of Louis XIII. The second, which superseded it in 1795, is clearly marked twenty francs.'

'And the gold napoléons?' he asked without that smile, but as if curious, as if he would gladly enter into a discussion about them.

'1857 followed by a second dated 1869, both denoting a twenty-franc piece.'

'And worth a lot more now, I guess, but it sounds as if you've been tracking the *marché noir* for the *Banditen*. Have you?'

Ah merde, had he known that too, or merely guessed? 'Coins are a curiosity, that's all.'

'Then you'll know all about the one I mentioned.'

'Since most are made of zinc these days, would it really matter?'

Having forced her up against the corridor wall outside her room, he made as if to turn away, only to turn back suddenly to touch her left cheek with the backs of three fingers. Pressing his middle against hers, finding an earlobe, too, he fingered it tenderly as a lover might and said at last, 'You like the Moët et Chandon, but are you easier after a glass or two?'

Everything told her to say nothing, but the temptation was too great. 'Was that why you chose it over the others when you climbed into the back of that van to toast your having killed those two?'

The smile he would give, decided Oenen, would be of the little boy who had just got the better of an older sister he rather hated when necessary, which was most times. '*Ah bon*, mademoiselle, I think we understand each other perfectly.'

Had he been taken through the house at home? Had the *Moffen* brought him there to better familiarize himself with her? Had he or they found another snapshot of Henki and herself at Zandvoort, like the one she had then brought to Paris last December, the one with that bottle behind them in the sand, Henki having opened it to toast their engagement? Or had he been shown the snapshot Henki would have carried not in his wallet, but hidden? 'Again, I must tell you I simply don't know what you mean. I've told Étienne nothing he didn't already know. I've even apologized for doubting you.'

And given without a quaver, felt Oenen, so he would angrily stiffen and tell her how it was, '*Eine Mischlinge, eh? Eine Halbjüdin, ja, Fräulein Anna-Marie Vermeulen?*'

The transformation to an SS officer had been instant.

Releasing her, turning brutally away to go down the stairs, he said as if throwing it over a shoulder to *gestapistes français,* '*Employez la baignoire avec la glace, mes amis.* Maybe the chill will loosen her tongue, but be sure not to drown her.'

Shade filled the rue Daru as dusk approached. Up from the Seine came the first touches of the evening's fog, but he wouldn't go along the street just yet, felt St-Cyr. He would continue along the rue du Faubourg Saint-Honoré, would keep mingling with others on foot and never look back. He had to be absolutely certain of not being followed, and that, of course, was only the start of it, for he had then to somehow leave convincing evidence for Anna-Marie Vermeulen so that she would agree to meet and not vanish if she did manage to get into Paris.

The Salle Pleyel had two secondary entrances on the rue Daru. The first, and nearest to him as he crossed that street, was just around its corner with the Faubourg Saint-Honoré. A courtyard entrance allowed those in private cars and taxis to be dropped off. The second, and more plebeian was, he knew, well along the street and all but next to the Cathédrale Alexandre Nevesky. *Artistes*— musicians, even Cortot perhaps—would enter there, dancers too, and those who worked in the studios. And across from that, of course, was Chez Kornilov, but was it not favoured also by those who ran Reichsmarschall Göring's biggest purchasing agency, the Bureau Munimin-Pimetex? It was, and yes, unfortunately Sergei Lebeznikov, alias Serge de Lenz of Rudy de Mérode's gang, would be all too familiar with it and with them, especially as Göring had astutely ordered that his purchasing agency be run only by Frenchmen.

'Since those will know where things are and have all the necessary connections,' he said as if to her. '*Merde*, mademoiselle, but you do have the linkages, and not just to Hector Bolduc via that mistress of his, or to Madame Nicole Bordeaux and the cream of Parisian society.'

Munimin-Pimetex was attached to Göring's Ministry of Armaments and Munitions, and bought hugely and constantly and still did, for the Reich desperately needed evermore quantities of everything. 'Including diamonds,' he softly said.

Hermann and Évangéline Rocheleau had let him off at the Quai de Valmy. Right away, though, those who would try to follow had been far more careful than last time. Taking the *métro*, crowded as it always was especially on a Sunday, had helped, changing trains as well, but could one ever be certain?

Coming to *place* des Ternes, he stood as if waiting for someone beside one of Guimard's marvellous art nouveau entrances. Évangéline Rocheleau had had a life history that had overflowed yet Hermann, being Hermann, had listened attentively and had made no attempt to stop the torrent. Indeed, he had *encouraged* it and hadn't even silenced her incessant questioning of their past and present lives and investigations. Instead, he had plucked bits of truth to commingle with the elaborate fiction he had concocted, this partner of his having to listen to it all while *crammed* into the backseat of his *own* car next to that woman's *three* suitcases.

Hermann was to show her a little of the city while there was still some light, and to find her an hotel where she could freshen up. Later they would meet in the foyer of the Hôtel George V and go into the Boeuf sur la Toit together to encounter the husband and Herr Ludin.

Quickly crossing himself at the thought, and the traffic circle to its island, he walked beneath the lindens searching for a café that would give him a view of the Faubourg Saint-Honoré. Every week, though not on Sundays, there was a flower market here, but now not even that and far too few pedestrians.

Bicycles and *vélo-taxis* did go round and round the circle. Wehrmacht trucks and staff cars would speed ahead of the *gazos* but with everything else, did give some semblance of cover. Tattered and faded, last year's poster still proclaimed the Salle Wagram's International Exposition, LE BOLSHEVISME CONTRE L'EUROPE. Lots had attended, but now the war in Russia had progressed to such a point, using that threat would avail the Occupier little.

Satisfied, he retraced his steps but would first head for Chez Kornilov where a *vélo-taxi* and a Mercedes were dropping off a few early diners, the women beautifully made-up and clothed in nothing but the latest the *marché noir* had to offer, the men perfectly dressed in suits, ties and polished leather shoes, their fedoras freshly blocked.

Anna-Marie Vermeulen had lived right across the street, a girl with a kilo of boart and another of borderlines, something those at Munimin-Pimetex would be more than anxious to obtain before any other purchasing agency did; the same, too, of course, for Lebeznikov and Rudy de Mérode and all the more reason to somehow convince her to meet with him.

Very quickly he would have to cross the street and duck into that artists' entrance, all the while wishing that Hermann was watching his back.

Lighting yet another cigarette for Herr Kohler, Évangéline knew her lipstick would again touch those lips and perhaps he would think of her in that way. Attentive, considerate, an excellent listener and always conscious of her presence, he had quickly shown her as much of the city as possible. Pausing on the *place* de la Concorde, he had let her see the obelisk with its strange and wondrous writing from the temple at Luxor in Egypt. 'More than 3,000 years old,' he had said. 'Imagine having to write like that. Slaves, concubines, pyramids, pharaohs and Cleopatra who came lots later but killed herself with an asp because she wasn't able to seduce Octavian who became emperor anyway. Look right down the Champs-Élysées to the Arc de Triomphe, Évangéline. My partner tells me this is by far the finest view and that it was a Frenchman, Jean-François Champollion, who, having dedicated himself to it at age sixteen, finally figured out how to read those and lots of other hieroglyphs on 14 September 1822.'

She had asked of an asp, and he had enthusiastically told her it was either one or the other of the Egyptian cobra or the horned viper. 'Instant, but painful,' he had said. 'I don't suppose anyone even held her hand.'

Outside the cafés and bistros, the waiters were now stacking the tables and chairs or stringing chains to be locked among those as darkness came on. Lots of pedestrians and cyclists were still about, a few German cars and trucks, two old wagons, one being pulled by an elderly couple, the other by a mare that desperately needed feed and water, and then a hansom being used instead of a bicycle taxi, and with two German officers sitting in the back, talking and smoking cigars and taking in the scenery as if it was the most usual of things.

Magazines, newspapers, posters and films, Paris seemed to have everything. On the Île de la Cité, they had both stood side by side gazing up to where the rose window of the Notre Dame had once been, that 'eye' as he had said, 'having been carefully packed away in case of a bombing raid.' Lots of the 'green beans' and the 'grey mice' had been around. 'Tourists,' he had said of the secretaries, typists and such from the Reich who had been very spiffy in their neat grey uniforms, their caps perched at absolutely the same angle, the hair never once touching the shoulders, but pinned up, tied up or simply cut short. 'And otherwise forbidden,' he had said. 'Love affairs, too, but girls will be girls, and everyone knows love never pays any attention, does it?'

Merde, did he know what she herself was thinking, but . . . but was he also *asking*?

Turning onto the rue de la Boétie revealed, through the growing darkness, she felt, the family mansions and former *maisons de
maître* of the wealthy, many of these now offering a choice of hotel.
But which would he choose for Eugène and herself, and would he
take her up to the room to tip the porter and close the door behind
himself? Would they face each other at last and in private? Eugène,
he had never taken the time with her like Herr Kohler must with his
two women, one at a time, of course. Always with Eugène it was in
and out, on and off, his jumping from the train at the last moment
to shoot the stork in flight, Maman always listening from the next
room to hear her daughter's desperate sighs of unfulfilled longing.

'The Wildenstein Gallery is in that hotel at number fifty-
seven,' said Herr Kohler, glancing again into the rearview mirror.
'It's being run by a very trusted employee, Roger Dequoy, who
sells scads of fabulous paintings and drawings for Wildenstein to
scads of buyers from the Reich and Switzerland, among others
like Spain, Portugal and Argentina—you name it and they come,
even with the war and especially because of it and the bargains.
But at number twenty-one, the former Rosenberg Gallery is now
the Institute for Study of Jewish Questions. Rosenberg was the
agent for Picasso, Braque, Matisse and others.

'*Ach*, there's the Hôtel Excelsior,' he said, glancing again into
the rearview, 'but there are also the Hôtels Rochester, Angleterre
and d'Artois, and lots of choice.'

He had slowed the car beside a fabulous house with white pil-
lars yet had said nothing of it, simply glanced again at it and then
into that rearview, and when she started to turn to have a look
behind, said so very gently, 'Just be the sensible woman you are,
Évangéline, and leave this to me.'

He'd drive right up the street and turn around and come back
at them, thought Kohler. Nicole Bordeaux lived in nothing but
a perfect mansion, defying change, the Occupation, the charges
of *collabo* and everything else. Unfortunately those two cars that
had picked them up at the Pantin entrance had stuck to him like
glue, and the worst of it was that the moment he parked Madame
Rocheleau in one of these hotels, they'd pounce to find out who
the hell she was and what he was up to. Having failed to remain
silent, that husband of hers had told her all about those shoes and
that bit of embroidery Louis was carting around.

There was only one thing to do. Park her where they couldn't get at her without a hell of a lot of trouble.

'Now don't worry,' he said, 'I know just the place. It's not far and you'll be right in the centre of things so that when the shops open tomorrow, you and the *garde champêtre* can have a field day. Breakfast first, though, overlooking the central courtyard and its garden. They've a fabulous restaurant.'

Strung with gold, there was a glass roof over the entrance whose brass doors shone, and a doorman in uniform with white gloves, all of which said that it must cost a fortune. 'Me, I . . . I couldn't stay in a place like that, Herr Kohler. I've not the clothes, nor the way of speaking like the people in there. Everyone would stare at me.'

A realist. 'Royalty, that's what you are,' he said, having laid a reassuring hand on hers, the car at idle, the doorman glaring at them. 'It's all in the mind, *n'est-ce pas?* Believe me, you have something many of those who are staying in there don't and want very much, so always keep that in mind. You're what you are, a woman of mystery.'

Ah mon Dieu, was it really happening? *Bien sûr*, the Hôtel Bristol, at 112 rue de Faubourg Saint-Honoré, was five-star and the room and the bed would be perfect, but . . . 'Won't I have to leave my papers at the front desk?'

'Not on your life.' The *Bonzen und Oberbonzen* from the Reich would think her perfect; so, too, the generals and other higher-ups. 'The American multimillionairess, Mrs. Florence Gould, lives here more or less permanently since her apartment on the boulevard Suchet, along with the Palais Rose that the Gould money built on the avenue Foch, was requisitioned by the military governor back in June 1940.[*] She's famous for her Thursday lunch gatherings where she brings together both sides of this Occupation to introduce those from the Reich to Paris society and has the finest of tables. Oysters, caviar, truffles and pâté for starters, then the soup, the duck *à l'orange* and all the rest. She's still married, but her husband decided back in July 1940 that he'd stay on the Riviera where it was warmer. Florence knows everyone: Marie-Louise Bousquet, editor of France's *Harper's Bazaar*, Suzanne Abetz, wife

---

[*] In April 1942, she rented a large apartment at 129 avenue Malakoff.

of the German ambassador, also Marie-Blanche de Polignac and Marie-Laure de Nouilles, the *marquise*. Those are names to keep in mind since they're all very fashion-conscious and intimately know each of the great dress designers and will be a huge help in getting you the very best of positions as a seamstress and designer. I'll have a word. Don't worry.'

Since all of them, felt Kohler, would know Nicole Bordeaux and could well have encountered Anna-Marie at one of that consumptive's Sunday 'cultural' gatherings.

Still worried, Évangéline watched as the doorman was forced to summon the head porter to take her suitcases and then to lead them across a magnificent foyer to the desk where Herr Kohler simply leaned over it to buttonhole a rather stern looking, much older maître d'.

'Kohler, Gestapo Paris-Central, with one of Boemelburg's "specials," so don't get huffy. The suite with the best view, since I know he keeps two of them free at all times, even if he has others staying with you, then a word in private with Madame Gould.'

Ah merde, Madame Gould must have said the wrong thing to the wrong person, the gossip gathering to bring on the deluge, felt Émile-Henri Dumais. No more of the special lunches and the 'At Home's' for those who liked to drop in 'unexpectedly' to stay the night. The young officers, and the not-so-young.

'Madame Gould will have been attending an auction and showing of paintings at the Jeu de Paume with the Oberleutnant Bremer and others, and is to dine at Prunier.'

Just to the west of the *place* Vendôme, at 9 rue Duphot, and the number one place for lobster, fish and oysters. 'Then for now, her secretary will do.'

It had really happened. It must have, felt Dumais. 'Madame Volnée visits with her mother on Sundays, returning to us at ten o'clock always.'

Louis would have said God had sent this one. 'Then I'll have a little chat with one of Madame Gould's maids. There are three of them, but only two share that *chambre de bonne* and the winter's cold up there in the attic, thanks to yourself, no doubt.'

But did this one also know what could well go on in that room if a little adventure was needed by one or two of Madame Gould's 'unexpected' guests and herself, or that those 'maids' could then come downstairs if desired? 'Mademoiselle Beauchamp will be in Madame Gould's residence.'

'Good. Stay here. Just give me the key to Boemelburg's guest suite and have those bags sent up.'

Louis, though he hadn't said anything of what he was going to do in that room at the Salle Pleyel, would absolutely have to be helped. No question.

Grâce à Dieu, felt St-Cyr, darkness now all but hid the rue Daru. One by one, the little blue lights above the Salle Pleyel's other entrances came on, and then that for Chez Kornilov. Pausing still, he would wait to make absolutely sure the coast was clear.

Ducking into the artists' entrance, he again would wait. *Merde*, had he *heard* someone?

More audible now, the steps came on. *Sacré nom de nom*, had he been so foolish as to have led those *salauds* to her very doorstep? *Bien sûr*, they had been good, but . . .

Holding a breath, he waited. Trying to silently unbutton his coat to get at the Lebel in his left jacket pocket, a button flew off. Irretrievable, of course. Irreplaceable, too.

Muted, the evening's traffic filtered in, the smell, too, of the one who stood out there facing him and not of tobacco, not really. Of herbs, rosemary in particular.

He'd use the Lebel as a club and would shoot only if necessary, but the steps started up again. Following, they led him to the Cathédrale Alexandre Nevesky. Vespers would be held on Sunday after sundown, the beginning of the Orthodox day. Incense is what he had smelled. *Incense*. Others would be arriving, the Occupation having filled the churches of every denomination.

Returning to the Salle Pleyel, he found Concierge Figeard at his evening meal, sitting in his *loge* at the head of a table on which were two place settings. Candles made of stubs were ready to light, wineglasses awaiting water from a small, stoneware pitcher. A plate of radishes, perfectly cut into fans, accompanied lettuce leaves and sprinklings of chives from the roof garden, the aroma now fully of rabbit stew with carrots, onions, the white of a leek, garlic, thyme, all from the roof garden, and rosemary too. A small dish of chopped parsley was at the ready, but no guest had arrived. Sadly, Figeard was fingering that empty bottle of Château Latour, the half of which had generously been shared last December on just such a return from visiting an ill mother in Rethel.

'Inspector . . . ?'

Touching the lips would urge caution. 'Please, a moment. I may have been followed.'

'It was only that boy from the cathedral. More candle stubs and questions of where Annette-Mélanie is and why she hasn't returned to bring him more of that rosemary. I've sent him away twice and have told him funerals take time, and that the house, it would have had to be closed up and left for her mother's attorney to sell, but he pays no attention. Instead, he tells me subdeacons, which is what he is, must decide whether to marry or not *before* being made deacons, and that afterward it is forbidden, but he hardly knows her. Annette-Mélanie has never spoken to me of him in that way and would have. Me, I would have seen it in her eyes and smile. *Bien sûr*, he has taken her to dinner at Chez Kornilov with his father early last February and then again more recently, but for him to be asking her to marry and she to be agreeing, it's just not possible.'

'The boy who prepares the incense?'

'*Oui*. The one who then feeds the censers and lights their little charcoal fires. Annette-Mélanie and myself do manage to grow some on the roof, but rosemary, it likes the heat and dryness. Even under the bell jars we have had but a modest success.'

'His name, just for the record.'

'Pierre-Alexandre Lebeznikov. I have it here. I made him write it down so that I could inform her of it correctly.'

The son of Serge de Lenz and not one but *two* meals across the road!

'Chief Inspector, what has she done? Come, come, you return at this hour and suggest you may have been followed? You still have that in hand, or had you forgotten?'

Tucking the Lebel away, there was, he knew, only one thing he could do despite the risk. 'Since I must take you into my confidence, I must ask that you tell no one of my visit.'

Or visits. 'Since she has been like a daughter to me, how could I not agree? Now, please, what on earth has she done to cause such as yourself to take interest in her: obtained rosemary for religious purposes from one of the gardeners at the Jardin des Plantes?'

The things one learned. 'Accidentally witnessed the murder of two bank employees and the partial robbery of their van.'

Yet there had been no news of such in any of the papers. 'Partial? Me, I will go upstairs with you since it is her room you wish to search, is it?'

Having missed a little something on the last visit—was this what Figeard was now thinking? 'Just stay where you are and stop any who might attempt to follow.'

'Unless there's a concert, I lock that side door at dusk and am just a little late this evening.'

The artists then having to ring for him. 'Then lock it and leave me to do what I have to, but tell me this: You mentioned part-time positions as an usherette here and as a salesperson at the German bookstore. Did Mademoiselle Jacqueline Lemaire happen to have anything to do with getting her those jobs?'

Since a beautiful dress, shoes and expensive underthings had been delivered to *that* address last year on 14 August by a shoe salesman. 'And the job every other Sunday afternoon at Madame Bordeaux's residence on the rue de la Boétie?'

And circles within circles. 'Yes, that one too.'

'Those shoes, though brand new and very expensive, didn't quite fit as they should have.'

'So you suggested she stuff some newspaper into the toes that fortunately weren't of the open style?'

There was no need to give the chief inspector the name of the paper or its date. 'Annette-Mélanie had never had anything so good as that dress, those shoes and the pearls.'

'What pearls?'

And sudden interest. 'The necklace she'd been given on loan.'

'By whom?'

And yet more interest. 'Mademoiselle Lemaire. There was also a bracelet of diamonds from Cartier. Of course Annette-Mélanie could not possibly accept such a loan. She said she would be terrified of losing them. Madame Bordeaux offered to keep them for her so that they could then be worn only at the Sunday gatherings.'

Diamonds and pearls, and with Jacqueline Lemaire and Hector Bolduc present. Hermann wouldn't hesitate. He would simply say, If you hadn't been so preoccupied using the cameras of the mind on your *first* visit, you'd have thought to ask Figeard about those jobs and all the rest.

The suite was magnificent, felt Évangéline. Never had she seen anything like it, and turning to Herr Kohler as he tipped the porter, thought to throw her arms about him but already he was indicating what he had arranged. Beyond the entrance room with its mirror, vase of flowers, stand for coats and place for walking sticks and umbrellas, there was the *salle de séjour* with a carpet so thick one wanted only to walk barefoot. Sofas, settees and armchairs seemed at every turn, a desk, too, with writing things. A liquor cabinet on little wheels had such a selection, the glasses for every sort of drink and all of crystal. There was a cocktail shaker and an ice bucket with tongs.

Attentive, Herr Kohler's generous smile said that he was delighted by her every reaction. In the bedroom, there was a mirrored armoire that would tell no lies and another facing the bed that would tell none of its own, either.

'There's also an *en suite,*' he said.

Bath, lavabo and bidet had their own room in white tiles and with towels, the bidet something she had seen only in torn catalogue pages used for somewhat the same but outdoors, of course. 'It even has hot water,' she heard herself saying.

'Real soap, too,' he said, letting her catch the scent. 'Soap like it used to be. Perfumes too. Samples. Lanvin's Mon Péché.'

He had chosen My Sin.

'The *parfumeurs* are still very much in business,' he said. 'Coco Chanel's shop still sells Chanel No. 5 and all the other things her firm makes, but she's decided to retreat a little and has holed up in the Hôtel Ritz with her German lover. Remember to try them all and when your visit's over, tuck a few into your purse. Guests always do. It's expected. The toilet paper, too, and the soap.'

There was no question Herr Kohler was used to such places and would know exactly what to do with a girl like herself, but first she would have to 'freshen up.'

'Check out the rest of the suite,' he said. 'Pack away your things. Just give me a few minutes to settle something, then we'll go down for a drink in the Bristol's lounge, or have one here.'

Évangéline would keep for the moment. Louis was going to

need all the help he could get, himself as well, and there was only one place and way to get it: give Mrs Florence Gould exactly what every arch-socialite desired the most. Gossip none of the others had, something new to talk about, but for later.

Diminutive, with soft brown eyes and long lashes, her uniform grey-blue and complete with white lace-trimmed cap and apron, Mademoiselle Beauchamp was not quite seventeen but probably thirty in experience. 'Is this the residence of Mrs. Florence Gould, the American who constantly avoids arrest and being interned in the camp for foreign nationals at Vittel's Parc Thermal?' he asked. 'The one who pays her way out of it but should be with every other American woman and girl over eighteen and locked up as in the autumn of 1942 along with all the British females, too, those who hadn't escaped when the Occupation first started in June 1940 and were summarily arrested then?'

Ah mon Dieu, mon Dieu, they had arrested Madame, felt Yvette, and would now arrest herself and the others, Madame Volnée as well.

'Hey, go easy, eh? Easy. I only need her help with the murder investigation my partner and I are working on.'

'A murder? In this hotel?'

'Not here, elsewhere, but perhaps if I were to come in, I could explain things in confidence.'

He had even looked both ways along the corridor to see if anyone else was listening. Like so many of *les Allemands*, he was big and tall but also wore the slash of the fencing sword from the left eye to chin. *Formidable*, Madame would have said of him. *Monté comme un étalon aussi.* 'Your name, please? Madame, she will insist.'

'Oh, sorry. Kohler, Kripo, Paris-Central. A detective inspector.'

And a womanizer but also one of Gestapo Boemelburg's men, that one having been to several of Madame's Thursday lunches, his people constantly listening in to madame's telephone calls. Those of others, too, both staff and guests.

'Mademoiselle Beauchamp, let me have your first name. It'll be easier.'

This 'Kripo' had closed the door behind himself and had even put the lock on. Well, one of them. 'Yvette.'

'Good. That's a lovely name and one I won't forget. Yvette,

we're after the killer of two bank employees. Apparently he had his mistress with him, for she left her shoes behind in the bank van he then robbed with the others of his gang. All the press need is a photo of something like those shoes, and me, I thought Madame Gould might have a pair and be only too willing to oblige.'

A gang, a killer and a mistress, a moll, *une nana de gangster.* 'Is it that you are hoping someone will come forward who saw something?'

Maybe she wasn't as 'old' as he'd thought. 'Detectives have to try everything.'

Yet he didn't have the shoes, only the memory of them. 'And the reward, *Monsieur l'Inspecteur*, does it include a little something for such assistance?'

Lieber Gott, had the Occupation corrupted her too? 'Five thousand for the loan of the shoes, ten if I don't manage to get them back to you.'

He had a thick wad of those notes. 'Back to my mistress, wasn't it?'

Louis should have heard her. 'Fifteen, then.'

Three big ones and she would stuff them down her front since that was what he would be expecting. 'The shoes, they are this way, Inspector.'

In a suite of rooms upon rooms with floor-to-ceiling damask curtains and paintings, sketches and pieces of sculpture, knick-knacks too, Florence Gould had one reserved for the clothes she wore, and in it, a wall of shoes and a pair probably for every day of the year.

'Perhaps if you were to tell me what was needed, Inspector, I could find them, since one of my jobs is to look after these and I might, I confess, have misplaced a pair under her bed or behind a settee or armoire, she having kicked them off in a hurry with one of her lovers.'

And a treasure. The shoes were perfect. Neither too big, nor too small, equally expensive and of but a slightly lighter shade of blue.

'Will Madame really have her name splashed in the papers?'

'Certainly. Invaluable assistance like this is always acknowledged. That encourages others to come forward.'

'Then if the shoes, they are not returned, madame she will remain pleased and grateful.'

A further 5,000–franc note was found. 'Just don't tell her until after the news breaks that we've finally apprehended the killer.'

'And the others also, *n'est-ce pas*, especially the mistress?'

Jésus merde alors was another 5,000-franc note being demanded? 'Them, too, but what's that scent you're wearing?'

That such a one should ask such a thing could only mean a tenderness hidden. 'Guerlain's Coque d'Or. Madame, she will wear no other. It's her signature and therefore that of myself and all the others, even Madame Volnée, so as to avoid any conflict.'

And the phial shaped like two truncated eggs standing side by side in gold with black covers and the central stopper in gold and bearing the name at the bottom, the design by Baccarat probably in the late 1930s.

Herr Kohler even held the phial as if what it contained was definitely appreciated.

'That partner of mine, Yvette, thinks he's an expert. Take any perfume and all he needs is a whiff to pin it down. Rose absolute, jasmine, clary sage and you name it. Splash a little on a white handkerchief, preferably one with a bit of embroidery. Tulips and daffodils, that sort of thing, and let me see if he's right.'

She would press the flat of her hand against the left side of his chest and would look up into those faded, lying blue eyes of his. 'Then that must, I'm afraid, be entirely one of my own.'

And yet another 5,000-franc note.

'Are those the shoes Eugène found in that bank van?' asked Évangéline.

'They are, but I thought you had better have a good look at them just to be sure. Try them on. Maybe they really do fit.'

The room in the Salle Pleyel building was as before, felt St-Cyr, its austerity all the more evident since the risk of doing anything was far too great. By simply taking Concierge Figeard into his confidence, he had already placed not only Giselle and Oona at far greater risk, but Gabrielle too, and all who were close to them, Hermann as well, and Chantal and Muriel. Every linkage Annette-Mélanie Veroche had forged said emphatically that she had to have been, and still was, no doubt, affiliated with an FTP *équipe* or some other such Résistance group. Help given on first arrival in Paris, false papers and all the rest, in exchange for help demanded. Watch, listen and report all you hear and see, and go back time and again. Ingratiate yourself and find out all you can.

And yet no one in that *équipe* could really know her true self nor what she had hidden. He would have to say it softly, as if she was with him. 'Kriminalrat Ludin is under huge pressure, mademoiselle, and will have no other choice than to call in reinforcements. Hermann and myself have no intention of telling him anything, but it's only a matter of time until Sergei Lebeznikov, on seeing one of those twenty-by-twenty photos of you from the Hague, tumbles to who he and his son have been taking to dinner. You will, unfortunately, have made a laughingstock of him, something both he and Rudy de Mérode will definitely not appreciate.'

If left on the bed in full view, the shoes would immediately cause her to grab that cardboard suitcase and head for the roof, pausing only to recover the nougat tin.

If left in the armoire with the dress, the same. Indeed, no matter what he did here, she would still head for that tin since Concierge Figeard, though trying hard not to indicate such, would inadvertently, through gesture or word, let her know there had been a visitor. But perhaps it was that she would never be allowed to return here even if that *passeur* did manage to get her into Paris, since that Dutch *mouchard* would stay far too close to her and would have to.

Frans hadn't backed off, felt Anna-Marie. As soon as she had come downstairs to supper in the kitchen, he had been waiting for her, surrounded by its everyday warmth and welcoming aromas. Sensing discord, Madame de Belleveau had insisted that Frans was to sit next to herself at the far end of the table to give as much distance as possible, but Frans was far too quick and took Étienne's place. Not even asking, he uncorked *le rouge* and filled her glass. '*Salut!*' he said. No grin, no smile, just: Say anything and see what happens.

The *potage parisien*, that standby of every French household, whether on the farm or not, reminded her of home so much, she felt like bursting into tears. She *couldn't* let Frans betray them but he was watching her far too closely. Was it fear that what was troubling him, though he had the only gun, or was it that he simply saw her as someone in the theatre with whom to compete? Oh for sure, to succeed as he had, talent had been needed, but that alone would not have been enough. The ability to lie convincingly would have been necessary, the twisting of things said or done, the denigrating of others whenever possible. 'He's good, that boy,' Papa had said of him, 'but I pity the women he encounters.'

Salome, Herod's daughter, and Herodias, that one's wife.

When Arie arrived, he set her walking shoes on the floor beside her and with but the flash of an engagingly mischievous grin, said, 'They might hold up, but you never can tell with shoes. One lace will break when you've already tied two knots. Then the other one goes, or a seam will split, or a heel come off just when you're racing to catch a bus or get to a film.'

He had even polished them and had made replacement laces out of leather thongs he'd worked on to get them to match the rest and not look too out of place even though lots in Paris were having to wear far worse.

'No more *Klompen*, eh?' quipped Frans.

'Arie, *merci bien*. They're perfect.' He had even cut insoles out of felt. Always he was doing something useful, had sawn and split lots of stove wood for Madame and would probably like nothing better than to work the land she must have leased to another who hadn't needed the barns and farmyard that were well behind the *potager*.

They would eat and when it came on, listen to the nine o'clock news from the BBC in London, the wireless secreted in a cupboard behind things, the aerial strung only for those times. The penalty, prison of course, or death.

The soup was perfect. 'Some chopped chives, perhaps,' her father would have said. 'A little of the *goudse boerenkaas*. Just a slice or two to nibble on and stop us from slurping too much.' The farmers' gouda, the *edammer kaas* as well.

She couldn't let it happen. She mustn't.

The chicken was superb, the sautéed potatoes Arie's favourite as they would have been her father's. He even cleaned the frying pan with a bit of bread, she herself having failed entirely to have touched her wine. 'You sure are worrying,' he said. 'It's completely understandable, but we *will* get you into Paris and I'll see that one of the bikes in the back has a Paris licence.'

And no tag stating that it, and the others, had been requisitioned by the Occupier in Liege, and then stolen from them. There were a dozen, but also ten-kilo bags of roasted, ground Belgian chicory root for coffee substitute, Ardennes hams, chocolates, pipe and cigarette tobacco, Trappist beer from Chimay, too, and the flat, round cheeses of those monks, eggs in water glass as well and lots of other things. 'Arie . . .'

'Let me have a look at that hand.'

He even ran a forefinger gently over the stitches.

'Maybe another day, maybe two, but when they're ready, I'll gladly tease them out and you won't feel a thing.'

It was Frans who said, 'That was touching but maybe he wants a little more.'

'Leave it,' said Étienne. 'It's almost time for the news.'

There was static, the Boche always trying to block reception, but Arie managed to tune things in and at once, having never heard it before in France, that call-sign of '*Ici Londres*,' filled her with hope. But in the Aegean, the Germans had taken the island of Kos, the only Allied airbase in that area. In Russia, the Soviet advance had been stalled along what had to be the longest of fronts. And in Italy, while the British had taken Naples and their commandos had landed at Termoli and would soon link up with their Eighth Army, the American Fifth had reached the southern bank of the Volturno River fifteen miles to the north where a major battle was shaping up along what the Germans called their Gustav Line. The Sixteenth Panzer Division had been moved into position.

In the Battle for the Atlantic, after a respite due to losses, the U-boats were again attacking the convoys from America and Canada. In September alone, twenty-nine merchant ships and escort vessels had been sunk with a loss of 156,400 tonnes of badly needed supplies and far too many lives. Worse still, the U-boats were now concentrating on the escort vessels first, but nine of those submarines had been sent to the bottom, 'And with good riddance,' Mr. Churchill said. 'Desperately needed air bases in the Azores will now be available, the Portugese having finally agreed to this.'

In the Far East, the Japanese had established a broad offensive in China, but on Kolombangara, in the Solomon Islands, American forces had found they had fled. Four airfields had been taken. Bougainville, the largest of those islands and last major Japanese stronghold there would now be next and difficult.

But in Corsica, after an armed civilian uprising on 8 September, French partisans, Morrocan Goumiers and American OSS agents had finally driven the Germans out.

'Spring will come,' said Arie as he switched off the set. 'It's just taking its time.'

Unfortunately the invasion of Europe would be far too late for them unless Frans could be stopped. *'Bonne nuit,'* she said. 'Tomorrow will come soon enough.'

'Then don't hurry it,' he quipped, flicking cigarette ash her way. 'Sleep tight. Don't let the bugs bite.'

There was no hope. There could be no hope.

7

In bursts of collective emphasis, noise echoed, the Hôtel George V resounding, felt St-Cyr. To the staid seventeenth- and eighteenth-century decor, art deco pieces from the Boeuf sur le Toit's former location on the rue du Colisée clashed, but no one else seemed to care. At 2120 hours and late for their meeting with Heinrich Ludin, there was still no sign of Hermann. He'd not been in the lobby as agreed. *Merde*, what was one to do? Walk among the crowded tables and ask or simply withdraw?

Waiters hustled the heavy trays or took away the empties, while thick on the air and emphasized by the half-light, the tobacco smoke had all but overwhelmed all other scents. Ackerland was on tap, Spaten Dunkel too, and Dortmunder Union, each glass or stein overflowing.

'There's even Einbeck Dunkel, Louis, and a Bock and Double Bock I'd recommend. The Führer may not like it that this brasserie of choice hasn't been shut down as ordered, but he sure does know his boys like their beer. It's flown in every day or sent by rail.'

'Hermann . . .'

So popular had the Boeuf sur le Toit been to the avant-garde and Bohemian wealthy of the Roaring Twenties, its fame had spread and in the autumn of 1940 it had immediately been adopted by the Paris SD, SS and Gestapo.

'You're late,' said Louis.

'I was held up.'

'Which table then?'

'That one at the very back that has two empty chairs facing the life-size bronze nude from the former location.'

Svelte and on tiptoes with uplifted breasts, the nymph had one arm extended high above her to release a dove of peace.

'The table with what look to be two *Grosskotzkerls*,' said Hermann, 'but don't be fooled, not by those two.'

The big vomit boys, those who, like Reichsmarschall Göring, would eat and eat. Both sinister, and like him in that as well. 'Berlin must have sent them.'

'Kaltenbrunner, I think.'

'God always frowns, Hermann, but our *garde champêtre* is taking the soup as if a last meal. *Ah bon*, he's afraid of what I might well do to him.'

'Just don't mention the shoes.'

'The *what?*'

'The ones he wanted for Évangéline.'

She of the plunging neckline, radiantly beatific and licentious smile, and the drenchings of one of Lanvin's latest.

'It's called Mon Péché,' said Hermann.

And on a first-name basis with her too. 'Me, I think I understand.'

'You'd better.'

Uniforms were everything to the Occupier, no matter how humble the station, felt St-Cyr. To the basic Luftwaffe blue of these two had been added the stiff-collared walking-out white shirt, black tie and vest, all of which indicated that they were Göring's. One even wore the *Deutsche Jägerschaft* badge of the hunting association and medals to prove deer had been shot and killed at exceptional range, the other no doubt fiercely jealous. Both, however, wore the party's golden badge of honour and red armband with white circle and gold-lined black swastika, indicating that Hitler also had a definite claim to them.

'Uniforms tell you only so much, Louis. They may even hate each other.'

Party functionaries and dyed-in-the-wool Nazis.

Neither bothered to even look up from the oysters in the half, the *pâté*, bread and wine. Indeed only Rocheleau seemed to have noticed their arrival and that of his wife. Having dropped his spoon and splashed his uniform, he had knocked over the glass of the red, which was now finding its way to his trousers. 'Évangéline . . .'

'Eugène, *mon cher, mon brave*.'

Kisses of repentance were necessary—was it really repentance?

wondered St-Cyr. Joyously the woman trailed trembling hands over that husband of hers while Ludin, having quickly downed yet another shot of the stomach bitters, gazed leadenly at them and said, 'Sit,' but in Deutsch, of course.

It was Hermann who dragged from his coat pockets a pair of shoes to ask, 'Would these be what you're looking for, Kriminalrat?'

'Eugène, *mon cher*, they're a little tight but it was wonderful of you to have risked so much for me, the young girl you married fifteen years, seven months and four days ago.'

'Those . . . Those, they are . . .'

'Beautiful and me, I would love to have them anyway. Dancing will loosen them up. Dancing in Paris, Eugène.'

'It's not allowed. It's against the law.'

'But there are lots of places where it does happen. French musicians and their ensembles play nothing but the latest tunes. Hermann took me to one. "Douce Georgette" is by Joseph Reinhardt and his ensemble, but Hermann, he says the piece, it is really called "Sweet Georgia Brown." "Irene," it is terrific, too, and very dreamy. André Ekyan and his ensemble do it marvellously. "Palm Beach" as well, and Monsieur Hubert Rostaing's clarinet, it is just as good as Monsieur Benny Goodman's in the "Saint Louis Blues" or was it "Smoke Gets in Your Eyes"? No, that one was Tommy Dorsey and his orchestra. A trombone, I think.'

Hermann loved to dance and listen to the Voice of America whenever possible, and he did like such music as did those ensembles, and of course they played in clubs and bars and even held outdoor concerts the Occupier also loved, though all of it was *verboten*.

'Tell the slut to shut up,' said Ludin to the husband who was now trying to claim the shoes he'd found had been of a darker shade.

'Eugène, *mon cher*, they are exactly the ones you told me of. The imprint, it says so. Hanan, wasn't it? Hanan of New York, at 43 avenue de l'Opéra.'

And no longer there since the Führer in his wisdom had declared war on the Americans on 4 December 1941.

'Are those the shoes?' grunted Ludin, clutching at a spasm that must have wrenched his gut.

'What else would they be,' said Louis in Deutsch, 'since they came from my coat pockets and we save everything we can from every case we have to investigate and this one, if I must remind you, is still very much a murder inquiry and not some circus.'

'Rocheleau, you idiot,' said Ludin, 'take that slut and get her out of here. Go home to where you belong.'

Somehow they understood.

'But first a little visit,' said the master of ceremonies, tucking three or four big ones into the woman's hand, she giving him a kiss on the cheek and the playfully lingering touch of her tongue.

Ludin lost all patience. 'These gentlemen have come all the way from Berlin to talk to you, Kohler, so you had damned well better listen.'

Blitheness was called for. 'And are they aware that you've a *Spitzel* aboard that *gazo*, one whose presence you've already advertised enough without having them come all that way?'

'One that may well need your help, is it, Kohler?'

'Hermann, let's hear what they have to say when they've finished eating.'

Unknown to her, for sure, Anna-Marie had just brought down the wrath of the Reich on them, felt Kohler, and reaching for the empty bottles, held two up for one of the waiters.

'Ah, the Châteauneuf-du-Pape, the 1921, Hermann. Of course, neither Herr Ludin nor these gentlemen could have known that after the Great War, the market was flooded by fake bottles of it, so much so that Baron Pierre le Roy de Boiseaumarie led a campaign to safeguard the name and his own. Ask for the Châtau Latour. Any year you like, but let's drink a toast to their health.'

And to that of Anna-Marie Vermeulen.

Frans was in the room and at the bed. He had given her an hour and a half to get to sleep and was now going through her pockets to find that coin and her papers. He had to know the name she was using in Paris.

Unable to find either, she heard him draw in an exasperated breath and then gingerly slide a hand under her pillow and her head. There . . . there . . . have you found them now, Frans? Have you?

Quickly leaving, he softly eased the door closed, but now if they *did* manage to get into Paris, she would have to make him follow her, for only then could Étienne, Arie and Martine be saved, since he must tell no one else *anything* until he had been forced to tell the right ones everything.

To the Boeuf sur le Toit, felt St-Cyr, there was nothing but increased noise and laughter, to this table with its two visitors from Berlin and Heinrich Ludin, but the desperate. All three seemed to be waiting for something or someone. Hermann *had* explained their having followed that truck's route to its link-up with the bank van and murders, but Ludin, sour and troubled as always, had been far from satisfied, the others simply belligerent.

'*Eine Halbjüdin?*' swore Ulrich Frensel. '*Eine Mischlinge,* Kohler?' Angrily, he stabbed an already loaded fork into the braised red cabbage that accompanied the roast pork and potatoes he'd been devouring. 'Are you and that *verfluchte Franzose* telling me that you know nothing useful yet and are letting a *verdammte Hure* get the better of a person such as myself? *Die Schlampe* will be stripped naked, I tell you! *Naked,* Kohler!' He jerked a butcher-size thumb back to indicate the bronze behind him. 'All questions will be answered. If not, I will personally see that she shits through her nose.'

Liebe Zeit, was he about to have a heart attack? wondered St-Cyr. Red in the normally florid and fleshy cheeks with double chin and brew-master nose, Frensel knuckle-wiped the Führer-like moustache that went with the haircut before lowering that fist to stab the fork in again.

'The black diamonds, Kohler,' seethed the other one, slab-faced and dark-eyed, and with the *boeuf bourguignon* and side dishes of caramelized onions and braised chestnuts. 'She *knows* where they are, I tell you! That filthy *Schweinhund* Meyerhof *told* her. That is *why* we had to let her run. That is *why* this *Sonderkommando!*'

And wouldn't you know it, thought Kohler, the myth of the so-called black diamonds, and both of these two from Berlin in on it but hating each other.

'*Ach*, this other one is Johannes Uhl, Louis, and none other than the person who almost single-handedly during the Blitzkrieg captured 940,000 carats of rough industrials, so pleasing the Führer that he . . .'

A long-fingered, agitated fork-hand was acidly raised for silence, sauce dribbling. '*Bitte, mein Lieber. Bitte.* There were an additional 290,000 carats of Congo cubes and other industrials I personally took off Belgian vessels in Antwerp's harbour. The Führer . . .'

'Was ecstatic, Louis, and gave him this medal and a photo spread in *Signal.*'*

Having leaned over the clutter, Hermann pressed a forefinger to one of the awards, and turning away as if to ignore it, said to the other visitor, 'And you must be in charge of gem diamonds. Herr Uhl of the industrials is from Frankfurt, Louis, where on the day we started this investigation, the RAF and USAAF did a round-the-clock, levelling a good part of the city and leaving more than 500 dead.

'Herr Frensel, is from Münster where, on 6 July 1941, and in *three* nights, that same RAF flattened a good quarter of the city, so like our Kriminalrat, they both have that added reason for wanting us to solve this mess they've created.'

Shock brought silence and then from Ludin, not looking up from the vichyssoise that had finally been set before him, 'As does Reichssicherheitchef Kaltenbrunner, Kohler.'

There could be no smile, felt Frensel. Instead, he would simply spear a chunk of pork and offer it to this *verfluchte* Kripo who was nothing but trouble. 'In Berlin, *mein Lieber*, though a million have been evacuated, we who are left still pray for the zoo to be hit. Lion testicles in a sauce perhaps, or elephant teats in their cream—it's said to be very rich. Some maintain that the giraffe will be stringy and must be tenderized by pounding as we do the war bread we are now having to eat with the turnips instead of potatoes; others that when plucked, stuffed and roasted, the ostrich will be a bit gamey, but a meal to walk on its legs. I believe, and you can correct me if I am wrong which I seldom am, St-Cyr, but didn't the population of Paris eat their zoo animals during the Franco-Prussian War we most certainly won?'

'The boa constrictors were said to be tasty. Grand-mère always swore that her portion was exquisite, like eel served with mustard, so, too, the Indian cobra, but fortunately without the poison sacks.'

Ach, gut, he had finally got their attention, thought Frensel. 'I,

---

* Hitler's picture magazine.

too, have received such a medal and commendation—five of them to be precise. In the Netherlands alone, Kohler, and well after having relieved those diamond firms and traders of all they said they had, you understand, I took from those held for transit at Westerbork and Vught more than 250 million guilders of gem diamonds.'

Even at 10 guilders to the pound sterling, that was still 25 million pounds and Louis would have figured it out too.

'Or at 4.4 American dollars to the pound, Hermann, about 110 million dollars or roughly now on the black bourse, at let's say 100 French francs to the dollar, 11 billion francs.'

'And more than enough, eh, to pay the Reich the 500 million a day they are now demanding in reparations, which are then, of course, immediately used to buy up all the loose diamonds and other things on offer.'

'You'd be surprised where some of those *Schweinhunde* thought to hide such things,' said Frensel, ripping off a chunk of baguette to mop up juices. 'A specimen of no name, but bare and bent over the table, had 187 carats up the one and 356 up the other, and both coming out her eyes.'

Oona and Giselle were at the mercy of such, Chantal and Muriel, too, and Gabi but neither Louis nor himself could dwell on this. They had to push these two and Ludin to get what they could before it was too late. 'And you've been keeping the traders in Lisbon, Madrid and Zurich happy, have you?' he asked Frensel.

The laugh was rich and full, felt St-Cyr, for Reichsmarschall Göring had insisted on fencing such stones, the Reich desperately needing foreign exchange and gold, since few, if any, countries would accept Reichsmark. 'Tungsten from Portugal and Spain, Hermann. Watches, microscopes and other precision instruments from the Swiss. Ball bearings, too, and machine tools.'

'Guns, Louis, even those on the Messerschmitt ME 109s that fired the cannon shells Oona and her husband and children had to dodge during the exodus. But the Swiss do need our coal to keep warm and to run things, so fair's fair and we'd better not question the matter.'

'Wolframite, Kohler,' said Johannes Uhl, sucking on a tooth.

'The name tungsten goes by,' said Frensel, stabbing a potato to slice off a morsel to add to the cabbage. 'Tungsten carbide is next to diamond in hardness and it, and its steels, if I may say so, are fast replacing many of the uses of industrial diamonds and putting certain people out of work. Grinding powders, Kohler. Grinding wheels, too, and wire-drawing dies. All formerly done by using industrial diamonds. I personally have it on the best of authority—the Reichsmarschall himself, you understand—that the Luftwaffe are having great success with tungsten-carbide, armour-piercing shells. Instantly they destroy the Russian T-34 tanks, making the Soviets shit themselves.'

'But . . . but there isn't nearly enough of it,' interjected Uhl, lifting the spoon he had taken to using on the sauce. 'The supply is vastly limited and the cost astronomical, especially when smuggled into France and shipped to the Reich. Wolframite concentrate's price just keeps shooting up and up and now fetches more than 130,000 Swiss francs a tonne, so the industrial diamonds I attend to still have a very definite place in our war industries.'

'An iron, manganese tungstate, Hermann, containing the industry-accepted sixty percent tungsten oxide. The British own some of the mines in those supposedly neutral countries of Spain and Portugal, and as a result it often has to be carried in sacks on the back and sometimes across not one but two borders at night and in the rain if lucky.'

'Or if you wish it,' went on Uhl, '28,886 American dollars, so you can, I trust, understand why the Reichsmarschall, who is also my friend and superior officer, requires what that girl knows and is carrying.'

And yet more information, felt St-Cyr, knowing Hermann would have felt the same.

Timidly dipping a crust into the vichyssoise, Ludin thought to sample it. Instead, he reached for the bitters and said, 'Josef Meyerhof also gave her, and this we know, Kohler, his family's life diamonds.'

He having had to cough up the information probably. 'And knowing this, even though you and that no-name SD colonel had a *Spitzel* aboard who left dribbles of coins for you to follow, you let her leave Amsterdam?'

'We had to wait until Meyerhof's contact person was finished dealing with her,' said Ludin.

'But by then she was already on her way?'

'In a stolen Wehrmacht truck, but this we did not learn of until later.'

'And in another note left for you by that *Spitzel*?'

'The first such note, yes, but one that I didn't leave with the coins for that Jew-lover Oona of yours to find.'

'Louis, that's why all the so-called secrecy. That's why it hasn't kept Rudy de Mérode and his gang from trying to follow us everywhere we go. That *was* Sergei Lebeznikov who just ducked into the kitchens, wasn't it?'

After having had a good look at who had come all the way from Berlin. 'He'll be asking the waiters if anything further can be added to what he has already discovered, Hermann.'

'They and the other *gestapistes français* must be wanting a share, or maybe even all of it if they can get to her first.'

Lenz and Mérode could well be useful, thought Ludin. 'Meyer-hof was director of the Amsterdam protection committee, Kohler. As such, he had the names and locations of all those they had black-listed for selling to the Reich. He also made frequent trips to Paris before and even right up to and into the Blitzkrieg, so would have had plenty of opportunity to illegally bring diamonds here to hide.'

'Thousands and thousands of carats, Kohler. Gems—industrials, too, of course,' said Frensel, having shoved his plates aside to rest forearms on the table, hands clasped tightly. Big hands, swastika knuckle-dusters in gold too.

'Millions,' said Uhl. 'I personally have uncovered the lies in the record books of all such firms. Each paper of high quality industrials, each packet or cloth bag, was to have been weighed and recorded, you understand, but many were not and I have recovered thousands they attempted to hide from me.'

Taking out a silver toothpick, Frensel went to work as he said, 'As I have myself, Kohler. Those diamond Jews were a close lot. All decisions were done in committee and no one else was ever allowed in, but no longer, of course. Now we have put a stop to it and to them.'

'There was a handkerchief,' said Ludin, having shoved the soup aside. 'A bit of childhood embroidery. This has not been mentioned, Kohler. Why is that, please?'

Rocheleau must have told him everything and some. Dismayed by the request, Louis had begun to fish about in his coat pockets. Laying the empty cartridge casings on the table, he then found the slugs only to go back for more.

'*Ach*, I have it, Chief,' said Kohler. 'It was drenched and I simply shoved it away. Perfume, but I can't tell which. Maybe you can.'

And a 'breather,' as the Americans used to say in that other war. 'It's called Sleeping, Hermann. It's one of Schiaparelli's. Very delicate, very feminine, and indicative of its user but not as decisively so as Molinelle's No. 29 or Muriel's Mirage.'

'But will it help to lead us to her if she does manage to get past the controls and into Paris?'

'Ah, one never knows, does one, *mon vieux*?' said Louis, quickly pocketing it. 'Even the smallest of things can open up an investigation. One tries. One simply never gives up and it is, after all this talk of diamonds, still very much a murder investigation. Gestapo Boemelburg has ordered us to find the killer of those two bank employees, *meine Herren*, Osias Pharand as well.'

'My boss and his,' said Hermann. 'Herr Uhl, to give us some idea of what is really involved, what's the current price of the lowest grade of industrial diamond?'

And on the *schwarzer Markt* where all such things were bought and sold. 'Boart is at 450 guilders a carat, having gone up from three in the summer of 1940 and just before the Blitzkrieg.'

'So in round figures a kilo would be worth what?' asked Hermann.

'In Reichskassenscheine about 2.25 million,' said Uhl.

The Occupation marks, and at twenty to one in France, about 45 million francs, or 1 million dollars or 225,000 pounds sterling.

'She was a borderline sorter, Kohler,' said Ludin, 'and will not only know of the value but which stones are roughly equal, either as gems or industrials.'

'A half-and-half sorting out those that are half-and-half, Louis. Either one or the other.'

'Ah here, at last, is Standartenführer Gerhard Kleiber,' said Uhl, jumping to his feet to raise an arm in salute.

'Who?' exclaimed Hermann.

'Exactly,' said Frensel, having also leaped up to salute.

'And the one, Louis, from the Warsaw ghetto uprising of April and May. The one who, under Brigadeführer Jürgen Stroop, who thought it would be all over in a day or two and not three weeks, volunteered to flush the last of the recalcitrants from the sewers.'

Kleiber didn't waste time or words. In rain-spattered cap and open grey topcoat, with Iron Cross First Class at the throat, Close-Combat Clasp in gold on the chest and silver Wound Badge for three or four, he slapped a letter down in front of Hermann and said, 'Read it to that "partner" of yours.'

Verdammt! felt Kohler. Lebeznikov was watching from the kitchen doors. Kaltenbrunner had signed and dated the letter, and had furiously stamped it with everything the Reichssicherheitshauptamt had including, in red wax, his signet ring. 'Flown in from Berlin, Louis. It seems we're now members of this *Sonderkommando* and are to be made a party to all of its secrets. If anyone, including that one who has just vanished out the back door of the kitchen, should try to horn in on things and stop us, all we have to do is show them this.'

Tree-lined and pleasant in the morning's growing light, with mist rising off the nearby Seine, the turning leaves of the avenue Foch gave impressionistic touches to those of the Bois de Boulogne. Behind the wheel for a change, St-Cyr told himself they should see it as it once was. After all, it could well be their last time.

Funnelled by the wide and beautiful avenue, the view rose gradually and magnificently to the more distant, wooded hills of the Fort Mont-Valérien, in Suresnes, and those of the suburb of Saint-Cloud. 'October is surely Paris's month, Hermann. Haussmann, as you can see, must have had this in mind when he laid out the avenue in 1854. A triumph, isn't it?'

'That fort's the main execution ground and those woods around it hide the hurriedly dumped corpses of far too many, as you well know, so please don't forget it. This summons has to mean trouble.'

Hermann had had a bad night. 'Maman was not overly tall, nor was Grand-mère. Their feet never extended beyond the foot of that bed, nor have my own.'

At 0646 the old time, 0846 the new, had come the fist-pounding, at 3 Rue Laurence-Savart in the 20th. It was now 0859 hours, Monday, 4 October.

Number eighty-four didn't hold the office of Brigadeführer und Generalmajor der Polizei/Höherer SS und Polizeiführer of France Karl Oberg, the butcher of Poland. That was at number seventy-two, but number eighty-four was also on the north side and just before the boulevard Lannes and the *place* Dauphine.˙ Though there was but a scattering of cars, all of the Occupier, one ancient hackney gave momentary thoughts of the *belle époque* whose sumptuous mansions these houses had once been, the street internationally famous. Indeed, the Palais Rose was at number fifty.

'Stop daydreaming!' said Hermann, longing for a fag.

'*Ach, Inspektor*, had you taken the time to notice, you would have seen that the *Standartenführer*'s temporary office is on the second floor.'

'That was him at the windows holding a Schmeisser and satchel of ammo while watching for us, was it?'

'Death in the offing by piano wire, is it, for having kept things from him and Herr Ludin?'

The office was in what had once been the billiards and smoking room. Firmly pressing a nicotine-stained forefinger down on the green baize and on Queen Wilhelmina's head, a disgruntled Kriminalrat shoved a coin toward them.

'When and where?' managed Kohler, picking it up and passing it to Louis.

'The Porte de Versailles at 0810,' said Kleiber, watching them closely.

Three of Bolduc's bank vans also used that entrance, as did a certain Werner Dillmann. 'But not arrested?'

'Half the load in payment as usual, I gather,' said Kleiber.

'The coin having been slipped to some trustworthy who was told to bring it here?'

'And now, since I have already had the safehouse where she is surrounded, you will soon see how things are done.'

From the avenue Foch to the Gare de l'Est was not far with the colonel at the wheel of his tourer. Serving northeastern France, Belgium, the Netherlands and beyond, there was constant activity: Wehrmacht trucks and men in plenty with duffel bags and rucksacks, staff cars, too, and *gazogènes*, buses, horse-drawn wagons, *vélos* and *vélo-taxis* and plenty of citizens with suitcases, some even with sacks of potatoes. To the west of the station, St-Cyr knew that along the nearby rue du Faubourg Saint-Denis were shops, cafés

---

* Now the *place* du Portugal and the larger *place* du Maréchal de Lattre de Tassigny.

and restaurants; to the east, where they were now heading, whole-sale garment works, haberdasheries and hosiers, and once off the rue du Faubourg Saint-Martin, rag dealers, stamp mills, machine shops and such.

A captain, an SS Haupsturmführer, crashed his heels together and gave the salute. 'All secured as ordered, Sturmbannführer. Those to be interrogated, waiting.'

The fool, felt Kohler. Under guard and down the street a little were gathered eighty or so from the surrounding flats and ateliers, all of them justifiably enraged and miserable.

The courtyard of 22 rue du Terrage was long and narrow and well chosen, the cheek-by-jowl houses and ateliers on either side of a ground floor and one storey, but a labyrinth. Broken shutters were above the door to a former stable into which that *passeur*'s truck would have been hastily tucked. Outside a carpenter's tin-plated atelier and home, salvaged lumber stood waiting. Old windows being refurbished were next to a glazier's, metal-work outside another. Bricks in front of a mason's, prevented anyone from easily stealing a chained cement mixer with two flats. Downspouts, electrical cables and wires seemed everywhere, even two old dogs that sensed that things were not quite right and had hidden under a broken bench.

'Totally of the people, Hermann, and not a soul now but ourselves.'

Only at the far end was there any sign of tidiness in flaking paint and bricks that climbed to faded, lace curtains. The courtyard's cast-iron communal tap constantly dripped. Laundry had been strung but could no longer be watched, and to the scent of leather tanning on the Quai de Valmy, came the not-too-distant pounding of a stamp mill.

'A "safehouse," Hermann, the Standartenführer having announced our presence well beforehand.'

All exits sealed. 'But safe for whom?'

'In April, our informant told us of this house, in July, of yet another,' said Kleiber. 'Both have been dealt with.'

'There isn't anyone here, Colonel,' said Hermann. 'The instant those trucks and cars of yours careened into the district, word shot out and the ones we want vanished. *Ach,* this is the tenth, *mein Lieber.* Belleville and Ménilmontant are nearby, La Villette, the largest of the city's abattoirs, but a little to the north.'

The steps were worn, the staircase narrow, the smells as would be expected, felt St-Cyr. Even the concierge, old, miserable and demanding to be left alone, knew little beyond that the owner was still in the south, in the former *zone libre* and that the rent had been paid month by month without question.

'The tenants they came in their truck and they left. Last April it was, the twenty-fourth I think and staying but till the Sunday, or was it the Monday? The memory, you understand. *Bien sûr*, they had items to sell—everyone does these days but me, who am I to question a good tenant when so many try to dodge the rent and wear out the legs, the lungs and the patience? Labrie . . . yes, yes, that was the name. Étienne, I think, but will have it written down, since that *is* the law in these parts, and I would remind you, monsieur, that a magistrate's order is required before anyone searches anything, even one such as yourself!'

It was the same at 34 rue de la Goute-d'Or in the 18th, a deep courtyard with many ateliers, the staircases leading down from the flats above and all lettered through the alphabet. 'Clearly our *Schmuggler* has used another safe house, Colonel,' said St-Cyr, 'but what is not so clear is why your *Spitzel* chose not to tell you of it.'

'Maybe he's had a change of plan,' said Hermann.

Frans was onto her; Frans *was* sticking close, felt Anna-Marie. Having let him steal that coin and her false papers, she had deliberately put herself at his mercy so that he would know he could follow at will because that was the way Frans was. Arrogant, domineering, very sure of himself, flip too, of course, and hopefully overconfident. But what she *hadn't* anticipated was that he would have *needed* a ready excuse to leave the others: her papers. 'Forgotten,' he'd have said, 'left behind in the rush to get away.'

Étienne had been firm. No one was to have left the house at 3 rue Vercingétorix until all was clear and he had checked things with the concierge. Arie had taken a bike from the truck and had asked if its saddle was at the right height and she hadn't waited, had simply hopped on and ridden down the courtyard and out onto the street. Now she pedalled like the damned, but she *couldn't*, *mustn't* lose Frans.

The rue Froidevaux ran alongside the Cimètiere du Montparnasse whose gates were now open. Flowers for the dead were on offer as usual, the Occupier lined up for a look at the famous. At *place* Denfert-Rochereau, the traffic was insane. Bicycles were everywhere and of all types, pedestrians too, for without the cars and trucks, people simply cut across the streets whenever they felt like it, bells ringing madly. But on the boulevard Arago, though still busy, the cumulative sound dropped off—fewer shops and smaller line-ups, more single pedestrians, the Café de la Santé always busy: *flics*, guards, Gestapo, SS and *gestapistes français*. Made to hold 200, the prison held more than 1,500, but she wouldn't look back to see if Frans was still there. She *had* to trust he would, *had* to appear as if taking her life in her hands by being so desperate as to ride along this street on a bike that didn't even have a Paris licence, because *that* was what Frans had to think.

Heading up the rue de la Santé, brought her to the boulevard de Port-Royal and Val de Grâce, the military hospital. Tempted to use it as a means of appearing to escape, the thought to turn up the rue Saint-Jacques came but she would continue on to the avenue Denfert-Rochereau. Severe, walled in by wood, brick and stone, that street gave no chance to look back or escape. Priests, nuns and the wealthy lived behind tall, often solid gates. Only when across the Île de la Cité and just to the east of Les Halles did she finally chance a look. A mountain of empty wine barrels was perched on a wagon whose horse was so thin it looked ready to drop. Hesitant streams of traffic parted as they passed, but *merde* there was no sign of him. In the window of a nearby *pâtisserie*, birthday cakes, *babas au rhum* and petit-fours surrounded a sumptuous wedding cake. All were so realistic few said they would have known the difference had that little sign not been there: TOUTES SONT IMITATIONS. ALLES NUR ATTRAPPEN, all sham. Papier-mâché, paint and endless hours of devotion to remind everyone of what could no longer be purchased.

Frans could just be seen behind a cart that was loaded with firewood twigs at which two tethered goats were nibbling. The couple with the tandem bike were selling the milk. Everyone in the line-up had their own container. Timidly some four- and five-year-olds were attempting to pet the goats, Frans having just fed one the last of his cigarette.

At the Gare de l'Est she again paused but wouldn't look back. To her left and west, on the original facade, were the statues of Strasbourg; to her right, on the newer wing, those of Verdun. Two wars, this quartier very much of Alsacians and Lorraines.

Heading to the *Arrivée*, mingling with the crowd who were hurrying to get home or to wherever else they were going in Paris, she walked the bike among the baggage handlers whose two-wheeled carts leaned this way and that awaiting customers.

Frans would know she hadn't a lock for the bike but what he wouldn't know is that she had something else.

Grâce à Dieu, those dark, oft-questioning eyes swept over her, she softly saying, '*Félix, un mouchard, le Buffet de la Gare, un pistolet, le Browning neuf millimètre.*'

Leaving the bike, she hurried into the station.

Street by street, courtyard by courtyard, sewer by sewer and underground tunnel or cavern, the avenue Foch's map of Paris and its suburbs wasn't just impressive. It was, St-Cyr had to admit, as Hermann would, a terrible shock and damning indictment. Everything noted was, of course, in Deutsch and quite obviously the *gestapistes français* and others, including the PPF, had been busy supplying the Occupier with the necessary.

'Well, where then?' demanded Kleiber, having spread the map over the still warm hood of his tourer.

'Another courtyard, Colonel,' said Louis, 'but I have absolutely no idea which. Any of a few hundred would compare with what we have just visited. Paris is Paris—tell him, Hermann. No matter where he looks, its history has to be navigated. This street, this rue de la Goutte-d'Or is that of the golden droplet. Wine, you understand. White wine but so famous in the 1500s, its name has stuck. Look uphill. Look up this very street. What is it that you see, and please don't tell me it's just the basilica. Oh, for sure, humility caused us to build that huge white encrustation in the years after the Franco-Prussian War we lost, but for the history you really need, you must go back further. Gradually those little farms, monasteries and vineyards became what we now see of the Louis-Philippe era from 1830 to 1848. Each house is of five storeys. All don't just face the street behind closed blinds and curtains but line up to the very pavement. Intermittent courtyards, however, are relics of the once deep gardens that led to the stables behind and to places for the help, and with, perhaps, a few back rooms to rent so as to ease the budget. But then

. . . why then, the times changed, and many of the houses became tenements, the flats smaller and smaller, while the courtyards were flanked by one- and two-storey ateliers. Coffin makers, funeral directors, photographers, print shops, ironworkers, et cetera, et cetera, off which all-but-hidden staircases lead to the concierge's *loge* and finally to those flats, yet still in districts like this, the citizens cling to their original dialect and village closeness. She could be anywhere, so if you would be so kind, please begin by telling us what you and Kriminalrat Ludin know not only of her but of those others we are supposed to be finding for you in top secret.'

Grâce à Dieu, and good for Louis.

'Ask a Frenchman, Kohler, and right away he has reasons beyond reasons for even the most simple of things. Heinrich, *mein Lieber*, having chosen him yourself, you will know far more than myself about this *Spitzel* of yours, Frans Oenen—Paul Klemper. Start with him while I have a look at those "villagers" who have been rounded up.'

The Buffet de la Gare was simply that: thin soup for herself, thought Frans, because she didn't have her ration tickets and papers. No salt either, nor even the usual 'ashtray' of powdered saccharine for the acorn water that passed as 'coffee.'

Though she was at his mercy and it felt good, he would still go carefully. *Feldgendarme*, looking for deserters, were grousing about, as were plain-clothed Gestapo, though after others, *flics*, too, and *gestapistes-français* types.

Lots of other French were about, but she had deliberately chosen to sit near a group of German officers. Spooning her soup, blowing gently on it, she was watching him approach her table, but a Hauptmann got up to ask if she would like his slices of the grey national, and with margarine too.

Managing surprise and a grateful smile, she said, '*Dank, Herr Offizier*, that is most kind of you.'

'*Sprechen Sei Deutsch, Fräulein?*' he asked in surprise, pleased by it too.

'*Deutsch lernen, mein Herr*. I'm taking classes through the Deutsches Institut.'

'*Ach, das ist keine Kunst, Fräulein. Viel Glück!*' There's nothing to it. Good luck!

'*Und gleichfalls,*' she said. And likewise with yourselves. The Hauptmann even bowed.

Breaking the bread, she dropped pieces into the soup but never for a moment looked down at that bowl and spoon, for now she knew for sure she hadn't managed to escape. Still, he'd play it as if having come upon her unexpectedly, thought Oenen, and leaning over her and the table as a lover would, put his arms about her for the embrace of embraces. 'You left us in such a hurry, Étienne insisted I come after you, but are we to call you Annette-Mélanie Veroche of the Salle Pleyel and from Rethel, was it, or is it still to be Anna-Marie Vermeulen?'

His lips had been dry, his fingers cold, he now taking a chair facing her, so there was no other solution. She would *have* to appear as if having given up, have to appear as if putting herself right into his hands. 'Please tell me what you want.'

She wasn't even trembling and should have been, felt Oenen, but he would smile again as a lover would and confide, 'Not to see you lying naked on the floor in the cellars of the rue des Saussaies.'

Gestapo and Sûreté headquarters and being hosed off. 'Or in those of what was once a lovely public school on the Euterpestraat?'

Where they would have taken Josef Meyerhof to finally get every last thing out of him. 'Either way, *ma chère*, you haven't a chance. No one is going to believe that you lost your papers during the Blitzkrieg when Rethel was virtually destroyed. The *Moffen . . .*'

'The Boche, your masters.'

'Won't go looking for tombstones with the Veroche name on them to verify these.'

Having hurriedly shown them to Étienne and Arie, but not necessarily the name, he had found excuse to chase after her and not have the two of them immediately go to ground in his absence. 'Good, then you can give me back my papers and while you're at it, that rijksdaaler.'

'Ah, the last of my little crumbs. Would it have told my "masters" that you had somehow been delivered, do you think?'

Must he always tease? 'Please just give me my papers and tell me what you want.'

'Finish the soup. You'd better not waste it.'

But was he waiting for the Germans? Had he somehow managed to tell them where she was? People were glancing at them, some suspiciously, others simply with the inherent curiosity of the French. Using the last piece of bread, she would, she felt, break off a few crumbs and set them before him, then push the soup plate aside.

'Well?' she asked. 'What is it you want in return for your supposed silence?'

There had been no such offer, felt Oenen, but he'd shove the papers at her and see what happened.

Immediately she checked to see that nothing was missing, but that didn't bring the grateful sigh it should have, simply a deeper suspicion. 'Well?' she asked again, defiantly too.

There would be no smile. Instead he would put it to her as if he had paid for her services. 'A share of whatever it is that they are after so badly they would order me to get it for them.'

'And what, please, would that be?'

Stripped, she'd soon cry it out. 'What Meyerhof told you of, the black diamonds.'

'The "hidden" ones? Me, I simply ask because there are also those that are really black.'

How cruel of her. 'Then those that our "friends" call black, but also those that you were given to bring to Paris for him.'

'Josef didn't give me anything. They would have already taken everything from him.'

'Yet he saw that Étienne was given those louis d'or up front to make sure you got back to Paris safely?'

She must let her shoulders slump as if in defeat. 'All right, but I'll have to take you to them.' Either Frans still had that coin in his pocket or he had, as they had entered Paris, slipped it to the enemy.

Feeling the rijksdaaler Ludin had let them keep, hefting it here in the rue de la Goutte-d'Or, St-Cyr felt that Queen Wilhelmina's expression was neither gentle nor severe, but rather earnest, as if questioning the loyalty of each of her subjects. 'But on the reverse, Kriminalrat, the initials *A M V* have been deliberately scratched with the point of a needle or knife.'

'*Ach*, I've no idea why. Oenen—Klemper—probably did it to amuse. He's like that.'

'Yet none of the others in this top-secret envelope of yours have those same initials or any other.'

'*Verdammt*, must you persist in carping?'

'Kriminalrat, Louis only wants to know if Oenen was trustworthy.'

'Then why *didn't* he say so instead of trying to get the better of me? Klemper—Oenen—was planted with Labrie and Beekhuis last February. Klemper's good, make no mistake. So far he has been able to tell us of three other such "packages," all of whom are currently still under watch, as are the *Hosenscheisser* who are helping them.'

A situation that wouldn't last, but those visitors from Berlin had definitely put Ludin off stride. 'Labrie and Beekhuis can't be allowed to feel anything's wrong, Louis, that's why the delays with those other "packages."'

'Yet we know so little of this Klemper, Hermann. Flesh him out for us, Kriminalrat.'

'Lay him on the butcher block, is that it?'

'Trustworthy?' asked Hermann.

These two had found out so little, it had to mean they were hiding things even though Kohler's women were being held hostage. Lighting another Juno, he would offer none. Coughing, choking, grabbing at his gut, the uttered gasp he gave had to be a warning, but it, too, would have to be ignored. 'Frans Oenen—Paul Klemper—is twenty-six, though appears much younger and uses that. Trust? He has only one thought, himself. Women? you might ask. Two, three and each believing firmly they were the only one until the others he had confided in would tell them the truth. An actor since the age of fourteen. Mother twelve years older, an avant-garde violinist and teacher of music with clandestine and not-so-clandestine affairs of her own in the Hague, now ended of course. Father older than her by fifteen years and a professor of psychology, some of whose students were, of course, much younger than that wife of his. A freer couple than most, you might think. Progressive, some might have said, not myself. When son Paul, at age twelve, took it upon himself to spend the summer with Gypsies he had met at a fairground, it was the mother and then the father who let him go, only to find out exactly where he was when he finally showed up two years later.'

Scheisse! 'Having travelled all over the Netherlands, Belgium, France and beyond, Louis, learning everything those good folk could teach him.'

'*Good*, Kohler?'

'*Ach*, I meant figuratively, Kriminalrat. How to shuffle cards or coins and play that guessing game where you gamble and lose. How to mimic others and even appear as if one of them, how to act but not just on stage, and how to do all the rest, including very accurately being able to instantly and correctly size people up. He'll also know how to hide things, how to deceive, how to find angles and get himself out of difficulties, since he'll have anticipated them before they even happen. Why such a one, Kriminalrat? Why when you must have known what he'd be like?'

'Because we didn't choose him; he chose the Reich. Back in October 1941, arrested and held with 483 others in the Joodsche Schouwburg awaiting transit to Westerbork, he offered his services to the SD and was so convincing, he was given a chance to prove himself. It was only after having successfully targeted several "divers" in Amsterdam and the Hague, that he was then infiltrated into Labrie and Beekhuis's service, and that is why, later still, Standartenführer Kleiber, chose to use him for our purposes. His choice, I must add, not my own.'

'*Ach*, Heinrich . . . Heinrich, *mein Lieber*,' interjected Kleiber, hurrying to rejoin them. 'It was yourself who did that and more recently told me that everything was in place for this *Diamantensonderkommando*—isn't that *korrekt*? Meyerhof was desperate you said, and when he saw that girl, a former employee he knew well, since she was the daughter of his lead cutter and much respected employee, you chose to let him speak to her through the wire that shut off that ghetto, and then . . . *ach* then, deliberately let him use a non-Jew who was free and whom he trusted, to contact not only her, but Labrie and Beekhuis.'

The bastard! 'Standartenführer, that non-Jew has since been arrested, interrogated and shot, as you well know since you yourself ordered it.'

The usual in such situations, felt Kohler, but animosities should be encouraged, for one never knew when they might be useful. 'Which of you gave Oenen that pistol he then used to kill those two?'

'Which of us is an accessory to murder—is this what you're wondering?' asked Kleiber. '*Ach*, I did. Don't you remember, Heinrich? Oenen specified what he felt would suit, and after you had agreed, I reluctantly allowed such a weapon to be released, but only on the condition that there be one full magazine and no extra rounds.'

How comforting. 'And the coins?' asked Louis.

Taking a deep drag and then another before dropping the butt to the paving stones and crushing it underfoot, Ludin looked defiantly at his superior officer and said, 'Oenen felt they would be a means of letting the Standartenführer know they had successfully gone through certain places along the route, places he knew of since Étienne Labrie had told him of the route that would be used. Oenen chose the places—prominent and easily found—and the coin recovered, but also secure. It seemed quite harmless.'

'Harmless or not, Heinrich,' said Kleiber, 'it was yourself who agreed.'

'As did yourself, Standartenführer, since the coins were, if I remember it correctly, on your desk when he told us of the route that would be used.'

The two of them must hate each other, felt St-Cyr. 'Could that girl have scratched her initials on that coin, Kriminalrat?'

Good for Louis. So often it was the little things that counted. 'As a means of identifying him to others, Standartenführer, assuming of course, that it would have had to have been returned to his pocket *after* she had scratched her initials on it.'

'But identifying him to whom?' asked Kleiber.

'Having lived with the Gypsies, Standartenführer, he would have learned how to follow someone as if glued to them even though at a distance,' said Hermann.

'In other words,' said Louis, 'did that girl have help here on first arriving in Paris and does she *still* have that help?'

'*Banditen?*'

'FTP?' said Hermann. 'It's just a thought, given the recent assassination of Dr. Julius Ritter, but if Louis and myself are to find her for you both and recover all the black and life diamonds those two from Berlin say are hidden, then it's a question that needs to be answered.'

Flipping the coin and catching it heads up, Louis climbed into the backseat of the tourer to let this 'Rommel' drive while they inhaled the secondhand cigarette smoke rather than beg.

FTP, thought Ludin. Was it time to release those photos of her to others who would be more likely to find her?

To the courtyard at 3 rue Vercingétorix there was nothing, felt Anna-Marie, but the stark reality of the ordinary for a Monday morning. Everyone—the carpenter, the tinsmith, the picture-framer, the mason—watched her as she walked the bike up to the very far end, the children, too, and one old woman at the communal pump.

Lines of washing were being strung from upstairs windows, the houses of one and two stories and occasionally a ramshackle third. Pigeons' nests, years old, still clung to narrow windowsills behind whose Second Empire railings a caged rabbit or chicken waited in hopes of nearby lettuces and herbs. Makeshift crepe paper blackout curtains still hung in some of those upper windows, and overlooking the courtyard from the rue de l'Ouest or the avenue du Maine was one of those wretched many-storeyed tenements from the 1920s and '30s.

A lone, mange-plagued cat paused. Staircase after staircase led into the adjoining labyrinths. Even the curtain of the concierge's *loge* looked as if permanently closed, the cloth having all but lost its original pink.

Plastered inside the glass were not only a pencilled, hand-drawn map of the courtyard, but a plan detailing the exact location and profession or other status of every tenant. All fifty-six of them. Étienne and Arie had been listed as 'furniture movers.'

Watched, she was certain, she went on. It was *crazy* of her to have come back. Frans must have told the Occupier where this safe house was. He'd not answered when asked, had simply smiled that smile of his and had made her cry out, 'Why? Why are you doing this?'

To which he had answered, 'That's for you to guess.'

Garages—old stables—and now often ateliers, were ranked side by side with their rusty, galvanized stove pipes clinging to the outer walls, cast-iron drainpipes too, and that inevitable clutter of things half-made and left, things still being made, and the desperately needed house repairs all too evident.

Ivy clung precariously to the flaking stucco above the door to the house at the far end, the curtains not moving.

'So you came back,' said Étienne, having stepped out of the adjacent stable, giving but a glimpse of Arie unloading things from that truck.

'I did, yes. I had to warn you.'

Right down the length of the courtyard, from the open windows with wet laundry in fists to the ateliers, everyone watched them.

'Warn us of what, then?'

Lame, a collie came straight to him and he paused to greet it warmly, revealing a side to him she would never have expected. 'Frans was going to betray you and Arie, not just myself. For all I know, he still might have, since I can't show you the coin. It wasn't in his pockets. He must have passed it on to someone when we went through the Porte de Versailles, but I really don't know. How could I, having been hidden like that, in the back of yours and Arie's truck?'

'What coin?'

'A rijksdaaler. He had left it on a post at that border crossing to the south of Reusel. That's why I cut myself. I *wanted* to tell you. I tried to but Frans, he always anticipated every attempt and you . . .'

'Wouldn't listen.'

Not for a moment had he taken his gaze from her.

'Leave the bike and come and meet Madame. It's necessary.'

'Let me speak to Arie first. Let me thank him and ask for a lock and a licence plate and registration number.'

'Not until she's decided.'

'Wouldn't it be wiser to just leave while you can? I honestly don't know if Frans has told the Boche of this place. He may have earlier, before you and Arie even agreed to bring me.'

'Have they photos of you?'

'Isn't that why Mijnheer Meyerhof insisted you agree?'

'Apoline is necessary. No one does anything here but that she knows who they are and why they're here.'

'Am I to be vetted, is that what you mean, she having made a terrible mistake with Frans?'

This one dragged information out of one. 'She has never seen him, nor does she even know of him because I never brought

Frans here. While Arie and I have other safehouses, this one I have recently been keeping in reserve, having used it very safely throughout 1941 and 1942 but not since Frans joined us.'

Abruptly she sat down heavily on the stone steps, and burying her head in her hands, wept with relief, the collie immediately nuzzling her. 'I didn't know. I couldn't,' she said. 'I thought I *had* to warn you even *if* it meant I'd be taken.'

Joining her on the steps, Labrie began to roll a cigarette, the others of the courtyard at last going back to whatever they'd been doing. 'You risked your life to warn us and I appreciate that, as will the wife and five children I dearly love yet have to keep elsewhere until this Occupation is over and done with, but Frans, where is he now? Don't hesitate. Just tell me since I really do have to know.'

And had just given her the reason. 'With friends. They'll know what to do. I'm not really one of their group. I simply find out things for them and from time to time pass that information along to my contact.'

'FTP? An "action" *équipe*?'

'I think so but really don't know because they have never asked me to do anything like that. I am, however, well placed, as least I was. Now I don't know what I'll do. Take it a step at a time, I guess.'

'Because they'll have photos of you.'

It was Arie who brought not just a glass of water but one of cognac, and taking a place beside her, said, 'Down a little of the first and then all of the other.'

Reaching for Étienne's cigarette when it was passed to him, he went on to say, 'You're going to need to wear fingerless gloves, but those I have are already a ruin and far too big. Gauntlets as well, and of leather.'

Immediately, Beekhuis felt her head come to rest against his shoulder. 'Madame will have seen there's been trouble, boss. Give this one a few more minutes. No one is coming for us anyway. Not yet.'

'Madame de Kerellec is a Breton but not, I emphasize, a separatist,' said Étienne. 'During the Great War, she lost her brothers, her father and the farm, and unable to keep her, the mother gave her to the sisters.'

'Eventually she washed up here in the quartier de Plaisance,' said Arie, 'and just around the corner on the rue Sauvageot to work for an uncle she had never seen. He owned a *crêperie* but decided she could earn far more than the wages he had promised. As a prostitute, she worked that same street and others, this one too, and then like so many, took to cleaning when the customers fell off. Married by then, beaten far too many times for being disobedient among other things, she secretly turned her husband in for the particularly brutal rape of a ten-year-old tenant he had killed to silence, earning him a knife in the Santé before the widow-maker could get at him.'

'That knife had been made from a fifteen-centimetre spike,' said Étienne, 'but neither the warden nor any of the guards could figure out how such a thing could ever have been brought into that prison and given to one of the husband's cell mates. She knows what we do and that's the way she likes it.'

'She's as discreet as a tombstone,' said Arie. 'Personally, I rather like her. Tough, but with a heart of gold if you can pry it open. Make friends with her canary, then talk to Madame. Try to gain a small measure of acceptance. She's not difficult. She just likes us to think she is.'

'We've been periodically dropping stuff off for her to sell ever since we started, but never with Frans.'

Who could well have followed them.

8

'Étienne Labrie—Stéphane Lacroix,' said Ludin, the Standartenführer having dragged these two *Scheissdreck* back to the office to sit across the desk from himself, Kleiber insisting that *he* be the one to tell them.

Shoving the photos across the desk, he would pause to open a fresh tin of fifty Lucky Strike, but take out only one. Lighting up, he took a drag and coughed again and again until . . . '*Ach mein Gott!*'

Clutching at his stomach, reaching for the bitters, Ludin took a swig and then another, even to shutting his eyes for a moment.

'*Ach*, now where were we? Age thirty-four. Former NCO. Escaped not once but twice and found his way to Rotterdam and Arie Beekhuis—Hans van Loos. Lacroix had worked for the tanker side of the Royal Dutch Shell; Van Loos had been in charge of the engines on one of them. A happy connection, you might say, since they had previously encountered each other several times before the Blitzkrieg interrupted their lives. Happy, too, since to get that job in 1937 when few others were available due to the Depression, Lacroix had to have been fluent in Dutch, Deutsch and English as well as his French. Father of five he's got tucked away somewhere in the former free zone. Wife an accomplished pianist, which should make it easier to find her and transport the family or use them as hostage.'

The son of a bitch, thought Kohler, but Kleiber, who was simply watching their reactions, had shoved the tin over to him, Ludin thinking to object but realizing he'd better not.

'*Dank*,' said Hermann, and lighting two, handed one to this partner of his.

Again it was Ludin who spoke. 'Lacroix's call-up papers must have come late due to his age and absence in the Far East at the time. After but the briefest of training, he was thrust into the battle for the Ardennes, which swept him up and should have put an end to him.'

'But didn't,' said Hermann, 'and eventually this *Diamantensonderkommando* of yours became necessary.'

There was a further gasp, Kleiber saying, 'Heinrich, I really must insist that you have that looked at. You've a peptic ulcer. Those bitters are only to help the digestion, not cure such a severe problem.'

A dismissive hand was waved. '*Ach*, later. After we have settled this matter and have the diamonds.'

Two photos of Arie Beekhuis—Hans van Loos—joined those of Labrie's and then the two of Anna-Marie before and during the general strike.

'Now either you find her within the next two days,' went on Ludin, 'or the Standartenführer, who has agreed, will order me to release these not just to the Paris police, but to others.'

'Like Rudy de Mérode and Sergei Lebeznikov, Kriminalrat?' asked Hermann.

'With the consequent risk of their stealing a good deal of what is then recovered?' said Louis. 'Hermann, it's long past the time I should have offered our condolences to the families of those two bank employees.'

Hector Bolduc and that secretary of his were going to need a visit, that mistress of his too. 'Me to check out how that coin could ever have found its way here.'

Sliding the photos into that top-secret envelope, Ludin said, 'For now, you can keep these since I have others.'

Serge de Lenz—Sergei Lebeznikov—was enjoying a cigar and leaning against the Citroën when they came out of number eighty-four.

'A word, *mes amis*,' he called out companionably with a wave of the cigar. 'Since your women are set to be transported, Kohler, I think you can use a little help and Rudy is quite willing to let bygones be bygones.'

One glance at either of those photos of Anna-Marie and Lebeznikov would immediately know who he and that son of his had taken to dinner. 'Ludin *would* give me this envelope, Hermann.'

'To absolve himself of all responsibility, just like he did with it and Oona. If we lose those photos to this rabble or any other— and that could well be what he has in mind—we'll be blamed. Let me just get the Purdey, and we'll hear what this bunch have to say since there are two other cars along the street, and they can't possibly yet know where she and that *passeur* and his firebox feeder are.'

Choosing ESCALIER M, whose door could never be closed since it didn't have one, thought Anna-Marie, Étienne led the way along a linoleum-floored corridor off which were doors and the steeply rising staircase.

The air in the room had been drenched with cologne but held traces of cabbage, sweat, the smoke of countless Gauloises bleues and other things. Overhead a single, naked electric bulb gave light to the woman whose lisle stockings had been rolled up to below the pudgy, work-worn knees across which the hem of a flowered housedress was draped. Strong, big, round in the contours and still of the streets, her bosom sagged, the dyed blonde hair a mass of curls and pins over heavily made-up eyes of the deepest blue. The complexion, once that creamy white of the Bretonnes, was now but pasty and blotched.

Under the woman's forearms and not quite hidden by the faded lace antimacassars, stuffing leaked from the chair, the canary silent in a spotless cage.

'*Ah bon, mon garçon*, it's about time,' she said, the accent so of Brittany, Anna-Marie felt herself smiling.

Swift to judge, the false lashes narrowed. 'Who are you?' asked the woman. 'Come, come, my beauty with the roll collar who hides the left hand in a pocket of those Norwegian trousers? From where do you come, Oslo or Narvik? Why are you here, what do you plan to do in Paris, is it legal or not, and why, please, having left us in such a hurry do you then return with the utmost caution? Were you expecting our friends to come here, having followed you, and if so, why?'

The puffy fingers wore garish rings.

'Madame . . .' began Étienne, looking as though silently laughing at her predicament.

'*Pauf!* Let the girl speak since speak she must.'

The room, the tiny world within the one Madame de Kerellec ruled, held a black iron cookstove, sink, drainboard, counter, pantry shelves with little but things old, a table, two chairs other than the one she was in, a bed that had yet to be made and a chamber pot that definitely needed emptying.

'It's early yet,' the woman said. 'Why hide your left hand? Is it disfigured, diseased or injured in some other way?'

'I've arthritis, madame. It was caused by my having to live in a garret where there isn't any heat and the ice, it forms in winter on the inside of the window and walls.'

'Arthritis . . . I have it too. The shoulder . . . This one. The shame of it all is that God, who could have done, did not make us perfect, but then He must have known what He was doing, don't you think?'

She would have to ignore the invitation to religious conflict, felt Anna-Marie. 'Your figurines are lovely.' Of fawns, dwarfs and fairies, all were in frosted bottle-blue glass but beautifully made, and they climbed, flew, danced and lived on shelves above that bed.

Étienne's newest friend notices everything, thought Apoline, but had Arie, who had lost the love of his life, secretly fallen for this one? 'Marcel Perrot, the glassblower, made those for me. He was a Picasso with glass and felt I would need the company once the cancer took him, so I named each of them after people we both knew, some good, some bad. Now yours, please, and show me that hand.'

Beside the bed, in a neat pile, were the lurid-jacketed originals of the cheap train-novel* series of *Fantômas*, all thirty-two of the arch villain's brutal and sadistic crimes.**

'I like to read,' said Apoline tartly. 'Every night I look forward to a new one, then I have it and I start all over again, now answer what I asked, or is it that the contents of my *loge* have so entangled that tongue of yours, you can't use it?'

There could be no hesitation since her papers said one thing and Étienne might still not know of it for he only had been given her real name. 'Forgive me, madame, but I love to read those,

---

* Paperbacks read and left at a journey's end.

** By Pierre Souvestre and Marcel Allain, the first published on 10 February 1911. Immensely popular, the original series sold more than 5 million copies and has gained readers ever since.

too, and pick them up whenever I can. Annette-Mélanie Veroche is my name. I'm from Rethel and am a student at the Sorbonne.'

Étienne had been impressed, but what lovely lies, if lies they were. 'Students, like artists, always suffer.'

There were a few crumbs on the saucer Madame had been using. 'May I?' asked Anna-Marie, and receiving a shrug, took a step over to the cage that hung behind and just to one side of the woman's chair.

'Napoléon has been bad,' said Apoline. 'He's being punished for having ignored me this morning. I'm going to call him Adolf—I really am, you little monster!'

When it sang, she was driven to tears, the mascara running, the glossy white Bakelite earrings catching the light. Wiping her eyes with one of the antimacassars, she said, 'Now what have you for me this time, Étienne, since I must confess I was greatly relieved to see that you and Arie were again staying here where you belong, even though the rent, it has been fully paid up month after month and you have always left things for me to sell for you and for myself and others, of course.'

'Eggs, cheese, coffee-chicory, chocolate, cigarettes, Ardennes hams and some of those wine-flavoured cheroots you like from Belgium. Annette-Mélanie is in a hurry to get to the Sorbonne, madame, but may come back to see us and even stay a night or two.'

'Is it that I should report such a thing to the Commissariat de Police as the law demands and the Victor of Verdun requires?'

Grinning, kissing her on each cheek, he dropped a wad of francs into her lap and said, 'Forget about the Maréchal Pétain. Here's 40,000 to help your conscience and cover the rent in future.'

Concierge's often being intermediaries in the *marché noir*, she was a good choice, felt Anna-Marie. Not a cross or crucifix were present, nor any of those garishly pious religious prints. Just one photo of the novice the woman had once been as a teenager.

'The sisters felt I would never be clean,' said Apoline, 'the fathers, that I was a sinner who needed to be taught a lesson. Naked, they beat me, and naked, I responded because I had to, which only got the Mother Superior and the other sisters all the more upset and jealous. Now go. Come back and come and see me again. We'll have a little anisette and you can show me that hand of yours because no one here will say a thing of you, but should Arie or this one take a notion to fool around with you without your permission, just leave them to me.'

Out in the courtyard, she said, 'I have to check on my place but will try to come back later after they've decided what to do with Frans.'

'*Un mouchard, ein Spitzel*, eh, Kohler?' said an unsmiling Lebeznikov, flinging the half-smoked cigar away. 'Two *Diamantenbonzen* from the Reich pay you a rush visit and still you and St-Cyr turn up your noses at our help? Rudy, tell them.'

The first of the two other cars had but four occupants. Mérode, having rolled the side window down, was behind the wheel and exhaling cigarette smoke while impatiently flicking ash, the suit, pink tie, gold fountain pens and swastika pin the same. 'Shoes is it, Kohler? Shoes that were left in a certain bank van by a girl that SD colonel is after? Shoes whose leather seems to have changed from a dark blue to a much lighter shade?'

Shit! Rocheleau, stern, smugly unforgiving and quite obviously unyielding, was in the back beside Van Houten, a known sadist and another of Rudy's 'Neuilly Gestapo.'

Weak, slack, her lips parted as if carnally guilt-ridden and definitely afraid of what that husband of hers might well do to her, felt Kohler, Évangéline Rocheleau turned away rather than let him see her like this. But her left hand was still resting atop Rudy's right, which had found, not her knee, but thigh, he having rucked up the hem of her dress.

'Madame Rocheleau insists that having never seen the original pair, she must have been mistaken, Kohler, so why not tell us before we let her burst that peptic ulcer of Heinrich Ludin's?'

It was Louis who said, 'Éugene Rocheleau, *garde champêtre* of Corbeny?'

'You know it's me,' countered Rocheleau, having leaned forward, 'but I no longer work for the *gendarmerie*. I have a new and far better job.'

'Good, that's marvellous but neither here nor there. Please step out of the car.'

Uh-oh. 'Louis . . .'

'Hermann, be so kind as not to interrupt a chief inspector in the process of carrying out his duties. This one not only tampered with evidence, he attempted to steal five bundles of 5,000-franc notes, for a total of no less than 2.5 million francs.'

'And ten tins of sardines, Chief, two coils of smoked sausage, six half-kilos of real coffee, two handfuls of fake black truffles and two rounds of the Brie de Meaux.'

All of which, noticed Lebeznikov, had come from Kohler's little black notebook, St-Cyr having placed the envelope he had been given by the avenue Foch atop the car.

Yanking the back door open, that Sûreté dragged Rocheleau out and flung him up against the car to slap the bracelets on.

'Don't!' said Kohler, having swung the shotgun toward the Russian. 'Just leave that envelope where it is since it's clearly stamped "top secret."'

Photos . . . Did it contain ones of that girl and the other two? wondered Lebeznikov. If only he could . . .

'The rue des Saussaies, Hermann. It's the cellars for this one,' said Louis, and hustling Rocheleau to the Citroën, shoved him into the backseat.

'Kohler, listen to me,' urged Mérode, his gaze still on Louis, 'this thing, it has to be big, *n'est-ce pas?* Thousands and thousands of carats of gem diamonds and industrials. Plenty to share and no one here or in Berlin the wiser.'

'Or it's all a lot of hot air, eh?'

Merde, but what would break the bastard? 'There was an embroidered handkerchief with a name on it. "Anna," I believe—wasn't that what your husband said, Évangéline?'

'Anna, yes, and . . . and something beginning with a *V*, he thought.'

'Really, Kohler, it wasn't kind of you to have got the Kommandant von Gross-Paris to consign that PPF hit squad to shovelling concrete on the Channel Islands, but even so, we are willing to let bygones be bygones. We've had the shop of those two old lesbians repaired, as asked, and have even left them with 250,000 francs in case anything was missed or stolen.'

There was only one way to stop them, felt Kohler. Reaching for the envelope, taking the letter out of his jacket pocket as if from it, he said, 'Then perhaps you'd better read this. It's from the Reichssicherheitschef and definitely tells you or anyone else to leave Louis and me alone to do the job we've been assigned.'

Putain de merde, even Heinrich Ludin couldn't go against such an order. '*Ah bon, mon ami*, we'll do as requested, of course, but continue to look ourselves, and if we should find her, why you can be sure we'll ask a few questions before turning her over to the proper authorities.'

'*Monsieur Figeard, c'est moi.* I'm back. How have you been? The chest, that cough, the sacroiliac? Did you go to Madame Duclos, the *masseuse*, as I told you to?'

Several broken matches attested to his having finally got his pipe alight. Startled, he looked up. '*Ah Sainte Mère*, is it really you, mademoiselle? A week, you thought. Ten days at most, and now the fourth of the month? Your dear mother . . . The funeral . . . Come in and sit down. Tell me everything. Let me have it while it's still fresh. Lean the bike against the corridor wall. No one will say a thing.'

'It's not mine. I borrowed it from a friend and must return it.'

A friend . . . A bike that had been made in Liege, but with a Paris licence that would have taken weeks. 'Did she suffer?'

'*Maman?* No, not at all. Indeed, she has recovered fully. That's why I'm late. The doctors all said it was because I had come to see her again and had stayed constantly at her bedside that she made such a miraculous recovery. Me, I'm just happy all my prayers were answered. Now tell me, please, how have the rabbits and the chickens been? Have they missed me?'

'Your hand . . . What have you done?'

Zut, she would forget, and like the good friend he was, he *would* notice. 'Ah, it's nothing. I just fell and cut myself on some gravel. It's fine. The stitches are to come out tomorrow.'

Stitched but not with cat gut, with what looked to be fishing line, but what should he do? wondered Figeard. Continue the charade or tell her what had happened in her absence?

Setting his pipe aside, he said, 'That boy, mademoiselle. That subdeacon, he's been here time and again and claims he intends to ask you to marry him.'

'Marry . . . ? Pierre-Alexandre? But . . . but I hardly know him.'

'My thoughts exactly. I tried to tell him, but the Russians, they can be very persistent. Apparently subdeacons must decide whether to marry or not before they are made deacons and never thereafter.'

'And all because I was able to obtain a little rosemary from one of the gardeners at the Jardin des Plantes? It's insane, Monsieur Figeard. We have hardly spoken.'

'And not even at those dinners he and his father took you to?'

Why had he to ask? 'Me, I knew it was a mistake to agree to let him and his father take me there. Oh for sure, the food it was magnificent and extremely expensive. Once perhaps, but twice . . . What *am* I to do?'

'Tell him he's crazy.'

'Of course. You're absolutely right.'

It would have to be said, felt Figeard. It simply couldn't be avoided. 'There was another visitor.'

Another.

Sickened, alarmed—ready to run if necessary—this girl he had trusted like a daughter, this Annette-Mélanie Veroche, waited for him to continue. 'A Sûreté. Chief Inspector Jean-Louis St-Cyr.'

Ah merde, merde, it had finally happened! 'Why?'

She had even darted a look behind and along the corridor. 'Please, mademoiselle, there is no reason for you to worry. Apparently they think you must have witnessed the murder of two bank employees and the partial robbery of their van. They will only want to hear what you have to say about it.'

'They?'

It would be best to just say, 'The Sûreté.'

Side by side, and looking as if Frans had put them there to mock her, the shoes were in the armoire beneath that incredibly soft and beautiful dress, but the one would lead to the other and that Sûreté would soon find that she had had a part-time job every second Sunday at the cultural-exchange gatherings of Madame Nicole Bordeaux.

Those would then lead him to Jacqueline Lemaire, mistress of Hector Bolduc whose bank van it had been.

Up on the roof, alone if ever she could be alone now, the nougat tin was still where she had hidden it. Surely if he had come up here and found it, that Sûreté would have taken it, but he *hadn't*.

Opening it, she heard herself gasp.

Black and of wrinkled leather, its braided thongs pulled tightly by those two wooden pegs, the pouch lay atop everything, and beneath it as if to emphasize what had happened, was the still wet, white paper packet of twelve flawless brilliants she had been given for herself. He hadn't taken *anything*. He had done the only thing he could to make her agree and not go to ground so hard all contact with her would instantly have been severed. He had also left the Opinel with which she had tried to defend herself at l'Abbaye de Vauclair, so must know everything.

Mademoiselle, we need to talk. Please agree to meet at the Jardin d'Hiver of the Jardin des Plantes between 2.30 and 3.30 Tuesday or Wednesday the fifth and sixth. You will know me by a brown suede tobacco pouch, which sadly remains empty but bears the scorched hole of carelessness and the letters AMPHORA. It was a gift of Agnès, my first wife, who had aspirations of my emigrating to America with her and becoming a detective there.

He had even known and trusted that great care would be taken with the note, since it could definitely identify him.

A Sûreté, a chief inspector, divorced once and married twice.

Funerals were usually in the morning but burials could be in the afternoon depending, of course, on the scheduling, this one being at 1400 hours, Monday's lunch having been postponed.

'The quartier de Bercy's burials are most often here, Hermann, where the departed can listen to the music of the arrivals. Be patient. It's necessary. God has granted us a reprieve and given us an opportunity.'

'We won't get a damned thing out of this bunch and you know it. Bolduc will have seen to that.'

Since losing his sons at Stalingrad, funerals had been difficult for Hermann, the lack of cigarettes simply adding an edge. 'Well, at least I won't have to break the news to the families.'

'You should have let me tear the heart out of Werner Dillmann!'

'Later. Even a Detektiv Inspektor from the Kripo should know that compromises are often necessary. Quite obviously I needed you here.'

'Rocheleau is now your sworn enemy.'

'But where he belongs.'

In a cell at the rue des Saussaies. 'I did ask Boemelburg to consider him a hostage but he said he'd have to ask Oberg who will, of course, simply tell him to release the *salaud*. Somehow I'm going to have to get Évangéline out of Rudy de Mérode's clutches before she and that husband of hers sink the two of us for good.'

'Perhaps she'd be suitable for that one's escort service?'

Arm in arm, Mademoiselle Jacqueline Lemaire—it couldn't be Madame Bolduc—was with the owner and president of the Banque Nationale de Crédit et Commercial. 'Who provided the gasoline, Louis. Otherwise the Occupation would have made certain those hearses were drawn by horses or a *gazo*.'

The Cimètiere de Charenton was just beyond the Gare de Nicolaï* and its marshalling yards that fed directly into those of the far larger Gare de Lyon.

'Since we're adjacent to the western edge of the Bois de Vincennes, *mon vieux*, there is at least the joy of its autumn leaves. *Bien sûr*, there are a few maples from Canada, other exotics from elsewhere, but by and large and most welcome are the steadfast oaks and beeches that the Prussians didn't cut down in 1871 as they did every last tree in the Bois de Boulogne. Perhaps they had it in mind to leave generations of the wealthy and upper middle-class Parisians thinking they were at a loss and envious, while the rest of us had this park.'

Louis always had to have reasons. 'The driver of that van did have a large family, just as Yvonne Rouget said. That has to be Madame Deniard.'

Seven children were ranked by age and height, and all looked under the age of twelve. 'Raymond Paquette, the assistant, had six, two sets of twin girls, and two boys, and all under eight.'

'The first victim and driver of that van bashed on the forehead with a jagged rock and shot in the chest at zero range.'

'The second, and assistant, in the back of the neck. Would the coffins have been open, do you think?'

Louis *would* ask. 'It's amazing what undertakers can do but you can be sure everyone, including that priest, will have had a damned good look.'

'Grégoire, the operations manager, but not residing in the bank's building, as does Mademoiselle Rouget, still takes her arm.'

'Steadfast like those trees, eh?'

---

* Now the Gare de Bercy.

'And no sign of Madame Bolduc, Hermann, or her daughters, Didi and Yvonne.'

'Kids don't like funerals any more than I do, but bankers love to show off their mistresses.'

The clay was gaping. 'And just like Rocheleau told us of his village priest, this one is adding a final deluge. Let's not hang around for the sprinklings of soil. Bolduc has arranged for a reception to take your mind off things and get it onto what's important.'

'Like the murder of those two and a whole lot else including why our Anna-Marie didn't want to step into that bank van or any other probably.'

Good for Hermann, Corporal Horace Rivet, custodian of the Berru lookout's ruins having said, 'I think her heart fell when she saw it and them.'

LES AMIES FRANÇAISES
BUREAU D'HOSTESSES . . . MLLE JACQUELINE LEMAIRE
DEUTSCHFREUNDLICH, DEUTSCH SPRECHEN

Alone in the corridor—taking a terrible chance to simply stand in front of the frosted glass of that door—Anna-Marie knew all was lost. Everything. The Sorbonne, the job here, the one at the Frontbuchhandlung and at Madame Nicole Bordeaux's.

She had to run, had to go to ground but couldn't, mustn't, would somehow have to work it through and try not to think of the loss of Henk Vandenberg and her parents, but of the promise she had made to Mijnheer Myerhof.

Mademoiselle Lemaire had tried and tried to get her to agree to becoming a 'hostess' but had led to Madame Bordeaux and Hector Bolduc whose vans had offered routes into and out of Paris without the need for *laissez-passers* and *sauf-conduits*.

Miliciens, PPF and others—those vans had been freighting them all so why not herself, Aram Bedikian had asked and said, 'You have to.'

And she *had* on that first trip to visit her 'mother' in Rethel last December though never again, but on the return with Étienne, Arie and Frans, something that no one could have foreseen had happened. *Bien sûr*, a roadblock control, but not a spotter plane and then, there in defiance of her ever having to use one of those again, had been that van at the ruins of the Berru lookout.

Étienne hadn't known, and she hadn't been able to tell him. She had simply said, 'L'Abbaye de Vauclair,' because she had known of it and a tiny village like Corbeny would have offered dangers of its own, and to do what they'd had in mind, those two would have stopped somewhere before it anyway.

Somehow she had to move her things—she couldn't just leave everything and take only the diamonds and the scraps from home. Yet if she were to take even a suitcase, Monsieur Figeard would know at once that she was not coming back, no matter what she said.

She must 'return the bike,' as she had told him, must then 'take the *métro* back but later.'

And that Sûreté? she asked herself.

That decision would have to be up to Félix and Aram and the others—FTP, all of them, and submarines as well.

Bolduc was far from happy to see them at the reception.

'Inspectors, I trust you are not going to be asking questions on such a sad and very private occasion. Please allow the families, their friends and associates, the decency of honouring their dead.'

'*Ach*, we wouldn't think of asking anything,' said Kohler, 'but perhaps you'd be good enough to tell us how much cash was lifted from that van of yours?'

'And why, if I might be permitted, did you, beyond the flimsy excuse given, show no interest in the absence of that van until we happened to tell you of it? Three days later, wasn't it, Hermann?'

'The porch. Come, come. Not here. Let them have their grief and a little sustenance. Yvonne, make excuses for me to Mesdames Deniard and Paquette. The latter is, of course, pregnant, the former no doubt as well, so the brutal killing of two of my most valued employees is very much on my mind.'

It must be. 'Go with him, Hermann. Let me find that priest.'

And circulate.

The *salaud!* thought Bolduc. 'Father Richaux no more needs to talk to you than yourself to him. He didn't know either of the victims nor even the families. He's a priest on call for such occasions. Jacqueline found him for me.'

'Jacqueline . . . Ah, Mademoiselle . . . ?' asked Louis.

'Lemaire, and yourself, Inspector?'

Hair: light auburn; forehead: average; eyes: brown, space: medium; age: 32, height: 1.7 metres; weight: 50 kilos; clothing, apart from diamonds: designer mourning suit from none other than Paul Poiret, cost on the *marché noir,* a minimum of 12,000 francs. 'It's Chief Inspector, and this is Detektiv Inspektor Kohler of the Kripo.'

'The one with the slash . . .'

She would impulsively yank off a glove, thought Jacqueline, to let a forefinger trace what the SS had given this one early last December, leaving everyone else who was anyone, to speak of it ever since, and he with his two women being held hostage at Gestapo Boemelburg's villa by none other than Kriminalrat Heinrich Ludin. 'The truth and nothing but it, eh? Hector, we shall have to be careful.'

Bolduc could sure pick them, felt Kohler. Clothed, as in the belle epoque of this place's decor, she'd be like that reproduction on the wall of Tissot's gorgeously seductive painting, *L'Ambitieuse.* Heady, just like that one, her fine hair swept up and back in defiance of the usual styles of the present day to reveal two of Cartier's *blanc exceptionel* drops to match the much larger brilliant at her throat even when in mourning, and what a throat it was.

'Hector, darling, let me leave you with the chief inspector for a little while I show this other one around.'

An open-air café or dance hall, in the old style of a *guinguette,* there were two parts to the restaurant on the Île de Reuilly in the Bois de Vincennes's Lac Daumesnil, felt Kohler. An inner room, still with the gaslights, was surrounded with end-to-end tables, place settings and Thonet bentwood chairs for eighty at least.

But beyond that room, equally spacious and with perfect views of the lake, the forest and a glimpse of the zoological garden with its six hundred animals and seven hundred birds, native and otherwise, was a latticed porch with climbing grapevines offering shade and temptation, and thoughts of the jungle.

One table had been set out here.

'Hector would have had us sit with the others, himself right in the centre, for he can be of them when he feels it necessary, but Yvonne, not appreciating my presence, felt this more appropriate.'

'Mademoiselle,' asked the waiter, 'the Moët et Chandon, the Taittinger or the Mumm?'

All three had been laid out on the tray, the glasses already filled and grouped accordingly, the hospice for the blind having been short-changed. 'The first, I think,' said Kohler.

'And an excellent choice,' said Jacqueline, he having chosen the very same as had been found broken open when Grégoire had gone to check the contents of that van. 'Now, please, while we have this moment of privacy, tell me everything you can about these terrible murders. Otherwise I will have nothing to say to others, and you know what that must mean to a girl like me.'

She was even wearing Guerlain's Eau de Cologne Impérial just like Yvonne Rouget would and had when Louis and he had broken into Bolduc's office to find out all they could. 'First tell me what you do?'

How did he even know she did *anything* other than please Hector? 'Me?' She would toss her head and give him an impish smile. 'An escort service. *Jour ou soir*, it's all the same. An entertaining, fully satisfying and most memorable visit. La tour Eiffel, the galleries, the Louvre and Catacombs, museums too, then a dinner or luncheon in nothing but the finest of restaurants.'

'The Folies-Bergère, Noctambule, Lido, Moulin Rouge or Shéhérazde?'

With bare breasts and bare bums. 'Those, too, if requested.'

'And breakfast?'

How mischievous of him. 'If necessary, since clients are seldom here for more than a few days.'

'Satisfaction guaranteed?'

'It goes without saying.'

'Any new ones of late?'

Zut, he *would* ask! 'There are always new ones.'

'Business good?'

Why had he to fire such questions at her? 'Business is seldom what one desires, but has been immensely gratifying. If one works hard and is known for what one does, one is sought, isn't that so? But me, I accept only clients of distinction. *Bien sûr*, my girls fulfil what the clients want. The experience, it is positive, you understand, or the fee, less expenses, is returned. I've two shifts of twenty at present and rotate them every two weeks.'

'Ages?'

Was he zeroing in on someone? 'Eighteen, twenty, twenty-four or -six, even thirty. It depends. Sophisticated, of course. Knowledgeable and not just of Paris. Fluent in Deutsch—that is essential.'

'Fee?'

Why, again, must he ask such a thing and so quickly? 'It varies: 4,000 to 6,000 for an afternoon or evening, and whatever is necessary is placed on top of that.'

With the bed, couch, chair or carpet underneath. 'Students?'

Ah merde. 'Sometimes but it depends more on their willingness to . . . shall we say, forget their studies and be accommodating. For instance, a student of the violin at the conservatory must set aside her love of the classical to genuinely appreciate and enjoy the latest jazz.'

'And dancing in a place such as this?'

'If necessary. Why not?'

His shrug could well have been that of the uncaring, but then he said, '*Ach*, you must know.'

Running a finger lightly down his sleeve, she would move in a little closer to gaze raptly up at him as if a girl wanting nothing else. 'Because it's illegal? As are many things, yet still they happen and most people don't even seem to mind. Now, please,' she tapped his chest as one of his two women might, 'a little refreshment and some sustenance. At least a *croquette ou canapé.* Surely those are not out of the question, or does duty prevent you from enjoying yourself?'

The hot, or the hot and the cold. 'Not at all when there's shaved ham from Reims and smoked sausage from Champagne or Brie de Meaux and lots else like sardines, but you still haven't given me the names of your latest clients?'

Damn him for his persistence! 'My secretary will have those. Perhaps you could drop by the office later? Here, let me give you my card. It has the address and telephone number. Call ahead, and I'll be sure to be there to answer fully whatever it is that you need and we can offer. Now tell me, please, about these terrible murders.'

There was only one way to let her know he wasn't yet done with her. 'Let's take a stroll and leave that partner of mine to sort things out here.' And grabbing a bottle of the Moët in case refills were needed, he took her by the arm.

Oeufs durs mayonnaise were among the hors d'oeuvres. Tempting, oh for sure, felt St-Cyr, but because of the Occupation's shortages some of the younger children had never seen an egg before. Terse explanations were being given. Bolduc had already said his piece to the assembled, as had Grégoire. Both were solicitously going from table to table offering condolences before rejoining Yvonne Rouget and himself.

'While I have you at my elbow, mademoiselle, be so good as to tell me why, if the illegal contents of that van were to have been sent over to the Hôpital des Quinze-Vingts, is there not only some of the champagne here, but the *vin rouge, vin blanc de blanc*, ham, cheese, eggs, flour for the *canapés* and *croquettes*, the smoked sausage, sardines, too, and even the truffles? And please don't tell me René Deniard was doing such an illegal thing simply to please his mother. We've already had that from your boss, and even Deniard's younger children knew what an egg was before they got here.'

Must this Sûreté be so impossible? 'Since a reception was called for, where else was I to have found such things? There's little enough as it is.'

'For the hospice of the blind, as suggested by your employer.'

'He *didn't* tell me that!'

'*Ah bon*, perhaps he forgot, as he did that van's being so overdue, but where, please, is Madame Bolduc and your two nieces: Didi, wasn't it, and Yvonne?'

Did he forget nothing? 'The girls are at school, my sister at home.'

'Hence Mademoiselle Jacqueline Lemaire. A beauty, *n'est-ce pas*? Trouble, too?'

'And to *what* are you referring without any possible evidence?'

Damage control having momentarily lapsed, she was all too aware of this but still distracted probably because of the absence of that very one. 'Me? I'm only searching for answers as to why she had to find him a priest.'

'The Church . . . The Bishop, he is . . .' *Ah merde alors!*

He would say it as if from the pulpit. 'Being difficult since Madame Bolduc consistently gives plenty and refuses absolutely to allow the divorce to go through uncontested.'

She would toss the hand of inconsequence at such a thing. 'Divorce has never been easy.'

He would give her a moment, then tell her how it was, since it had been done to stop the disgruntled and/or unfaithful wives of prisoners of war, or those prisoners themselves, from seeking such. 'And under our Government in Vichy, forbidden as of 21 September 1940 unless, of course, the Maréchal Pétain, his advisors in Vichy, and the Bishop agree.'

Must he? 'Oh for sure the Sûreté, they have never been pleasant, but with yourself, you compound it!'

'Fortunately you didn't need to worry about such a formality, since your husband "sleeps in his coffin."'

Touché, the *salaud*! '*Excusez-moi*. I must find Jacqueline.'

Before she says something she shouldn't.

To Yvonne who was now standing at the end of the dock, there was but dismay, felt Jacqueline, to Herr Kohler at the oars, the grin of the urchin he must once have been.

'Wave,' he said, 'then she'll know we'll be heading back in a few minutes or an hour if necessary.'

'You wouldn't!'

Anger made her even more attractive. 'I will, so start by telling me why that lover of yours felt those two *Diamantenbonzen* from Berlin needed to be escorted around the sights and probably free of charge?'

For whatever information could be pried out of them, but had it been a lucky guess? 'I've no idea who you mean. How could I?'

'That's precisely my thought, but if your escorts are, why that would indicate you know far more than you want to let on.'

'I don't. Hector never tells me anything, nor does that one!'

Yvonne Rouget. 'Aren't Hauptmann Reineck and Leutnant Heiss overseeing that bank of his?'

And flying with him early on Thursday to the Côte d'Argent and Côte Sud des Landes for a little pot-shooting and to deliver the bank's gift of a brand-new flying boat. 'They are, but what have they to do with the other two?'

'Since buying and fixing up cars at that garage of his to sell in the Reich shouldn't matter? If one is in the know, isn't the other, and since when would those overseers and the owner of a bank not be interested in diamonds?'

And that *Sonderkommando* whose roadblock to the east of Reims had led to the murders. 'All right, I did offer to see that Ulrich Frensel and Johannes Uhl were shown the sights, but that really only started yesterday. It's to be for a few days.'

'Since they're waiting around for those diamonds to be found.'

The black ones that Josef Meyerhof and others must have hidden in Paris, but Herr Kohler wouldn't tell her who it was that *Kommando* were after. Indeed, though he might now have a name, not an alias, and even a photo, he might still be just rowing about in his own little lake, searching for answers.

Kohler knew he couldn't jeopardize Anna-Marie by asking, but as sure as this one was facing him, she'd had an eye on that girl if only as a potential hostess. Nor could he ask about those vans of Bolduc's ferrying PPF and *Miliciens* and others past the controls while smuggling stuff into Paris.

He's at a loss for words, felt Jacqueline, and letting a hand trail in the water, playfully flicked some at him, since it was her turn to smile.

'Maybe I should tell you what those two were up to before they were shot.'

Turning the boat, deliberately taking his time, he began to slowly head for the dock, she to finally say, 'Well, tell me. Don't just keep me waiting.'

Still he didn't say a thing. He just looked and *looked* at her in that way of his as he rested the oars until, in anger, she heard herself blurting, 'Damn you, were they chasing that girl? Is that why Deniard was hit on the forehead with a rock?'

It was Yvonne who caught the painter and tied the boat up, Yvonne who said, 'We mustn't keep Chairman Bolduc waiting.'

Notebook open, pen to its side, Louis was sitting at that table on the porch, having tucked into the hors d'oeuvres and facing Bolduc and Georges-Arthur Grégoire who was looking far from calm. Thin, greying, wise no doubt in keeping track of the bank's vans and what they were up to, this operations manager waited for more questions, hands clasped, elbows on the table, a sure sign that he expected nothing but trouble.

'Ah, Hermann, things are not as bad as thought. Mademoiselle, did you enjoy your little voyage?'

She was looking positively ill, thought Kohler, but Yvonne Rouget immediately went into damage control by yanking out the chair next to Louis. Indicating that Mademoiselle Lemaire should take it to avoid having to directly face detectives but her lover instead, she then took her own place with Bolduc and Grégoire on the other side of the table. To proceed wasn't stated, but felt.

'Only eight bundles of the 5,000-franc notes, Hermann.'

Two being from the poor box at Corbeny, five from Rocheleau's sachel and one as grease money for Dillmann, thought Kohler, but now was not the time to mention this.

'But forty-six of the bundles of hundreds, Hermann, eighty-two of those of the twenties, fifty-five of the tens and two hundred and three of the fives, for a total of 4,780,500 francs. The thieves must just have quickly grabbed whatever they could.'

'Inspectors,' blurted Jacqueline, 'I must use the lavabo!'

'Run!' said Hermann. 'And the insurance claim, Chief?'

Hand to mouth, she rushed off, alarm all too evident in the others. 'Slightly more, of course,' said St-Cyr.

These two, they'd strip away everything, felt Grégoire, interjecting quickly, 'To balance things out, Inspectors, we always add a little. It's accepted.'

'Is it?' demanded Hermann.

'Thirty percent, *mon vieux*. We've yet to go over the rest, but there are olives from Provence that we missed, and this too. It brings tears. It's the greatest of the blue cheeses. My Agnès had a terrible passion for it. *Ah, excusez-moi*, the first wife. I seem to keep thinking of her of late. There's also some Picodon. This one's either from Département of the Drôme or the Ardèche, the name itself taken from the *langue d'oc*. It means spicy.'

'But indicates travel from much farther afield, eh,' said Hermann, 'and why is that, Monsieur Grégoire, given that those vans of yours have definite limits to their travel?'

Yvonne, as usual, had been absolutely correct, felt Grégoire, and now this madness of Hector's was going to bring all of them down if not careful. 'Deniard had relatives from Saint-Rémy-de-Provence who are now living in Paris. Perhaps if you were to ask them after the reception, they could tell you . . .'

'Inspectors, can this not wait?' demanded Bolduc.

'Murders never do,' said Louis, 'but if I must, let me remind you all that this is most definitely a murder inquiry.'

With the Abwehr all but gone and worrying about its last days, the Höherer SS and Polizeiführer Oberg would have to deal with these two, felt Bolduc. Yes, Oberg and his deputy. The full force of the avenue Foch, even if he himself had to go down on the knees! 'Then begin by telling us what happened at those ruins. Deniard hit squarely on the forehead *before* being shot?'

Hector *would* demand the obvious, felt Yvonne, therefore she would have to get him the answer he needed. 'But hit by whom, Inspectors?'

'And isn't that the one Herr Kaltenbrunner's *Sonderkommando* are after?' asked Grégoire. 'Well, isn't it, and if so, who was it?'

'Louis, I think I'd better visit the toilets.'

Clearly Bolduc was to be left out on a limb, felt St-Cyr, but care must be taken not to rush things. 'Mademoiselle, messieurs, Hermann and me were able to pick up the trail of that van prior to its arrival at the ruins.'

'Where?' demanded Bolduc, his fists clenched.

'Berru lookout where it was joined by the *gazogène*-powered truck in which rode the killer, and since both were carrying goods bound for the *marché noir*, perhaps you'd be good enough to tell us what had been arranged.'

'Since the one, slow as it must have been, chased after the other only to find those two trusted employees of yours chasing after someone else,' said Hermann, having hustled Jacqueline Lemaire back to the table.

'Did they have a disagreement with that someone?' asked St-Cyr.

'A severe one,' said Kohler. 'It must have been. Mischief certainly. Rape, probably, so start talking.'

Had Jacqueline said something she shouldn't, wondered Bolduc. 'Me, I have no idea of what you're saying. How could any of us? Deniard and Paquette wanting to fool around with whom?'

'Tell them, Mademoiselle Lemaire,' said Kohler. 'If you don't, I will.'

With but that look of his, Hector would destroy her if he could, felt Jacqueline, but she would have to answer, have to endure Yvonne's faint and knowing smile, Georges-Arthur having unclasped his hands to place them flat on the table in judgement. 'Annette-Mélanie Veroche.'

The stupid *chatte* would say it! thought Bolduc. 'What the hell was that girl doing in one of my vans, Jacqueline? Come, come, let us have the proof of it.'

It was all over for her. Everything! Hector would kill her now if he could.

'Well?' demanded Bolduc.

'Hitching a ride,' said Louis, 'but now that we have a name, mademoiselle, could we not also have an address and a little more?'

One must grin and throw out the hands in a gesture of good-will, felt Bolduc. 'Look, Inspectors, it's really a very simple matter. Annette-Mélanie had to go home to Rethel last December to visit her mother who was desperately ill in hospital with pneumonia. You both must know how things are at the Kommandantur during the pre-Christmas rush. A day, two days, three probably in the line-ups and then the quotas, the turn-down. Me, I . . .'

'Let her hitch a ride in one of your vans,' said Louis, 'so as not to have to bother getting the necessary *ausweis*: the *laissez-passer* and *sauf-conduit*.'

'Was it the same van, Monsieur Bolduc?' asked Hermann.

'It was,' said Yvonne, having laid a hand gently over those of Georges-Arthur which again had been clasped.

'Then, I take it, that girl knew of both Deniard and Pacquet,' said St-Cyr.

Somehow Yvonne and himself had to save the bank, felt Grégoire. 'They would have recognized her, but neither Mademoiselle Rouget nor myself were aware of what was going on behind our backs.'

'You . . .' began Bolduc.

'Monsieur, must I caution you?' said Louis.

'And is she the person that *Sonderkommando* are after?' asked Hermann.

It would have to be admitted so as to gain time, felt Bolduc. 'We have been led to believe so, yes, but have not yet said anything of it to others. Like yourselves, we have been trying to put two and two together.'

'Good,' said Kohler. 'First by asking questions of those two overseers and friends of yours who are swimming in the know because they have to be even though the Abwehr is on the skids, and now by the two most recent clients of this one's escort service.'

But did it go even deeper than that? wondered St-Cyr. There was only one way to find out, though not here. 'Show them the letter from Kaltenbrunner, Hermann. Let them see that if they say anything of this matter to anyone but ourselves, the Reichssicherheitschef will hear of it.'

'Inspectors . . .' said Yvonne, taking the letter.

'Save it,' said Hermann, taking it back. 'Mademoiselle Lemaire, the address of this person who must have witnessed the murders?'

Hector would be only too glad to see her body dragged naked from the Seine, she having been beaten, violated, all those things so as to but increase the gossip, felt Jacqueline. Georges-Arthur, he simply looked at and through her as though saying, You fool, and Yvonne as if, *Salope*, now you've really done it to that future 'husband' of yours, haven't you? But there was her pride, most certainly. 'Inspectors, let me show you since she lives in the very building where I have my office and have a file on each of my escorts, as well as every client that one has sent to me.'

Both Yvonne Rouget and Grégoire seemed relieved, felt St-Cyr, as they looked questioningly at their chairman who gave them but the cruelest of nods. 'Then for now, we will break off this discussion. Be prepared to answer fully and truthfully when time—our time—allows.'

'Jacqueline is far too upset,' said Bolduc. 'Perhaps if Yvonne were to . . .'

'She can't come with her, can she?' said Kohler. 'Since everything we do has to be kept a secret none of you had better reveal.'

It was Arie who took the stitches out and gave her a pair of light grey gloves from which he had cut each of the first joints and re-knitted them perfectly; Aire who said he was glad to see her back safely and that she was to keep the bike and leave it here if needed; Aire who asked if she had found things okay at her place.

There was no sign of Étienne.

'He's gone to move his wife and children. I told him he had to, that I'd stay to help you if needed.'

'He's not coming back, is he.'

'We were going to split up anyways, but after what you said of Frans, we both knew he should get out of Paris while he could. This war, this Occupation is going to end, Anna-Marie. It's months now, not years. It has to be, and when they're kicked out, the *Moffen* will be far from friendly, and the locals, the *collabos* or not, every bit as bad. Stay clear of those who have been helping you. Go to ground as soon as you can. Don't get mixed up in anything more. The SD, SS and Gestapo want you, and unless you're awfully careful, they'll get you.'

'Is that really why you stayed?'

'It is, and I still have the truck to take care of. I don't know where Étienne's keeping his family. I never did, not since the defeat. We had met before the war and had got to know one another, and then, having escaped from a prisoner-of-war camp in the autumn of 1940, he found his way to Rotterdam and we decided to do what we could. You're the last of several and now if I could, I'd say let's take in a film, but we both know what that could mean.'

Since the Occupier, the Paris Police and others regularly raided the film theaters to grab anyone they could for the Service du Travail Obligatoire and the wanted ones especially.

'There is one thing I'd like to know. When we met up with that van at the Berru lookout, did those two know of you? Me, I ask only because I heard you suck in a breath and softly gasp, "Ah, no."'

'I recognized them, they myself, but I couldn't say a thing because Frans had that pistol.'

'You must have been terrified.'

'I was. I had used that van before, but please don't ask when or how. There isn't time.'

'Then tell me about Frans. Tell me where he is and what's to happen to him.'

'Obviously I can't answer but I can tell you those who have helped me are good people. Frans will be questioned, and I know I will have to be there. They've not insisted, you understand. They will simply expect it of me and I mustn't do otherwise because that's the way they are. "*Tous pour un, un pour tous.*"* It'll be dark—

---

* All for one, one for all, and from D'Artagnan, in *The Three Musketeers* by Alexandre Dumas, 1844.

it always is—and I'll be using my own bike because I still have to get it, but could I come back here afterward?'

Since her concierge would question things when awakened. 'Of course. Apoline will hear of it and think what she will and be delighted, but you'll have to go and see her first thing in the morning. It wouldn't be right not to. I can come with you, though.'

To back up whatever was said and Madame de Kerellec might think. 'Then we'll do that. Now I must head for the *métro* on foot and try to figure out what to tell my own concierge since I've only just arrived and he'll not be expecting me to leave again.'

The *métro* . . . 'And if they have posted photos of you?'

Impulsively he had reached out to gently take her by the hands causing her to feel what? wondered Anna-Marie, only to answer, In another place and at another time perhaps, but not now. 'Just don't wait up. Just leave the lock off and when I've brought the bike in, I'll take care of it.'

Beekhuis knew he might never see her again and that if taken, she would try to keep the rue Vercingétorix from them for as long as possible.

Twelve hours was the wish, but few could hold out that long.

The file was easily located, the office tastefully finished, felt St-Cyr, even to having a more private room behind it: a home away from home or of the spur of the moment with a day bed, a settee, drinks' cabinet and such just in case needed.

And this one? he asked himself of Jacqueline Lemaire. *Bien sûr*, she was ambitious but was she vindictive enough to save herself and sink Bolduc?

Having irritably lit a cigarette as soon as they had arrived, she sat pensively where her secretary had been, he having told the girl to come back in an hour, but he couldn't have Anna-Marie finding him here. Concierge Figeard had been difficult and could well warn her he was not just in the building but in this office.

'"Annette-Mélanie Veroche, age twenty-two years, eight months," mademoiselle?'

This one would know only too well what such a file should contain. 'I don't need it *read* to me.'

'"Blonde, blue-eyed and a little above average height? Figure, perfect, if a bit thin? Father, deceased, German; mother, of French

Huguenot extraction? Home address: *bis* thirty-two (a) *place* de la République, Rethel, Ardennes?" Did she give permission for you to record any of this?'

'Of course not! Why would she?'

'She refused when asked, did she?'

Ah merde! 'I . . . I never asked, not beyond seeing if she'd like to join Les Amies.'

'So you went after the information elsewhere, having been prompted to do so by your lover?'

Must he? 'Yes!'

The Paris address was given, also a student, her dissertation being primarily on those early Cistercian monasteries, but he must hurry, thought St-Cyr. All too soon Hermann would be confronting Oberfeldwebel Dillmann and then what? Dillmann to Heinrich Ludin to tell him this half of the *Sonderkommando* must be onto something big.

Recent and not so recent photos showed Annette-Mélanie on foot and on her bike or at her studies in the Bibliothèque Nationale's reading room, poring over what had to be a very early illuminated manuscript written on velum in Latin; others at Chez Kornilov with none other than Sergei Lebeznikov and what must be his son. The hungry student, the *Mischlinge*, the *onderduiker* was even wearing the dress and no doubt the high heels but not the diamond bracelet and necklace of pearls.

'Mademoiselle, in none of these would that girl have realized she was being photographed.'

What more did he want? Having ushered Camille out the door in an instant, he had closed and locked it and gone straight to that filing cabinet.

'Well?' he demanded.

Hector would make certain it all ended for her. There would be no more salons and soirees, no more dinners or telephone calls from Suzanne Abetz, Nicole Bordeaux, Florence Gould or any of the others, no more perfect clients with unlimited cash. 'Oh for sure, there are photos. Don't men like to see what they're getting?'

'But they weren't "getting" this one, were they? "Refuses to join us, gives excuse after excuse, the studies, the part-time jobs, the mother . . ." et cetera, et cetera.'

Everyone who was anyone would banish her.

'Mademoiselle, it's not good to keep me waiting, especially at a time like this.'

'All right, all right! Hector had someone take those. He had met that girl here and at Madame Bordeaux's and had thought she'd be perfect for Hauptmann Reineck or even Leutnant Heiss, who is married and missing his young wife.'

'And the photographer, mademoiselle?'

He would want everything! 'The Hauptmann found someone, and when batches of photos had been taken, it was he who brought the prints here for me to keep.'

But not the negatives, and therefore an Abwehr-West photographer. Someone so reliable, Anna-Marie would not have known. Also, of course, Reineck would have been a client of this escort service, to which Hermann would have said, How cosy. 'And has your lover copies of them?'

'No! He . . . he looked at them here from time to time.'

'And the part-time jobs, did you help her get them?'

'Only the one with Madame Bordeaux and because Hector thought it would be good to show her off. The other jobs she got herself. First the one here in the autumn of 1941.'

'After having moved in.'

'And then in the summer of last year, the one at the bookshop. Nicole met her here at the concerts and there, too, and that settled the matter. Me, I made sure of it.'

'Because Bolduc insisted on it?'

'Yes, damn it!'

'A student doesn't usually have the clothing in these?' He had held up two from Chez Kornilov.

'Nicole had those things delivered here.'

'When?'

Damn him! 'Mid-August of last year. I . . . I then loaned the girl a few trinkets but those she always left with Nicole. That's why they're not in the photos.'

'And did either or both of Bolduc's bank overseers meet her at one or more of the salons at that *maison de maître* on the rue de la Boétie?'

She would have to say it. 'Reineck wanted her very badly and Hector loves to tease and constantly needs favours from them, they from him.'

Ah bon. 'And the boy in this photo?'

Not the man, not the *gestapiste française* and second-in-command of Rudy de Mérode's Neuilly Gestapo. 'The son of the other. Pierre-Alexandre Lebeznikov, a subdeacon or something. She takes rosemary to him for the incense burners.'

'Grown where, please?'

Why on earth did he need to know *that*? 'The Jardin des Plantes, one of the assistant gardeners.'

'Name, since that lover of yours would have had you find that out as well and Hauptmann Reineck would have had that photographer make certain of it.'

Ah, mon Dieu, mon Dieu, this was all going wrong! 'Jacques Leporatti.'

An Italian, a former Communist probably. 'Bolduc certainly got you to check up on this girl, so perhaps you'd be good enough to tell me why, beyond what you've already admitted?'

It would have to be said. 'Hector moves people into and out of Paris in those vans of his. The service is far from free, you understand, but please don't think it's completely illegal and against the wishes of our friends. Hauptmann Reineck and Leutnant Heiss both knew of it long ago, and when Annette-Mélanie told Hector on 28 November last that her mother was very ill and she had to get home in a hurry, Hector offered to help and she went to meet him at that garage of his.'

'Those overseers of his also having known of this?'

'*Oui.* Those two have always closely watched everything Hector does, including his affair with myself, and his putting the money up for this escort service.'

'And at that garage whichever drivers and assistants were present would have seen her?'

Had he thrown her a rope? 'Hector letting them say what they would of her to themselves and then joking about it and telling them that was exactly what she needed.'

The knife at last! 'And she returned when, please?'

'The tenth of December.'

'Having used the service twice—out and back into Paris?'

'*Oui,* but . . . but it didn't happen then, and this time she . . . she lined up at the Kommandantur for hours to get the necessary papers and took the train to Rethel. This I know because he had me check.'

'He wanted to know why she hadn't asked him again?'

'Most certainly.'

'And that then caused him and those overseers of his to question the matter further?'

Hector would definitely not be happy with her. *'Oui.'*

'Now let's be absolutely clear on this. Would Deniard and Paquette have recognized her after an absence of eight months?'

'Me, I have to think so.'

'But would they still have tried to do what Bolduc felt she needed?'

'To please him? *Ah mon Dieu*, does it really matter so much? She's just a student and has nothing but a dissertation on those damned monasteries and monks.'

Ah bon. 'You've been in that girl's room, have you?'

This was not good. 'Only for a look. She . . . she has nothing, Inspector. Not a thing from home, just the cork from a champagne bottle on her bedside table.'

'But did that lead to the broken neck of another in the back of that van, mademoiselle?'

'It must have, mustn't it? That's what Hector and his overseers have just come to believe, and now they want that girl more than ever since she will be able to lead them to all those diamonds, but she's out there somewhere and they don't know where.'

9

Having just arrived back from the *métro* where things had been difficult to say the least, felt Anna-Marie, she had found Monsieur Figeard adamant. Nothing would suffice but that she immediately leave and go next door to tell Pierre-Alexandre that she couldn't marry him.

'Mademoiselle, that boy has to stop pestering me. I can't have him coming here at all hours begging to know if you've returned. I've told him nothing, you understand. *Absolument rien!*'

'I'll just go up to my room, then I'll go to see him.'

St-Cyr was still in the building! 'Don't! Go now and quickly.'

For emphasis, he glanced at the ceiling, instantly letting her know there was a far greater reason. 'Should I take my bike?'

Grâce à Dieu, she had understood. 'That would, I think, be a good idea, but hurry.'

She couldn't leave her suitcase, couldn't leave the diamonds, yet could take neither at present. 'If I can, I'll duck in to let you know how things go.'

'In ten minutes I'll be waiting at the artists' entrance.'

Ten and not a moment longer. A black, four-door Citroën, its engine at idle, was parked outside Chez Kornilov, the two leaning against it wearing the broad-lapelled suits and snap brims of *gestapistes français* and smoking cigarettes while waiting for their boss. All of which was terrible, but had Arie had a premonition of it?

'Arie,' she said, only to realize she had just kissed the heel of her gloved left hand.

Having retrieved the Sparta and its trailer from the cellars, she now had to walk them under the eyes of those two. Every second told her they would cross the rue Daru to grab her and the bike, but they didn't. They just looked and looked, seemingly as men will.

There was a side door she usually went to during the week when services were not being held. Opening onto a small grove of trees and a garden, it offered respite and a modicum of seclusion, but she wouldn't have to knock and wait for Pierre-Alexandre. The door was propped open by an upended wooden shoe, not Dutch but Russian from the days of the Revolution.

Monsieur Sergei Lebeznikov—she couldn't think of him as Serge de Lenz—was listening attentively to his son's baritone which melodiously filled the cathedral. On seeing her, he smiled generously and softly said, 'He's good, isn't he? It's his calling.'

'Monsieur, can we speak outside a moment, please?'

Did the girl not *want* to listen? 'Mademoiselle, the boy will be glad to see you back safely. Was it bad—your mother?'

'Not at all. Perfect, really. A miracle, but . . .'

He had taken her by the arm.

'There will be no *buts*. When he's finished, we'll cross the street and have a little celebration. I'll get the others to do what I was going to.'

The others—those two. 'Monsieur Lebeznikov, please speak to Pierre-Alexandre for me. I can't marry him. Maman is deeply of our Church; my father was too. For me to do such a thing would be to go against everything they've taught me. Besides, I hardly know him.'

Perhaps if he gently told her how it really was for most? 'Knowing often comes. It just takes its time.'

Why must he be so impossible? 'There's the war; this Occupation. Everything is so uncertain. Please, I have to hurry to the dentist. I can't be late. Tell him I'll see him later but he mustn't bother Concierge Figeard anymore.'

'Leave the bike. My men will give you a lift.'

'It's not far but afterward I must go to the Bibliothèque Nationale to renew my place in its reading room. If I don't, I'll lose it and I can't have that, not now, not when my dissertation is almost finished.'

She was going to have to listen. 'Mademoiselle, you're perfect for him and come very highly recommended by the very best of Parisian society. The boy's desperate. If you won't marry him, he's determined to leave the Church and I can't have that. Not with the way things are developing.'

Things . . . 'He's safe here, is that what you mean?'

'You will be too. The Church guarantees it, and you'll have everything you need. A flat in Neuilly, a place in the south, cash in the bank and lots more.'

'Please, I really must go. I *will* speak to him later, I promise.'

'Can I tell him you'll think seriously of it?'

'Of course. If that will help, then certainly.'

'Now I must rush off myself to the rue de Vaugirard and Porte de Versailles. An Oberfeldwebel who's been up to mischief. Be good to Pierre-Alexandre. Be gentle. He really is smitten with you, and I don't think either of us would want to see him hurt.'

The rue de Vaugirard and not far from the rue Vercingétorix. That coin Frans should have had in his pockets but hadn't. An Oberfeldwebel.

At 1650 hours the Porte de Versailles was busy, noted Kohler, but when dealing with the venomous even detectives who have shown mercy in the past had better tread carefully. Finding a café with a view, he ordered a coffee. Dillmann was doing the usual. Dillmann didn't give a damn about anything else, even to ratting on them to Ludin about the partnership's probably meeting up at Chez Rudi's during Saturday's *cinq à sept*. If he had to, Dillmann would probably choke his mother or sell his sister. These days, he had never had it so good.

Three of the Tabac National's trucks were sent on their way with a rap on the hood and, '*Ach*, I'll see you later.' A farm truck, a *gazo*, took more time. After all, there were papers to glance at, questions to be asked, and were the *flics* and the Vichy food controllers taking any notice? But would this one and those tobacco trucks be sent to the horse abattoir, or had that son of a bitch changed his drop-off?

Without a cigarette to nurse, Kohler knew he could only wait and be reminded of Schütze Hartmann and those from the previous encounter. Having dropped Louis and Jacqueline Lemaire off at the Salle Pleyel, he had gone straight to Boemelburg's villa in Neuilly. That letter from Kaltenbrunner had worked its magic— he'd only to show that SD Head Office stamp and that signature— but it had been a mistake, of course. Oona and Giselle were being well looked after but had been more than anxious and not just about themselves, about Anna-Marie, and he'd known he'd have to be truthful. Somehow Louis and he were going to have to get them out of there and away from Heinrich Ludin.

All of which meant first dealing with this cobra.

When a black Citroën *traction avant* exactly like the one he had parked out of sight on the boulevard Lefebvre nearby, headed in to have a word, he knew the worst. Sergei Lebeznikov was greeting that bastard as though a long lost friend. Questions were being asked and talked over, answers too readily given, the agreement settled with but a clap on the back and handshake.

Louis would have said, God really doesn't care, Hermann. There are always two sides to any coin.

And we're not on either, he'd have replied. There was nothing for it but to try the horse abattoir and hope it was still being used. Anna-Marie Vermeulen had sure dug a hole for them and with no bottom in sight, was it to be nothing but a free fall?

'Monsieur Figeard, what is this you are saying?'

That ten minutes had stretched into a half-hour, and having lied to him again and again as she must have, did this girl he had trusted deserve anything further? wondered Figeard. 'Mademoiselle Veroche, you have challenged my very judgement, and certainly if he were to know that I had even listened to you, Chief Inspector Jean-Louis St-Cyr of the Sûreté would be grateful.'

Grateful? 'Please just tell me. To stand out here on the street with my bike is not good. Pierre-Alexandre, he has refused to listen and might . . .'

'Was that his father who roared by earlier in that car with those other two?'

'It was.'

'And having "witnessed" two murders, is it that you are in trouble with one such as that?'

'And others, but only because of a promise I made to a very dear man who was about to be sent away just as were my parents.'

Ah mon Dieu, what was this? 'As he left, the chief inspector said, "Tell her the tobacco pouch is still empty."'

Meet him in the Jardin d'Hiver but not today—tomorrow! 'Let me get my suitcase and say good-bye to the rabbits and chickens.'

'And the Boche, if they should arrest you?'

'Will simply be told you knew nothing.'

'Mademoiselle Lemaire is still in the building.'

'Then I must wait until she has left or hope the door to her office is closed.'

'What's she got to do with things?'

'Everything, probably.'

'Then let me go ahead, and I'll make sure it's closed.'

'Don't speak to her. Don't tell her anything, for if you do, all will be lost.'

'Mademoiselle, there is something else you should know. The chief inspector has a partner. While he's definitely not the usual, he is still of the Gestapo.'

Blinking at him through the autumn sunlight, Dillmann's keeper of the horse abattoir's sheet-iron doors said, '*Ach*, Herr Kohler, the Oberfeldwebel told me that if you should come by, I was to give you a few packets of cigarettes. Run the car in, and I'll open a box.'

The tobacco trucks had just left as had the other one, the smell of the gasoline given clear enough, as were the sacks of potatoes, squash, cabbage, carrots, onions, et cetera. 'And you are?'

'Gefreiter Weiss. We're about done for today, so he should be here soon.'

There was no point in asking anything else since Werner would have taken steps to keep what he knew to himself, but it was interesting that he had been expected.

'We've matches, too,' sang out Weiss, having shouldered the Schmeisser. 'Here, take a few of these as well.'

'*Dank*. I'll just borrow your flashlight and have a little look around. You never know when it might be useful.'

What the hell was Kohler after? He hadn't switched off the Citroën, had parked facing the doors so that he could beat it as fast as they did. Only now and then was the light needed but when it shone fully on the walkway door that gave out onto the rue Brancion, the thought came that he must want another exit. Checking to see if it was locked, which it was with a sliding bolt above the handle, the Detektiv released this and opened the door a little.

Satisfied, he let what darkness there was return, but only now and then were his footsteps heard beyond the background noises of this place.

'Gefreiter, that Oberfeldwebel of yours is on his way. If you'd bothered to put a hand on the concrete beneath those boots, you'd have felt the vibrations.'

Scheisse, he had come up right behind him and had a hand on the Schmeisser!

'Open the big doors and tell Werner to leave room for me to get out ahead of him. He can then close the doors himself when the rest of you are in the truck.'

As if on cue, the truck turned in and when told, Werner heaved himself out from behind the wheel of that chariot and, tossing away a perfectly good cigarillo, said, 'Hermann, *mein lieber Kamerad,* what is this?'

'You tell me and then we'll both know, but while you're at it, where's Schütze Hartmann?'

His little informant with the steel-rimmed specs. '*Ach*, it was felt Russia would be good for the boy, but the medics got him first and guess what they found?'

The son of a bitch! 'A massive dose of the clap.'

Gregariously, what was left of those hands were thrown out in a gesture of sympathy. 'So he's taking the cure, my Hermann, and if he's lucky, his mother won't hear of it.'

'When she gets the usual, eh?'

The death notice, but had Hermann seen him talking to Serge de Lenz, was that the cause of the trouble?

'Well?'

'Who am I to question what the brass decide?'

'But you did tell them the boy was anxious to prove himself in battle with eyesight like that?'

Such a concern had to be but a diversion. 'Doesn't one say what one has to before such people?'

The shit! 'There's the matter of a coin you should have told me about. You let that *Schmuggler* through the Porte de Versailles at 0810 hours this morning and didn't feel it necessary that I should hear of it. Instead, knowing you as I do, you would have dropped everything here and personally hand-delivered that *Spitzel*'s little calling card to Heinrich Ludin and Standartenführer Gerhard Kleiber at the avenue Foch.'

'But . . . but what else was I to have done? Countermanded an order from Kaltenbrunner?'

'How much did they pay you?'

'Nothing. I was told I was just doing my duty.'

While repeatedly taking half of every load he could in exchange for the grease, oil and gasoline needed, Kleiber having put it straight to him, no doubt. 'And the coin?'

'Of silver, but as to my not having immediately sent word to yourself, perhaps if you were to ask that "source of all gossip" he would tell you that I most certainly did.'

'Rudi?'

While not yet true, such things could always be fixed, especially as Hermann was far too anxious to pull fish from the river. 'I immediately sent word to Herr Sturmbacher at his restaurant. You can't have been in to see him, but now that we've got that little problem settled, tell me what this pigeon they're all after knows and is carrying?'

'It's nothing but a lot of hot air.'

'The two biggest diamond gatherers in the Reich arrive and everyone talks of a half-Jew submarine from the Netherlands, a bank van, two killings, a *Spitzel*, a *Schmuggler* and a *Sonderkommando*? Anyone who is anyone says she's carrying a fortune and knows where the black diamonds are hidden, Hermann. Billions, I tell you. Isn't it up to us to grab a piece of it?'

Ludin would have told Werner to report any further contact with himself but Dillmann wouldn't have said a word of a little something else, namely: 'Fifty-fifty, eh, so long as I pay Rudi his share out of my own?'

'Is not a deal a deal when cut?'

'Having wiped the slate clean for you once, don't expect me to this time.'

'*Ach,* is it threats now, Hermann? If so, please don't forget that Rudi also has friends and friends of friends and a telephone, and no doubt our Rudi also loves diamonds, so let us make a little piece between us. You to let me know, as agreed; me to help as promised, and no one else the wiser.'

This one had told that other Rudy everything he had said to him during that first encounter here: the festering wound, the need for that first-aid kit, et cetera, but these days everyone lied, so another lie wouldn't matter. 'Agreed, but if Louis and I do manage to get our hands on the diamonds, shouldn't we use one of Bolduc's vans?'

'Is that one in it so deeply?'

Werner hadn't known. 'Just answer. Don't complicate life.'

'My truck.'

'And here, Werner?'

'Where else, but you'll have to let me know ahead of time and I have to ask, are you going to let me know?'

'With a gut like yours and that moustache and connections, what else could I do? Just keep using this place and checking in with that gossip fountain but don't be telling anyone else. That would only spoil things for yourself, and we wouldn't want Kaltenbrunner to know of it, would we?'

'I'll just help Weiss open the doors, and we'll all look forward to seeing you again.'

'Louis, we can't eat in a place like this. I'm hungry!'

'We can and must, so don't be worrying about my car that you've let me drive. Just relax. This is one of those restaurants a Parisian would be proud to call his place.'

A *catégorie D** in the 13th on the boulevard de la Gare** and right across from the massively sprawling Gare aux Marchandises and just to the south of the Gare d'Austerlitz-Orléans.

'*Ach*, in an age of mystery meat and leavings' soup, what is it we're to get, eh? Stewed roof rabbit and mashed rutabaga?'

In the Reich, cats were called that and Goebbels offered tasty recipes, while in France, Pétain warned of eating them, since they killed rats and might carry disease. 'Patience is required, *mon vieux*, and we can't do what we have to at Chez Rudi's. There are things I need to show you and talk over and they require uninterrupted peace, not Occupier after Occupier with their *petites amies* and Rudi or that sister of his leaning hungrily over our shoulders. Which you've guaranteed, by the way, as has Werner Dillmann.'

'I was thinking of Rudy de Mérode and Sergei Lebeznikov barging in to find out what we're up to.'

---

* From the verb *se débrouiller*, to make do.
** Now the boulevard Vincent Auriol.

'Even they wouldn't dare. Not here unless they want repercussions.'

Uh-oh. 'Then there's more to it than peace and quiet?'

'Oh for sure there often is, but Agnès can be trusted, as can her second husband, myself having been the first.'

'So now, at last, I know her name too, eh? You told me she had run off with a travelling salesman, or was it a truck driver?'

'Neither. Agnès felt she would be happier with a chef who wanted a place of his own to which I contributed 10,000 francs. Since the money was as much hers as mine, it was a present, and yes, I attended the wedding.'

The things one hadn't known even after all the time together since 13 September 1940.

'Guy Beauchamp is an excellent husband and marvellous cook, Hermann, especially as every day he has to leave their kitchen to seek out and buy the necessary. They've two boys, now seven and ten, and a daughter who is five. I was the mistake; never Agnès.'

Who couldn't stand not knowing if he'd ever come home in anything but a coffin.

'That's another thing experienced detectives have to deal with, Hermann, but since we really do need that quiet, let's not worry about my car. No one will dare to touch it here.'

'Is Beauchamp an FTP, seeing as the railway yards are close by and railwaymen frequent this place?'

'*Ah bon*, you're beginning to understand.'

A brunette who was plump, short, bespectacled and busy, Madame Beauchamp stopped cold when she saw Louis raise a cheery hand. Swiftly she set the loaded plates aside, pointed to other customers to deliver them to still others, and came on like a rocket. Kisses on both cheeks were out of the question.

'Jean-Louis, you said you would never come here with that one. Are you not to be trusted?'

'These days, *ma chère*, necessity causes even the most trustworthy to occasionally break their word. A quiet table, the *prix fixe* but without the ration tickets since I haven't been able to stand in line for new ones, and if that's not possible, the soup. Coffee as well, and since it's not a day without alcohol, a *pousse-café*,* but

---

* A liqueur, a cognac.

first the *vin rouge ordinaire*. It's always excellent, Hermann, for the Halle aux Vins* is but a stone's throw away.'

'You . . .' she began, only to change her mind and shout with a toss of a hand, 'This way then, Chief Inspector. Who am I to deny a Sûreté and his Gestapo partner no matter how decent the first says he is, but you may not sit with everyone else. This I insist. *Vite, vite*, the table at the back where I normally do the accounts, a task that I hate with a passion.'

Younger than Louis by a good ten years, she must have been a lot of fun whenever he happened to be home, but a hand had been laid on that Sûreté's forearm.

'Me, I was sorry to hear of the loss of your new wife and little son, Jean-Louis, but must confess that I consoled myself, for if I had stayed in that house of your mother's, I'd have been the one that bomb would have taken. Would you have missed me, I wonder, knowing that I would have forgiven you for not having warned me of those troublemakers?'

The Résistance, but it had been the Gestapo's Watchers who hadn't removed it, thought Kohler, but Louis would tread lightly.

'Even they have hotheads that can't be controlled, Agnès. What is needed is that big asparagus but also the SOE.** Hermann is one hundred percent. Oh for sure, there's no way I could ever make him into a Frenchman, as will definitely be needed when this Occupation ends, but I have been trying.'

'I'll get Guy but can tell you it's dangerous for us. On the one hand, those who don't want the Occupier will see this Hermann and think what they will of us, on the other, those who support the Occupier will wonder if we're playing a double game, so you do see, I hope, that you have presented us with a dilemma.'

A wise woman now backed up by the cleaver and butcher knife Beauchamp held threateningly. Grinning from ear to ear, he told everyone to relax, that they were both okay.

Louis didn't wait. 'Guy,' he confided, 'Hermann needs a message taken to the Club Mirage on the rue Delambre. Either

* The huge wine store that, after it was torn down in the 1960s, became the location of the Sorbonne's Faculty of Sciences.

** Charles de Gaulle but also the Special Operations Executive who dropped agents into France.

of the Rivard brothers who own two-thirds of that club will do. They're to tell the third owner that absence makes the heart grow fonder.'

'Absence?' asked Agnès.

'*Oui*. The message will be understood.'

'But not by that one's lover, Jean-Louis. By your own, I think. Is that not so?'

She had always been sharp. 'That, too, then.'

'Good. You need someone solid just as myself did, but you wouldn't listen when you settled on that new one, that Marianne. This time, I sincerely hope you've found someone who understands you as I did, and maybe you'll be lucky enough if you understand her, too.'

'Agnès, please. I knew you desperately wanted a family, but on my salary, and with the life I had to lead . . .'

An earful, all of which Hermann, being Hermann, took in.

Shown to a table at the back in a far corner, they had a full view of the entrance, the stand-up bar, coffee machine and all the rest. Solid comfort and the kitchen door to hand if a sudden disappearance was needed. '*Ach*, now I really do want a cigarette,' said Kohler, 'and we damned well don't have any.'

'But we do have this.'

The *mégot* tin of Arie Beekhuis, the alias of Hans van Loos.

From the Salle Pleyel to the Quai d'Orsay, and from there to the rue des Gobelins in the 13th was not the shortest or easiest of rides, thought Anna-Marie, especially as she'd had to pass by the Santé again. Concentrating on the silhouettes she would need during the blackout, she tried not to think of what others would see of her and think: a girl with a suitcase strapped down in her little trailer and a colourful shopping bag up front; a girl who was in a terrible hurry because she had not only to fix those silhouettes in mind for tonight, but watch out for everything else at the moment. She *couldn't* be arrested, not yet.

Rank on the air came the stench of the tanneries. Though none of that work was now being done in the one they used, there were others close by, small factories as well and a warren of them among the soot-blacked, derelict old houses, the former *hôtels particuliers* of ages gone by.

When she saw the solid, six-sided stone tower she wanted, its roof rising above the five attic dormers of the ancient house to which it was a part, she paused, and when she came to the arched entrance of number seventeen, with its crowded, cheek-to-jowl buildings and forbidding gate, the lock had been broken years ago, but *Dieu merci*, the chain that was used had its padlock facing the street and not the courtyard. Félix and those who had helped him had definitely brought Frans here, bound and gagged no doubt, and now still guarded.

Otherwise that padlock would have faced the courtyard.

The family Cavoye had been contemporaries of the Gobelins and had built their 'house' here in about 1520 atop the ruins of an even earlier château. The first had been that of Blanche de Provence, daughter-in-law of the king of Castille; the second named that of the *reine blanche*. But in far more recent times it had been turned into a tannery until the occupier had finally taken so much, sufficient hides had no longer been available for this one and the building had been shuttered.

Turning down the crooked and narrow rue Léon Durand,* there was a further and even better view of that tower from number four, but *merde*, would she be able to find the right place in the dark? Those little blue lights above occasional street names gave but fragments of help and often slowed her.

Turning back to the rue des Gobelins where all was of light industry and grimy, but with its residents also, she said to herself, A lone girl on a bike with a suitcase and a fortune in diamonds shouldn't hang around.

Arie would be happy to see her and could be trusted—she was certain of this, but would have to memorize all of those silhouettes as well, as she headed for 3 rue Vercingétorix.

And then? she asked herself. What then, after Frans's fate has been decided? Was it to be a meeting with that Sûreté in the Jardin d'Hiver tomorrow?

'Hermann, that girl doesn't have a chance. It's only a matter of hours.'

They hadn't even touched their wine. Louis had just managed to roll them a cigarette and had handed it to him to light.

---

* Now Gustave Geffroy.

The spread of photos from that file of Jacqueline Lemaire's wasn't just impressive. Dating from last December and Anna-Marie's first visit home, there were periodic groups of them since and they all engendered nothing but a deeper and deeper sinkhole. 'Whoever took them must have come to know her well, Louis, and not just where she went, but the routes she'd take and even how she would watch out for others like himself and try to cover her tracks.'

'Many have been taken with a telephoto lens, but never once could she have realized he—or perhaps it was a she—was onto her.'

Louis always had to grasp at straws, but maybe it could have been a woman. 'Jacqueline Lemaire might have known of such a one, but it's highly unlikely, given the shortages of film and that to get it without permission, one has to hunt the *marché noir* and draw attention to oneself.'

The cigarette was handed back. 'Hermann, Hector Bolduc got Hauptmann Reinecke to handle the matter.'

Shit! 'He then finding someone who knew exactly what they were doing, and that has to mean an Abwehr-West photographer.'

Ah bon, Hermann had finally realized what they were now up against. 'A *Parisien ou Parisienne*, who wouldn't have stood out, since others would have noticed and she would have seen that they did for she would have been watching constantly for just such a thing. Reinecke would have had a good look at the prints when he delivered them to Jacqueline, but are these the only copies? That is the question.'

'And since Abwehr-West have forbidden their members all contact with the SD, SS and avenue Foch, Ludin and Kleiber won't know of it yet and may not even have guessed.'

A problem for sure. 'Start the car and give me a minute. I'll just apologize.'

Agnès had the soup in hand but Hermann insisted on taking the bowls from her to set them aside and couldn't resist saying, 'You and your Guy have brought us exactly what we need, but now we have to run.'

Must the past continue to haunt? 'Take care of him, then.'

'As he does myself.'

Again as before, felt Anna-Marie, the courtyard at 3 rue Vercingétorix, with its ateliers and one-, two- and even three-storeyed places, was incredibly deep and cluttered. And at its far end was that almost insignificant house with its flaking stucco and clinging ivy, the former stables and garage immediately to the left, while overlooking everything was the back of that tenement, a perfect silhouette especially if the moon was out.

Fewer were about, but all noticed her—the tinsmith in his *bleus de travail*, the mason in his, two old women at the communal tap as well as a young mother who was nursing her baby. Kids, cats, that old collie, all shyly or curiously watched and she said hello to each and gave her name as Annette-Mélanie Veroche, student, they taking note of it and asking, 'Has Madame agreed to let you stay with Monsieur Arie?'

'I'm to see her in the morning.'

'Mornings are never her best.'

'She'll be at her supper. Is Napoléon happy?'

And so it went, she trying to memorize the location of all the staircases, the smells, the drains, the downspouts, the iron bars on some of the windows that gave directly onto the pavement. She mustn't trip in the dark, mustn't drop the bike, must walk it up the centre and hope no one was waiting for her because she was going to have to leave the diamonds with Arie, was going to have to give him a note and an address he could quickly destroy if needed, something like, If I don't come back, take this tin box to . . .

He had been about to reheat an omelette for two and had been watching the courtyard for her, but . . . 'I don't think I could eat. As soon as it's dark enough, I have to leave. You're not to try to follow. You're to stay right here and look after this for me. I haven't told anyone where I'm now staying, and I won't no matter what happens.'

The early evening's traffic was the usual, thought Kohler. Hordes of cyclists constantly dinged their bells, the occasional ribald bangs of a *gazogène* were heard and to those came the hurrying click-clack of the hinged, wooden-soled shoes everyone hated because small stones, twigs and mud would cause them to jam. But no French pedestrian would ever set foot on the pavement directly adjacent to the Hôtel Lutétia at 43 rue d'Assas without one of the Occupier. It was forbidden.

'A gigantic sugar cake of art nouveau and art deco, Louis,

whose rooms and suites were all cut up into offices in the summer of 1940 for counterespionage agents and all the rest. A former bastion of Left-Bank luxury, with ground floor, five storeys and attics, and since the defeat, the home of Abwehr-West who let so many out of jail and gave them jobs and purchasing agencies to hide behind. And considering what's now happening to the Abwehr, if that's not irony, what is?'

Though in a hurry, it would have to be said. 'Irony? Look across *place* Alphonse Deville and what do you see?'

'The military prison of the Cherche-Midi.''

'Had the Church not agreed to the sale of the Convent of the Daughters of the Good Shepherd in 1847, Hermann, *that* would never have been built to remind us all of the shame of Dreyfus having been arrested and the injustice now of far too many others.'

'Let me deal with the sentries here.'

A last, fleeting glimpse of the setting sun gave the nearby Bon Marché, Paris's first department store and one of Agnès's great pleasures, but . . . 'Speaking of irony, Inspector, was that not a forest-green Cadillac Sixty Special you just parked my car behind?'

'*Liebe Zeit*, the things one misses when in a hurry.'

Both sentries had machine pistols, so security must have been beefed up. 'Kohler, Kripo, Paris-Central, *meine Freunde*. Hauptmann Reinecke and Leutnant Heiss. It's urgent.'

'And a murder inquiry,' said St-Cyr. 'Show them the letter, Hermann.'

But a glance was needed.

'They're in the darkroom, in the cellars. Go left at the main foyer and desk, and immediately take the staircase down. Shall I ring them?'

'It's to be a surprise,' said Hermann.

'The darkroom, Hermann, and not in records?'

'Not the usual, then. Not a top priority. Incidental, even just a notion about someone, but there will be the negatives and at least one print of each.'

The little red light was on and the door locked. 'Let me,' said Louis.

'Don't expect me to find liniment to rub on that shoulder.'

---

* Levelled in 1966 and since 1968 a school of higher education and social sciences.

'It won't be necessary. The solution, if you had taken the trouble, is readily available.'

A bucket of sand represented the tonic for incendiaries should any happen to fall on the hotel and make it to the cellars. Taking it up, Louis rammed the lock, the door flying open to reveal two startled uniforms who immediately dropped what they'd been holding and reached for holstered pistols.

'Don't!' said Kohler. Reinecke was the taller, Heiss the younger, though both were under the age of thirty. 'Chief Inspector, slap the bracelets on that one, while I do this one. Both have been up to enough mischief for the Führer to want them shot.'

'No pistols, please, gentlemen,' said St-Cyr. 'No handcuffs either, but where does Hector Bolduc want you to deliver these?'

Prints and negatives of that girl were scattered about, thought Kurt Reinecke, but this Sûreté and Kripo, though hated by the SD, SS and Gestapo, were on the best of terms with the Kommandant von Gross-Paris, who not only despised those others but revered the Abwehr.

'Well?' demanded St-Cyr.

'This is a top-secret Abwehr investigation. If I were you, I'd back off and leave Leutnant Heiss and myself to deal with it.'

'Top secret, Hermann.'

'And a nice try, Chief, so they can join us if they like. Now where are these to be delivered, Hauptmann?'

The time to take care of these two would have to come later. 'That garage of his.'

'Good!' said St-Cyr. 'Let's fill that wastebasket with every negative and print of her, and when we get there, why we can have a look at them to see how valuable they'll be to our murder investigation and no other.'

'You to take the negatives and the prints, Chief, me to drive the Cadillac and take these Abwehr so that I can answer any questions they might have of what's to happen to them if they don't cooperate.'

'But will follow, Hermann. Otherwise you might never find it, and I'd have to find you and then that girl after everything else with these two and Bolduc has been settled.'

Always in the rue des Gobelins during the blackout, thought Anna-Marie, there would be the sudden and not so sudden sounds of nearby industry; always, too, one of the *hirondelles*—the swallows—a cape-wearing *flic* on a bicycle who would do his best to see that not a glimmer of light was showing, this one a sadist at it.

On and on he came, the squeaking of ungreased axle and sprocket lamenting his passage and irritating him but giving warning, as did the blinkered, blue-washed headlamp he would often switch off so that, leaving the bike, the hunt for her could begin.

Alone and dwindling, that red taillight at last found the rue Léon Durand to vanish southward toward the Gobelins itself. But now the gate at number seventeen wouldn't open. Now, when she felt for it, the padlock was on and facing inward. Frans wasn't here. Frans had been moved. Something must have happened. Had the *Moffen* done a razzia? Had that been why that *flic* hadn't bothered to search for her? Had they all been arrested, Frans as well?

Letting go of the padlock, it struck the iron bars.

'Mademoiselle, you endanger Félix with a matter you should have taken care of yourself. Now you expect us to do your housekeeping when you have jeopardized the lives of all of us. Were you followed? Did you even consider going back out to the boulevard Arago to have a final look and listen?'

'Aram . . .'

'Have you understood what I have just said?'

'I was desperate. I . . . I didn't even know if Félix would be at the Gare de l'Est.'

'But took a chance.'

'Yes.'

'And were you once an apprentice borderline sorter for the Diamant Meyerhof in Amsterdam?'

Frans must have told them. 'Yes.'

'And do you know where these so-called black diamonds are hidden?'

'Definitely not.'

'But you do have some to deliver?'

'Simply to an address I must keep to myself. They're not the black diamonds, not really. Those are something else entirely, and I really know nothing of them.'

'Chosen, were you?'

'When one is very desperate, one seeks help that can be trusted absolutely.'

Hence Félix. 'But that is not the answer I want.'

'Then by a very dear man who, for all I know, may no longer be alive.'

'And is this Meyerhof to cause us all to lose our lives as well?'

Though she didn't know him well, Aram had on two occasions left her with the impression that he tended to go around things to come at them indirectly, thus throwing a person off, so as to find out as much as he could. 'I was given some to use if necessary but was told to sell them a little at a time so as not to attract undue attention.'

'Yet already you have attracted far too much.'

Only then did he pause to quicky light a cigarette, hiding the flame in cupped hands but giving the briefest glimpse of that high and narrow brow, the jet-black hair, darkest of eyes and close-cropped beard. Having lived through not one but two horrible genocides, those of 1906 and 1915–1918, Aram Bedikian did everything he could to stop another. Nothing, though, could have disguised the accent.

Unlocking the gate, he let her in, then put the lock back on.

'Some couldn't make it, but there are enough for you to face a quorum.'

'And Frans?'

'Will answer your accusations. We're not uncivilized. We try to do things correctly.'

The Cadillac was a honey, felt Kohler, but this investigation, where was it all to end? Oona and Giselle held hostage, Louis's Gabrielle threatened with the same and now these two from Abwehr-West who not only had thought they'd the right to do what they wanted with Anna-Marie but would presently strip her of the diamonds if they could in order to save their own miserable asses.

Reinecke and Heiss had tried to lay it in on in the car: *Gleich-schalten, ja?* Himmler's bringing everything and everyone into line, the Abwehr vanishing into the Sicherheitsdienst, so of course, they were, they had tried to claim, working secretly for the SD, having jumped ship before it was too late.

Russia deserved them, but as sure as that God of Louis's had made mice to get caught in traps, he'd have to show them and Bolduc that the partnership didn't piss about.

Ah nom de Dieu, felt St-Cyr, what the hell had happened en route? Hermann hadn't hesitated. He had gone straight for the Purdey in the Citroën's boot as Reinecke and Heiss, looking smug and self-satisfied, had got out of the Cadillac.

Side by side under the dim blue wash of the garage's light at 2010 hours on this Monday, five of the bank's vans were in. Beside these, its back door open, was the one from the robbery, and next to it, two gasoline-powered trucks with engines still running.

The dogs were nowhere to be seen or heard. Instead, heavily laden with wine, champagne, hams, cheeses, sacks of potatoes and tins of cooking oil, et cetera, et cetera, two dealers and four helpers had been caught red-handed. *Bien sûr*, it was definitely a moment of decision.

'BOFs emptying that storeroom ahead of us, Louis.'

'And in a hurry, *mon vieux*, but for now we had better stick to priorities. Messieurs,' he called out, 'Sûreté and Kripo at your pleasure. Leave while you can if you wish, since we have bigger fish to fry.'

Bolduc wasn't in that office away from the office. He was distant from it in a veritable Ali Baba's cave and clutching two magnificent hams by the bone. Seeing them, he angrily shouted, 'Inspectors, what the hell is the meaning of this? Another invasion of my privacy without a warrant? I demand an explanation.'

'Which we will be only too glad to give. Hermann, please ask his overseers to find us a little pâté, some cheese and biscuits to go with those pills you must have taken and what this one has yet to set aside.'

'You can't arrest those two,' said Bolduc. 'They're Abwehr-West and are working on a top-secret investigation.'

'To which you were a party, monsieur—is that how it was, and you not even supposed to know they were even Abwehr?'

'They're not budging anyway, Louis, not with this in my hands, but will be trying to figure out how to make life a little more difficult for us.'

'Good, but grab something to eat. Messieurs, that office *immédiatement*.'

Tough to the last, Bolduc set the hams aside and said, 'Kohler, there's really no need for that upland twelve. I know perfectly well what it can do since it happens to be one of those that I, like everyone else, had to turn in.'

Yet had, in a way, managed to keep. 'Don't argue. Just do as you've been told. We're the ones who ask the questions. You and the others are supposed to give the answers.'

Louis had them sit across the table from him, he with the darkroom's wastebasket on a chair and that Secret-Reich-Business envelope Oona had looked into, directly in front of him with the file from Jacqueline Lemaire's escort service.

Cigarettes were reluctantly offered, cognac poured, for Hermann, being Hermann, hadn't hesitated to give each of them and themselves a goodly double.

Setting the two twenty by twenty prints from Hague Central of Anna-Marie facing them as a reminder, St-Cyr said, '*Geheime Reichssache, meine Lieben. Ein Diamantensonderkommando*, yet you have failed entirely to tell us of the photos you had someone take.'

'We were getting those together to take to Kleiber and Ludin,' said Reinecke.

'And even the negatives, but bringing them here?'

'It was en route.'

'Then let's all have a look at them, shall we?'

Digging into the basket, St-Cyr selected a few to hold up for Kohler, but which ones, wondered Bolduc, for that Sûreté then set them face down on the table beside himself. Hated now more than ever by the PPF, who would have immediately formed another hit squad, they were now also the sworn enemies of Rudy de Mérode and Serge de Lenz. Four hundred thousand francs might do it, a million if necessary, but somehow they would have to be silenced and quickly. Most wouldn't give a damn anyway beyond sighs of relief. Jacqueline could entice them to meet somewhere with the offer of yet more information, and would gladly go down on her knees to beg forgiveness from him and prove it.

One of the photos had been placed between the two from Hague Central.

'The reading room of the Bibliothéque Nationale, messieurs,' said St-Cyr. 'A student diligently at her studies, the manuscript centuries old. That alone should have caused you to pause.'

'Why?' demanded Bolduc, tossing off the last of his cognac

and wiping his lips with the back of a hand. 'So what if she's good at languages? French, Dutch, German, even English. The little *chatte* has a gift for them.'

'And the English, monsieur, where, please, did you overhear her speaking it?'

'Must you try to suck up evidence like a carp?'

'A noble fish upon which the Cistercians who did not eat meat depended.'

'Give him the answer,' said Kohler, helping himself to the rest of the chairman's cigarettes and lighter.

'I heard her speaking it to Florence Gould at one of Nicole Bordeaux's cultural gatherings.'

'And this photo, monsieur, when would it have been taken in this girl's room?' asked St-Cyr.

Sacré nom de nom! 'I have absolutely no idea. Why should I have?'

'Hauptmann Reinecke, I gather Jacqueline Lemaire informed you, or the lieutenant, of when it would be appropriate to illegally enter that room.'

St-Cyr would never back off and neither would Kohler. 'That is correct, but as to when that photo was taken, perhaps the lieutenant might know.'

'I'm sure he does, especially as Abwehr-West are known for thoroughness and have fortunately left nothing to question.'

Methodically, as if laying out the tarot cards of their fortunes, Louis began to place photo after photo in front of himself.

'Early this year,' said Leutnant Heiss.

'You're not quite correct.' Turning it over, he let them see the date and stamp. 'The fifth of December last, messieurs, but by then, according to her concierge, she would have been visiting her mother who was extremely ill with pneumonia and in Rethel. When she returned on 10 December, Monsieur Bolduc, either yourself or Deniard or Paquette very generously gave her the half of a bottle of the Château Latour, whose vineyards you could well have an interest in. But surely knowing what you must of Rethel, Hauptmann Reinecke and Leutnant Heiss, either one or the other of you would have looked a little deeper?'

'We now know she must have gone on to Amsterdam.'

'Having gained exit past the Paris controls in one of Monsieur Bolduc's vans, *n'est-ce pas?*'

'But not with this latest trip when she went to find out why her fiancé hadn't come to Paris to join her as agreed,' said Leutnant Heiss.

Everything in her room had been recorded—that cot, the all-too-evident student poverty, even that champagne cork, but Hermann and himself would still have to go carefully, felt St-Cyr. They couldn't reveal anything more than what had been gleaned from Mademoiselle Lemaire's file and Concierge Figeard or the murder site. They mustn't betray what they really knew.

There was even a shot of a pair of laundered and carefully mended step-ins and a brassiere, both laid out on that cot.

'Jacqueline likes to tease,' said Bolduc, giving them a slum-landlord's grin.

'And René Deniard and Raymond Paquette, monsieur, did they, too, like to tease?'

'Look . . .' began Bolduc.

'Just answer,' said Hermann.

'Even I can see the date.'

'Precisely,' said Louis. 'The first of October and *after* the robbery and murders, not before them. A diagram of none other than the ruins of l'Abbaye de Vauclair, Hermann, the photo taken of a sketch map in her dissertation, I gather. There's even a notation—*l'eau potable.*'

'And yet . . . and yet, Louis, he didn't even think to question why that van of his hadn't returned on schedule? Instead, he simply told Yvonne Rouget that they'd better give Deniard and Paquette a few more days.'

'You *knew*, monsieur, that we would discover they'd been illegally hauling things for the *marché noir.*'

'Precisely 65.25 million francs due in, Louis, and yet he didn't have a care.'

'From which only 4,780,500 were taken,' said Bolduc. 'Why so little?'

'Because they, too, were hauling goods for that same market,' said St-Cyr, 'and like yourself, didn't want it known that they had had any connection whatsoever to the murders.'

'But they had a *mouchard* that they didn't know of,' said Kohler.

'*Ein Spitzel*,' said St-Cyr. 'One who knew of this Annette-

Mélanie Veroche and was to follow and report on her where-abouts to that *Diamantensonderkommando* because they had let her go with a little something they should never have let go.'

The stairs were many and of the rue des Gobelins, and they spi-ralled upward in that ancient tower, felt Anna-Marie, until at last they came to Frans. Forgotten hides, long-mildewed, hung from wooden rods, crowding in on either side of him. Bound hand and foot, gagged and blindfolded, he sensed her presence.

Kupka, the thirty-year-old Czech Communist from the Sude-tenland, handed the knife to her. 'Not the gag, mademoiselle, not the wrists either, and not the blindfold. He's to face us only when all are gathered.'

The butt of a Webley Mark IV, .455 calibre revolver, a Résis-tance standby and leftover from the beaches at Dunkirk in 1940, protruded from Kupka's belt, but to say Frans's name was still too much. 'You'll have to let me take you by the arm. The stairs are steep and you'll not be able to hold on to the railing.'

Violently shaking his head, struggling to speak and yanking himself away, he indicated a need to pee, Kupka tapping him on the shoulder and saying, 'All right, I'll unbutton you and hold it. Mademoiselle . . .'

Turning from them, she couldn't help but hear the flood and wonder at what was to become of her, but it was as if Frans was grinning at her discomfort, for he wouldn't have to face them with wet trousers.

Down and down they went, the air increasingly rank not with urine but the eye-stinging stench of this place until, in the cellars, they came to stand before the others amongst the silent wooden hoists and beams the tannery would have used, the heaps of scrapings from the hides as well. A lonely chair had been placed apart, and on either side of it was one of the emptied rectangular concrete vats that had been sunk into the floor to hold the sodium sulphide and hydrated lime that had been used. Repeatedly steeped in a solution of those for days on end so that the hair could be easily scraped away, the hides would then have been de-limed by washing and soaking in a solution of brine and concentrated sulphuric acid.

Forgotten, perhaps deliberately so, were rows and rows of ten-litre glass jugs of that acid. Aram, she knew, had on two occasions given them a curious look as if to wonder what they could be used for.

Emmi, from Neukölln, a working-class and formerly Communist suburb of Berlin, always wore her thick blonde hair braided into the *Knoten* much-favoured by the Nazis. Tall, big across the bust and shoulders, big, too, in the heart, she could quote Schiller, Goethe, Heine and others, notably too, the Führer, but if ever there was one the Occupier should be concerned about, it was her. *Eine Brünnhilde* with thighs, knees, heavy grey woollen stockings, black jackboots and tight grey skirt, she invariably wore the uniform and side cap of a *Blitzmädchen*, one of the *Helferinnen*, the helpers. Secretaries, wireless and telephone operators and such, she looked as if of the 'grey mice,' even to switching rank, top-coat, cap and all the rest when necessary, but preferring the boots since they were more comfortable at times than the regulation black leather shoes. Black or grey gloves too, and no others.

André Beauchamp, dark-haired, dark-eyed and always looking hungry and younger than his twenty, had been on the run since mid-1941 and not just as now for so many others, from the Service du Travail Obligatoire.

Félix Vérando took his place among them, as did Aram. Light was offered from a can of motor oil with a wick.

Seated before them, Frans waited, Aram indicating that she should cut the gag and remove the blindfold. But again there was the thought that she had never done anything like this before and that from now on things would be very different for her.

Unaccustomed to even such a light, Frans blinked. Swallowing tightly, he asked for water, but was it to be but a ploy for time?

Aram indicated that she should comply but when the mug was held, Frans pulled away to look up at her not as the condemned—never that with him—but as one who laughingly mocked.

Unsettled, she very quickly accused him, but of course there was no coin.

There was only one way to escape this, felt Frans, but first they would have to be told how things had really been. '*Bien sûr*, I'm a *résistant* and I helped Étienne Labrie, the alias of Stéphane Lacroix, and Arie Beekhuis, that of Hans van Loos, to move hunted individuals such as yourselves through from Amsterdam, the Hague and elsewhere in the Netherlands to France and on to Spain and Portugal or North Africa. Whatever destination suited, since cost was seldom a factor. Our motive was to deny the enemy those they most wanted.'

This one was clever, felt Bedikian, for he hadn't denied the accusation as most would. 'And were you yourself ever held in the Hollandsche Schouwburg as she has claimed?'

Standartenführer Kleiber and Kriminalrat Ludin would appreciate getting their hands on this bunch. 'What the *Moffen*—the Boche—in October 1941 forced the Dutch to rename the Joodsche Schouwburg? Yes, I was, and yes they knew me as Paul Klemper, an actor, and yes I was first taken to Gestapo HQ-Amsterdam in that requisitioned public school on the Euterpestraat, and yes, I did manage to escape from that theater as she's claimed. Though the date is a little hazy, I think it would have been around the 17 October 1941. A Friday, and yes, a good forty or so of us, not just myself, simply buggered off as soon as the guards got distracted by searching for valuables and forgot that some of us—myself in particular—would have known that theater well and would lead the others out.'

A hero, felt Emmi. If given the opportunity, he'd take all night to slow them down and make leaving this place more difficult than that theater had soon become. 'And when recaptured, what, please, did you do, monsieur?'

He mustn't smile, felt Frans, though dressed like that she only needed a beer stein. Instead, he must look steadily at her and say, 'I was never "caught," Fräulein. I remained on the lam until, having kept the *Moffen* from Étienne and Arie not once but twice, Étienne then asked me to join them last February.'

A year and four months of betraying others before that, no doubt, but she'd have to tell them what had happened to him, decided Anna-Marie. 'This one was, apparently, grazed by a bullet.'

'The scar of which, if the sight of me is not too traumatic for her, I will willingly reveal, if you'll but let her cut my wrists free. It's high up and near the shoulder and I was, I admit, rather lucky, since they had dogs as well.'

'Yet when we grabbed you at the Gare de l'Est, you tried to get at this pistol of yours, and when you couldn't, cried out for help,' said Félix.

'Wouldn't you have done? *Merde alors*, monsieur, how was I to know who you were? *Gestapistes français, peut-être*, and not just an end to myself and Étienne and Arie, but this one, too, especially since she has been hiding so much from you all.'

'A trainee borderline sorter, Diamant Meyerhof, Amsterdam,' said Kupka.

'But has she told you what she's been carrying? Lots and lots of those, otherwise why would the enemy want her so badly Kaltenbrunner in Berlin would clamp such a lid of secrecy over it all?'

If he could, this Frans would turn them against Annette-Mélanie, even to using her real name, but still he would have to be heard, thought Bedikian. 'Did you and Labrie or Beekhuis know anything of what she was carrying?'

They could use the diamonds and this one was now thinking about that, so good. 'Not until we got to Paris. We only knew that she was desperately wanted and that we had to get her out.'

By her expression alone, felt Emmi, Annette-Mélanie couldn't hide the dislike of what she was being forced to do, accuse another whose life was in the balance. 'Out and away as fast as possible, monsieur, and how, please, did the three of you manage that? I'm not a Fräulein, by the way. I'm a widow but no longer wear the ring because those who shot my husband, who was a Communist like myself, stole it from me. Now answer, please. We haven't got all night and you know it.'

The slut. 'At my suggestion we played dress-up as NSBers, the Dutch fascists, the Nationaal Socialistische Beweging, and we— that is myself who was playing the captain—told the Wehrmacht at the Amsterdam depot that we were to deliver one of their trucks to the internment camp at Vught. We had forged papers for it, certainly. Good ones too.'

But had those on guard at that depot been told to let them have it? wondered Kupka. 'And where, then, if I may ask, did you finally leave that vehicle?'

So that others could then be held responsible and shot, eh? 'We had parked our own, a *gazogène*, with a reliable farmer well inside the Belgian border, but of course we didn't leave the Wehrmacht's truck anywhere near him, but next to the farm of a well-known *collabo*.'

This one would have answers for everything, decided Bedikian. 'So you made the crossing just to the south of Reusel, was it?'

Again he had better not smile. 'And that is where she claims to have cut herself as she retrieved that coin I was supposed to have left for the enemy to find. A rijksdaaler, *mes amis*? A silver coin any would gladly pick up, and with no guarantee it would ever be found by those she claims were intended. Now is there anything else, Anna-Marie Vermeulen, or would you prefer Annette-Mélanie Veroche, and I do hope and trust you'll tell them all about the diamonds.'

'After you had killed those two, you climbed into the back of that van and broke open a case of champagne. There were three types, the Taitinger, the Mumm and the Moët et Chandon. Constantly since, I have asked myself why you chose the one you did when you had the others.'

'She had a fiancé, monsieur,' said Emmi.

'And how the hell was I to have known that? We're only given very minimal details of any we move, and speed is of the essence, secrecy too, so who had time to spell that out?'

It would have to be said. 'I think you had been shown a photo of Henki and myself, taken at our engagement in the dunes at Zandvoort. The bottle of Moët that Henki had somehow managed was upright in the sands behind us.'

How touching. 'And is it that I didn't simply choose quickly so as to salute your happy escape from the rape those two had intended?'

'What is this, he's saying, Annette-Mélanie?' asked Aram.

Frans had known that she wouldn't have told them anything of what those two had intended. 'I knew that they'd be up to something because they had recognized me from that previous journey you asked me to make with them, and when I saw them at that Berru lookout, I suggested to Étienne that we use the ruins of l'Abbaye de Vauclair because I knew something of it from my studies. I think, too, but can't be sure, that their boss, the chairman of that bank, Monsieur Hector Bolduc, may have encouraged them, for he's been wanting me to join the escort service of his mistress whose office is in the building where I used to live, and I have been constantly refusing because I knew that what he really wanted of me was to please the overseers of that bank of his.'

'Why didn't you tell me?' asked Aram.

'Because I felt I could handle it myself, as I have in the past.'

'Now perhaps she'll be kind enough to tell you exactly why the *Moffen* want her so badly.'

It would have to be admitted. 'It's true that I was an apprentice borderline sorter and that I happen to have diamonds I'm taking to someone, and that I was given a few for myself to use if help was needed. But I haven't any of them with me, and I intend, at all costs, to keep that information entirely to myself.'

'Then perhaps, *mes amis*, that is the answer you need. Enough to buy the necessary weapons, cars, trucks, travel papers—you name it, and much more—and she knows it, too, otherwise she'd have told you. She's afraid you'll make her sell those diamonds or take them from her.'

'Again, I haven't any with me, having deliberately left them with someone I believe I can trust, and that's not to say I don't trust yourselves, but I do have this. It's the note that was left for me by the chief inspector of the Sûreté who is after this one for the murders he committed.'

'An informant,' said Louis while looking across the table at Bolduc and fingering that rijksdaaler Ludin had let them keep, 'and this photo, Hermann. The Jardin des Plantes and an associate groundskeeper who is, unless I'm very mistaken, handing her some dried rosemary, the date taken being 7 April of this year.'

'And a good month and some after those first photos with Sergei Lebeznikov and son at Chez Kornilov,' said Kohler.

Picking those up, Louis said, '*Ah oui, mon vieux*, they certainly did know of this happy gathering, she being introduced to whom, please, Monsieur Bolduc or either of you two?'

That coin could only have been taken out to remind them of what was at stake, felt Reinecke, but it wouldn't hurt to answer since both would already know. 'Rheal Lachance and Émile Girandoux of Munimin-Pimetex, with their secretary, Lucie Jourdan.'

Age twenty-four. 'Who takes turns showing no favourites and sleeping with both, Louis, the husband being in a Stalag.'

'The most dominant purchasing agency of Reichsmarschall Göring's Ministry of Armaments and Munitions, messieurs,' said St-Cyr. 'Metals, industrial machinery, pumps, generators and all the rest, including food stuffs, platinum, radium, gold, of course, and diamonds most especially. This Annette-Mélanie Veroche looks as if delighted to meet them, doesn't she, Hermann?'

'We didn't—couldn't—have known then that she would come to have anything whatsoever to do with the black diamonds,' said Bolduc. 'To us, she was simply a young and very attractive girl who wasn't willing to cooperate with Jacqueline's service.'

'Or yourselves, but you *did* encourage Deniard and Paquette to do what they attempted.'

'Jacqueline often embellishes.'

'But now you do know of that girl's connection to the "black" diamonds, and my partner and I will, of course, have to inform the others of Herr Kaltenbrunner's secret commando. We have no choice, Monsieur Bolduc, just as we have none with that little side business of yours.'

'Louis, I'll get the tape and seals from the Citroën. Take over the Purdey.'

'With pleasure.'

'Inspectors, wait,' said Bolduc. 'Surely we can come to a compromise?'

'Not if you're about to try to buy us off,' said Hermann. 'It would spoil our reputation.'

Merde! 'Stay quiet and we'll help you extricate those two who are being held hostage, and will move them out of Paris to wherever you think safest.'

'You do need us,' offered Reinecke. 'Kriminalrat Ludin can't let them go, not now. They're to be sent to a KZ because Kaltenbrunner has demanded it. I've seen the telexes. Abwehr-West have been running a check on the Reichssicherheitschef ever since he was nominated last January to replace Reinhard Heydrich."

'Didn't one of your women marry a Jew, Kohler, and have two children?' asked Heiss. 'Kaltenbrunner was notified by Kleiber who hasn't missed a chance to let the Reichssicherheitschef know everything.'

All of which might or might not be true, felt Kohler. Louis would, too.

---

* Killed by a grenade thrown by Czech partisans on 29 May 1942, Heydrich was buried on 9 June of that year, Hitler then waiting eight months before replacing him with Kaltenbrunner.

'Don't be difficult,' said Bolduc. 'Be reasonable.'

'Collaborate?' asked Louis, pocketing the coin. Putting all of the photos and negatives back into the wastebasket, he added Jacqueline Lemaire's file on Anna-Marie and the Hague Central's *Geheime Reichssache* manila envelope, which also had the photos of Étienne Labrie and Arie Beekhuis. 'Get the tape and the seals, Hermann, while I keep this bunch in line. Hands on the table, messieurs. That way they won't wander to pistols that should stay where they are.'

Everything that was anything was now in that damned wastebasket, felt Bolduc. Oh for sure, underlings in the food control would rejoice at his downfall, but such a charge would never be laid. Others could take the rap if paid enough. Jacqueline would have to be forgiven to silence her, the marriage put back on the stove, but if Kleiber and Ludin were to discover that he and Kurt and Eric had been having photos taken and had known where that girl could be readily found, all would be lost. 'At least let us have another cognac, Chief Inspector. Kurt, would you? Doubles, I think, and a cigarette, if that's possible.'

Grâce à Dieu, thought St-Cyr, Bolduc had seen the need and taken the bait but would he also find, as Heinrich Ludin had done with Oona, that an opportunity when presented often leads to temptation? 'No trouble, please, gentlemen. Just let Hermann and myself seal that storeroom with the Gestapo and Sûreté's tape and seals, and we'll depart until necessary. Don't leave Paris, though. Be ready to offer up answers when asked.'

It took but a moment, felt St-Cyr. Once the back was turned, at least two of them did the necessary with their cognac, the other adding the lighted match and for the moment unwittingly saving Anna-Marie and that source of the rosemary, Labrie and Beekhuis also.

10

Wearing the mud-caked rubber waders of a sewer worker, the *bleus de travail*, blue jacket, cap and lamp on a bandolier across the chest, Jacques Leporatti had finally arrived. Frans shuddered at the sight of him, for there was a finality to that arrival that was understood only too well. Nearly in his sixties, Monsieur Leporatti had been on the run for so long, he understood exactly what it was like. A passionate gardener, especially in the Jardin des Plantes, he yearned for nothing else and immediately reached out to her, she saying softly, '*Merci*, I'm so glad you finally got here.'

Giving her arm another reassuring squeeze, he smiled and said, 'You were worried about me and I am honoured. Aram, two things. First, in reprisal for the killing of Dr. Julius Ritter, Standartenführer Helmut Knochen of the avenue Foch has selected fifty hostages to be shot at the Fort de Romainville.* Secondly, the car you requested awaits.'

Tossing him the keys, he took his place. *Les égoutiers* being among the very few who would have papers allowing them to be out after curfew, Monsieur Leporatti would have used his backup identity papers, even with a name change.

It was Aram who said, 'Annette-Mélanie has had a note from a Sûreté, Jacques, but for now we must deal with this one. Frans Oenen—Paul Klemper—is there anything further you would like to say in your defence?'

'She really does have those diamonds, like I said, and though she will continue to deny that there are others, she has to know

---

* An adjacent suburb just to the east of Paris.

where fortunes more are hidden. The Boche wouldn't otherwise have clamped such a lid of secrecy on the hunt for her.'

'And yourself, it appears,' said Emmi. 'Aram, let me have a look before we put our heads together. Annette-Mélanie be so good as to lift this one's feet so that I can examine his shoes. We'll start there.'

Frans grinned. He couldn't resist, and as each shoe was then taken off to have its sole examined, and then the insoles removed and the leather linings scrutinized, he watched Emmi intently with amusement, only to finally say, 'Are you now satisfied, Frau Widow?'

'Not yet. Patience is necessary and Anna-Marie Vermeulen has to learn this, for one can never tell, can one?'

Feeling the turn-ups of his trousers between thumb and forefinger, Emmi went carefully around each, only to then take something from her topcoat and hold it up in the palm of her hand. Spring-loaded, the SS blade leaped and with it, she slit the fabric and removed the tiniest slip of tissue paper. '*If arrested, contact Kriminalrat Heinrich Ludin.* There, you see, *mein Lieber*, it's a night for notes.'

'I didn't betray any of them. I simply followed her to the Gare de l'Est to tell her she wasn't to worry, that I would never have told them anything. That's why they still can't know of the safe house she and the others are now using and where she must have left those diamonds.'

A nice try, but it was Aram who said, 'Anna-Marie, please take this and tuck it under his shirt.'

It was, she knew, a stick of Nobel 808 and it stank of bitter almonds so badly, she automatically flung back her head but could no longer bring herself to say Frans's name, had had to become another person. 'It'll give you a blistering headache. The skin absorbs it just as fast as the lungs.'

She couldn't, felt Bedikian, allow herself to refuse, and had quickly come to realize it. 'And now this, Anna-Marie. Stab it into the end of that 808 and crush the necessary.'

'Red gives a delay of one-half hour, depending on the temperature,' said Félix. 'The colder it is, the slower the chemical reaction.'

Of about fifteen centimetres in length, the 'pencil' was about six millimetres in diameter.

'It has a thin glass vial of acid,' said André Beachamp. 'When crushed, that dissolves a wire that holds back a spring that then fires the detonator.'

'Protecting the vial, there's a ridge that has to be pressed hard,' said Emmi.

Feeling as though she could hear it break, Anna-Marie knew she had to do this, for they'd never forgive her if she didn't. Quickly inserting it into the end of the doughy brown 808, she emptily said, 'You may have about thirty-five minutes, since it's colder here than outside.'

'Surely you're not going to leave me like this?'

Gagged, he was taken to the car, but were there now even twenty minutes left? she wondered. Time pencils were known to malfunction, some either detonating far too soon, others far too late.

Floored, the car shot out of the courtyard and up the rue des Gobelins through the blackout, the tires squealing horribly as they reached the boulevard Arago and then the boulevard Saint-Marcel, Aram heading for the pont d'Austerlitz.

Running its control, crossing in a matter of seconds as the Wehrmacht detail tried to use their rifles, he turned onto the quai Henry IV to follow the river, but within two or three minutes the tires were again squealing, they having turned to the right, Aram saying, 'The avenue de l'Opéra, I think. Yes, that should do nicely.'

André sat up front with a Schmeisser, Frans in the back between herself, with Fran's pistol, and Emmi who had a Luger. Reaching *place* de l'Opéra, doing a loop, they barely missed the low, white-painted traffic barricade in front of the darkened Kommandantur. Skidding to a stop, now facing the equally darkened Café de la Paix, where late-nighters in uniform with their *petites amies* and others would still be hanging on in that favourite haunt of the Occupier, the engine idled, Emmi getting out as Frans valiantly tried to resist. 'Shove him,' said Aram.

Totally in darkness, the nearby steps down into the *métro* would be closed off, for those last trains would have departed at 2200 hours, but now there were lights from the café and yells, too, in Deutsch to halt, get out of the car and put their hands up.

Slamming the door behind herself, Emmi breathlessly said, *'Neun Sekunden,'* as shots were fired, and they hurtled west along the boulevard des Capucines.

Nine seconds. Not content to trust the time pencil, Emmi had stuffed a pattern-24 stick grenade behind Frans's belt. Ashen, Anna-Marie knew she mustn't cry, but when held and kissed on the forehead, cheeks and eyelids, broke down. They *couldn't* have detonated any of that near the tannery, but could have shot Frans and left him anywhere else. Instead, Aram had chosen the very place to most enrage the Occupier. 'They'll kill us all,' she wept. 'They won't stop, Aram. Not now.'

'But it will bring the worms out,' said Bedikian as they raced back across the river. 'You're truly one of us at last, and the lesson learned is that savagery *will* be met with savagery.'

Floodlights lit up *place* de l'Opéra at 2315 hours. Truncheon-wielding *flics* and helmeted, rifle-bearing Wehrmacht held back the curious which included Rudy de Mérode, Sergei Lebeznikov and other *gestapistes français*, namely the towering, white-fedora and white silk–suited Henri Lafont of the rue Lauriston, an old acquaintance, felt Kohler. And among them, of course, were the *pompiers*, the ambulances and even three salad shakers. Louis and himself had finally been about to get something to eat when a harried Rudi Sturmbacher, having just heard the news, had rushed to tell them.

To the right were the collective brass in their greatcoats and military caps; to the left, waiters from the Café de la Paix urging patrons to return to their tables since the imminent threat of another bomb had passed.

Picking their way through the entrails, their high heels and silk stockings clear enough since the hems of their evening dresses had been hiked, *les horizontales ou petites amies* paused to have a closer look. After all, it wasn't every day such a thing happened. And of course, someone had notified the press who were having a field day.

'Kohler . . .'

It was the Kommandant von Gross-Paris.

'Get rid of those parasites, then come to see me alone and with St-Cyr.'

'Immediately, General.'

All wore name tags either on the chest or tucked into their fedoras, and among them were *Paris Soir*, the most widely read daily, *Le Matin*, too, a close competitor as was *Le Petit Parisien,* and all were fierce rivals even if tightly controlled, but there was only one way to shake them off.

Je Suis Partout, that insidious weekly that sought out and published the hiding places of wanted Jews and others and clamoured for their arrest, loved nothing better, like the others, than to reveal hidden caches for the *marché noir*: sixty kilos of sugar in a baby carriage; one hundred fifty–kilo sacks of potatoes in a convent, eighty of butter in a stove for which fuel could seldom be found. But news like that seldom, if ever, targeted the BOFs who could buy their way out, only the *lampistes*.

'Hermann, at least let's consider the ramifications.'

'We've no choice. We need Boineburg-Lengsfeld now more than ever. Hey, you two from *Je Suis*, and you from *Pariser Zeitung*, do you see that bank over there on the boulevard des Capucines? Yes, that's the very one beyond that gleaming white Bentley of Lafont's. Well, my partner and me have just come from the mother lode of *marché noir* caches, and guess where we found it?'

There were even offers of money, which only showed how shallow the press were, felt St-Cyr, but Hermann told them anyway, and out it all came in a rush. 'Take a few *flics* with you and be sure to tell them to bring an army from the food control. Eyes are going to be opened and not just your own.'

General Karl-Heinrich von Stülpnagel, the military governor, was with Brigadeführer und Generalmajor Karl-Albrecht Oberg, the Höherer SS und Polizeiführer of France whose bottle-thick glasses were catching the light. Boemelburg, head of the Gestapo, was beside them, and beside that one, Osias Pharand of the Sûreté and Talbotte of the Paris Police. All were far from happy, as was Heinrich Ludin. Only Standartenführer Kleiber looked as if in his element.

'But I'm seeing the headlines, Louis: Assassins Butcher SD *Sonderkommando* Informant. '

'Who let them know all that?'

'You should be using the cameras of the mind that you keep preaching.'

'Just tell me.'

'The Kommandant von Gross-Paris.'

But Heinrich Ludin was now passing out extra copies of the two photos that the Hague Central had sent him. 'And in case you haven't yet noticed, Hermann, Lebeznikov is livid.'

Clouds hid the moon, but from the utter darkness of the boulevard Arago came the ever-increasing sounds of not one, felt Anna-Marie, but two of the swallows. They were just starting to pass the Santé now and had she not heard them, would have been onto her.

Huddled against that brick wall, the Sparta pulled in close, she waited. Both were smoking cigarettes and she could see those little lights above their blinkered headlamps and even gauge the height of each. The taller, by his voice alone, seemed the older and when they paused, the sound of their brakes was clear enough, the root smell of their tobacco also.

'*Sacré nom de nom*, Henri, what's it this time? Me, I just want to get home.'

'My lamp caught a glimmer. Along this way, Jacques. A silhouette.'

Though it had hurt, Aram had been definite: 'Sell that kilo of boart or else. The money won't just buy everything needed. It will cause other *équipes* to flock to us and we can then do the necessary.'

'Then at least sell a little at a time. Even 50 grams is still 250 carats and far too risky. At 9,000 francs a carat, that's 2.25 million.'

'We haven't the time and they know it. Use the Bureau Munimin-Pimetex. Göring's bunch will go for it right away if only to lord it over the others and keep them from getting the diamonds.'

'*Mademoiselle, montrez-moi vos papiers, s'il vous plaît.*'

Ah non. '*Messieurs les agents*, I haven't done anything. The cleaning wasn't easy tonight, and I simply stayed until it was done so that I wouldn't lose my job. I'm a student at the Sorbonne. Tomorrow I must be at the Bibliothèque Nationale first thing and then must present my dissertation to my professors. Please don't cause me to lose a whole year and consign me to cleaning the toilets at your Commissariat de Police for a week or ten days.'

'She even knows the usual sentence, Henri, but not that we can now consign her to the Service du Travail Obligatoire for two years. Maybe if we detain her long enough, she'll sing another tune.'

'Please,' she begged. 'I really haven't done anything and have a good reason for being out. Why not . . .'

One of the flashlights was switched off, that of the older and by his accent, definitely from this district. '*Vos papiers, mademoiselle,*' he said again, this time with a hand extended. 'Maybe it's your night to get lucky, Jacques. She's young enough and pretty.'

As with Aram and the others, so, too, was there now no other choice. If they yelled, they'd bring several from the Santé. 'Please carefully turn around and then switch off the headlamps. Unless I have to, I won't shoot, but please don't make me. I've already done enough for one night.'

Neither Aram, nor Emmi, Félix or any of the others would have hesitated to silence them, but elsewhere and far enough away if possible. Merely being in this street would give the Boche and all their friends the districts to ruthlessly comb, and it would only be a matter of time until the tannery was discovered.

But at the rue du Faubourg Saint-Jacques, one suddenly ran and leaped onto his bike to head to the left, the other to the right, leaving her no other choice. She couldn't go back to the tannery to warn anyone, for all would have already left, and she mustn't head for the rue Vercingétorix yet either. To do so would only lead them to Arie. At the least she would have to create a diversion and be seen, and that meant riding as far from here as possible to widen the net. Only then could she head for that safe house.

But she mustn't go anywhere near *place* de l'Opéra.

A bit of sash cord, once white, revealed that the wrists had been tied, likely behind the back.

'*Ein Spitzel*, Kohler,' said Boineburg-Lengsfeld, nudging the scrap with the toe of an immaculately polished jackboot. 'And a mere girl has caused this—Dutch, was she?'

The *pompiers* were uncoiling the fire hoses to wash away what the ambulance crews had failed to remove. 'An under-diver, General, but one my partner and I have come to believe has FTP connections.'

And quite obvious! 'But she also has other connections, Kohler?'

Because of their deliberate burning of the photos and negatives to save themselves, Bolduc, Reinecke and Heiss would now definitely be planning to use what they knew. 'Yes, General. Hector Bolduc, owner and chairman of that bank and its van.'

'And two from Abwehr-West, General. Overseers of his bank and accomplices in both Bolduc's *schwarzer Markt* activities and in his smuggling of individuals into and out of Paris for a substantial fee with or without Abwehr-West authority or any other.'

'Both are also buying up cars that Bolduc's garage then get ready for them to sell in the Reich.'

And with fuel in such shortages the Wehrmacht in Russia were having to destroy perfectly good vehicles. Was there no end to the duplicity and disgrace those two were shedding on the Service? 'Their names, Kohler. Admiral Canaris' will have to be informed. Would a tour of duty in Russia suit?'

Had that God of Louis's finally quit throwing rocks? 'As soon as possible, General, to prevent them and Bolduc from interfering with our investigation. They'll now be determined to find her for themselves so that they can lay hands on the black diamonds before anyone else, including Ulrich Frensel and Johannes Uhl.'

And yet another two of the Führer's infernal riffraff. '*Ach*, do those diamonds even exist?'

'It's highly unlikely, General,' said St-Cyr.

'Yet this whole investigation centres around such a fiction?'

There was no point in avoiding it, felt Kohler. 'On Thursday, General, Reinecke and Heiss are to deliver, with Bolduc, the flying boat his bank has donated to the Luftwaffe. '

'They'll also take in the fall pot-shoot, General, and visit a few of the properties the two of them and that bank have been investing in.'

'The properties, Kohler?'

'Yes, General. Promising resort areas along the Côte d'Argent and Côte Sud des Landes, and vineyards and châteaux just to the north of Bordeaux in the Haut-Médoc and Médoc.'

'Well, we shall see about that. You will, of course, still have to find her. We can't have banditry like this going on under our very noses even if it *is* over a fictitious cache of diamonds Kaltenbrunner and others insist on claiming exists. Now go and deal with those superiors of yours and then with that Kriminalrat and his. None of them will have taken it kindly your both having first talked to myself, so be sure to tell them I have important matters to attend to and must now take my leave.'

The salute he gave was not the usual but that of the soldier he'd been in that other war.

'We have to leave with him, Louis. We can't pass up the excuse Lebeznikov and Mérode have given us and need to keep hiding what we know.'

For as long as possible since Ludin and Kleiber were also leav-

---

* Head of the Abwehr, also arrested for the 20 July 1944 attempt to assassinate Hitler. Unlike Boineburg-Lengsfeld, Canaris was executed 9 April 1945.

ing to follow those first two. 'Then let's hope she's found another and far safer place.'

Midnight had come and gone. It was now, noticed Anna-Marie, 0022 hours, Tuesday 5 October. The headquarters of Abwehr-West was in total darkness, the Prison du Cherche-Midi also. *Bien-sûr*, this didn't mean there were no lights on in those and other such places. The interrogations and the torture would go on for hours and hours if necessary, but above her and still with their tantalizing mystery, the stars were fully out, the air so clear, there was that lovely scent of falling leaves.

Sometimes there were controls on all of the bridges across the Seine, sometimes on only one or two or even none. Somehow she had to let the Occupier know that she had crossed the river, for only then would they broaden their search for her beyond the 13th arrondissement, the Gobelins, and the 14th, the Observatoire.

There were two on guard and by their silhouettes, *Felgendarme*. They'd shoot. They wouldn't hesitate. Both were smoking cigars and that could only mean they must have had some luck and perhaps had been given or taken a bottle or two.

Walking the bike toward them, she would have to do the totally unexpected, and as the sound of her bell broke the silence, one called out, *'Halt! Was wollen sie?'*

Momentarily blinded by their flashlights, she shielded her eyes. *'Nicht schiessen, Herr Offizier. Nicht schiessen. Meine Name ich heisse Annette-Mélanie Veroche.* I'm a translator, you understand. I'm late again but only because I had to work and there wasn't anything I could do about it. There never is.'

'Eine Dolmetscherin?'

'Jawohl, Herr Offizier.'

'Französin, Fräulein?'

'Aber natüralich, Herr Officier.'

'Yet you speak Deutsch?'

'And do what I can to help with the interrogations, but it's very late and I must get home.'

'Ihre Papiere, Fräulein. Bitte.'

Verdammt, a stickler. *'Ach, einen Moment.* I've a letter that's signed and stamped by Brigadeführer und Generalmajor der Polizei Karl Albrecht Oberg and also by Gestapo Boemelburg.'

'The *Oberbonzen*, Rolf. She won't have heard a thing of that blast and all those cars and trucks that raced to it. She'll have been indoors.'

'In the cellars at the Santé, *meine Herren*. A difficult session. Three men, all of them *Banditen*.'

An angel, and a blonde. '*Ach*, Rolf, so few speak our language, and here's one who helps with the arrested. *Auf Wiedersehen, Fräulein*. Morning will come soon enough.'

On the pont Royal, the two were busy with others and didn't even hear or see her ride past to reach the Left Bank again and finally head for 3 rue Vercingétorix.

The rue Daru was not entirely in darkness. Next to the artists' entrance of the Salle Pleyel, their lights still blazing and engines running, were the cars of Sergei Leneznikov and Rudy de Mérode.

'There's no sign of Ludin, Hermann.'

'Not yet and that can only mean one thing.'

Kleiber had gone for reinforcements. 'Then let's get this over with as quickly as possible.'

'Those shoes, Louis. Have they come back to haunt us yet again?'

Hermann hadn't been told. 'I left them in the armoire, but she may well have taken them if only to help us, for there was a suitcase packed in readiness under her bed, and if my guess is right, she'll have taken it, too.'

'And that note you left?'

'Most certainly.'

None of the Neuilly Gestapo had bothered to summon Concierge Figeard. They had simply fired shots into the locks, thrown shoulders against the door and burst in to head for the *loge*.

Torn from his bed, pistol whipped into silence, Armand Figeard, in his long underwear, gloves, toque and scarf, lay propped against a wall, blood pouring from a forehead gash. 'Me, I didn't tell them *anything*, Chief Inspector. It's an outrage what they've done! What has happened to the Paris I once knew and loved?'

'He's going to need stitches, Hermann.'

Things like this did happen, and for all they knew there'd be a heart attack.

'I'm fine. Go and give them a taste of what they've given me.'

Lebeznikov and Mérode hadn't waited with that room either. Smashed, overturned, dumped out, whatever, they had left only that dress hanging neatly in the armoire and had rushed up to the roof, thinking to chase after her.

'Louis, I should have brought the Purdey.'

'And now you've decided to tell me?'

Up on the roof, the rabbits had scattered, their cages in ruins, the chickens also. Trampling broken bell jars, Lebeznikov and Mérode urged the flashlights of others on and over the Himalayas of the adjoining roofs.

'Call them back,' said Louis. 'She's long gone.'

'*Espèce de salaud*, you knew who she was!' said Lebeznikov, turning his light on them. 'A pair of shoes whose colour wasn't the same? A monogram that was nowhere what it should have been?'

'And the shoes, please, where are they?'

'Not here,' said Lebeznikov.

'But you were lying and I'm the proof positive!' shouted one of the others in a brand-new fedora and topcoat, and armed with, of all things, a Lebel Modèle d'ordonnance 1873. A little man with damned big glasses whose black Bakelite frames now made him look even more owlish, thought Kohler. 'He didn't stay locked up for long, Louis.'

'There's blood on that Lebel, Hermann.'

'Don't! Not yet. How's Évangéline, my fine one?' asked Kohler, pushing the Lebel aside.

'Working the streets where she belongs,' spat Rocheleau. 'Ten a night. That's the minimum or it's another damned good thrashing like the one I gave her.'

'Now it's your turn, Louis, since he threatened you with a revolver.'

Felled, blood pouring from a broken nose and opened forehead, Rocheleau lay stunned as the Lebel was pocketed and then Louis's own before that Sûreté calmly turned back to ask Lebeznikov the name that girl had been using. 'Or is it, that you were in such a hurry, you saw only the room number?'

'*Embrassez mon cul, salaud*. When we find her, I personally am going to tear her apart.'

'Why? To be in such a rage you must have a reason?'

Did they not know? wondered Lebeznikov. 'My son was fond of her.'

Louis seldom if ever backed off, even when facing a gathered mob. 'And he is where, please?' he asked as if but the usual inquiry.

'A subdeacon at the cathédrale.'

'And a neighbour. This gets more interesting by the moment, Hermann. His name, Monsieur Lebeznikov?'

Louis had even hauled out the notebook and pencil, having put a foot down on Rocheleau.

'*Foutez-vous le camp, trou de cul,*' said Lebeznikov. 'There are far too many of us and we won't hesitate, not now that we've been given permission to hunt for her and the offer of fifty-fifty of anything we find.'

Just like Dillmann, thought Kohler, and a deal when cut is always a deal.

'When we find her,' cried out Rocheleau, 'we'll let you watch!'

And Évangéline but a decent woman deprived of a little fun, thought Kohler, and a career she had desperately wanted. '*Mädchenhandler*, eh? That's another offence, Chief.'

White slave trader.

Dragged up and turned around so that Louis could slap the bracelets on, he blurted, 'My nose. I must hold the handkerchief.'

'Let him go,' said Mérode. 'There are far too many of us and you know it.'

'But I'm also a chief inspector. Stand aside so that I may exercise my duties.'

This would only get far worse, felt Kohler, though now there was the sound of hastily arriving trucks and cars in the street far below.

Reluctantly, so as not to waste them, St-Cyr unlocked the bracelets and pocketed them, even to emptying that extra Lebel before handing it over. 'The street, Hermann. Ourselves first so that when confronted by Heinrich Ludin and his colonel we will have the answer for them.'

It wasn't just the rue Daru that was being cordoned off. It was the cul-de-sac of the avenue Beaucour, too, and a touch of the avenue du Faubourg Saint-Honoré.

'The full door-to-door and staircase by staircase,' said Kohler.

'But she hasn't gone across the roofs, Colonel,' said St-Cyr. 'If anyone had bothered to reasonably ask Concierge Figeard, they would have discovered that she had left yesterday. She's out there somewhere and if the avenue de l'Opéra is any indication, has no intention of letting us find her.'

'But you will,' said Ludin, lighting a fresh fag from the butt of the last one. 'Otherwise, Kohler, you can watch that train as it leaves from Drancy.'

The son of a bitch. 'Are Oona and Giselle no longer at the villa?'

'Let's just say we'll give them a few more hours. Then you can choose the cattle car.'

'Louis . . .'

'The hospital first, with Figeard, Hermann. It's necessary and we mustn't disgrace ourselves by not attending to a badly injured and totally innocent bystander.'

'I'm warning you, Kohler.'

'And I've listened, Kriminalrat, but we really do need time, so down another slug of that latest bottle and lay off the smokes. We'll be in touch, but if you move Oona and Giselle as threatened, everything is off.'

'And you'll never find Annette-Mélanie Veroche,' said St-Cyr, 'because I think this time you really do need us, Kriminalrat, if you and the colonel are to save yourselves.'

Morning had come, and with it this duty call, felt Anna-Marie. Apolline de Kerellec was smoking one of the wine-flavoured Belgian cheroots Étienne had brought her to sell and enjoy. Propped up in bed at 0950 hours, the suggestion of a cold coming on, she had done her hair and face as before, the knowing intensity of that gaze not just of the streets, but of the concierge she was.

'So,' she said at last, 'here you finally are, and with Arie, but you didn't sleep late. Instead you must have come in at a forbidden hour, only to leave at all but the same, and now to return but not as if on your knees. That left hand, please. Take off the fingerless glove this boy has made for you, perfect though it is.'

She'd been reading the day's *Le Matin* but was clutching a volume of Fantômas, the title deliberately turned away until . . . *Ah non*, it was *La Fille de Fantômas*—Hélène, the daughter of, and volume eight in the series.

Napoléon was singing.

'Apolline . . .' began Arie, only to have a silencing forefinger raised.

'Mademoiselle, I suggested a little anisette when we first met, but as the bottle now finds itself empty, we shall have to forgo such a courtesy. A student, you told me. Arthritis, I believe.'

The book was left lying beside her, its jacket illustration shockingly lurid, the blue glass figurines above the bed as if watching.

Cold and pasty-feeling, the thumb that now probed the scars and counted the stitch marks wasn't going to go away until she had been told the necessary.

'Barbed wire,' came the confession.

'And where did you go this morning with such urgency?'

Only a straight answer would suffice. 'The Gare de l'Est to warn someone that a certain place might no longer be safe.'

'And were you able to "warn" that someone?'

'Yes.'

Still gripping that hand, she then asked, '*Quel est un Diamantensonderkommando?*'

'A special commando.'

Jeanne d'Arc would not have given any sign of fear either. 'And the one who was executed in *place* de l'Opéra last night?'

The press had let it out, and that could only mean the *Moffen* had allowed them to release details. '*Un mouchard* who was working for the Occupier.'

The Fantômas should now be fingered as if searching for clues to her psyche, felt Apolline, since she notices everything. 'You don't fool around, do you?'

'I didn't want to do that to him. Others decided and did.'

'Others, and you let them. Are there photos of you posted in every Commissariat de Police? Am I, and all here at 3 rue Vercingétorix, to expect a visit?'

She'd never agree. How could she, but it would have to be asked. 'I need to stay for just a little longer, madame, but must come and go. I've a task to do, a promise made.'

And again, said just like Jeanne. 'What task, what promise?'

'I'm to contact someone and give them something.'

'Anything else?'

'There's a job I have to do for those "others."'

A job. A sigh should be given, a distant look as well, and then the forefinger trailing itself across the book. 'And this one and Étienne and that *mouchard* brought you all the way from Amsterdam.'

'Did the newspapers say that?'

Ah bon, she was worried about Arie, for she had instantly glanced at him. 'The papers are rubbish. No one believes them and there wasn't a photo of you. Not yet, but the press are like men with virgins. They invariably get what they want.'

'Give me a day or two, that's all I ask, then I'll leave and if they catch me in the streets, I'll run like my Henki did and tell them nothing.'

'Her fiancé,' said Arie.

'What's this?'

'She was engaged.'

And just like Arie who had lost the love of his life and their little baby, but now he had reached out to take her by the hand, so things, they could well be on their way. Then, too, of course, there could possibly be diamonds. 'Avoid the days, come only after dark.'

It couldn't be argued, but sealing the bargain might be useful, especially as it would have to be broken. 'Here is my dissertation, madame. Please guard it closely, but if you could have a read, I'd be interested in your opinion, especially as it looks as if I will never be able to present it until after the Occupier has left, if then.'

After the *épuration*, which would come as surely as any dose of salts and with all of its hurrying even if bound up like concrete. 'And you've not even tried to buy me. Arie, stuff this newspaper into the stove for its warmth. I've not seen it and know nothing of this matter—*Absolument rien!*—But will read this other anyway, just to see how good it must be.'

Fifteen hundred hours and the Jardin d'Hiver would come soon enough, felt Anna-Marie, but for now there was that promise and its delivery and she mustn't let Arie come with her.

From the Arc de Triomphe and Tomb of the Unknown Soldier with its crowds of visiting soldier-tourists and its circling bicycles, *vélo-taxis*, handsome cabs and occasional staff cars and Wehrmacht trucks, the avenue de la Grande-Armée would take her to Neuilly-sur-Seine, the Bois de Boulogne and the boulevard Maurice Barrès. Directly along from the Jardin d'Acclimatation, the children's zoological garden, which had an entrance on that boulevard, was number seventy-two, the headquarters of Rudy de Mérode. None of his henchmen were outside giving bonbons to the children, something they often did to garner favour. No cars were parked there either. Indeed, along from it, the boulevard, apart from three women on bicycles and a few others on foot, seemed all but empty except for herself. But were they all out combing the city for her, thinking, of course, that she would have seen the newspapers and would never have come anywhere near here?

Sickened by what she had heard of the utter sadism that went on in that headquarters, she turned away, and when she got to the address Mijnheer Meyerhof had given her, the villa on the rue Victor Noir was lovely. Its gardens would run right out to the Cimetière Ancien de Neuilly where Anatole France was buried, and oh for sure it would be like living as near to silence as possible, but Monsieur Lebeznikov and that gang of Mérode's were far too close.

Anxiously pressing the gate's bell, which made no sound, she waited. Far along the street two women were approaching and as they continued speaking, they noticed her. Remaining locked, the gate left only the questions of, Go back to Arie? Head for the Jardin d'Hiver? Wait? Hope?

Stern and unyielding—instantly suspicious—the deep brown eyes of one of those two surveyed her. *'Mademoiselle, que désirez-vous?'*

Cook, housekeeper and probably far more than that, the woman looked dependable. 'A word with your mistress.'

The hand that held the key was abruptly tossed, the words coming in a rush, *'Il n'est pas possible.* The perfume distillates. It's an important time and the business, it cannot be left untended.'

Not with the demand being what it was, and the implications not good, yet the shopping bag looked heavy and there was a copy of *Je Suis* protruding. 'Please tell her Mijnheer Meyerhof sent me.'

'Josef? That's impossible.'

Hastily the woman crossed herself, and looking quickly back along the street, found it now empty and said, *'Vite.* The bicycle inside. Fortunately that was Madame Horleau, who has two boys in a prisoner-of-war camp. She'll not talk to anyone about you until she has had a word with me.'

Instantly relief fled through this girl in the cocoa-brown beret, scarf, serviceable jacket and skirt, so perhaps, felt Claudette, she wouldn't have been seen by others.

Baccarat crystal and Russian silver scent bottles were mingled with Roman ones, noticed Anna-Marie, and on the walls of the *salle de séjour* were absolutely gorgeous paintings by Henri-Fantin

Latour, Pierre-Joseph Redouté, Jan van Dael and others, all of which served to indicate that Léon Guillaumet must know exactly where to park his money.

Pausing on the staircase to study this girl, Geneviève Guillaumet let her linger over the photos on the mantelpiece, knowing only that she should have hidden them. 'That is our daughter, Michèle, Mademoiselle Veroche. She's with my brother and sister-in-law, and at school in Taunton, Somerset. When the Blitzkrieg came, Michèle was unable to return, and now, of course, we wait for letters.'

The designer suit was perfect and of a soft, warm grey linen, the broad-collared white silk blouse, poise and looks those of a former mannequin, the diamond necklace from any of those on *place* Vendôme, for Mijnheer Meyerhof would have had to repeatedly call on them over the years, but had mention of his name caused her to wear it?

Now in her mid- to late thirties, Madame Guillaumet had the pallor of one who not only hadn't been out of doors in years but was also very afraid. Unable to resist it, the woman snatched up the copy of *Je Suis* to hurriedly scan the columns, only to close her eyes in relief and say, 'You're not from them. You can't be, but they will do things like that. Send someone as if from a loved one. Have you news of Josef?'

'Sadly it's not good, madame. I have to believe that he and Mevrouw Meyerhof will have been transported, but it's your daughter I've come to see, and I know, because he told me this, that she's not at school in England.'

Abruptly the woman sat down, and bursting into tears, hugged herself only to finally gain a measure of control and say, 'Forgive me, please. Every night has its nightmares. Our papers aren't stamped *Juive*. We don't have to wear that star. Léon, he takes care of everything by paying the *préfet de police de Neuilly-sur-Seine* and others to keep us off the lists, but for how long, since they constantly ask for more?'

Even Mijnheer Meyerhof hadn't thought of such a thing ever happening in France, but to leave the diamonds with her, wouldn't be sensible. 'And Michèle, madame, where is she?'

Must this girl persist? 'We're both Catholics. We both wear one of these.'

A silver cross, but every district would have its alphabetical list of those to be hunted down. 'Please, madame, I need to know. It's what he wanted.'

Trust was everything, but now especially, even that could and often was broken. 'I can't tell you. I'm sorry, but I mustn't.'

'Both of my parents were taken, madame, because my mother refused to let my father go alone. I'm a *métisse*.'

A half-and-half. 'Michèle is with Monsieur Laurence Rousel, Josef's Paris notary, and my husband's, though with what's happened to so many of his clients, he decided in protest to retire. She's in Barbizon, at the former home of his mother. The house, it has no name, but is directly across the rue de la Grande from the little museum of the Barbizon School. From time to time Laurence comes to Paris, and if Michèle needs anything, I send it with him. Books that Josef, the "uncle" she has always loved, gave her. Other things, too, and yes, I can see that you consider the arrangement far too fragile, yet what else could we have done? Laurence is a very dear friend. He despises what Vichy and the Germans have done and are continuing to do, but has to remain silent, of course. However, in her day, his mother was midwife to the village. Aloof, oh for sure, but known and both feared and respected since she knew the first moments of so many and could judge them by those, and of course Laurence as a boy grew up amongst them.'

Madame Besnard, the housekeeper, brought *le thé de France*, the china paper-thin and magnificent, thought Anna-Marie, remembering the Nieumarkt's Sunday antique fairs and the searches she would make to find something that really, really would surprise her mother.

'Josef gave that china to her,' said Geneviève. 'Always when in Paris, he would take her out and they would find things—concerts, art galleries, museums, so many, many places, and always there would be a little something special for her, the daughter he loves as much as does my husband. That piano. Each of these paintings. If Michèle kept returning to gaze at one of a gallery's paintings as if she couldn't leave it, he would, without her knowing, have it sent to her, to the daughter I had with and for him, Mademoiselle Veroche, on 9 June 1928.'

'My father was one of his diamond cutters, myself a trainee borderline sorter.'

'If you've brought diamonds for my daughter, please take

them away. We've far too much to contend with and those who would destroy us need no such encouragement. The weekend before Poland was invaded, Josef pleaded with us to send Michèle to England. Just before the Blitzkrieg we had a last visit, a Sunday, 5 May 1940. Michèle and I were at Mass and when we came out, he was waiting. I hadn't seen him like that since Kristallnacht.[*] Everything told him there would be war and that, though neutral, the Netherlands and Belgium would also be invaded. We simply weren't prepared. The German military, of which he knew a great deal because he had had to sell to the Krupps and other industrialists, was just too modern, well equipped, and far too keen. He also begged Léon to leave France and take us to America, but my husband, though he respected the advice, had faith in our generals.'

Like so many others. 'Did Mijnheer Meyerhof ever speak of diamonds?'

'Constantly. *Ah mon Dieu*, he *was* of diamonds and certainly he told us of what some of the Amsterdam and Antwerp traders were doing or planning to do. But his position as director of the Amsterdam protection committee made things difficult. On the one hand he couldn't be seen to be running from the threat lest their be a stampede, on the other, prudence demanded that he consider it.'

'Did he ever ask your husband to hold diamonds for his firm?'

'The so-called "black" ones? Much as he admired and valued my husband's friendship and business acumen, Josef would never have put us in such a difficult position. Whatever stocks are hidden, if any, will be found in America just like the paintings, pieces of sculpture and other such things of the lucky.'

There being no way to avoid it, thought Anna-Marie, she would simply have to ask. 'Do the Germans and their friends know who your daughter's real father is?'

How stark of her. 'They may or may not. Though I was single when I had her, and the name of the birth certificate was Vilmorin, as was mine, Léon, on Josef's advice, took care of it in 1935. A lost certificate, a new one, new papers, too, and money on the side. The Church records as well, although that was by far the most difficult.'

But would it take the *Moffen* and the Paris police long to dis-

---

[*] 9–10 November 1938.

cover the truth? 'She must really miss being here with you. I know I would.'

'As she was life to Josef and to myself and my husband, so were we to her. Even on that last, brief visit, he somehow found a way to bring her a little gift to tell her that everything would soon be all right, and she had no need to worry.'

'And that, what was it?'

'An aquarium with tropical fish.'

And brought through all that chaos. 'Might I see it?'

'Of course, but why?'

'I'm simply trying to trace the route he may have taken.'

The room overlooked the rue Victor Noir, and on a table in front of the windows was everything that would be needed, all left in readiness for when the Occupation would end. 'There's no sand.'

'Michèle knew the fish wouldn't survive without her. After Claudette—Madame Besnard—had dealt with them, my daughter buried them in the cemetery, and when she came back, said that was what Josef would have expected her to do.'

'And the sand, did she bury that too?'

'Some of it is in the cellar. Before she left us to stay with Laurence, she made us promise never to throw any of it out.'

'Sand is sand,' impatiently said Madame Besnard, having brought two twenty-kilo cotton bags up to the kitchen.

'But it isn't,' said Anna-Marie, digging a hand down to the bottom of one to feel about, since diamonds were heavy, and with all that vibration on the train, would have settled, and Josef would have known that too, had he not put them there first, but there were none and that could, or could not mean Michèle had taken them with her. 'This is perfectly clean. It's the extra Mijnheer Meyerhof must have brought. It's from Zandvoort, a resort town on the Noord Zee. The beaches are fabulous and behind them, ranked one on another, are superbly sculpted dunes of this pure white sand. My Henki . . .'

'Henki?' asked Claudette.

'My fiancé, but . . . but he was then shot by the *Moffen*. A *résistant*.'

Out on the rue Victor Noir, and still with the diamonds, there was, felt Anna-Marie, now no longer any choice. She would have to meet with that Sûreté who, having found what she had hidden, had understood there had to have been a reason and had left them for her, the shoes as well.

Wide open, the gates to the driveway of Gestapo Boemelburg's Neuilly villa awaited, and as he drew the car in, Kohler swallowed tightly, for two small suitcases sat in readiness. Boemelburg had flatly refused to intervene because of Kaltenbrunner.

'Oona, Louis. Giselle . . .'

Drancy first, then Dachau, Mauthausen, Auschwitz or any other of the *Konzentrationslager*—they both knew absolutely what all of those would be like, having experienced Natzweiler-Struthof in Alsace last February.

Shattered, Hermann still couldn't seem to move. Reaching over to switch off the ignition, St-Cyr said, 'Easy, *mon vieux*. Easy, eh? Together we'll sort this out.'

'How? That *verdammt eingefleischter* Nazi with the peptic ulcer's in there waiting for us to see the smile on his face.'

Sharing a cigarette might have helped. 'Stay here. Let me find out what's happened, and please don't take any more of those damned pills. Even Messerschmitt night fighters get shot down.'

'He's onto us. He's found out that we must have known where Anna-Marie was living and the name she'd been using, and now knows you must have been in that room of hers and up on that roof, too, to have a look.'

'But perhaps not where she might quite possibly be meeting me.'

'We *can't* let him send Oona to a KZ, Louis. Giselle will go out of her mind and Oona *won't* be able to hold her together.'

Two women, two loves, and when Hermann glanced into the rearview, he said, 'That black Citroën of his is now behind us. Here, take this stupid letter from Kaltenbrunner and keep it for us. Otherwise he'll be after me for thinking I could use it again to see them and will be demanding it back.'

The cloud of cigarette smoke, shabby grey fedora and overcoat were the same, the expression that of Frankfurt's having received a round-the-clock flattening yesterday.

'Well, Kohler, you and that *Französischer Schweinebulle* have been lying to me. I've just been to see a concierge who was pistol-whipped and guess what he had to tell me after a little persuasion.'

'He was a veteran of the Great War,' said Louis.

'*Verdammter Franzose*, when I want anything from you, I'll ask. It's this *verfluchte* Kripo who is to answer. You have a choice, Kohler. Either you will be shot or you'll do your duty to the Führer *und Vaterland*.'

'Let me take the suitcases.'

'And your two women?'

The son of a bitch. 'Louis, put the bags in the car and go and get Oona and Giselle.'

'So that I won't be able to hear what you say, Hermann?'

'All right, I'll ask him first if he's spoken to Hector Bolduc's former mistress and then to Bolduc himself and those two overseers of that bank of his. After all, Kriminalrat, this is still a murder investigation and that girl was a witness or as close to it as we can get so far.'

A gut-wrenching spasm caused a desperate gasp and cry, the cigarette falling to the pavement. Another was fiercely lit, the latest bottle found empty and flung aside.

'Since you're not listening, Kohler, perhaps it is that you should come with me. That girl was seen and stopped outside the Santé late last night, armed, too, and with, I believe, the very pistol our Frans Oenen had been allowed. So if it is a murder investigation you're wanting, then his will suffice. Standartenführer Kleiber is presently commanding a rigorous house-to-house and there is every indication he will find and arrest her. *Banditen*, Kohler. *Banditen!* Even the Kommandant von Gross-Paris can't argue with that.'

'Louis . . . Louis, do the best you can.'

Built in 1938, the Jardin d'Hiver was beside two much older greenhouses from which the plants and trees had been moved here to make way for others. Cup-of-flame, passion flower, trailing orchids and the hanging flowers of the pitcher-plant were so close, St-Cyr felt he could touch them from where he was sitting. Lianas climbed to reach the sunlight. Coconut palms spread their fronds. Papayas, grapefruit trees, silk ferns and tree ferns seemed everywhere, and the irony of it was, that like the artist Henri Rousseau, who had visited greenhouse after greenhouse, the Jardin d'Hiver had become his very own jungle. Whereas Rousseau, in *The Dream*, could place a beautiful and very naked young woman lounging naively oblivious to all threats among jungle plants, so, too, was he naively waiting. Self-taught, having never left Paris, Rousseau had been a customs clerk whose paintings had been dismissed as 'nonsense,' but he had painted what he had *wanted* others to see and feel. The strange and varied leaves, the bright and often wildly coloured flowers made larger and bolder by himself and all but lost in his jungle, more apelike than human, a recorder-playing savage who, one supposed, was trying to entice that maiden to himself.

Until he and Anna-Marie met—if indeed they ever did now that photos of her were out there and everyone who could was looking for her—he wouldn't know how to proceed, for what really, had he and Hermann to offer, especially with Giselle and Oona so threatened?

Alone beneath a jacaranda whose fernlike leaves threw shadows, the fragrant soft-purple flowers drew his undivided attention. Lots of the *Moffen* were about, the sounds of their voices, and their French companions and others, periodically clashing with the warmth, the humidity, the closeness and the faint but gentle murmur of trickling water.

Two of the remaining buttons on his open topcoat hung by threads and when he took it off because it was so warm, he was careful not to lose them.

A scorched hole, right through where the zipper ended on that brown suede pipe pouch was evidence enough. Fingering it as though longing for its daily ration of tobacco, he made sure the letters AMPHORA could be seen. A Sûreté chief inspector. Divorced once—wife Agnès—widowed next from wife Marianne, and their four-year-old son, Philippe, due to a Résistance mistake the Watchers of the Paris Gestapo had deliberately left in place.

Aram had been thorough.

'He has chosen one of the most secluded of places,' confided Emmi, 'but one from which it will be impossible for me to get you out of there if I have to.'

The gravel path that led to that bench found it in the tightest of cul-de-sacs where leaves of every shape and shade of green sought the myriad panes of glass. 'Then I'll do it now since Aram has given me no other choice.'

'Just don't force me to have to shoot our way out of here.'

Emmi hadn't wanted to come; Aram had insisted, yet now

that she was alone with the chief inspector, he still hadn't realized who it was and had definitely been expecting someone else.

En français, she said, 'Monsieur, may I sit beside you for a few moments? These shoes of mine, they don't quite fit, and my friend has tired me out.'

Caught off guard and momentarily perturbed, the deep brown eyes under those bushiest of brows instantly became curious only to soften. '*Ach*, of course, Fräulein.' And moving the shabby coat onto his lap, went on to say, 'This is lovely, isn't it? One yearns for peace and harmony.'

Had he still not realized? 'It reminds me of the paintings of Henri Rousseau.'

At first he didn't know what to say, so struck was he by her comment, but then, gesturing with the hand that held the pouch, he said, 'And the irony of that is, Mademoiselle Vermeullen, that I, too, had been thinking the very same thing. The *Blitzmädel* uniform, side cap and black-and-silver *Blitz* brooch of a signals operator are perfect, the black leather shoes as well, but please don't ever be caught in that uniform. The *Moffen*, the Boche, the Occupier, the green beans, SD, SS, Gestapo or whatever would not be appreciative. Even knowing you from so many photos, I didn't think it could be yourself.'

'So many photos?'

Her expression was one of utter dismay. 'Please don't worry unduly. My partner and I believe they now have only the two that were sent from Hague Central and date back to the general strike. Hermann and I made others destroy all copies of what they'd had taken.'

'Others?'

Merde, were they to delve deeper and deeper into this when time was so short? 'You hitched a ride last December in a bank van and then recently.'

'And Monsieur Hector Bolduc had someone secretly taking photos of me in Paris, did he? I thought so on three occasions—I felt it, you understand—but could never prove it. Always whoever it was would vanish. All I did come to know was that Monsieur Bolduc must have been talking about me to his overseers and that mistress of his, and to those two with the van, for when they unlocked and opened that back door at l'Abbaye de Vauclair, the younger one grinned and said horribly, "Now you're going to get what our chairman has repeatedly said you damned well need!"'

But would Bolduc ever be held responsible? 'And in *place* de l'Opéra last night?'

'I did what I had to and yes, I tucked that stick of Nobel 808 inside Frans Oenen's shirt front because if I hadn't, those who have helped me so much would have turned their backs on me. I would *never* have killed him if left alone. I'd have tried to buy him off with what Mijnheer Meyerhof had given me for myself. Those twelve *Hochfeines Weiss* you also found at that spring, in their paper.'

She must have decided to be absolutely straight with him, but . . . 'You didn't give Oenen the grenade?'

'That was Emmi, the one I'm with, and to make certain of the other which had a time pencil.'

FTP backup leaving nothing to chance, but she'd have to be warned. 'You were stopped late last night outside the Santé.'

'Fortunately I was able to tell one of the others that the place we used was no longer safe. At least, I hope what I said to him reached all of them, the boss especially.'

'You've a pistol in that handbag?'

'Frans's gun. A Browning FN Hi-Power, the Pistool M25, No. 2. There are eleven rounds of the nine-millimetre Parabellum left and if I have to, I'll shoot myself.'

She had meant it too. 'I'm not a threat and neither is my partner. We're on your side.'

How dangerous of him to have said it, for if captured and tortured she could well cry it out. 'I've brought you something and am now going to open that handbag. It's also from Belgium, but Arie Beekhuis, the driver of that truck, felt we'd better not give you the tin, only its contents, so I've wrapped it in a kerchief of mine.'

A fortune. 'Old Belt Virginia, but with added touches of an Oriental and a little Perique and Latakia. It's superb and I am totally in your debt. *Merci bien.*'

Already he was packing that pipe of his. 'Having found the life diamonds and the others that I hid at that spring, Chief Inspector, why did you then leave them for me with all my little scraps from home and that kilo of boart and the one of borderlines?'

Having lit the pipe and appreciatively paused, felt St-Cyr, he would tell her exactly how it had been. 'Because those scraps speak volumes, mademoiselle. My partner and I, having discovered where you were living and under what name, have been desperately trying to keep that information from the special commando that are looking for you.'

'They having deliberately left me free to leave Amsterdam because they had an informant both Arie and Étienne, and myself at first, didn't know of. The "black" diamonds don't exist, in so far as I know. What I have belongs only to the daughter of Mijnheer Josef Meyerhof. Enough, he hoped, for her to get Diamant Meyerhof restarted when this war is over. Until he had told me of her, however, I would never have thought it of him, for he was, I'm sure, very much in love with Mevrouw Meyerhof and they did have a son. Unfortunately, Michèle is not in Paris with her mother and stepfather, but is in Barbizon at the home of Monsieur Laurence Rousel, Josef's former notary. The house is right across the street from the small museum that celebrates the painters of the Barbizon School, but . . . but I don't know how I can possibly get to her.'

'We'll help if we can, but I should tell you that Barbizon has its nest of collaborators and is a much-favoured spot of the Occupier especially because of those painters.'

'And is that partner of yours not of the Occupier?'

'Hermann is simply Hermann and unique, but they've made things exceedingly difficult. They're holding his Oona and Giselle hostage and threatening Drancy, and it has to be weighing heavily on him, but we've been up against such people before and he has always pulled through.'

Yet now, what now—was that what was worrying the chief inspector? 'Where is he—watching your back as Emmi is watching mine?'

'Would that that were true, but he's near the Santé. Another house-to-house, not because he wants to be any part of it—please don't misunderstand—but because, like myself, he has continually to walk a knife edge.'

The 14th and far too close to the Gobelins and the tannery.

11

Louis would understand. He would have to, felt Kohler. Miserable as always, Heinrich Ludin was still behind the wheel but had been far too silent, and the rue de la Santé ahead could not have been bleaker. Devoid of foot traffic and bicycles, there was, but far along from them near the intersection with the boulevard Arago, nothing but two horse-drawn delivery wagons half-loaded with firewood no one should have left untended and one lonely *gazogène* truck that looked as if its little fire had suddenly been extinguished.

'He isn't learning, is he, that colonel of yours, Kriminalrat? *Ach,* this is Paris, not the Warsaw Ghetto on a second visit to its sewers.'

'And you have yet to learn that I've had enough of the shit you and that partner of yours have been trying to feed me. That girl was stopped last night and we now know where those *Banditen* must have met before and *after* they killed Frans Oenen.'

Cigarettes lay in full view between them—Camels this time, but there was no point in even asking. 'Maybe that girl will try to make contact. Have you even thought of that?'

'Contact, after what they did last night? Those two women of yours will be in Drancy tonight, and in a railway cattle truck tomorrow at 0500 hours. I've already given the order to send them to Mauthausen, and it's been ratified by Reichssicherheitschef Kaltenbrunner.'

'And here I am, trying to tell you something but neither you nor the colonel will listen.'

'Two of the Paris police stopped that slut near here at 2337 hours last night, just after she must have left their hideout.'

Ludin had finally turned onto the boulevard Arago and they were now slightly to the east of the Santé. Salad shakers were being loaded. Half-naked and totally, the models and other arrested females were, of course, verbally sounding off, the kids too, their fathers having been hammered.

'Artists, Kohler!' shrilled Kleiber, pistol in hand. 'Communists!'

Even reason wasn't going to help, but he'd have to try. 'The Cité Fleurie is but one of several such colonies, Colonel. There's another nearer the Gobelins and on the rue Broca,* at Number 147. There the Cité Verte is even more dilapidated than this, since artists never waste anything and scrounge what they can. Everything needed to build these shacks and glaze them came from the Universal Exposition of 1867. Picasso once had a studio here, Modigliani, too, and Rodin. Others as well, lots of them and still maybe thirty or forty. That's why the big, north-facing windows and the makeshift skylights that always seem to leak. The porches are so that they could haul their paintings outside to have another look.'

Louis, being Louis, had brought him here in the autumn of 1940. Vegetables had been harvested again this year from every scrap of the now retilled soil, refurbished constantly of course with outhouse waste to await spring planting. Rabbits were caged indoors in whatever had been to hand, chickens, too, and gerbils, which were really very tasty when fried, or so Louis had claimed necessity was causing some to eat. One lonely goat looked bone dry, though there were no cats and dogs, since every scrap of food was needed.

Studio after studio held the usual, and often degenerate art just to inflame Nazis like these two further. Jackboots smashed the hours of patient labour. One weeping woman had given birth and was in urgent need of help. 'Get her an ambulance. They're not here, Standartenführer. Artists are only interested in their own art and that of their friends and competitors, and would have told you everything by now if anyone else had been here.'

Even the trees had been stripped of all but their highest branches, the stoves in such need. Near the shaded cast-iron water trough and pump, someone had lost a tooth. 'Louis will have answers, Kriminalrat. Back off and rescind that order.'

Still cloistered in this pseudo jungle with the enemy constantly near and himself smoking his pipe at last, St-Cyr listened intently

---

* Now the rue Léon-Maurice Nordmann.

as Anna-Marie spoke softly but with an earnestness that was humbling.

'All of the diamonds would be weighed and entered into the firm's ledger, but the day before the Blitzkrieg struck we had a shipment of industrials that came in from the Congo and South Africa. I was going over the lesser ones and when Papa came to see me, he turned his back on the others in the room and shoved that kilo bag of boart and the other of borderlines at me. I was simply a trainee and normally everyone when leaving for home would have to go through security but not that day for myself, and he must have known this. As soon as he got home, he put them into a fruit jar and after dark we buried it in the garden.'

'And with his pocket watch?'

'When he knew he and my mother were to leave, he left it there both to tell anyone else that they were Meyerhof diamonds and also in the hope that I would find it.'

'Were other diamonds taken?'

'If so, he never told me. Fortunately those who then ransacked our house failed to find them, even though they dug up the garden, too, but I felt I could no longer leave them there, so brought them to Paris last December.'

'Only to then find that you had to make a second visit.'

It was now time to tell him, felt Anna-Marie, and taking a small twist of cloth from her pocket, handed it to him, he feeling its contents and immediately knowing what it contained. 'Chief Inspector, the *équipe* are asking that you and Herr Kohler arrange for the sale of that kilo of boart to Munimin-Pimetex. Its lead purchasing agents, Rheal Lachance and Émile Girandoux, have both met me at Chez Kornilov on two occasions. You're to tell them full price on the *marché noir*: 45 million francs but not in 5,000-franc notes or 1,000-franc notes. In these.'

Having dug it out of another pocket, she let him unfold it. Distinctively big—eight inches by five—and white, but with flowing dark black script, the banknote was well worn and bore the usual cashiers' stamps, this one of Lloyds and Barclays, and the hastily scribbled notations of bookmakers, shopkeepers and others through whose hands it had already passed, they having jotted down who had passed it to them in case of forgery. 'Fivers,' he said. 'That's what the British call these, their most beloved of banknotes. Hermann and myself have encountered them before, but still . . .'

' Monsieur Lachance had a wad of them from which he paid their bill at the restaurant, and ours too, to impress Monsieur Lebeznikov and his son and myself. He then gave me one and wished us well.'

'You then handing it over to the leader of your *équipe*.'

'Who told me they must have come from the bank vaults of the occupied territories, that Reichsmarschall Göring would have made certain of getting his hands on plenty. The Belgians alone had apparently hoarded stacks and stacks of them.'

As foreign currency reserves but still forgery, too, was possible, and certainly both he and Hermann knew well enough that the SD and Abwehr used them to pay off informants and others. 'Your choice of purchasing agency is appropriate, but if so, how many of these would be needed?'

Was he going to agree? 'Forty-five thousand, tied in bundles of one hundred and packed in three medium-size suitcases, the drop-off and exchange to be made tomorrow, but arranged by yourselves.'

How businesslike of her. 'And I'm to relay the time and place when and where?'

'Tomorrow at 1000 hours. There's a *Lokal* on the boulevard Saint-Michel and just around the corner from a *Soldatenheim* on the boulevard Saint-Germain. Go into the *Lokal* on the pretext of looking for Herr Kohler. Take out your pipe and tobacco pouch, and wait. You'll be contacted, if not by myself, then told where to meet me.'

A district she would know well as a student, a hostel for visiting soldiers on leave and the canteen they would go to, but still a terrible risk for her, even though *Blitzmädchen* also used them. 'And if we refuse? Things are difficult enough as I've already told you, and I don't honestly know how my partner will react. Before I came here to meet you, we had just seen the suitcases of his Oona Van der Lynn and Giselle Le Roy packed and ready waiting for the truck to take them to Drancy, this evening probably.'

Aram hadn't told her what to say to such a thing, but was an offer being demanded? 'And where, please, might those have been seen?'

Taking out the letter from Kaltenbrunner, St-Cyr knew he had to do what he had to, she seeing the signature and the stamps and knowing immediately how valuable they would be to those who forged papers. 'They're in Neuilly, on the corner of the boulevard Victor Hugo and rue de Rouvray. The villa Gestapo Boemelburg keeps for special prisoners.'

'When?

'The sooner the better.'

Drawing the Citroën to the side of the road, St-Cyr fingered the rijksdaaler that had tipped her off, but could she and Emmi do the impossible, and could Hermann and he really make such a deal and then see that all that cash was handed over to an FTP *équipe*?

Along the street, all was in chaos. Harried and dismayed, Hermann was trying his best to reason with Ludin and Kleiber, but they simply weren't listening.

Ancient like its former *maisons de maître*, the rue Broca was much nearer to the Gobelins. Blocked off with trucks, salad shakers, *flics* and Wehrmacht just like the Cité Fleury apparently had been, the Cité Verte, at number 147, was another artists' colony. Here, though, the studios were in the centre of the garden that those early artists had taken over as squatters back in the latter half of the last century. Even more dilapidated, fire must have seemed the only solution to former city fathers, the present ones too, and certainly the Standartenführer gave every indication of helping things along.

Lined up on the clods of overturned earth, resident males faced resident females, both in all states of dress and undress, teenagers too, and young children, as well as grandparents and others, and shouldn't those kids have been in school?

Kleiber and a Parisian interpreter were progressing between the two rows. Held back by the rifles and Schmeissers of the helmetted and the batons of the *flics*, the forty or so adults were far from happy, but obviously had been beaten into submission.

Flames leaped from the still growing mountain of canvases, easels, paints, brushes and such, the troops rejoicing in their task by first smashing things.

'Louis, these people will only hate the Occupier far more than they already do, and when I have to pack up and leave, it's not going to be pleasant. Oona and Giselle . . .'

It was, of course, heresy for him to have said any such thing in such company. '*Doucement, mon vieux*, let me roll you a cigarette from that *mégot* tin of Arie Beekhuis. You've not taken more of those pills, have you?'

'Beekhuis? She didn't make contact. She couldn't have.'

What a slender thread that was and Hermann had felt it snap, but there was no time to tell him what had happened. Struck hard across the face by Kleiber, a woman in the line-up shrieked, *'BOCHE POLTRON, SOYEZ MAUDIT!'* There was silence at that greatest of insults, and through it came the crackling of the flames as Ludin settled on her ten-year-old daughter. Holding the child by the left hand, he drew on his cigarette.

'Don't, Kriminalrat,' pleaded Hermann. 'Leave her. She won't know anything.'

Gut, a little panic could but help, thought Ludin, giving pause to things.

'Kohler, the Vermeulen girl must have come from somewhere in this district last night,' said Kleiber. 'It's only a matter of time until one of this scum coughs up the answer.'

'They were hiding here last night, weren't they?' Ludin asked the child in Deutsch, the interpreter translating.

Soulful, deep brown eyes lifted to him from under dark brown bangs, and a seriousness came to those tender years, the freckles and the thinness. *'Ah non, monsieur,'* she said gravely. 'Those people, they don't hide in places like ours where there are far too many coming and going all the time except for after the curfew when it's illegal to do such a thing. They hide in the Bièvre.'

'What's that?' demanded Ludin.

'Tell him in French, Louis.'

Had she been reading *Les Misérables*?** wondered St-Cyr. 'A stream whose banks were lined with tanneries, dye works and factories, all of which dumped their effluent into it until the stench became so rank it was covered over in 1910 and made into part of the sewer system in the 1930s.'

All this was duly repeated in Deutsch until a sigh was heard. 'There,' she said, 'Now you know. Tanneries stink and so does that sewer system into which that hidden river pours especially when

---

* Boche coward, be cursed!

** Victor Hugo uses the area several times in the novel.

it rains a lot, and when those people you want have to come up to walk along the boulevard Arago you can *smell* them especially when they're not *even* wearing their big rubber boots.'

'*Les égoutiers?*' asked the startled interpreter.

'*Ah oui,*' she answered, scrunching up her nose to indicate the stench, 'but me, I think there are others too.'

'All hiding in the sewers?' asked the interpreter.

'Oh for sure they're down there, monsieur. Lots and lots of them, and they come out at night because they *like* the darkness.'

'*Ach*, she's making it all up, Kriminalrat,' said Hermann. '*Mein Gott*, what else would you expect her to do?'

'The Bièvre, as a sewer, does flow into the one that runs under the boulevard Arago to join others, Kriminalrat,' said the interpreter, 'and from there you can get to virtually any place in the city.'

Dropping the butt, Ludin lit another. 'A buried river.'

'The sewers and a tannery,' said Kleiber, having made the mother kneel, the muzzle of his pistol now pressed to the back of her neck.

'To the east of us a little,' said the interpreter. 'There are several just off the rue des Gobelins. Ask the *flics* to show you.'

The tannery was in the Parisian usual, how could it have been otherwise? felt Kohler, uneasy at the thought of this warren of butt-to-butt, corner-to-corner, courtyard-to-courtyard buildings, some ancient, others not quite but all pinch-penny and needing repairs. Towering over it all was a nearby tenement from whose upper-storey windows possible accomplices could look down on everything, while against the sky the oft-struggling forest of rusty metal chimney pipes from the ateliers and small-scale factories below sought relief.

Otherwise, the whole damned area had fallen silent, Kleiber having readied the troops.

Number 17's courtyard ran straight in and south from its iron-barred, padlocked gate. A hexagonal, grey-stone tower was at the nearest corner of what had once been *la maison de la reine blanche*, but it didn't look inviting.

'*Ah mon Dieu, mon vieux,*' said Louis, 'that tower simply holds the staircase to the first and second storeys and those attic dormers. That's why there aren't any windows. The courtyard does, however, if I remember it correctly, take an abrupt turn to the right.'

Trust Louis to have said it but not, 'And out of sight.'

'*Ah oui*, it ends in a cul-de-sac where there is, indeed, a manhole cover, but also iron-barred windows and locked doors. That's where, on 13 June 1935, I was . . .'

'Later, Louis. Later. Colonel, there are still far too many avenues of escape, not just the sewers.'

'Is that cowardice I'm hearing?' asked Kleiber, checking to see that all were finally in place. 'If so, I can only warn you.'

Probably never having ridden in a car before, the woman's daughter had been ordered into the back of the tourer and was now too afraid to even look out its side windows. 'She knows she lied, Louis, but given the way I'm feeling, there could well be an element of truth.'

'Let's let them go ahead. We have to talk, and the sooner the better.'

'There isn't time. Ludin's ordered me to stick close to Kleiber, and has already made certain Oona and Giselle will be in Drancy and on their way to Mauthausen tomorrow at 0500 hours. I could have stopped it, Louis. I didn't and am hating myself.'

'And for that Anna-Marie would thank you.'

'You *did* meet?'

'Have a whiff of this but don't let any of them see you.'

His tobacco pouch, but the lock on that gate had been cut and the rush was on, the entrance to that former mansion being given just enough plastic to lift away the ornate bronze doors of antiquity.

Down in the cellars, six plain wooden chairs stood in a semicircle facing a single one. Brimful, and reeking of sodium sulphide and hydrated lime, two of the vats that had been sunk into the floor were on either side of that chair, and from the wooden rods that lay end-to-end across them were steeping cowhides that when lifted, looked as if things had just begun.

Effluent would run along the drain that led to a manhole next to the far wall. Elsewhere the vats were empty.

It was Kleiber who found the blindfold and gag that had been cut away, Ludin who noted that beside an outermost chair in that semicircle, whoever had sat in it must have been wearing mud-caked boots.

'*Ach, Kriminalrat,*' said Kleiber, 'there is also the note you insisted be sewn into the turn-ups of Oenen's trousers in spite of my having definitely told you not to do such a thing.'

Scrapings from hides lay about, wooden barrows, too, one of which looked oddly out of place and as if, in spite of the tannery's having been closed, it had recently been used.

So, too, an oil can and its wick.

'Louis, I wish our Anna-Marie was here to tell us what's different.'

'These cowhides are mildewed.'

Sounds came from the art gallery above and then the sounds didn't, thought Anna-Marie. The voices were in Deutsch and French and accompanied by footsteps, and always there was this desperate need to listen should any be on the stairs to these cellars. Yet there was also this equally desperate need for haste when apparently none could be taken.

Emmi was among those in the gallery; Emmi who had found the contact who had brought them here, yet to the pencil and tracing paper there was but total patience, for no line, letter or shading could be out of place or overlooked.

Monsieur Auget, for that was the name he had given, had placed the letter from Kaltenbrunner on the light table and had fixed the tracing paper firmly above the stamp mark of the Reichssicherheitshauptamt. Later he would make a woodcut or rubber stamp of it, but for now the tracing paper copy would have to do.

The Galerie Dumail, formerly that of its original owner but now run by his assistant, was but one of several scattered amongst the antiquarian bookshops of the rue Guénégaud. A favourite haunt of the Occupier, as were those on the rue Mazarine off which this street ran, the quartier de Saint-Germain-des-Prés readily confronted one with its history. La Monnaie, the Mint, was just across the street. 'And handy,' Monsieur Auget had said. 'Skilled engravers, as I was myself until a year-and-a-half ago, but those people wouldn't dare do work like this, would they? Instead, it's been left to myself to whom Maréchal Pétain himself pinned this in that other war.'

The Médaille Militaire.

'But in this one with the defeat, he has had no need of me.'

Shoving his eyeglasses up to perch precariously on his brow, he said, 'Now stop watching what I've been doing. Look away and think of something vastly different. A piglet or a chicken. Describe it to yourself in detail. That little fellow isn't just greedily suckling, squeezed as he is amongst his brothers and sisters. He's dug his hind legs into the straw and is pressing them firmly against the floor so as to get an even more possessive grip.'

Arie would have said, 'I was thinking of a goat.'

He kissed his fingertips and threw that hand. *'Chèvre,'* he said with longing. 'A Chabichou du Poitou from the Loire. It has a delicacy that is sublime and is perfect with a freshly sliced, fully ripened pear and a glass or two of the Pouilly-Fumé. My Leah and I when on holiday would always enjoy such a repast right after our swim, then enjoy each other, of course.'

'Your wife . . .'

'She was there at home and I was here: 17 July last year. Operation Spring Wind, they called it—who would have thought of anything other than a pleasant stroll?'

The Vel d'Hiv round-up.

'Now forget that goat and look again at what we've before us. Concentrate hard, for lives depend on it, not just your own. Is there anything I've missed? Anything, even the tiniest of nicks or a gap across one of the letters that might indicate that the typeface had been worn or poorly cast?'

The tracing seemed perfect.

'Now let me show you something you may need to know when people like me are no longer available.'

Turning the tracing paper over but now using jet-black copy ink and pen and that same care, he produced a mirror image of the stamp's impression, but in reverse. Blowing on it a little, he then held it positioned over the letter he had written and typed up on a German machine, an Olympia, and carefully turning the tracing paper over, laid it down where it absolutely had to be and gently pressed the heal of his hand against it before teasing the tracing paper away.

'Now for the signature that will free those two if, and I say this with great respect, you manage to get there before the real truck to Drancy does. But please, even with such a need for haste, don't distract me. Take a look at your newpapers and start to memorize the details. You are now Annette-Marie Schellenberger from Cernay in Alsace. It's a small town just to the east of Thann and it suffered greatly in the Great War, so you will know all about its cemeteries. Just to the north is Hartmannswillerkopf, what the French *poilus* called Vieil-Armand. It was Alsace's Verdun, so look into it if you have time since your mother must have told you repeatedly where and how the father who never saw you had been killed. Oh, I almost forgot. I've given you a few years you don't yet have, but they might just help. Who knows?'

The photo of herself, taken and developed by an assistant, showed her as she now was dressed: severe and uncompromising.

Taking up the letter he had typed, he said, 'I've put the two you are to collect and take to Drancy as down for the Stutthof KZ. It's in what was once north-central Poland. An administrative centre and forced-labour camp, it has at least a hundred sub-camps, so there will be plenty for your two to do should they ever reach such a terrible place. The SS have one of their armament's factories there and it's rumoured, we understand, that early next year work will begin on a Focke-Wulf aircraft plant.'

Kaltenbrunner's signature when compared with the original was perfect.

Pushing across the table two of the diamonds Mijnheer Meyerhof had given her for herself, she saw Monsieur Auget shake his head. 'That's generous, but you've brought us something of inestimable value and certainly it was the reason I immediately agreed to drop everything and see you, but one will be sufficient. You might need the other yourself.'

'My life diamonds.'

'And a very apt name. *Bonne chance*, Fraülein Schellenberger. Take a few moments to mingle with the gallery's crowd, then quietly leave with your associate.'

For now she would have to hang onto her old papers as well since to get to Arie and the truck, she had first to change out of the uniform and only later, back into it. But would those two have already been taken, and if so, what then would they find at that villa?

Emmi hadn't been able to contact Aram to even ask his permission.

From the cellar of the tannery the sewer must run out to the rue des Gobelins, felt St-Cyr, to then connect with that one and from there, link up with the larger that carried the Bièvre, but it wasn't good. A pair of worn-out leather work gloves had been left near that manhole grill as if quickly cast aside, the cover itself not quite settled back into place and indicating that someone—a *résistant, ein Bandit*—had thought to tightly close it after himself, but hadn't quite managed.

'Louis . . .'

'Hermann, it's far too deliberate. Refuse to do what Kleiber's ordered. Tell him he has to first send in a Wehrmacht mine-disposal squad, orders or no orders.'

'Kaltenbrunner is insisting I be the one because of my trip-to-heaven bomb-disposal experience at Vieil-Armand, but what Klieber has failed to notice is that whoever filled those two steeping tanks and left the rest for us to find, also uncovered enough of his background to know that the sewers would tempt him.'

'*Bien sûr*, but we're obviously dealing with someone who knows exactly what to do.'

'If I let him.'

On his hands and knees, and with everyone else having taken cover, Kohler ran his fingers lightly round the grill that dated from 1869 and just prior to the Franco-Prussian War, not that Kleiber or Ludin would give a damn about such an irony, but that wire might be of interest if left and so might the other one. A good five centimetres below the first, it ran along a seam between the paving stones and down into the sewer so that when the first was safely removed, the second would take care of things.

Both took time, as did climbing down into the sewer to work his way carefully forward. Passing a red-brick lateral that must date from two hundred years ago and drain other areas into this one, he felt it had better be left for now, though it could well have been used. But when he found uncapped ten-litre glass jugs of concentrated sulphuric acid resting on a wedged-up plank above, they were balanced so lightly it could only mean there could well be others.

More than half-full, the sewer was blocked by something. Prodded from behind by Kleiber, he said, 'Pass these jugs back and up and be careful. He'll be long gone, given what he's already left.'

'Is it that you're refusing to continue?'

'*Ach*, don't be so dyed-in-the-wool. With these flashlights, if he was down here, he'd have shot us. Since he hasn't, he must want something else or has simply buggered off.'

'He's hiding, or hiding something he doesn't want us to find.'

Above, and endlessly chain-smoking, Ludin kept his gaze rivetted to that open manhole, noted St-Cyr, as did the others, their machine-pistols cradled. Using a rope, one of the men carefully hoisted a full jug of acid and set it to one side, then another, the wooden workings of this steeping floor remaining fixed in position as if but waiting for the whistle. Yet there were rows of empty steeping tanks in the floor.

Hides were in the blockage, hair from the scrapings, too, felt Kohler. Thick, heavy and waterlogged, the mush had been deliberately dumped into the sewer, but why? Simply to slow them down?

When he found the charge, he knew the worst and said, 'I think we'd better leave while we can.'

'Defuse it.'

'*Ach*, listen, you. He's waterproofed it with a *Kondom* to make sure the time pencil and plastic remain bone dry. Since we've no idea of the pencil's setting, I'll either have to leave it here or take it up above, so which is it to be?'

'Cut it open.'

'You must really want a hero's death, but those diamonds don't even exist. They're nothing but a rumour.'

'Then understand that when arrested in Nice, Meyerhof's son said otherwise. Under the reinforced interrogation of his wife and children, he readily confessed.'

Naked, she would have screamed at her husband, as would the kids.

Cutting the rubber away, Kohler heard himself saying, '*Scheisse*, it's white. Two hours but glass broken when? Get out of here, Colonel.'

Teasing the pencil out, he handed the charge of plastic to this *eingefleischter* and ducked down under that clotted mass to lay the pencil as far from them as possible. 'If it goes off next to my foot, that's it, *mein Lieber*, so we really should retreat.'

Kleiber hadn't listened. He had gone up that brick lateral and would now have to be told. 'Standartenführer, maybe we should talk to Louis first since he met with that girl this afternoon.'

Darkness had fallen, and when the truck finally came to the villa in Neuilly where Gestapo Boemelburg kept such prisoners, Anna-Marie felt the touch of Arie's hand on her own.

The gates to the drive off the rue de Rouvray were wide open as if expecting someone, but had those two the chief inspector wanted already been taken to Drancy, or had the gates been left this way for new arrivals?

Blinkered, the blue-washed headlamps of the truck revealed so little, the thought of what lay ahead filled her with dread.

'I'll keep the engine running,' said Arie. 'If I have to, I'll ram anything that tries to block us.'

He'd be shot, and he knew it, and maybe he wanted this, especially if she and Emmi were taken, but when told at 3 rue Vercingétorix of what was to come, he hadn't objected, had simply reached out to her and had said, 'If it has to be, then that's what we'll do.'

But now? she wondered. Was it all to be but a desperate gamble, *Blitz* uniforms or not, forged letters too?

'Sitting here won't solve things,' said Emmi.

There were no suitcases waiting at the kerb, and when that little light above the door went out, the gates behind them began to close.

For some time now, nothing further had been heard from Hermann or from Kleiber. Though not necessary, St-Cyr knew he couldn't help but say, 'Oil of vitriol is most unkind, Kriminalrat. In situations such as this it is very doubtful if even immediate assistance would be of any use.'

Irritably flinging his cigarette away, Ludin turned on him. '*Verdammter Franzose*, is it that you think I haven't realized that? If Kleiber's killed, I'll be blamed far more than anyone. There have been no such screams.'

'*Ach*, that is precisely what I'm implying: *Das auslösende Element.** Had you counted them, you would have discovered that there were originally thirty-two jugs of that acid in those rows over there against that wall. Circles in the dust indicate that six have been removed.'

'And since two have surfaced, four remain unaccounted for.'

Sickened by the sight, Kohler let his gaze sift carefully over everything as light from the torch glinted from the bottles. Upright on a bricked recess in the lateral, two of them faced Kleiber whose back was to the opposite wall and who must have dropped his torch. A third was right above the colonel, a fourth just upstream and weighting down the makeshift raft on which it rode.

Wired, and with another of the white time pencils ticking its little life away, this fourth bottle had two 8-ounce cartridges of Nobel 808 taped to it.

The voice that came was far from steady.

'Kohler, I'm caught on something.'

---

* The trigger element.

'*Ach*, don't try to talk. It's a loose strand of barbed wire and it's hooked to the back of your waders.'

'HE'S A SADIST! CORROSIVE BURNS AND UTTER AGONY, ARE THOSE WHAT HE WANTS?'

'Easy. Just go easy, eh? Try not to move or we'll both go up.'

'I've shit myself.'

'I would too.'

Slowly, carefully, deliberately, felt Kleiber, Kohler got his hands around behind until there was but the embrace of death.

'It's rusty, Standartenführer. Made to look as if just something that had been tossed in here years ago.'

'The Reichssicherheitshauptamtchef is demanding that we get these *Banditen*, not just the diamonds. Both will put you back on your feet. Loyal to the Führer, Kohler; loyal to the Greater Reich.'

'And Oona and Giselle?'

'Our Heinrich has made far too many mistakes already. That was one of them, and I will personally see that it is corrected and they are returned.'

The lying son of a bitch, but there was no sense in worrying about it now. First one barb was freed and then another, but the mush of hair and hides in the main channel was causing the water here to back up and rise, only to then suddenly fall, and this last hook just couldn't be freed. Not yet. 'There's unfortunately a little something else, Standartenführer.'

Under probing fingertips that barbed wire had been fixed to another that was plain and not rusty and ran up the bricks behind Kleiber and across the top and down to those two bottles, behind which was yet another eight-ounce cartridge of the 808 but not a time pencil. Here, and leaning a little to one side so that its hand-clasp would definitely slip away, was a No. 36 British Mills grenade. Pull the pin and count but remember there are only four seconds until its spring-loaded striker detonates it.

'Standartenführer, I can't defuse this. I haven't another pin nor could I pull the one out and insert another fast enough even with the torch in my teeth.'

'Free me then. Once this is cleared, we'll find out what that bastard was hiding.'

'A cache of weapons, a wireless set, who gives a damn? Just

bugger off while you can, now that I've unhooked you and not hooked myself.'

'Before you reached me you shouted something about St-Cyr and that Netherlander.'

Shit! 'Only that we should talk to Louis since he might have found out something.'

'I thought you said he had met with the *Schlampe.*'

'Me? In the spot you were in, you'd have thought anything.'

'Then when we have her, we'll use her to get this one.'

In the foyer of the villa where Giselle Le Roy and Oona Van der Lynn were being held, there was a telephone, and as two *gestapistes français* joined him, this SS Captain Oster finished reading the letter and saw the stamp and signature. Pausing to reconsider something, he finally said, 'Fräulein Schellenberger, this states that they are to be sent to Stutthof KZ, yet my instructions specifically state their final destination is Mauthausen.'

There was only one way to handle this. 'By whose order?'

'Kriminalrat Ludin.'

'But is an order from the Reichssicherheitshauptamtchef to be countermanded by anyone other than the Führer?'

'*Ach*, of course not, but always we must check to see if a mistake has been made. *Einen Moment.* I will telephone Gestapo Boemelburg. Your papers, please.'

Now what were they to do—shoot him, shoot the other two and the cook-housekeeper, then search for still others?

'*Ihre Papiere, Fräulein.*'

'*Entschuldigen Sie, bitte!*'

'*Dank.*'

But Herr Oster didn't use the telephone here. Instead, he started for another.

'*Zum Teufel, Haupsturmführer,*' called out Emmi, 'these two bitches are not the only ones we have to collect tonight. This *is* Neuilly, isn't it and still the home of far too many?'

The tall one with the shoulders and the years, having stayed closer to the door and exit, had at last spoken. 'Then give me the order papers for those as well, Fräulein.'

'You have no authority to even look at those,' swore Emmi. 'Don't overstep.'

'Surely Herr Kaltenbrunner's letter is sufficient,' said Anna-Marie, 'or is it your wish that the report I must file should fully detail the reason for such a delay?'

These two . . . Both wore the uniforms of signals auxiliaries in the Wehrmacht. Neither were SS or from the police unless undercover, and the younger one who had been doing all the talking until the other's outburst, had forgotten to snap her handbag closed, Madame Décour having indicated this with but the slightest of nods. 'Herr Boemelburg will be at Maxim's. It will take but a moment for a waiter to bring him a telephone or lead him to one.'

Silently, as if needing replacements, felt Anna-Marie, that cook-housekeeper had returned to gazing at her slippers, while the two Parisians were simply watchful and Oona Van der Lynn and Giselle Le Roy sat side by side knowing only that Drancy awaited. Packed and ready, their small suitcases were next to the door, and yes, Mademoiselle Le Roy looked as if she had recently fallen or been badly beaten. But what was to happen when the real truck arrived and would it find Arie's still in the drive?

Unbearable, this waiting was an agony, but when Oster briskly returned, he snapped her papers into her hand, brought his heels together, saluted and said, 'Fräulein Schellenberger, *Alle ist korrekt.*'

But was it? Had he even used the phone or had he just had a good look through her papers and noted down the essentials?

He would keep the letter—he had to, felt Anna-Marie, wishing that she had first considered the ramifications of their doing this when the chief inspector had asked it of her.

To the city and the darkness there was, felt St-Cyr, but thin bicycle traffic and an occasional car, while along the adjacent pavements many of those who remained hurried to the *métro* or to closer destinations, or waited for an *autobus au gazogène* that likely would never show up because the Occupier had the use of most of them.

On the rue Daru there were several gasoline-powered cars parked ahead alongside Chez Kornilov, while across the street, the artists' entrance to the Salle Pleyel had lost its wire-caged little blue light, probably to theft, Concierge Figeard being unable to attend to it.

Behind the wheel, Hermann was far too quiet. 'Easy, *mon vieux*. Take another puff.'

'It's your pipe!'

'But it might help and that is what I believe Arie Beekhuis thought when he suggested she give me that tobacco.'

'You made a deal. You *told* her that if she would attempt to rescue Oona and Giselle, we would arrange for the sale of that kilo of boart and see that an FTP *équipe* got its 45 million francs but in fivers! Are you crazy, after what I've just been through?'

Somehow he was going to have to get Hermann's mind off what had happened. Four of Kleiber's men had been torn to pieces by the blast, others badly burned. 'You know as well as I that the SD and others, especially purchasing agencies such as Munimin-Pimetex use notes like these to purchase quantities of things and pay off others. Had we a quartz lamp, its UV light would, I'm all but certain, show the bluish-grey of the false, whereas the real would be soft-blue. It's a preferred currency, *mon vieux*. No one wants Reichsmark or francs if they can be paid in these.'

Though the Americans had, in mid-1941, suspended international trade in dollars, those, too, would be equally useful.

'And with the British naval blockade, Hermann, the chances of any of them ever reaching the Bank of England for checking are minimal, and what others might suspect, if indeed they ever did, won't matter since the notes would immediately be used to buy the tangible and SD-Berlin must have plenty of them.'

The crinkle was good, felt Kohler, a sound so distinctive, bankers the world over used it to identify the real.

'The sheen is also perfect,' he said, having briefly flashed a light. 'It also has the deckle edges of handmade paper.'

'And the ink is clearly Frankfurt black, as the Bank of England would have used, the pigment made from German charcoal, from grapevines that had been boiled in linseed oil.'

This wasn't good; it was terrible. 'The SD must be having them made in one of the *Konzentrationslager*. Few will know of it, certainly not two dumb *Schweinebullen* like us. If we do what she has asked, we leave ourselves wide open to knowing of something that is so secret, only Kaltenbrunner and a few others know anything of it.* And that can only mean, even though they already have enough on us, Kleiber

---

* Known at war's end as Operation Bernhard, more recently as the Bernhard Pounds.

will be sure to mark us down for the piano wire, and if not him, Heinrich bloody Ludin or Kaltenbrunner himself.'

They *did* have reason to worry. 'We still have to try.'

'She might not have been able to do anything—had you even considered that?'

'Yes, but how else are we to solve this investigation and negotiate a way out of it not just for ourselves, but for Oona and Giselle, if rescued, and for Gabrielle? A murderer who is murdered but with the help of a victim like that? Diamonds that *do* exist and others that may or may not, but will have to remain hidden if they do? Surely she deserves our continued help.'

'You sound like a saint but have forgotten to mention the robbery of that van and that Sergei Lebeznikov took his son *and* that girl to this very restaurant.'

'I am merely saying that we have no choice. We need to find and speak to Rheal Lachance and Émile Girandoux before Kleiber or Ludin try to stop us. Besides, it's late and this place has a reputation.'

Pungent with the collective aromas of food, perfume and tobacco smoke, Chez Kornilov was also loud, and through the din came the sounds of cutlery and plates, the shouts of white-bloused waiters wearing peaked peasant caps, colourful sashes about the waist and trousers tucked into brown leather riding boots. Crossed cavalry swords, Cossack uniforms with bandoliers, beautiful carpets and displays of knives adorned the walls, with brass samovars seemingly everywhere. And on the wall facing all who entered, a large colourful map showed Saint Petersburg and the Bay of Neva and river of the same—Leningrad to the Bolsheviks, and no mention of the endless siege being briefly lifted on 18 January of this year, the population dying at a rate of 20,000 a day.*

Instead, there was a portrait photograph of Czar Nicholas II and family, and the silver-headed eagle of the Romanovs.

'It's like a monument to the past, Hermann.'

Picnic after picnic, palace after palace, thought Kohler, and not a reminder anywhere of the brutal murders of that family on 16

---

* The siege lasted from 8 September 1941 until 14 January 1944, though Moscow didn't announce its relief until the 27 January.

July 1918. France had opened her doors to fleeing White Russians, among them the young teenager Louis's songbird had once been.

An absolutely gorgeous hostess wore a tightly belted dress of dark blue woollen herringbone with silver threads that emphasized her figure. Brushing aside a lock of ash-blonde hair, her amber bracelets catching the lamplight, she gave them a slightly puzzled but knowing look and said, 'Messieurs, I am Ulyana Alexandrova, but are you here to dine or make an arrest?'

'Kohler, Kripo Paris-Central, mademoiselle or madame, and none other than my immediate boss, Chief Inspector Jean-Louis St-Cyr of the Sûreté. Since a meal here must cost more than 2,000 francs, please show us to that crowded table. *Ach, ja*, that's the very one with the secretary who looks as though she's being shared by both of her bosses.'

'That would be Madame Lucie-Marie Bélanger.'

'Do those of the Organisation Todt also share her?'

The builders of the Atlantic Wall and lots of other things, but this one needed a suitable answer. '*Peut-être*, but please wait here until I have asked if such as yourselves would be welcome.'

Did their curiosity extend to diamonds? wondered Ulyana. Diamonds, since everyone else was talking of them and these two were the sworn enemies of Serge de Lenz, the alias of Sergei Lebeznikov whose son, Pierre-Alexandre, had adored that student and had even hoped to marry her and been rejected.

Hundreds and hundreds of thousands of carats that no one knew of except for those two from Berlin, Herr Ulrich Frenzel and Herr Johannes Uhl who had claimed, Sergei had said, that the student was a *Halbjüdin* from the Netherlands named, not Annette-Mélanie Veroche as she had claimed, but Anna-Marie Vermeulen, the very girl, however, that Mademoiselle Jacqueline Lemaire, former fiancée of the banker Hector Bolduc, had wanted desperately to join her escort service so that his two friends and fellow partners, the overseers of his bank, could have the use of her.

Un mouchard, a bomb in *place* de l'Opéra, and now . . . what now? she wondered.

Sergei would be more than pleased to learn of their presence, as would poor Hector whose vans would so often drop off things necessary to keep a place like this going, but would they ever find that girl and those diamonds, and if they did, would they be willing to share a few?

Arie had tucked the truck out of sight in the former stable next door and now, thought Anna-Marie, they were alone in the safehouse at the end of the courtyard at 3 rue Vercingétorix. But it wouldn't do to reach out to him in relief, though she desperately needed to. Instead, she must say it plainly.

'I want you to leave early tomorrow morning right after the curfew has ended. You're to take the truck, and a bike, and use that same entrance we did with Étienne and Frans.'

She was in earnest, but . . . 'Why not come with me while you can?'

'Because whoever it was Frans gave that coin to will know who I am and be watching for the truck, and we mustn't leave it here. Also, I still have to do what I have to, but when I ordered those two to climb into the back and Emmi threw their suitcases in, that cook-housekeeper deliberately made sure she had a good look not only at its licence but that it was a faded red Renault 3.5-tonne with canvas tarp, so it's only a matter of time until they find it. Give whoever it was this, and make sure you tell him I'm still very much in Paris, and he'll let you go because he'll understand, I think, that something far bigger must be afoot.'

It was a beautifully cut, clear-white diamond.

'Then as soon as you can, ditch the truck and use the bike but keep to the back roads. Try for Martine and the farm, then vanish, but know that if I could, I believe I would come to love you as much as I still do my Henki.'

Instantly she held up both hands to stop him.

'It's neither the time nor the place and I can't for a moment forget what I have to do.'

'And the cash from that bank van?'

Étienne had taken some. 'Leave it beyond what you need.'

'Apolline won't like your walking out of here in that uniform.'

'I won't but must come and go for a little. In the morning I'll make sure she understands why you left without saying good-bye, and that she really has no other choice, but since I still have ten of those, a few will convince her. I won't tell her of the cash. Let's let her find it later.'

'And the things in that tin you trusted me to look after when you weren't here?'

'Will just have to take care of themselves, but with me.'

Tray after tray, plate after plate went to that table where Hermann was getting to know everyone: roast pork, grilled beef and mutton on skewers, a terrine of chicken with pork, then something called salmon *kulyebyaka*, baked cod, too, with horseradish, and finally a glazed pike-perch in aspic under a garnish of sliced cucumber. And the wine . . . *Ah, mon Dieu*, the Château Lafite, Château Mouton and Château Latour and wasn't Hector Bolduc interested in châteaux and vineyards near Pouillac and Bordeaux, and was that who Ulyana Alexandrova was now trying desperately to reach on a telephone that would most certainly be listened in to by the Gestapo's Listeners?

Accompanying everything, there were potato dumplings, omelettes, buckwheat *kasha*, beetroot casserole with sour cream, cucumber salad, beet salad, lentil soup and borscht.

Anna-Marie had eaten here not once but twice, so Ulyana would know something of her and would most definitely have found out more.

Taking out the coin, he ran a thumb over where she had scratched her initials thinking it the only way of saving herself from that informant. 'Two and a half guilders in silver and among the last to be minted,' he said to himself and as if to her, knowing she would have looked at the hors d'oeuvres just as he was, shocked that there were so many when children were terribly underweight, undersize, and athletic classes had had to be cancelled.

Having loaded two plates to capacity, he started for that table, the girls gorgeous French and Russian *Parisiennes*, all beautifully dressed and with jewellery they had obviously been given, their petty jealousies and rivalries all too evident.

Guerlain's Shalimar, named after a Mogul's garden in Kashmir, was distinctively being worn by the secretary: sandalwood, patchouli, vanilla and musk.

'And just a touch behind each of her ears, Louis, and on *le mont de Vénus*. But these are none other than Rheal Lachance and Émile Girandoux, and these are Horst Lammers and Heinz Springer, the number one buyers for the Todt. Carload after carload of French lumber, tonnes and tonnes of her cement, too, and steel reinforcing rods, copper pipes and electrical wiring. Diamonds also, I think.'

Had he popped more of those damned pills?

Alone in his car, Ludin wondered what the hell Kohler and St-Cyr were up to at Chez Kornilov. Was he to find Kleiber first or simply go in and confront the two of them?

Kleiber had blamed him for everything that had gone wrong, and now there were the deaths of those who had tried to defuse the bombs, also the excruciating acid burns of still others, all of which Kleiber was having to report to Kaltenbrunner *after* he had first answered why they had yet to have arrested that girl and recovered the black diamonds.

Hilda would have advised him to leave for Switzerland while he could, that all dogs piss where others have, and since he had never liked dogs, he should avoid them.

Had they met with that girl? Had she made contact, as Kohler had suggested?

Sleep wouldn't come—how could it? wondered Anna-Marie. Photos . . . so many photos, but had there been others still, others that hadn't been destroyed, and had Hector Bolduc seen some of herself with Jacques Leporatti at the Jardin des Plantes?

Jacqueline Lemaire would have looked at each of those photos and would know exactly who was in them and where they had been taken because whoever had taken them would have had to find out. But would she remember the faces, would the photographer? Emmi had had to be told in any case. To have not done, wouldn't have been right, and Aram, though furious with her for such carelessness, would deal with it if he could, but wouldn't wash his hands of her, not yet. Not with 45 million francs or 225,000 pounds sterling in fivers: 45,000 of those, with 15,000 in each suitcase, the numbers easy, the rest nothing but a disaster waiting to happen.

Ulyana shuddered. It was one thing for St-Cyr and Kohler to have come here unexpectedly, quite another for this sour-looking individual to have followed. As if in constant pain, and endlessly sucking on a cigarette, he pointed to that table and said in Deutsch, 'How long have those two *Scheissdrecken* been here?'

To cross him would not be wise. Better to give him an answer but in a way that only she could. 'Long enough for each to have polished off two heaping plates of the *zakuski* and a half bottle of vodka. Herr Kohler's *otbivnaya* and *pelmeni* . . . oh, sorry. His veal schnitzel in sour cream, with a side order of the Siberian meat ravioli, and the chief inspector's trout with walnut sauce, will not be ready for another ten-and-a half minutes unless I'm a little off.'

The *Schlampe*! 'Cancel those. Now use that telephone to call 84 avenue Foch. Tell the duty officer to find Standartenführer Kleiber and have him sent here immediately. It's urgent. Don't and I will shut you down and put your ass and everyone else's here on the Russian front.'

Oh là là, son cul, and he had meant it too. 'Would you like to order something to eat, mein Herr?'

Pistol in hand, he had already turned away.

The plates had been shoved aside, noted Ludin, the whores to the other end of the table and all now pissing themselves and falling silent at the sight of himself, the others still not having realized they had a visitor.

Huddled over what could only be a British five-pound note, and with St-Cyr still holding a twist of cloth, were four of the so-called purchasing agents—the 'slackers' the Führer had tried to get rid of last February. Spread out were about thirty or so Congo cubes, a gram, their small size, shape, colours and dimpled surfaces indicative of that very origin.

'A kilo . . .' blurted Rheal Lachance.

'How are we to get clearance for a sum like that and in those?' demanded Émile Girandoux.

'*Ach*, we can help, can't we, Heinz?' said Horst Lammers. 'Essex and SS-Rome will also want to come in and be glad of the opportunity.'

Himmler's purchasing agencies! *Merde*, thought Girandoux, how could he have said such a thing? 'Better to keep it to ourselves since that's what she wants, isn't it?'

'It is,' said Kohler.

'But still, Émile, how are we to get clearance for that much and of *those*?' asked Lachance.

'Easy,' quipped Kohler. 'Everyone knows Reichsmarschall Göring is in the Führer's bad books. This foolish offer of sale is going to guarantee him a huge comeback. Once the Standartenführer Kleiber hears of it, he'll know that we can use that kilo not only to get that girl and everyone else who is with her, but the other diamonds she still must have and the black ones too.'

Good for Hermann who was now pulling out a chair for the Kriminalrat. 'Three medium-size suitcases, messieurs,' said St-Cyr. 'Each to be packed with the notes tied in bundles of one hundred.'

'You've met with that girl,' said Ludin.

'Correction,' said Louis. 'She met with me and quite unexpectedly. You see, Kriminalrat, I was in the Palmhouse,* at the Jardin d'Acclimatation which is, if you will allow me to explain, the children's zoological and amusement park. The headquarters of Rudy de Mérode is quite near to its entrance.'

'And you just happened to be there, did you?'

Somehow the assistant gardener at the Jardin des Plantes with whom Anna-Marie had been photographed had had to be protected. 'Not happened, Kriminalrat. I was following up a lead and in search of the source of the dried rosemary this Annette-Mélanie Veroche had kindly been obtaining for the son of that one.'

Lebeznikov was heading for them and far from happy.

'Perhaps if our receptionist could find us a private room, Louis, it might be better than to broadcast the *Sonderkommando*'s business any further, since Parisians the city over seem to know enough of it already, thanks to this one and his colonel.'

'No one is going anywhere,' said Ludin. 'We will wait here for the Standartenführer and I will let him decide.'

Kleiber would, of course, insist on using that temporary office of his at 84 avenue Foch with plenty of SS backup and holding cells in the cellar.

Lighting yet another cigarette—Pall Malls this time—Ludin laid the pistol temptingly on the table in front of himself and said to Louis, 'How could that girl whose photo is everywhere have met you in such a place or any other?'

'It's a place for children and she was immersed in them and holding hands with two of them—a school-class visit, I believed, and we quickly spoke Deutsch, the children and the teacher not knowing a word of what was being said.'

---

* Predates the Musée de l'Homme, which has since been torn down and replaced by the Musée des Arts et Traditions Populaires.

'Cut the *Schmarrn* or I will cut it for you.'

'Certainly. She was with a group of schoolchildren and used them to conceal her presence, but we did stand apart under one of the palms and very quickly she told me what had been asked of her.'

'Sell that boart and get the money to her and those other *Banditen,* but how?'

'We're working on it, but they've been using her, Kriminalrat, just as you and the colonel have been.'

'She would have had no other choice but to obey,' said Hermann, reaching for Ludin's cigarettes and lighter only to have a hand laid on them.

'Your weapon, Kohler, and yours.'

'Not with what we have to do. You need us, Kriminalrat. She won't deal with anyone else and neither will those who are telling her what to do.'

But how *could* that girl have gone to such a public place and not have been spotted and arrested? wondered Ludin. Blonde, blue-eyed, a little taller than most, and very Aryan, attractive too, and fluent in the language.

Of course. That had to have been it. And as for these two, they had been constantly evasive, even to lying about those damned shoes. Rocheleau—hadn't that been the name of that rural policeman and didn't he now work for Mérode and this one to whose son she had given that dried herb?

'Kriminalrat . . .' called out Hector Bolduc, hustling that former fiancée of his toward them, she resisting, her overcoat undone and hat askew. '*Ach*, but I'm glad to have found you. Jacqueline has something you need to know. The Jardin des Plantes . . .'

Scheisse! thought Kohler. Now it was all going to come out.

But Kleiber followed, and wearing a black armband to honour those who had been lost at the tannery, didn't hesitate.

'Kriminalrat, you're finished. Mistake after mistake, I tell you. The Reichssicherheitshauptamtchef is furious and is demanding your immediate recall, so I've taken the liberty of booking you onto the early morning Lufthansa. Here are the necessary papers.'

Out on the street, sitting in the Citroën he'd been allowed and enveloped in the darkness, Ludin said to himself, A student. The Left Bank, the Sorbonne, the boulevard Saint-Germain. Places she would know only too well, yet a uniform, a *Blitz*. No one would have thought to look for that, Kleiber least of all.

The storeroom to which they were shown was yet another Ali Baba's cave, felt Kohler, this one obviously also having had Hector Bolduc's help, for chagrin clouded the banker's expression, malicious delight that of the former mistress. But photos had been secretly taken of Annette-Mélanie Veroche, both when alone and not. Later they'd been deliberately burned, along with the Mademoiselle Lemaire's file on that girl, and Louis had made a point of telling Kleiber not only why that had happened but by whom and when.

Angrily tossing a fist, Bolduc said, '*Sacré nom de nom*, that was not how it was. Who am I to tell my bank's overseers what they can and cannot do? It was *they* who had those photos taken, not myself who has never even *looked* at any of them, but when Jacqueline heard of it, of course she wanted prints for her file on that girl. Tell them, *chérie*. You must.'

Be forceful and I'll take you back—was that it, eh? wondered Jacqueline. Yet if Hector could be convinced, would his having 'begged' her to return not wipe away rejection's shame and cause Nicole Bordeaux and the others to admit they'd been wrong to have said such hateful things? Nicole who had bought that girl the dress, the shoes and had suggested time and again that what Annette-Mélanie really needed was *une sacrée bonne baise*. 'Hector is absolutely correct. I did mention the snapshots, but we were in a hurry and he said he would look at them later but never did.'

Trust a woman scorned to have said it, thought Kohler. 'And Hauptmann Reinecke and Leutnant Heiss have been recalled, I gather.'

'And sent to Russia, I think,' said St-Cyr, 'but as to my not having gone to the Jardin des Plantes to look for the source of that rosemary, I had had it in mind.'

'But not now, Louis. You'd only tip them off. We'll have to leave it until after we've made the exchange and the dust has settled.'

'What exchange?' asked Kleiber. 'Surely you don't think I'm going to agree to . . .'

There had been no time to talk to Louis about it, but something would have to be said. 'The boart for the cash in fivers. *Ach*, don't worry, Standartenführer. It can be done and will get you everything the *Sonderkommando* needs, including that girl.'

'Let Rudy de Mérode and me take care of her,' said Lebeznikov. 'We have the men and know the city far better even than those two.'

'Later,' said Kleiber. 'First, let's hear what Kohler has to say.'

'Yes, let's,' said Rheal Lachance, 'since it is through Munimin-Pimetex that such a purchase must be made.'

'Reichsmarschall Göring will okay it, *mes amis*,' said Girandoux. 'We'll telex him tonight and by 0700 hours tomorrow will have the necessary via the early-morning Lufthansa or an ME 109.'

The fivers, and one could have relied on Girandoux to have said it, thought Horst Lammers. 'The Todt would still like to come in on it. Two organizations will lend weight.'

'Oh for sure, we'll be only too glad to convey your interest,' said Lachance, 'but will have to let the Reichsmarschall decide.'

Göring? Was Lachance crazy? wondered Kohler. If the Fat One couldn't get his hands on those black diamonds, no one else was going to. 'Three medium-size suitcases, Standartenführer, each to be packed with fifteen thousand of the notes, and all with a little something else.'

'*What?*' demanded Kleiber.

Now for the crunch. 'Didn't I hear somewhere that the Philips Works in Eindhoven had come up with a very small but powerful transmitter?'

'One that's easily concealed,' said Kleiber, lifting a forefinger in pause. 'Preset, I think, to something in the range of 3,000 to 4,000 kilocycles per second. *Ach*, I like it, Kohler. Wherever those suitcases are taken, the locations can be pinpointed by our wireless tracking vans.'

And just like clandestine wireless sets, thought St-Cyr. To give Hermann his due, he had tried, but this . . . How could they possibly work for and with the enemy yet ensure that Anna-Marie and others of her *équipe* weren't arrested? 'Surely those suitcases will have to be opened and the cash payment examined before the boart is handed over, Hermann?'

'*Ach*, don't argue. The pitch is far too high for anyone to actually hear it. All three of the transmitters will be sounding away in unison and allowing the tracking vans to lock onto them right from the start. We do the exchange with no one else near, Colonel. Everyone to be held well back until I give the sign, since we don't want to scare them off. Just let that girl come in to hand over the boart and take the fivers, which will then nail down whatever safe house or houses they've been taken to, just as you've stated.'

Apart from broadcasting all of this to Lebeznikov of all people, and the others, Hermann had forgotten entirely about Heinrich Ludin who would be furious about having been so summarily dismissed. Then, too, there was the leader of that *équipe* and what *he* might think of such a scheme.

But Hermann wasn't quite finished.

'With all that cash, Louis and me can't be expected to carry it around in the Citroën. We'll need one of your bank vans, Chairman Bolduc. You to drive it and that one—yes, you, Lebeznikov—to ride up front. That'll see that the cash gets to where the exchange is to be made and the boart then safely taken to the avenue Foch first and later to Munimin-Pimetex.'

Unfortunately Hermann had to be flying on those damned pills and wouldn't have listened anyway.

'We'll do it toward the end of the day tomorrow,' said Kohler. 'Let's say 1830 hours and still lots of light.'

'And where?' asked Kleiber.

'The Vaugirard horse abattoir. It's currently empty and is out of the way enough not to arouse suspicion and give lots of routes of escape if needed, which will ease her mind. She'll arrive, Louis and me will make the exchange, and when all of that's been done, you can then track those suitcases or move in with the troops. Better still, why not ride in the back of that bank van so as to be right near the action and judge things for yourself? You can then check the boart and either be the one who grabs or follows her.'

Lebeznikov could shoot Kohler and St-Cyr and put an end to them, thought Kleiber, the girl to be given a reinforced interrogation and then executed. A clean slate, just as the Reichssicherheitshauptamtchef had demanded, including every one of those *Banditen* who had been associated with her. More diamonds, though, than could ever have been imagined, Herr Frensel and Herr Uhl to return to the Reich with them, the Führer not just grateful.

A Knight's Cross of the Iron Cross with Oak Leaves and Swords for sure.

12

The comings and goings at that *Lokal* on the boulevard Saint-Michel were clearly in view, Hermann having drawn the Citroën over to the side of the boulevard Saint-Germain not far to the west of its intersection with the other. It was Wednesday, 6 October, and they'd been on this investigation since the first of the month, yet it seemed a lifetime, felt St-Cyr. It was almost 1000 hours, and in but a moment he was going to have to do what that girl had asked, yet there was still this huge uncertainty over Giselle and Oona and it clouded everything. 'Hermann, she will at *least* have tried to free them.'

'Or been arrested. Had you even thought of that?'

'Constantly.'

'Just remember that if you *are* met, you tell her that she has to come alone and with that bike's trailer.'

'*Ah mon Dieu*, but why?'

'How else is she going to cart away three suitcases?'

'You've thought of everything, have you?'

'What I have in mind might just work.'

'Yet you've not had the guts to fill me in on the details or even to discuss it! *Bonne chance, mon vieux. Bonne chance!*'

Having had but another terrible night in that house of Louis's mother's, they were both bitchy, felt Kohler, Louis out of the car before anything further could be said and quickly losing himself among the pedestrians, the foot-traffic the usual for this time of day and midweek. Students, too, of course. Lots of those on bikes and on foot, but mostly female, the boys either dodging the forced labour or having already gone into hiding. 'But it's coming, isn't it?' he called out. 'The end, eh, and they all look as if they can hardly wait.'

'"Spring," *n'est-ce pas?*' said an urgent female voice. 'Floor it and pull over where suitable.'

Ach, she had ducked into the car so quickly, he hadn't even heard her open the door. 'Aren't you supposed to be meeting Louis?'

'This is safer.'

Ramming the accelerator to the floor and leaning on the horn, he didn't say another thing, just headed straight to the Halle aux Vins which wasn't far and just off the rue de Jussieu, next to the Jardin des Plantes. The rue de Bordeaux was busy, that, too, of the Côte d'Or. Settling on the rue de Bourgonne, he found a quiet place, and turning in and out of sight of most, left the engine running and said, 'Now tell me what the hell you meant.'

'Something—I don't honestly know what—told me not to go in there, and when I saw him hurriedly leave the car, that same instinct told me not to call out, but to speak to yourself.'

Had Louis walked right into it? If so, how could he possibly be freed? 'Did you manage Oona and Giselle?'

'The shop Enchantement. Madame Van der Lynn said to tell you Muriel and Chantal would hide them.'

Giving but the deepest of sighs, Herr Kohler very quickly told her where and how the exchange would be made, and how very tight the timing would have to be. And when he said, 'You've a trailer for that bike of yours. Be sure to use it,' she knew that he could only have seen it in those photos that had been destroyed.

He didn't ask where she was staying, simply said, 'I'll drop you off at the Jussieu *métro* station. In that uniform you'll ride free and the sooner you vanish from this quartier, the better. Louis may need me.'

Fewer and fewer were in the *Lokal,* the increasing emptiness seeming only to focus attention on himself, felt St-Cyr. No one had come to tell him where to meet Anna-Marie. Believing they were meeting, Hermann would have gone on to the Porte de Versailles to connect with Werner Dillmann, but was that whole house of cards of his to now fall in on them?

Emptying his pipe—making sure no little fire remained—he tucked it away, and forcing himself to do so, decided to wait another two minutes. Had she seen that their meeting here was out of the question? Had she been arrested?

Cold, hard, heavy and well known but not his own, the muzzle of a Lebel Modèle d'ordonannce was pressed to the back of his head. 'Hands flat on the table, Sergeant.'

'Ah, Rocheleau, and here I thought you would be busy elsewhere, but if you're intending to cause trouble again, let me remind you of the consequences.'

The blow must be excruciating, felt Rocheleau, the suddenness of oblivion instant!

Blood poured from the *salaud*'s head. 'Was that hard enough, Inspector, or do you want another?'

Not being able to understand more than a few words of French, Ludin impatiently said in Deutsch, 'Remove that pistol of his and hand it to me, then use his handcuffs.'

'*Ah bon*, the bracelets. Those will teach him another lesson.'

Two *Blitzmädchen* had collected Kohler's women last night, Ludin now knew, the one with papers that had given her name as Annette-Marie Schellenburger. She'd been blonde, blue-eyed and younger than the twenty-eight those papers had stated, but beyond that it hadn't taken much to figure out where she might well be wearing that uniform and meeting with St-Cyr. Not only was there a *Blitzmädchenheim* on the rue Saint-Séverin and just off the boulevard Saint-Michel, there was a *Lokal* on the latter and not far from a *Soldatenheim* on the boulevard Saint-Germain, and with lots of students from the Sorbonne as a reminder. But he had needed help, and there really had been only one person he could have used.

'Kriminalrat, this turtle will tell us everything. Just give me a few moments with him at Rudy de Mérode's. *Les joyeuses, n'est-ce pas*, then the bathtub with iced water and he'll soon cough up the answers, if not, a few lessons with the rawhide to mark him like that partner of his.'

Virtually all of what had just been said made little sense. 'Just clamp a handkerchief to his head and get him into the car. Kohler can't be intending to collect him. He'd have been on top of us by now, but we'll take no chances.'

Lying on a table in the *Lokal*, amid scattered cigarette ashes, saccharine and a wash of acorn water, were the bloodstains and a flat, almost full and forgotten bottle of Jägermeister.

Pocketing this last, Herr Kohler didn't hesitate. 'And this Frenchman who hit him?' he demanded.

'Owlish with black Bakelite specs, a broken, sticking-plaster covered nose, new suit, fedora, tie and topcoat, and relish at what he'd just done.'

One of the Wehrmacht's career losers, this unshaven, un-anything fifty-year-old 'cook' was waiting for a handout. 'Now tell me where they were taking him since that Kriminalrat was supposed to be on his way back to Berlin.'

While that was interesting, felt Karl Ludwig Hoefle, all he really could do was to give a shrug and then . . . '*Ach*, after I had helped the frog to get your partner into the backseat of that car, he scribbled something down and handed it to me. Now what the hell did I do with it?'

'What?'

'A scrap of paper with an address. *Ach*, he said that his wife was now working there and needed lessons, and that if I would give her "the works," I was to tell the boss-madam he would pay for it.'

'His wife?'

'Évangéline.'

'What house?'

Now this *was* far more interesting and haste was, of course, necessary but . . .

Peeling off a 500-franc note, Herr Kohler finally handed it over, and when told a 1,000-franc note would help, uncovered the answer. 'My French isn't too good but I think it was the *Lupanar des garennes*.'

The brothel of the wild rabbits and one of the forty that were reserved for the Wehrmacht's rank and file but obviously also owned by none other than Rudy de Mérode.

'Apparently the house is on the rue Vignon,' said Hoefle.

Known as Hookers' Alley, and just off *place* de la Madeleine and its boulevard, which all too soon became *place* des Capucines and home to a certain bank. Were things coming full circle? Heinrich Ludin wouldn't dare take Louis there and would have to find a place where no one would bother them, but could Louis hold out and stall them long enough to get what needed to be done before the search for him could begin? 'Tell no one you've given me that address, *mein Freund*. Mention it to anyone and I'll find you.'

Another 500-franc note was handed over, but to seal such a bargain, a further 500 was found.

Louis would have to be taken somewhere, but where, since Ludin was now disobeying Kaltenbrunner's orders and that could only mean one thing.

Fumes were what had finally brought him round, felt St-Cyr. Gasoline fumes, not the voices he now heard, but he'd keep his eyes shut. The engine had been switched off, a side window rolled well down—the driver's side: Heinrich Ludin's. Rocheleau was the one who was rapidly talking and therefore still feeling his oats.

'Kriminalrat, if you don't want to take him to Rudy's, let's find a quiet spot in the Bois de Vincennes.'

'*Verfluchter Franzose, Sei still!* Kohler has to have gone somewhere. *Ach*, my gut! Has it burst?'

A moment of quiet was needed, flecks of dark blood perhaps seen on a hastily clutched handkerchief, Rocheleau irritably finding himself another cigarette but crying out when the match either broke or showered sparks into his face.

It was Ludin who again gasped and, doubtless signaling, said in Deutsch, 'See if there's another bottle of that stuff, then check to see if you haven't killed him.'

Ah bon, felt St-Cyr, the wrists had been linked in front, but *merde* the bracelets were far too tight. Danger that he was, Rocheleau continued to suck on that cigarette, disregarding entirely the fumes and that the prisoner's face was still crammed uncomfortably against what could only be a hastily filled jerry can of gasoline, apparently one of three or four.

Holding the cigarette well away from himself, his nervous fingers probed for a pulse, that hand being grasped and yanked hard, the head being butted by an already wounded one, Rocheleau yelling so hard his face hit the jerry can, blood erupting from his nose and lips, the cigarette having thankfully fallen to the road.

Slamming him down yet again, took care of him, but now a Walther P38 was threatening from the driver's seat.

'Shove him out,' said Ludin, 'and lock that door and the other one.'

Good riddance, was it? 'No one will touch him, Kriminalrat, because of yourself and this car, but he does need medical and dental attention.'

'Where the hell are we?'

'Is it that you're wondering about all those blacks?'

'Just tell me.'

'Certainly. All are French citizens, the men veterans of that other war and many of those, the Chemin des Dames and the ruins at l'Abbaye de Vauclair, the absent younger males now prisoners of war in your country and/or enduring the forced labour. Quite by accident, you've turned south, and having crossed *place* de Jussieu and driven right past the back of Halle aux Vins and that also of the Jardin des Plantes, are on the rue Geoffroy Saint-Hilaire and all but at the entrance to the Turkish baths that are in the cellars of the Paris mosque.'

'What's Kohler got in mind?'

'Hermann? Believe me, if I knew I would gladly tell you.'

'Where's the Bois de Vincennes?'

'Make a left at the corner and I'll guide you.'

That Louis would be needing him was all too clear, felt Kohler, but it was already 1047 hours and the Porte de Versailles was still so busy there had to be another high-priority. Long lines of heavily laden farm wagons, gazo trucks and a few cars awaited entry, while over to the east and nearest the Parc des Expositions, cyclists and foot traffic were also being given the thorough. No one was going to get into or out of Paris, but had Kleiber grabbed that girl and called for a clamp-down or was it simply random?

Scanning the entrance, taking the time when such was no longer available, the cause of the trouble continued to elude him, but over to the west was a little something. Right in Werner Dillmann's territory was a faded red, 3.5-tonne Renault whose canvas tarp had been flung aside to reveal nothing but an apparent emptiness.

That broad, carefully combed moustache, the shrapnel scars, missing fingers, deceitfully wary blue eyes, and all the rest were the same, the look one also of knowing a little but wanting to know a lot more and expecting everything.

'*Ach*, Hermann, *mein Lieber*, am I glad to see you. Corporals Mannstein, Weiss and Rath, take over. It's another of those controls. Like the power outages and the raids on the unlicensed brothels, they never tell us until it's too late, but where is that partner of yours?'

Had he heard something or was he just fishing? 'Busy as usual and preparing for the pay-off at 1830 hours sharp and not a moment too early or late, understand?'

'Of course, but is the Vaugirard horse abattoir still necessary?'

Now what the hell had happened? 'Isn't it the most perfect of places?'

'Most certainly, but the boys tell me there are others who are showing a decided interest in it, though those have yet to approach it too closely.'

Kleiber hadn't listened. Already he must be getting men into position, but the location couldn't be changed, not with Anna-Marie having been told of it. 'Just remember the time. In and out, and faster than fast.'

A cigarette was necessary, and after three deep drags, handed over. *'Dank,'* said Hermann whose gaze, it had to be admitted, had repeatedly flicked to that empty truck.

'Three suitcases stuffed with forty-five thousand fivers, Werner.'

Those big, beautiful white notes of the English, but had he heard him correctly? Enough not only to buy one's way out of France and into Spain, but to retire in comfort forever. 'In exchange for what?'

As if he didn't already have a good idea. 'A kilo of boart.'

The cheapest of the cheap and at an agreed-upon price like that? 'And you need me.'

'Definitely. Few others would know how to do it.'

'Then perhaps we should first consider that truck I stopped early this morning. Nothing in the back, my Hermann, but two small and rather shabby suitcases, forgotten, I think, in the haste to leave it. A bicycle as well.'

Scheisse! 'And the driver?'

That was better, and even more humble when handing the cigarette back. 'His papers leave a lot to be desired and when questioned not only was he evasive, he tried to buy me off with this.'

A baguette brilliant, a beautifully cut oval, clear-white, and of about two carats.

'Perhaps it is, my Hermann, that this girl you and that partner of yours have been chasing, felt I might weaken and let him go, but of course, when a whole city has been turned upside down looking for her by a *Sonderkommando* straight from Kaltenbrunner himself, even such as myself and my men have no choice but to do our duty.'

'So you've kept his papers, taken the keys, told him to sit tight and have been waiting for me to show up.'

'One Arie Beekhuis who sounds as if from of all places, Rotterdam—that is close to Amsterdam, is it not?'

'Close enough. And those two little suitcases?'

Gut! 'Nothing but scatterings of female underclothes, an extra blouse or two, a toothbrush that must have been shared—that sort of thing. And the bicycle, of course. A Belgian one, which is curious in itself, as was the city's name on it. Did that truck happen to come through Liège?'

There was nothing for it but to beg. 'Let him go, Werner. Handing him over will only complicate what I have in mind.'

'And that is?'

Did he need to hear it again? 'The boart for the cash.'

'But he's insurance, my Hermann, and I will need such a release in writing from you, stating, of course, that you have indeed checked his papers most thoroughly and have ordered me to release him, or is it that you . . .'

The son of a bitch. 'How much?'

That was better, considering the risk. 'Two of those three suitcases you mentioned, the last for yourself to do with exactly as you please.'

'And still to pay Rudi Sturmbacher out of my share? *Ach*, I think I've got it.'

'*Gut.* Just don't try to cross me.'

'*Liebe Zeit*, how could I even think of such a thing? Just be there when needed. No sooner, no later than that 1830 hours and over and done in such a rush, no one but us will be the wiser.'

Downing three of the Benzedrine, spitting out the pocket fluff, he got back into the car.

Eighty-four avenue Foch was busy: cars and motorcycles out front, armed men in uniform and not and going to and fro, orders being given, and upstairs in that temporary office of Kleiber's, the billiard table as nerve centre.

Enlarged, a detailed street map of the eastern half of the Vaugirard clearly showed the abattoirs, arrows pinpointing the entrance off the rue des Morillons, but there was also a photo of the two life-size bronze bulls that still marked it in spite of the Reich's incessant scrap-metal actions. Apparently nothing was to be left to chance. The routes in by foot, and the rail line which ran along the southern edge, were all indicated, the fences too, for it wasn't a place for the casual. Another enlargement detailed the sewers and pointed out suspected and known caverns, caves and tunnels in the Left Bank's bedrock that had supplied so much of Paris with its building stone, but had Kleiber thought of everything? He was using a cue to point things out to Johannes Uhl and Ulrich Frensel. And at the far end of the table was one of the suitcases: alligator leather, not inexpensive, and with the *LV* monogram of none other than Louis Vuitton.

By the travel stickers alone, its former owner had had a penchant for taking the waters: the Friedrichsbad in Baden-Baden, the Grand at Italy's Montecatini Therme, the Hôtel du Palais in Biarritz, Vichy, too, and Vittel's Parc Thermal where last February Louis and he had come up against nearly 1,700 British and a 1,000 American females in that internment camp.

'Kohler, *ach* you're just in time. Two of the suitcases are being fitted with their transmitters. That was an excellent idea of yours. The Reichssicherheitschef was most impressed and has given his full support. We are to let those *verdamte Banditen* believe they are getting away and will track them with the wireless-listening vans. Already those are in place, others on patrol, and still others on foot with the hidden listening devices up the sleeve or in the fedora for the close-in work. Already, too, and I must inform you of this, we have located one enemy wireless which will be taken out as soon as our *Mausefalle* has sprung.'

Louis would have sadly shaken his head and said of the irony, Didn't Hector Bolduc use freshly baited mousetraps in that garage of his? But real coffee, schnapps and *Lebkuchen* had been laid on, the warmers holding sausages, with mustard, sauerkraut and dill pickles to the side, and another with no less than strudel: the cherry, the plum and the apple-and-raisin. Freshly whipped cream, sweetened with real sugar, was to help that last one go down and stay there.

'Those were for that traitorously incompetent Kriminalrat,' said Uhl. 'Herr Frensel and myself were unaware of his having been recalled in such disgrace.'

'There will be no more of his mistakes, Kohler,' said Frensel. 'Now we are to accomplish the inevitable seizure of the black diamonds those filthy *Juden* tried to hide from such as myself. *Mein Gott*, you'd think they might have learned. *Ach*, they even tried to use their children, thinking that I wouldn't know where to look!'

In bundles of one-hundred notes, and piled in a heap, even with some still in the pale green linen packets they had come in, the fivers were near that suitcase. Each packet had been sealed with red wax, stamped with the swastika signet and labelled *Geheime Reichssache.*

Stark white against the flowing dark black script, each note had Britannica on a throne in its upper left, the signature of K. O. Peppiatt, chief cashier, in the lower right, and in those and elsewhere would be the hidden security checks that would expose the counterfeit. Additionally, of course, there were all the marks and signs of having been well used: those of the banks each had passed through, the shops, the scribbled signatures, et cetera, and the consequent wear.

All the packets were addressed to Munimin-Pimetex and though Göring must have had them sent, all had come directly from none other than Heinrich Himmler. But even knowing of these, if not of the privileged, would carry the death sentence, to which Louis would have said, And didn't I tell you we were digging a bottomless hole for ourselves?

'You'll be checking in with Bolduc, will you, Kohler?' asked Kleiber. 'Be sure to tell him that the van, with himself as driver and Serge de Lenz as assistant, is to be here and ready at no later than 1500 hours. I must be absolutely certain that everything is in order. We've clocked the route several times and will be using the Pont d'Iéna and an average of seven minutes, thirteen seconds. French traffic police are already stationed at every interchange to clear the way, the speed not too fast, you understand, so as to avoid unnecessary attention.'

Given the repeats and the traffic *flics*, lots would be sure to watch.

'I'll have the suitcases for you, Kohler, and right inside the rear door of that van. I'll hand them out and take the boart in, you then closing that door and handing them the cash.'

'A kilo,' said Uhl. 'It'll be in a white cotton bag with the usual tie.'

'Only one of those suitcases will need to be opened for checking, Kohler—that one,' said Kleiber. 'Here's the key. You can tell them it will open the others.'

If bought at the same time, Louis would have said. Also, *une souricière du diable.*

'Doubtless they'll be using the same car as at *place* de l'Opéra when they executed that fool of an actor Kriminalrat Ludin insisted on using,' said Kleiber. 'A Ford Model C Ten, the same as were made in the Reich from 1935 to 1940.'

'The Eifel accelerates from zero to 80.5 in 18.2 seconds, Kohler,' said Frensel. 'Cruises at no less than 106.2.'

'Has three forward gears and a four-stroke, side-valve, four-cyclinder engine,' added Uhl.

'Witnesses have sworn that the car's wheels were not wire-spoked, Kohler, like those of the British models,' said Kleiber.

A probable guess and nothing more, though a terrific car, but it was now all but 1200 hours and there was still far too much to do. 'I'd better be getting over to Hector Bolduc's bank, Colonel. Louis will be wondering where I am.'

'Eighteen thirty hours, Kohler, and make sure Lenz is with Bolduc. Since I've decided to bring Mérode and the rest of his gang in on this, they'll be watching the flank areas. Sealed, I tell you, Kohler. This whole area and the rest of the city as well.'

'Eighteen-thirty it is, Standartenführer. *Meine Lieben*, until later. Chez Kornilov, I think, and the champagne first, then that partner of mine can get to sample the trout with the walnut sauce that he ordered last night but had to miss and has been complaining about ever since.'

Now here, now there, occasional mushroom seekers scavenged this part of the Bois de Vincennes, hoping to find what the weekend's traffic might have missed and what the last few days and nights of new growth would have produced. Sticks were immediately snapped into small pieces so as to be hidden in rucksacks, acorns quickly pocketed since it was illegal to gather anything save those feelings of being outdoors and the Bois was exceedingly popular, especially on weekends.

Two bicycles, not where they should have been, were locked, the chain linking them having been wrapped around a tree trunk and given a further padlock, bicycle theft being a major concern these days.

Ludin had unfortunately found the needed: a somewhat out-of-the-way dead end leading to one of the Bois's inevitable road closures that favoured wilderness walking. Leaves were settling on the windshield, and for once the sun was being cooperative, and were it not for the present circumstance, an afternoon in the forest would have been a delight, but there had been absolutely no opportunity of breaking free. The wrists were not just linked by Sûreté bracelets; those of the Gestapo had been used to tie the first to the grip-bar that had been installed above this seat in the autumn of 1940 for use in high-speed chases. A more awkward and increasingly uncomfortable position could not have been found.

Hermann would have said, Rocheleau should see you now, but Hermann would have other things on his mind and had probably downed still more of those damned pills

Side windows open, the Kriminalrat was giving the 'Toasted' Lucky Strikes a brief rest and the present circumstance considerable thought.

St-Cyr would have to be persuaded to tell him everything, but how? wondered Ludin. 'A kilo of boart for what?'

'Forty-five thousand fivers.'

Himmler would have had to agree. 'And then?'

'Is that why the jerry cans of gasoline? Are you on the run, eh?'

'Don't taunt. Just tell me.'

The Walther P38 was again in hand, but while a delay might mean a few more hours of life and perhaps a chance to deal with him, to answer correctly would be to put at risk all that Anna-Marie had sought. 'If I knew, I would tell you, Kriminalrat, but since she didn't show up at that *Lokal*, I haven't a clue.'

'Would Kohler have met with her?'

'Since she had never seen him?'

'Just answer.'

'Then that is rather doubtful, especially as Hermann had things to do and tends always not to hang around once he's dropped me off someplace.'

'Meyerhof did move diamonds for others. Thousands and thousands of carats. Those two from Berlin were certain.'

'And since they kept whispering such a fiction to others, especially to Kaltenbrunner, a *Sonderkommando* was needed, otherwise, that one would have had to answer to none other than Heinrich Himmler. Come, come, Kriminalrat, surely the Sicherheitsdienst can do better? A girl shows up quite by chance in Amsterdam, not once, but on a second visit and Josef Meyerhof who is constantly being watched and behind ghetto wire just happens to see her and make contact and entrust her not only with the family's life diamonds but the route to whoever knows where all those so-called "black" diamonds are hidden? Why not the son, please?'

'Meyerhof knew it was chancy enough trying to get the boy and his family through France. Once they were safely in Nice and the Italian zone, things could change.'

'But then that zone was no longer safe and the son and family arrested.'

'So Meyerhof had to find another way of hiding what he valued most, and with all the other diamonds he had already hidden not just for himself, but for others. By the way, I gather you and Kohler got that girl to free those two I had consigned to the KZ at Mauthausen, not the one at Stutthof.'

Grâce à Dieu! 'I hadn't known.'

'And now you do, so you will tell me where that girl will have to run to once that supposed sale has been concluded?'

If it ever would be. 'Shoot if you like, but give me a moment since I must argue with my conscience and everything depends on Hermann.'

Somewhat empty, the courtyard off the rue Volney and right behind the bank should have been warning enough, felt Kohler. Having parked the Citroën, he finally realized what he'd forgotten in the rush. It being a Wednesday afternoon, the *verdammt* bank would be closed and locked up tighter than the Santé. *Merde*, now what was he to do, let the whole thing collapse, and with Louis out there somewhere as a *prisoner*?

Pounding on the door did no good, hammering at it with the butt of his Walther P38 little more, but at last a shout was heard, and then, '*Espèce de salaud*, if you and those other *couillons* think to continue to torment me, you had better think again. Me, I am about to teach you a lesson you will never forget!'

Flung open, forced to face down the twin barrels of another upland, one had to shout, 'It's me, Kohler!'

The rolled-up shirt sleeves, muscular biceps, loosened tie, open collar and absent jacket were those of the desperate.

'I thought it was those parasites again. Where's St-Cyr?'

'Busy.'

'*Sacré nom de nom*, must you two smash everything? My bank? All that I have worked for? Major clients threatening to pull their accounts unless I give them the advantage of my being under duress? Those curs of the *petite bourgeoisie* demanding their paltry savings? The press, they are like leeches, I tell you. Never happy, always clinging. Did you and St-Cyr not realize what you had unleashed when you sicked them onto me? Those things I did were as nothing these days. *Nothing*, I tell you. If that Annette-Mélanie Veroche, or whatever it is she's now calling herself, had gone along with Deniard and Paquette and offered up her little capital, there would have been no murders, no half-baked attempt to clean out that van—yes, yes, that's the very one that has just turned in. The little *chatte* would have been back in Paris, Kohler, safe and sound, I tell you, and enjoying life to its fullest, not hiding diamonds for others and knowing things she may or may not!'

'And you wouldn't have been able to collect the insurance.'

'We can't. They're claiming it's a criminal matter and now, thanks to you and St-Cyr, I'm to be hauled up before Hercule the Smasher. *Hercule* whom I had counted among my closest associates and most loyal of friends. Bottle after bottle of the Vieille Réserve; cork after cork of nothing but the finest from the Haut-Médoc and Médoc, the hams, the truffles . . .'

Président du Tribunal Spécial du département de la Seine, Vichy's top judge and hatchet man in Paris, and an old acquaintance from last February. Louis should have heard him.

'Hercule presides over the black-market violators, Kohler.'

'And the night-action courts.'

Those where *résistants* and other troublemakers were tried and sentenced, Hercule loving nothing better than to condemn them. 'Photos, Kohler, and not just of myself, my garage, the tenements I own and my vans and bank, but of the wife, too, with the threatened divorce, and my little Didi and Yvonne. Both of the girls are constantly in tears.'

His daughters, the one named after his secretary and primary line of defence but obviously no longer present, since the wife was her sister.

'*Paris-Soir, Le Matin, Le Petit Parisien*—even *Le Cri du Peuple*. All have been running photo after photo and column after column of sensationalism and outright lies.'

That last being the PPF newspaper to which he had donated plenty.

'And now, you ask? Oh for sure it will be *Je Suis Partout* this coming Saturday. They're always berating the police to arrest those guilty of such things and telling them where they can be found. *Pariser Zeitung* will also be at it, as will Radio Paris, even Radio Berlin. The shame, the humiliation—am I to be stripped naked and paraded through the streets before stretching the neck under the widow maker?'

Sanctimonious as always, Vichy's Ministry of Provisioning must have needed a scapegoat to calm the masses. '*Ach*, it'll soon be forgotten. Heros are what's needed and Louis and me are about to make one of you. Just have than van over to Kleiber in good time—1500 hours is what he wants—and don't forget to lock him into the back. We don't want anyone holding you and Lebeznikov up and stealing all of that cash or those Congo cubes.'

'That one's a gangster and you know it.'

'But for what I have in mind, he's perfect and he'll keep Mérode and the others at bay. Now I'd better find Louis. This is going to need all of us.'

The rue Vignon wasn't far but the Wehrmacht's boys were two by two right up the staircase and along the corridor to that little kiosk at the far end where the cash was taken, the room assigned, and the regulation grey *Kondom* and postage-stamp towel handed over, jugs of disinfectant being in the rooms.

Évangéline Rocheleau, the flimsy negligée open and revealing all, couldn't have cared less. Reddened, soon to be giant bruises on her breasts, and a newly swollen left eye and chin, were evidence enough. That husband of hers was far from happy and still favouring a broken tooth and battered lips of his own. Louis hadn't just made himself an enemy. He had guaranteed it forever.

'That Kriminalrat will have taken him to the Bois de Vincennes,' spat Rocheleau, having at last wiggled the tooth free. 'He'll have given the *salaud* exactly what he deserves and me, I'm glad, do you hear? Glad!'

Ten minutes . . . would it take that long to find Louis and could he really leave her under a thumb like this?

Hauling Rocheleau out into the corridor, he told the boys to do the necessary, since this 'husband' of hers had spoiled their fun and ruined her income.

Closing the door, he said, 'Get dressed. I'll be back. I guarantee it. Pack what you still have and we'll find you a job as a seam-stress, but if he touches you again, I'll kill him.'

Louis would have said, Hermann, don't you dare make such promises, given what you now have to do.

Had he done the unpardonable? wondered St-Cyr. Had he given away innocent lives in but a stark gamble that Hermann would not only pull off that sale and bring Anna-Marie here, but some-how deal with this ulcer of a Gestapo?

Dark blood had now found its way thoroughly into Ludin's handkerchief, each cigarette butt bearing further evidence. That the spasms were not only more frequent, but all the more intense was clear enough, the lack of that last bottle of bitters a regretted moment of forgetfulness, but not by this prisoner.

Shackled—chained with that Bois-de-Vincennes extra bicy-cle chain and the bracelets too, and tightly—he was unable to straighten and had to remain squashed up against the passen-ger door and its window. As if to mock him—and God would do things like this—the late afternoon light over the Barbizon plain was everything that Millet and others of the Barbizon School had found. Sketching out-of-doors had not been common in the mid-1880s. Scandalous, mocked too, they had carried on anyway, but was there nothing he could do? Ludin wouldn't just kill him, he'd shoot that daughter of Josef Meyerhof and Monsieur Laurence Rousel, the notary who had risked his life to hide her. But would Ludin wait first to see if Hermann did get here with Anna-Marie?

'That ulcer of yours has eaten its way through the lining of your stomach, Kriminalrat. You're not just in urgent but desperate need of medical attention. Are those spare cans of gasoline to get you to Lausanne? If so, make sure you can still drive a car and that you don't ignite the fumes!'

'*Sei Still!* If this is another of your lies, I'll shoot now, rather than later.'

'Since the gun is yours, it's either one or the other and of no consequence, but you will never make it to the Swiss border on your own. Take my advice and use the train. There's a *rapide* every now and then. The station at Avon is only two kilometres from Fon-tainebleau, and that is not more than twenty from here. Let's just hope the Résistance don't leave a little something on the tracks.'

Instantly the fear of being shot was all too clear. 'Now show me where Kohler is to bring that girl.'

'There's really only one long street, this one, the rue Grande, and it cuts right through the centre of the village since there are only about six hundred residents. Plus the Occupier, of course, for it's a favourite of theirs, as it is of Parisians, myself included in the old days before the defeat. Rommel, Keitel, Stulpnägel and others have all dined at the Hôtel Bas-Bréau and Hôtel les Pléiades, and stayed overnight, for the cuisine is still said to be exceptional even with all of the terrible shortages.'

'And the name of Meyerhof's notary?'

'It won't be on any nameplate, but I do know where the house is.'

A few small shops, one general grocery, a *tabac*, a PTT, a scattering of other restaurants and a small museum that celebrated those painters all drew the camera-totting Wehrmacht who were on holiday. Cars were of interest, though, to everyone, the locals tending to avoid the tourists since those constantly behaved as though they owned the place and emptied the shops.

Of a storey and a half, ancient and of stucco, the house stood right up against the pavement as did most others, even to the windows that were closed off by shutters. 'That wooden gate to the courtyard, Kriminalrat, will but offer a tight a squeeze and be solidly locked in any case. Pounding on it will only attract unwanted attention.'

Unfortunately a lane ran alongside the property. Masses of tall lilacs, climbers and a stone wall gave further privacy, the picket fence and its gate at the back, one of stout limbs, though offering access for a car.

Unlocked, the shackle-chain was removed, the Sûreté bracelets left on.

Wild flowers, exactly like those painted by Théodore Rousseau of that school, not the Henri of that name, grew in profusion, though most had gone to seed. Beyond these lay a vegetable garden which showed every indication of diligent tending. Rabbit hutches held four does and a buck. Under worn canvas, and with no tires, but up on chocks, Ludin having flipped the tarp back, was a Citroën convertible and another life, another time, and proof positive that Laurence Rousel did indeed know how to drive.

'You're out of luck,' said Ludin, only to choke and gasp, and smother a cry.

A chicken coop and run with seven hens, half hid the garden-er, a gentle dark-haired, dark-eyed girl of fifteen whose gathered apron held the carefully harvested grass and wildflower seeds she had been about to scatter.

Terrified, she noticed the pistol.

Seeds showered as she stood helplessly, defeat registering in silent tears. Bolting for the house, she went into what must be its kitchen, failing entirely to close its door.

'On your knees,' said Bohle. 'I've had enough of you.'

Could he not even cross himself? 'If I were you, Kriminalrat, I would wait. Your French is nonexistent and you're going to need it if ever you're to find those black diamonds. While there may well be German soldiers who would come to your aid, for you to call on any would, I think, be most inadvisable. Hermann will . . .'

Reeking, the abattoir waited for it all to happen, the gobs and mounds of greasy-yellow fat, the hooves, the constant dripping of those *ver-dammte* taps. Kohler knew he had really done it this time. Kleiber had the whole area covered: supposed chimney sweeps on the surround-ing roofs at resident chimney pots and pipes that couldn't possibly have much soot; *égoutiers* lifting manhole covers they'd obviously never had to lift before; *flics* who weren't *flics* and others who were, and all on streets that were otherwise empty in any case, the locals having had the good sense to stay the hell out of the way.

Anna-Marie would see only snipers on those roofs. She'd know beyond a shadow of doubt that while she might get in through that side door that gave out onto the rue Brancion, she'd never leave by it or any other. Kleiber would ask, and she'd try not to answer, and then, Louis would have said, What will you do? Oh for sure, as usual you think you've considered everything, but is it that you've been so overconfident and in such a hurry you've missed something?

Verdammt, what?

That FTP *équipe.* Did you honestly think they would leave her alone to just come in here on of all things, a bicycle, and with not only a kilo of boart, but that of borderlines and those Meyerhof life diamonds? *Think, mon vieux.* You must, before she gets here and it all goes wrong.

There wasn't time. Bolduc was turning in. Lebeznikov was be-side him and probably cradling a Schmeisser. Kleiber would be in the back, shut in by all that armour plate and that lock, and able only to peer out the single armoured gun-portal on each side of the van, and the small, iron-meshed glass window into the cab up front or the one in the very back.

'*Monsieur l'Inspecteur, je suis là.*'

In the all but absent light over by that side door, she having closed it, she stood with hands on the handlebars. There was a rucksack on her back, a small suitcase in the trailer, and as she came hesitantly toward him, avoiding the offal and all the rest, he saw that the pistol she held was cocked and knew she was going to kill herself. And why did you not *think* of that, too? Louis would have asked.

Everything in her expression said it, but Louis wasn't here to help.

Clearly there were plenty of potential weapons in this kitchen that hadn't seen a touch of modernization in the past fifty years, and just as clearly Heinrich Ludin knew exactly how dangerous any of them could be. Alone, he sat in a far corner, pistol in hand, cognac and cigarettes nearby, and not for a moment did he take his gaze from the three of them.

Thin, tall and well into his sixties, and wearing the suit, vest and tie he no doubt always would, Laurence Rousel exuded the notary so much, one didn't need a second glance. Reserved, cautious—wary to the extreme, given the present circumstance—he sat at the near end of the table, spoon, napkin and glass of *vin rouge* all waiting. Head not bowed, not yet.

Michèle Guillaumet, housekeeper, gardener and cook, had found some inner strength and had obviously told herself to concentrate on the meal ahead. Giving the soup yet another stir and sampling, she removed it from what had to be one of Godin's original cast-iron ranges. Wood was added to the firebox, the contents of the oven checked, for she was drying the seeds, having sprinkled a little of the precious salt over them first. Ladling the soup into two plates and one of those ghastly china Pétain mugs, she added a sprinkling of chopped chives and said, 'There, it's ready. *Bon appétit,*' Ludin insisting on a translation, which as prisoner still in handcuffs, was dutifully given.

'I think the mug might be easier for you, Inspector.'

She had applied the iodine and precious sticking plasters to the back of this twice struck head, had tried to make him as comfortable as possible and would have lived in fear for well over two years that something like this might happen. Oh for sure she and Rousel would have talked it over many times, and yes, there would definitely be those who would question such an arrangement as her living here with a man nearly five times her age. In any village, not just this one, she could not have remained hidden without others knowing. Monsieur le Père for one and probably feared by most, the mayor *aussi,* the schoolteacher, too, for there was a pile of books and notes awaiting her concentration. Then, too, the grocer, shopkeeper, and in Barbizon, not a *garde champêtre* but a préfet with two *flics* at least. None, however, would dare to intervene, given that Citroën *traction avant* out there, and while there would be those who regretted it, others would say, Me, I told you so, as word of that car spread, and still others who would claim, It's about time someone cashed in on her!

Additionally, of course, she obviously had come to love to cook and that could only mean that someone had been teaching her. 'The aroma is magnificent, mademoiselle. Onion, of course, but shallots as well and a diced potato, am I not right?'

'And?' she asked, uncertain of what he was up to, Ludin getting the full translation.

'Chicken stock and the small pumpkin, again neatly diced, and all put through the French mill when cooked to give such a perfect purée. Not too thick, but just thick enough for that delicate yet complete fullness of taste. Ground cumin is a natural, but to this you have given it that rarest of things these days, a tender grating of nutmeg, black pepper as well, and equally rare, lastly the chives. I envy you your chef, Monsieur le Notaire. This is superb and something I haven't tasted in years. Grand-maman would make it for me once a year, sometimes with ginger—she said it was a Russian thought—at other times with caraway instead. The Russians do like pumpkin and caraway, don't they?'

This, too, was translated, since it had to be, the Gestapo having become increasingly agitated at the length of the discourse and wondering what the inspector was up to. Apologetically she would whisper, 'We were going to smash all of those mugs and that portrait when the Allies got here.'

Yet again, came a translation, Ludin immediately shouting, *'Ruhe!'* and vomiting blood.

The portrait hung above the crucifix, indicating that the

household believed Pétain considered himself that way toward the crucified. Ludin had, of course, earlier asked about the black diamonds and had received vehement denials of such a foolishness from Rousel, but would keep returning to that thought and had yet to search the house.

Hermann would have to arrive and if and when he did, he had better not rush into things, otherwise Ludin would kill the girl and her guardian and then this Sûreté.

Smoke poured from a nearby abattoir, one of the earliest, for apart from its sheet-iron roof, it had been made of wood. Billowing—filling the roadways among the buildings—the smoke brought the clanging *pompiers* and those, the ambulances, and through it all raced that green camouflaged Wehrmacht truck of Dillmann's, but would Werner do as thought? wondered Kohler. The bank van was on his own right, Kleiber locked in and peering out through its back window, but would he, too, do as thought, and what about Anna-Marie?

She had seen Kleiber and had put the muzzle of that pistol into her mouth! *'Don't!'* he cried. 'Please. Louis needs you. That's why he isn't here.'

Moving—not trying to stop her anymore—Herr Kohler ran to the cab of that van to grab the keys that had been thrust at him. Now he was unlocking its back door, was going to let the one in there arrest her just as Aram had felt might happen, he insisting, 'You will have to kill yourself. We can't chance your not telling them everything.'

The suitcases were being lifted out, her own being shoved in, Herr Kohler shouting, 'Standartenführer, wait! Give me five, then check that bag for the boart.'

Closing and locking that door—leaving the key in it—he gathered up the suitcases and hurried toward her, but of course three of them could never have been fitted into her trailer and he'd have to be told. 'Put the one on top and tie this around them.'

She had even thought to bring a rope! 'Let me have the pistol. He'll expect me to take it from you, that's why Sergei Lebeznikov isn't already out here. Kleiber's told him to stay put for the moment.'

Opening only one of the suitcases, he showed her what had to be a fortune's worth of those big white notes, Aram having wondered why the SD would ever agree to do such a thing, Herr Kohler saying, 'Don't worry, the other suitcases are the same. This unlocks them all.' But now brakes were being slammed, a sergeant leaning out from behind the wheel of that truck and shouting, '*Gefrieter Mannstein, Weiss und Rath, schnell machen!* Bike, trailer and angel into the back!'

Racing through the *pompiers*, clipping one of the ambulances, Dillmann headed for the exit even as Kleiber must have opened that suitcase of hers and given the little string tie of that kilo bag a tug.

The flash in the rearview was every bit as thought, felt Kohler, the sound the usual. Plastic for sure and probably the equivalent of at least five or six sticks of 808, and so much for the Reich ever getting their hands on that boart.

Speeding after Dillmann, he turned east onto the rue des Morillons. Others were giving chase but as yet without wheels. Street by street it wasn't far, but *place* Denfert-Rochereau was busy. Too many bicycles and *vélo-taxis*, pedestrians crossing where they shouldn't, buses off-loading Wehrmacht for late visits to the Catacombs, a gazo truck, a horse-drawn wagon . . .

Ach, Dillmann had stopped. Bike, trailer and angel were being set on the pavement, that deceitful son of a bitch having done exactly as thought, even to tossing him a joyful wave and yelling, '*Vielen Dank, mein Hermann.* See you in Spain,' and keeping all the cash.

'Into the car,' he said.

'I can't leave my bike. I mustn't!'

Liebe Zeit, what the hell was this? 'Are you crazy?'

'It's all I have.'

Those tracking vans were coming, police cars too, but Louis would have said, Do it, Hermann.

Using the rope, they tied it onto the back bumper but had to shove the trailer into the car.

'Barbizon,' she said when asked. Just that, but first a little detour to the north to where some architect had, in 1934, installed big windows around the cinema Studio Raspail so that the apartments he had built would be all the rage and look like artists' studios.

Shattered, there was glass everywhere, scorched fivers floating down, the collective citizenry still cowering, for Werner hadn't been able to resist the temptation and had done exactly as felt, Kleiber having also done the same to make certain none of those *verfluchter Banditen* ever got away no matter what.

Having jerry cans of gasoline to pay off those in the *marché noir* wasn't helping. The fire trucks would soon be here, those tracking vans as well. 'Barbizon,' he said. 'Maybe Louis will be there and maybe not, but I sure hope he is because he'll have to admit that this time I really did think it all through.'

At 2147 hours Hermann still hadn't arrived. Maybe it was just the blackout and driving far too fast on roads that ought to be familiar to him after *three* years of this Occupation. But maybe, too, he hadn't pulled things off at that abattoir, maybe they had gone terribly wrong just as they had here.

Oh for sure, Ludin was now desperately ill. Having vomited fresh blood again and again, he had forced Michèle Guillaumet to her knees and had put the muzzle of that pistol to the back of her head. Tearful prayers were being rapidly given, the neck-chain's silver cross being pressed to those lips, the girl begging God for forgiveness of sins that could never have amounted to much.

'Michèle, you must,' urged Rousel. 'If you have hidden *any* such thing—and Kriminalrat, I knew nothing of it—please tell us. Josef would never hold you to account. Not Josef. Did he give you *anything* to keep for him?'

All was dully translated, Michèle finally blurting, 'Only that sand in the cellar.'

'But . . . but those bags were for your aquarium at home?' stammered Rousel.

Again, Ludin, having snatched up the towel, vomited; again he cried out and clutched at his stomach, then harshly said, 'Get it!' to Rousel.

No translation was necessary. Four bags of sand, each weighing a good twenty kilos, were placed on the table, each bearing the name tag of a tropical fish: TETRAS, DANIOS, GUPPIES and HARLEQUINS.

It had to be a code, felt St-Cyr, each representing the name of the firm and its owner or owners, Meyerhof having been persuaded on that last trip to Paris before the Blitzkrieg to do as others had begged, though doubtless never for himself and his firm.

Each had to be emptied before the hidden could spill: gem rough of all sizes, fancies among them, the clear whites mingling with the exceedingly rare emerald green to soft rose and ruby-red, the sky-blue as well and deepest of sapphire-blue, the citron-yellow, too, even those subtle shades of what were known as the naturally occurring black.

Having hurriedly managed to light yet another cigarette, Ludin dug a hand into them and began to laugh only to cough, panic and vomit repeatedly. Dropping gun and diamonds, he collapsed, hitting his head on the edge of the table.

'Ah merde,' swore St-Cyr, leaping up from the chair to press fingers to that neck, 'now he's even more of a problem and Hermann . . . Hermann is nowhere near when so desperately needed, for how am I alone to deal with this and keep you both and all you have from the Occupier?'

Clutching two rabbits he had been about to gently toss into the kitchen to cause havoc of their own, Kohler nudged the black-out curtain aside and stepped into the kitchen, Anna-Marie right behind him and quickly closing the door to shut out the night.

'Walter, Hermann. What are we to tell him?'

Ludin was definitely dead, but in death was there not the answer or answers?

To the cellars of the rue des Saussaies, there was but a rending scream, from the front desk but the brutal snapping of fingers. Known here by all, they were not only to show their identity papers but to leave their weapons.

Formerly the headquarters of the Sûreté before the defeat of June 1940, the rue des Saussaies had become that of the Gestapo *and* the Sûreté. Major Osias Pharand, that acid little boss of Louis's, had been shoved out of his palatial office and down the corridor to that of his secretary, Boemelburg having tossed out the arty clutter and plastered the walls with maps of Paris and the country.

Teleprinters were never silent, telephones constantly ringing, orderlies coming and going, that beautifully carved Louis XIV lime-wood desk of Pharand's having been enlarged with plain pine planks to hold the accumulated clutter of the Occupier, the death notices of the 'troublemakers' as well.

They wouldn't even be allowed to sit, felt Kohler. Those rheumy Nordic-blue eyes didn't lift from the document in hand. The dome of that blunt head bristled with all-but-shaven iron-grey hairs. Quite obviously beyond the threatened retirement and having gained weight as a result, but with muscles, too, as head of SIPO-SD Section IV, the Gestapo in France, Boemelburg knew Paris like the back of his hand, having in his early days been a heating and ventilating engineer here before returning to the Reich to become a cop. A good one, too, Louis had always insisted.

The sagging countenance was just as grim as the tired lifting of those eyes. 'Well, Kohler, what have you to say for yourselves? Five dead Wehrmacht, including Standartenführer Kleiber, now a national hero, one banker and one of Rudy de Mérode's most trusted henchmen? No black diamonds, no *Halbjüdin* either, and especially no other *Banditen*. Reichssicherheitschef Kaltenbrunner is demanding the fullest of explanations before your court-martial and execution, but has reluctantly agreed to allow me to at least hear what you have to say.'

'Walter . . .'

'Louis, just because we worked together on IKPK* cases before this conflict, please don't presume you can speak.'

Was it to be the end of them? wondered St-Cyr. They had dropped Anna-Marie and her bicycle off at a *maison de compagne* to the west of Sézanne. A Madame Martine de Belleveau and Arie Beekhuis, the alias of Hans van Loos, had been overjoyed to see her. Hermann and himself had spoken to the *préfet* of Barbizon and had hopefully cleared Laurence Rousel of any connection to what had happened, a gravely ill Heinrich Ludin having simply dropped in to the house to ask directions and needing a rest. But they had had to leave all those diamonds hidden with Michèle Guillaumet, the Meyerhof life ones as well, until after the Liberation, had tried to cover all tracks, but had had no other choice but to come here, having first taken care of Évangéline Rocheleau.

It was now or never, felt Kohler. Louis would expect it of him, but would have to be given the opportunity to tuck things in as needed. 'Standartenführer Kleiber's plan was excellent, as the Reichssicherheitschef has stated himself, Sturmbannführer. It should have worked and netted not only that Dutch girl and the rest of those *Banditen*, but . . .'

---

* The international police commission, the forerunner of Interpol.

'Herr Ludin, Walter. He got Oberfeldwebel Dillmann to intervene.'

'And when Dillmann dropped that *Mischlinge* off, Kriminalrat Ludin was ready and waiting for her,' went on Hermann.

'He forced her to tell him where these were, Walter. It's about a kilo, I think, but Herr Frensel and Herr Uhl will be able to advise.'

'The stones are known, I think, as borderlines,' said Hermann. 'Of equal value either as gems or industrials. Half-and-halves, if you like.'

And just like that girl. 'But a kilo? *Ach, mein Gott*, Kohler, that's at least twenty times the value of the boart!'

'Exactly,' sighed Louis. 'Twenty or thirty million American dollars.'

And everybody happy. 'Those are definitely at least some of the "black" diamonds, Sturmbannführer. When we finally located Kriminalrat Ludin in his car at the Avon railway station on the other side of Fontainebleau, this first-class ticket to Lausanne was still in his hand.'

'This tin of Lucky Strikes was on the seat beside him and this all but full bottle of bitters,' offered Louis.

'And these,' said Kohler.

Two twenty-by-twenty photos of that girl, in the one she having dyed and cut her blonde hair.

'For the national strike, I believe' said St-Cyr.

'Dead, you say?'

'Of a peptic ulcer,' said Louis.

'But definitely heading for Switzerland and a hospital instead of obeying orders and returning to Berlin with that kilo,' said Hermann.

These two . . . *Ach*, though not the thousands and thousands of carats as thought, the diamonds would certainly help, felt Boemelburg, for they would prove beyond any shadow of doubt that the Reichssicherheitschef and the others had been absolutely *korrekt*.

Searching among the many papers, he finally found what might do. 'It's a little place to the northwest of Dijon. An archaeological dig of some sort. Bones and bits of rusty iron. A hillfort probably. That of a Gaul, a Ver . . . something or other.'

'Vercingetorix, Walter?' asked Louis.

It was just what was needed to get them immediately out of Paris and far from anyone here who might care, but also in under an umbrella if needed to save himself in Berlin. '*Ach*, that's it exactly. One of Himmler's people, a cousin as well. Someone's been taking umbrage with what he's been up to and has not only been stealing his artefacts and spoiling the results, but killing his assistants.'

A dig. 'Old bones and new ones, Louis.'

'And time, Hermann. Time to factor in the present with that of the past.'

'A timeweaver, then, *mon vieux*. A knitter of years.'

THE ST-CYR AND KOHLER MYSTERIES

FROM MYSTERIOUSPRESS.COM
AND OPEN ROAD MEDIA

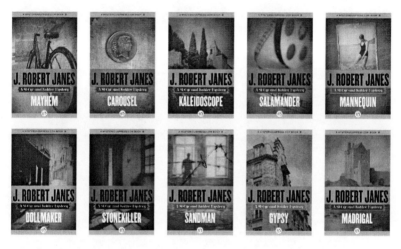

These and more available wherever ebooks are sold

MYSTERIOUSPRESS.COM

Otto Penzler, owner of the Mysterious Bookshop in Manhattan, founded the Mysterious Press in 1975. Penzler quickly became known for his outstanding selection of mystery, crime, and suspense books, both from his imprint and in his store. The imprint was devoted to printing the best books in these genres, using fine paper and top dust-jacket artists, as well as offering many limited, signed editions.

Now the Mysterious Press has gone digital, publishing ebooks through **MysteriousPress.com**.

MysteriousPress.com offers readers essential noir and suspense fiction, hard-boiled crime novels, and the latest thrillers from both debut authors and mystery masters. Discover classics and new voices, all from one legendary source.

FIND OUT MORE AT
WWW.MYSTERIOUSPRESS.COM

FOLLOW US:
@emysteries and Facebook.com/MysteriousPressCom

MysteriousPress.com is one of a select group of publishing partners of Open Road Integrated Media, Inc.

THe MYSTeRIOUS BOOKSHOP, founded in 1979, is located in Manhattan's Tribeca neighborhood. It is the oldest and largest mystery-specialty bookstore in America.

The shop stocks the finest selection of new mystery hardcovers, paperbacks, and periodicals. It also features a superb collection of signed modern first editions, rare and collectable works, and Sherlock Holmes titles. The bookshop issues a free monthly newsletter highlighting its book clubs, new releases, events, and recently acquired books.

58 Warren Street
info@mysteriousbookshop.com
(212) 587-1011
Monday through Saturday
11:00 a.m. to 7:00 p.m.

FIND OUT MORe AT:

www.mysteriousbookshop.com

FOLLOW US:

@TheMysterious and Facebook.com/MysteriousBookshop

OPEN ROAD
INTEGRATED MEDIA

Open Road Integrated Media is a digital publisher and multimedia content company. Open Road creates connections between authors and their audiences by marketing its ebooks through a new proprietary online platform, which uses premium video content and social media.

Videos, Archival Documents, and New Releases

Sign up for the Open Road Media newsletter and get news delivered straight to your inbox.

Sign up now at
www.openroadmedia.com/newsletters